MISFITS
& HEROES
WEST FROM AFRICA

KATHLEEN FLANAGAN ROLLINS

ISBN 1453755039
ISBN-13 9781453755037

For Mary Clare and Quentin

Several wonderful books helped me understand the importance of numbers and geometric patterns in Africa, including *Geometry from Africa: Mathematical and Educational Explorations*, by Paulus Gerdes, as well as his article, "SONA: Sand Drawings from Africa," and *Africa Counts: Number and Pattern in African Cultures*, by Claudia Zaslavsky. Ms. Zaslavsky's workbook, *Multicultural Mathematics*, is a great introduction to different number systems.

PART 1 – ALONG THE RIVERS

- in the area around two major river systems
in West Africa, about 12,000 BC

INTRODUCTION

Long ago, when West Africa was still unbroken rainforest and the Sahara was grassy steppe, two leaders had the same vision: a network of villages united by a vast river system. One, a warrior known to his enemies as the Black Rhino, was in the north. The other, a woman known as Dwyka, or the She-Eagle, from her sign, was in the south. It was a time when all great plans seemed possible, but great plans wind up being accomplished, or thwarted, by regular people, and sometimes the plans sweep those regular people into unknown places, with unforeseen effects.

This is the story of some of those people.

CHAPTER 1
THE OUTLINE OF A MAN

He was stretched out along the dark branch, taking in the night sound and smell. It was the smell that had brought him here, to this village, the complicated, heavy smell of men and women and children, and life as he had forgotten it. It had drawn him through the bush, where there were no paths except those the animals used, and each day it had grown stronger, more complex, and easier to follow.

When he reached the clearing, only the stars and the waxing crescent moon, the Healing Moon, lit the circle of sky above him, but he could make out the enormous silk cotton tree at the center of the village and the huts arranged in a circle around it. Raising his head, he drew in layers of smells: burned palm oil and resin, packed dirt floors, damp thatch, old cookfires, smoked meat, marula nuts, bitter melon, drying gourds, monkey oranges. Beyond the huts, off to one side, he could smell baboon, and to the other side, trenches of fermenting sorghum. But most of all, he smelled people.

While the village slept, he climbed the great tree, his hands in front of his feet as he ran up the ridge of one of the buttress roots and leaped from branch to branch until he found the one he wanted, thick and solid, reaching out over the village center. From his perch there, he could see without being seen, and, perhaps, find whatever had called him there. So he waited, listening to the night world move around him. Once, he heard leaves stir above him. As he looked up, the dark shape of an owl dropped down and flew over

1

his head, blocking out his view of the starfield before it flew on, soundlessly.

When the eastern sky lightened, four hunters headed out of the village, speaking in low tones as they passed right under his tree. Then it was quiet again until the dawn pierced the leaf cover and howler monkeys roared in nearby trees, waking the rest of the village. One by one, the people stepped into their day world, going through their routines with the ease of habit. No one saw him, lying there, watching them. It was only another day to them. But it was a shock to him.

At the base of the tree, a woman sat down, resting the small of her back against one of the buttress roots. Humming, she set out her coils of dyed reeds and took up her unfinished basket. Her long fingers worked the reeds easily, rhythmically, over and under the spines, as her humming became clearer, not a tuneless whistle, but a fine, clean sound that filled the air. The melody, the human sound, pierced him, resonated inside him. It wasn't simply a repeated melody; it was a story without words. It was the story she was putting into the basket, changing colors of reeds, switching seamlessly, so that the basket seemed to be forming itself under her fingers, playing out in colors and patterns the tale she wove with music.

He hadn't heard human music in a very long time. There was a day, many days ago, when he'd been part of a village, and he'd taken its life for granted, but he didn't remember it as beautiful. Perhaps there had been singers there, and dancers around the bonfires, and happy laughter of lovers, but he couldn't recall any. Mostly he remembered being angry. *Naaba again,* the townspeople would whisper. *There's something wrong with him.* And then, the last of many times he'd been beaten for breaking the laws, no one had stepped up to help him home, not even his family, or his initiation group members, the ones he was supposed to bond with for life. There was only the taste of the fine black dirt in his mouth, and the searing pain where the switch had cut into his skin. He couldn't even stand up. Eventually, when everyone had left, he'd crawled away into the bush, alone.

Memory, especially that not colored by nostalgia, is a dangerous box to open, and he'd worked very hard to keep it closed. But now, hearing the woman humming her story, he felt the box ripped open. Piles of images crashed into him at once, spilling into his mind, pieces of sights and sounds and sensations, bits of a life he used to know, all recalled at once. There were fights with the boys in the village, his older brother shrunken with fever, his father, mad with grief, beating his mother, then beating him. There was the theft of so many things, and the bird that always sang in the tree next to their hut until he hit it with a stone, his mother's hands shaking, the bad smell in their hut, the incredible dark red sky, the rancid taste of fear in his mouth. They went on and on, the rush of memories, moments recalled without invitation. And the weaver's story went on, humming its way through the dark and light patterns forming beneath her hands, carrying him along.

When he'd crawled away from his village, anger was his only strength. He turned on everything in his path, smashing it with rocks, or setting it on fire, or breaking it, and when he was done, and he was surrounded by broken egg shells and feathers and blood, he found the black smoke still curled through his insides, so he turned on himself, cutting at his arms and legs, watching the red streams running down in wavy lines. Then he sat in the river, letting the water flow over the ragged scars, not caring whether he lived or died.

So the bush punished him for his arrogance and then for his despair.

The fevers that took him left him so broken that he lay where he had fallen, shaking cold, even after wrapping himself in long raffia leaves. In the middle of the cold, fire burned through his mind. He dreamed he was once again stealing the shaman's sacred staff and medicine bundle, both the doer and the watcher as he saw his own hand take hold of the objects, even though he was forbidden to touch them. The man in the hood was watching him, but he took the staff anyway. And then he was beaten, and the man in the hood laughed as he beat him.

In his fever, he lost track of days and nights, awaking sometimes, vaguely surprised to find time had gone by without his notice. One day, when he found some ackee fruit, he tore into it, gulping down hunks of the orange flesh, but later, dizzy and weak, he threw it back up. As the world spun slowly around him, he dropped to the ground and drifted into a sick sleep.

Much later, when he woke, the full moon was up, its light falling in shafts through the canopy. In an open space left by an old brush fire, the light spilled across the still grasses. Drawn in, he climbed onto a flat rock and sat there, letting the night flow around him. Every blade of grass was tipped in silver, shadowed in black. At the edge of the clearing, a giant rat moved through the leaf litter, seeking out grubs. When it reached the open area, it raised its head, pulling in the scent of the man, but the man didn't move, so the rat went back to its foraging, not realizing a more dangerous predator was watching. A pair of ghostly eyes flashed pale green as a massive head and shoulder cleared the underbrush so quietly, in a motion so fluid, that the leaves barely rustled. Then the big cat stopped and raised her head slightly, reading the air, sorting out the many scents, including the man's and the rat's. She stood there and he sat motionless, unable to look at anything except her. As she moved out into the clearing, he saw the black rosette markings on her hide, the long body and powerful legs, the long tail curved up at the end. The rat, suddenly aware of the leopard, panicked and ran, scurrying through the underbrush, but she exploded into motion, her long body covering the ground between them in three strides. Then she was on it, strangling it with a single bite, and it went limp, its life extinguished in an instant.

With the body of the rat still hanging from her mouth, she turned her head and looked at the man for a long time, reading him, considering him. With one great paw on the rat, she ripped off a hunk of meat and swallowed it, its blood marking her jaw. Then, after a final look at the man, she walked off into the underbrush, back into her world. As she moved away, he could see the white tips on the back of her ears and the white tip of her tail. Suddenly, he wished he could follow her, follow those white patches as her pups did, and learn the world as she knew it. But she'd already spoken to him. The language was unfamiliar, but her meaning was clear. For reasons he didn't understand, she'd chosen to share her kill, with him. She'd measured him and given him a gift, but not as people do, in expectation of a return gift, or at least a sense of debt. Her gift was a judgment, and a bond.

He ran his finger through the bloody meat and drew it across his face and chest and down his arms and legs in long lines, one after another, over and over, marking himself with her gift, taking its power and its faith to him. Then he wrapped the body in broad leaves, and buried it in the clearing. Lying down on top of it, he felt the power of the offering there, below him, travelling up the roots and filling up the grasses underneath him, mixing with the moonlight above him, washing through him from the top and the bottom, as quietly and certainly as the river, filling him, spilling into all the empty spaces inside him until they overflowed. Then his mind emptied of everything he used to know, and he slept.

He dreamed he was seeing the world through the leopard's eyes and speaking through the leopard's blood-spattered mouth. He was in the clearing, looking at himself sitting on the rock. Everything had a pale yellow cast. As he approached the man sitting on the rock, he said, "Now that you have died, what will you do with your life?"

The woman who was singing her wordless story nodded as she worked, her fingers always moving, always in the same rhythm. A host of images flooded his mind; they were all jumbled together and they all seemed to be equally important, even the very small ones: the slow sound of the adder emerging from under a log, the flash of red on red as two red-necked falcons ambushed a carmine bee-eater, the pattern of dead-white branches laced into the dark sky, the swirl of eddies in the river, the salamanders burrowing in the wet dirt, pushing their bodies under the stone where there couldn't possibly be any room for them, the fine taste of the rough-skinned plums he'd found, gifts from the tree that grew underground. Only the branches stuck up into the air, as if someone was hiding behind a wall and only a hand appeared, offering this treat to the passer-by.

The memories were all images, sounds, and smells: watching the strange wriggling of the parasite larvae he had to cut out of his swollen feet, noticing too late that he was walking across a line of warrior ants, sitting on the sandy crescent where the river bowed around him while a crocodile watched him from the water. But for all his memories and all the seasons he'd spent in the bush and all the things he'd witnessed, he was still only an outline of a man. The bush air was all that was inside him. He looked around and saw only the palm leaves turning in the breeze or the parrots flashing through the canopy. He couldn't see himself, even when he bent over the river to drink. So the bush sent him away, far from the world he had come to know. It sent him here, to this village, to hear this woman's song.

He thought he'd like to say something to this woman, if he could think of what to say, but of course he didn't. It wasn't his village. He was only a visitor, a spy, really, in a world he'd forgotten, and, at this moment, a world he couldn't remember ever having visited. So he listened to her melody until it was dulled by the other sounds of the waking village: a baby crying, spider monkeys chittering in the treetops, a woman breaking up sticks for a fire, children yelling while they raced along the path, a couple arguing, a man pounding a wooden stake with a hammerstone, one man calling across the village to another - so many sounds that they crowded each other into a general mass of noise, and the sweet humming of the weaver's story was absorbed into it and lost.

Then, suddenly, it was too much for him, too many sights and smells, too many sounds, too many people, too many memories; everything was pounding on him. He put his head down and closed his eyes, but the sounds still pulsed through him like too many heartbeats. At the same time, the village drummers started pounding insistently, three beats and a pause, three beats and a pause, and on and on. As the man waited, motionless, the basket weaver set down her work and joined the others as they gathered at the entrance to the village. The four hunters were returning with their kill, and the villagers shouted their welcome, pounding on whatever they could find. Straining under the load, the hunters carried an already gutted eland tied to a platform of narrow logs. Its cavity was stuffed with ferns and stinging nettles to keep away the insects, its long spiral horns and red coat displayed proudly as the hunters paraded it through the village to the cheers of the people and the insistent beat of the drums. Almost all the villagers crowded along behind the hunters, so they could watch the butchering of the big antelope that would feed them all handsomely. The heart and liver would be set out for the gods in thanks for this gift. The rest would be served up at a feast, and the air was already festive.

The man watched, but he felt distant now. As the procession moved away, he found his way down the tree, ready to leave the village behind. At the base of the tree, he stopped and picked up the weaver's basket, running his fingers along its intricate patterns before he set it back down. As he stepped away, a little boy started yelling for his mother, saying a wild man had jumped out of the tree and stolen a basket. When his mother ran up, she looked around, saw no one there, saw the basket still sitting where the weaver had left it, and spanked the child for lying.

"He was right there just a moment ago," the child insisted as his mother pulled him away.

CHAPTER 2
THE WATERFOOT

The sun was very hot when he left the village, and the wind sweeping up behind him carried with it sounds of the pounding drums, the smells of game meat and blood. But not everyone was at the celebration or even in the village area. In a small clearing, not far in front of him, stood a young woman, her hands clasped awkwardly behind her back because they were tied together at her sash. The rope went from her hands down to her feet, which were bound at the ankles. He stopped still. The two of them stood there, not moving, not recognizing the other, until the woman said, "Are you the wild man of the forest?" She hadn't looked at him or even turned in his direction.

The man searched the clearing, thinking there must be someone there with her, but there was no one. Only the woman, motionless in the white heat, gazing off into the distance.

He hadn't spoken in so long, he had to remember words to use. "Why are you bound?" The words went out into the hot wind like a whisper, but she turned to him when she heard them. Her eyes were so strange they were shocking. In the sunlight the irises looked golden, and flecks around the edges glowed in the sunlight. He stared at her, watching the long twists of hair with bits of hollow bird bones woven into them catch the wind.

"Because I'm a wanderer."

Still, neither one had moved. He pointed to the ropes binding her hands and feet. "Who did this to you?"

"The man my father sold me to," she said, studying him, this tall, thin man with his cat-like movements, his dark face and wild look.

The hot sun stripped the shadows from the meadow, leaving everything in tints of white and yellow. The man knew if he cut her bonds, he'd be involved in the very place he wanted to leave behind. But if he didn't, the memory of her standing there, in the clearing, tied up like a prisoner, would haunt him. So he made a decision. She never moved as he approached, but her yellow eyes followed every move as he took out his knife and cut the bonds on her feet first, then her hands, and then stood back. They both waited for the other to speak, to ask questions, to move.

"How do you know I wanted to be free?" she asked, finally breaking the silence between them.

"If you don't, you can easily re-tie the bonds," he replied, "but from the marks on your ankles, I think you would rather be able to move."

"He beats me when I wander, the man I was sold to. But I still wander. This time he tied me up, but I left anyway."

In the bright sunlight, the wind snapped the white-tipped flowers back and forth. "I don't like that man or sharing his hut," she said, "but that's not why I wander."

He waited with his left foot resting on the side of his right knee, but she didn't explain. "Then what are you looking for?"

"I'm a waterfoot," she said, carefully, as if it was a dangerous thing to admit. "I feel the water moving under my feet, even the smallest trace of it. I can find it, even when the land is dry. I'm taken along its path. My feet line up with it, and I go with it. That's all. I'm standing on the water right now. Not the little spring we use. A full river. It's what I was following. It's under the ground, but it's there, I know it's there. If I were to dig straight down between my toes, it would be there. And I know it's going that way, to join other water I've never seen, like raindrops on the tiny high branches of a tree running down to the bigger branch, then joining others, until they all flow onto the great trunk." She turned her golden eyes on him. "I'm sure you think I'm crazy or I'm lying, but it's the truth."

"No, I don't think you're lying. If I thought you were a liar, I wouldn't have freed you. Lies are poison, and they poison everything that comes after them." He looked away, to the far side of the meadow, and to the dark bush beyond. "I can't say who's crazy and who isn't. People simply are who they are."

"Then who are you?"

"I don't know. My name is Naaba. I lived in a village once. I was punished for breaking the laws," he paused, turning so she could see the lumpy scars that crisscrossed his back, "so I left. A leopard was my second mother. But now," he tilted his head slightly, looking at her, "I wander. I've been following the river for a while; I don't know how many days. Then I ... came here." He didn't add that he had followed the smell of something he couldn't name, and it had brought him to this place.

"Where will you go?"

"Back to the bush, back to the river, I suppose."

"And if someone else were to go to the river as well -"

"But your people, your friends - You have food and shelter here. Safety."

"I have nothing here. I can go with you, or I can go on my own. My feet won't stay in this village. Eventually, the people here will kill me for it. Having others wander away challenges their happiness."

"Won't you be followed?"

"No. I won't be missed."

"Then I'd welcome your company."

So, at first, it seemed easy to go. Since she had no possessions she'd risk returning to the village to retrieve, she told him she'd leave without them. It was a moment she had thought about for a long time: being free, free to follow her feet, free of the man who had bought her, free of her old life. She thought she'd be happy, very happy, or at least relieved, but the truth was she was afraid. Her question to the man had been sincere. She wasn't sure she wanted to be free. It's easy to hate your bonds, to dream of what you'll do when they're loosed, but it's hard to actually break them, or to continue once they're broken. And what of the village, the only home she'd ever known? What of all the sights and sounds she knew so well? There were good people there, in the village, and she was sorry she hadn't said goodbye to them, hadn't told them how much she'd appreciated their kindness. In that moment, she even missed her father, whose compulsive gambling had caused him to lose everything, even his own daughter. And this strange, wild man, what did she know of him? What would she do, all alone in the forest with a man who called himself the son of a leopard?

In her fear, she thought about telling the man it was a mistake and she had to go back. But she watched him move off, his long strides covering the ground so lightly, and she pictured what would happen if she went back. The man who had paid for her would beat her again, and the villagers who cared would ask why she was always wandering when it only got her in more trouble. *Why don't you just stay put?* Then it would start again, and soon her feet would take her, as they always did, along the path of the river underground. The difference would be that this man, this wild man, wouldn't be here, in the hard sunlight, to cut her bonds. He wouldn't be here because she would have chosen to wear those bonds forever.

With the smallest of backward glances, she wished the people of the village happiness. In a way, she envied them their contentment. In another, she knew she'd never feel it. Perhaps it didn't matter; some were meant to stay and others to go. So she tried to think about the river, but even so, she was pulled in both directions for most of the first day.

At the end of the day, she built a fire and cooked the wild yams they'd found, wrapping them in leaves, setting them in the fire, then covering the fire with dirt and leaves. They said very little. But after eating, the man went off and lay down on a long, smooth branch, draped over it just like a big cat. Unsure what to do, she sat down on the ground by the fire pit, wrapped her arms around her knees and tried to sleep, but she couldn't. She wasn't used to being in the bush at night, and it was full of sounds she didn't know, the snap of twigs from unseen feet passing, quick squeaks, the calls of the wild dogs, the piercing cries of their prey. Insects whined around her ears and crawled up her legs. Nervous and miserable, thinking she'd go mad before morning, she stood up, ready to go back to the man she hated. But the moment her feet connected with the river and she felt it flowing along under the ground, she got her breath back. She waited, letting the river calm her, letting it take over her body.

From the branch, the man watched and waited to see what she'd choose. When he knew she'd stay, he said, "You'd be safer sleeping up in the tree. It's just as comfortable as the ground, once you get used to it."

She looked doubtful but knew he was right about sleeping on the ground, so she found her way up to a large branch and wedged her back up against the trunk. Eventually, fatigue overcame her fear, and she fell asleep.

When she slept, his eyes closed as well.

It wasn't exactly true that she wouldn't be missed, but because of the celebration over the successful hunt, she wasn't missed until the next day. Then, the man who had bought her searched for her briefly. He found her shuffling tracks leading out of the village and the two sets of tracks heading out of the clearing, but he didn't follow them past there. With a shrug, he told everyone he was tired of her and her wandering, but inside, it stung that someone had gone off with his property. Still, he didn't care enough to try to get her back. "She won't survive out there anyway," he told the people who asked.

The weaver knew someone had been in the tree and had stopped to look at her basket - his footprints were clear in the fine dirt - but she told no one. She just hummed a beautiful new melody as she wove the story into her basket. The boy who had seen the man told everyone, but no one listened. For a few days, the woman's flight was all the talk of the village, but then there was other news, and the tale of the disappearing wanderer became just one more of the stories the people told.

As the days passed and they walked farther and farther from the village, the woman, Asha, felt her fears lift. With every step, she realized she was going where she had always been meant to go and that something that had been asleep inside her had awakened. After calling her for so long, the power of the moving water surged up through the ground and spread through her. Her feet lead her, but her heart followed, singing like the river she couldn't see. For the first time in her life, she felt everything was exactly, perfectly, as it should be. It was an unnerving realization.

For the man it was strange, at first, to have company, especially her company. Sometimes he found himself watching her move, watching the curve of her body as she walked or the sun catching the edge of her arm. She said very little while they were travelling, but she sometimes sang or told stories when they made camp. Then he'd forget that he had gotten used to travelling alone because it seemed so right to have her there.

As they went along the path of the underground river, where it came closer and closer to the surface, Asha became more agitated. Periodically, they'd pass depressions where the water seeped to the surface, and she'd stand in the muddy water with tremors running through her legs. "All the sacred places," she said, "the great council trees, the caves, they're all connected by water, you know, all connected by underground water passages. Power is flowing through here, and it flows right through the tallest trees and up into

13

the clouds, where it comes down once again. It's the original power, from the shed skin of the sky serpent."

"Water is the difference between life and death," he said.

"Water *is* both life and death," she replied.

When they reached the outcrop where the underground spring reached the surface and became the stream that flowed out of the earth, Asha felt the current sweep up through her feet, right through her body, answering some long-forgotten question, something she had perhaps been aware of as a child and then forgotten in the confusion of adulthood. She stepped into the water, raised her arms, and danced as if she had always known this dance, as if the river had taught it to her years ago in her dreams. She was taken up by the water's flow, swaying and turning sinuously, her movements liquid, as if she had no skeleton but was made only of the river currents that ran through her. She moved easily, beautifully, her face shining, ecstatic, her legs covered in the muddy splash. She drew him in also, and they moved together in the water, the first water of the river, his hands on her hips, her hands on his waist. They stepped and twisted and swayed, spinning slowly apart and together, the man untying her wrap as she spun, running his hands along her body, feeling her hands cool and wet against his skin, her hair falling on his shoulder, her breath on his neck, his hand gliding down the center of her back, drawing her in.

"I will call you Naaba, son of the leopardess, walker in the forest," she said.

"And you are golden-eyed Asha, the waterfoot, who dances the beauty of the river."

CHAPTER 3
A SNAKE AND A PATTERN

For days they wandered, Naaba and Asha, along the tributary, like the first people at the birth of the world. They watched fruit bats taking nectar from the pink flowers of trees older than time, silk cottons larger than twelve men could reach around. And little potos, with their big eyes and long tails, eating stinging ants and centipedes that would kill a man. Geckos darting along the rocks. Jumping spiders dancing so extravagantly, throwing their front legs up and swaying back and forth. Tiny orange butterflies landing on them, tasting their sweat. It was a world they had been invited into because they were brand-new, without any community except each other. When Naaba leaned over the river, he saw his reflection, and hers, dancing together in the water.

From the tall and slender Kola tree, they picked the seed pods that looked like turtle shells and dried the seeds in the sun, picked cassavas and plantains, collected termites and caterpillars. Sometimes, Naaba set out his trap in the river, and Asha cooked the fish, steaming it over hot rocks in the fire pit. It was a fine life they had on the little river that they shared with parrots and pythons, mustached monkeys and yellow baboons.

When they were covered with leeches and mud and mosquito bites from a difficult swampy section, they bathed in the clear-running river, Naaba rinsing the dirt from Asha's hair, Asha running her hands over Naaba's scarred back, erasing its memory of pain. Naaba didn't tell her how big the river got later on, or how dangerous. It was enough that it was theirs at the moment. It was enough to catch a fine perch for dinner while the brown ibis watched from a branch nearby. Or watch the giant hawk-moths as they sought the nectar of the white orchids. Or hear the sawing bark of a leopard.

One afternoon, as they walked, Naaba put his hand on Asha's arm and waved her over to the side, where he silently climbed a tree, motioning her to follow. As she did, he moved out to a branch and held out a hand to guide her. There, on the game path beside the river, a young leopard with a very full stomach was sitting, watching a new-born duiker. Its mother was nowhere in sight. The young duiker was still wobbly-legged and fell often, its feet splaying out beneath it. The young leopard tilted its head and reached out a paw to it, but the duiker stood back up, and instead of running away, it walked up to the leopard. The two stood watching each other, almost nose to nose. When the duiker stumbled again and squawked as it scrambled to get its legs under control, the leopard sprang toward it, pawed it, but stopped short of grabbing hold of it. Again, the baby struggled to get its weak legs to go somewhere, and the leopard watched. The duiker wobbled away, eventually, and the leopard lay down, casually licking its paws.

Asha was amazed.

"The leopard wasn't hungry," Naaba commented, as the duiker wobbled away. "Another day it would be a different story. I've seen a leopard hide, almost flat, in the grass, and then leap up and attack a full-grown antelope, staying with it as jumped and twisted, overpowering something far larger than itself and then hauling the body home for its young." He paused. "Her young."

When they set up camp that afternoon, Naaba had a strange feeling. He assumed it was the encounter with the young leopard that set him on edge, but the feeling stayed, even as they built a fire and ate spice plums and the catfish they'd caught. The spot they'd chosen for their camp was incredibly beautiful. Down the river in front of them, a pair of grey-crowned cranes walked along the far bank, their long legs moving slowly, their fans glowing as their heads bobbed low, looking for insects. Then a third crane came soaring in, honking its arrival, its wings spread wide, black tips flared out.

Behind them was an ancient fig tree, its tall, sinuous roots rising from the ground to halfway up the massive trunk, its foliage arching high over them. It was more than a tree; it was a presence. Another time, he would have loved to spend the night in its care, sharing this giant with the green pigeons and fruit bats that fed so voraciously on its fruit, but on this afternoon, even in the middle of all this beauty, there was something else flowing through the great tree. He watched, waiting for a sign, but when it came, it was so slight, so faint, that he doubted he had really seen it. The deeply folded surface between the high walls of the roots left large sections of the trunk in shadow, and it was at the edge of one of these sections that he had seen something, but when he looked again, there was nothing there. And what had he seen, anyway, but the smallest flash of grey on grey? Slowly, he rose, motioning Asha to move behind him, though he still couldn't have said why. Then he stepped quietly to his right, searching the tree's shadow where he had seen something that wasn't the trunk of the great tree. There was nothing but the soaring height of the fig tree, and its high, twisting roots. He moved again, this time looking deep into the creases of the roots where they met the trunk. Near the trunk, the roots stood so tall, they were as high as the walls of a room, and it was impossible to see over. But he knew this was the right place. Carefully, he went from one root crevasse to the next, also searching the trunk above as he moved. Once again, it was only a flicker that caught his eye, but he knew, then, what he had felt. It was almost invisible. Its long grey body, longer than two tall men, was lined up with a dark crease of the trunk; only its narrow head crossed over into the sunlit part. Even then, the grey head blended perfectly with the grey bark. Only its flicking tongue gave it away.

It was looking at him.

Naaba sucked in his breath. The snake hissed and opened his mouth wide, showing its black mouth. Naaba froze. He knew about these snakes; everyone did. Their venom could kill a grown man in a matter of moments. They were lightning fast and aggressive. Even standing still, Naaba knew he would be considered a threat. He motioned to Asha to back away slowly. Then he looked at the snake. With its jaws wide, it raised its head and fixed its black eyes on Naaba. He felt as if he couldn't move, as if the snake was holding him there. There was a knife tucked into his wrap, but he was so shaken, he didn't think he could hit the snake with it. He knew he had to move. Even with its incredible speed, the snake would have to lunge to bite him. The fig tree wouldn't give it as much support as it would have on land. Then again, maybe it would. He backed up, still watching the round black eye that was watching him. One step. Another. Another. He wanted to run, to head down to the river as fast as he could, but he couldn't turn his back, couldn't stop watching that eye, so he just stepped back, hoping Asha had already gotten away.

But she too was mesmerized by the snake, and once she had backed up, she had stopped and watched, so that he bumped into her as he backed up, and there was a commotion, and the snake slithered down the tree and along one of the long roots, lifting its head and spreading its hood as it hissed, its great dark mouth spread wide.

"Run!" he yelled at Asha. "I'll meet you at the river!"

With a cry, she tore herself away and ran for the river, stumbling over roots and stones, slipping on the bank, afraid to look back, afraid to think. She ran right into the water and stood, shaking, but even then, at that moment, when fear had hold of her, she knew she had to go back. Frantically, she glanced around, looking for an answer. There had to be something useful here, something, there had to be something. At her feet, the rounded river stones reminded her of the game she used to play with the other children, the one where they'd set a stone in a sling, whirl it around their head until they got the right speed, then let it fly at a target. Once she was very good at it, but it seemed like a long time ago. The sling was just a long, folded leaf tied together so the stone was held in the bowl made by the rounded middle. Her fingers trembled as she picked out stones and scrambled up the bank with them. The leaves, she couldn't remember what kind of leaves they used, but there had to be something. She searched the old trees by the riverbank, but all their leaves were short. Farther along, there. They'd do, not as well as the original, but they'd do. They had to, she thought, as she ripped several from the drooping branch. She folded the long thin leaf over several times and tucked the edges in, whispering, asking the tree for its help as she fitted the stone in the sling and wrapped the long end through and around her hand.

At the tree, Naaba still hadn't moved. Torn between terror and fascination, he was held motionless by the black mamba. Its power, the ability to kill instantly, made it famous, but it made itself fearsome. Everything about it was meant to arouse fear: its great length, its terrifying black mouth, its spread hood, its hissing cry, but its shining black eye was where it really held the victim hostage. It didn't blink.

Asha crept to the other side of the tree and began throwing her stones. Pebbles at first, just enough to make the vibrations travel through the tree to the snake's sensitive skin. Then she moved closer, lobbing a larger stone into the crease where the snake was hiding. At once, its head swung to her and it moved its incredible length smoothly up the tree and out of the crease. Wrapped around a branch, it moved around the trunk and faced its new foe, opening its black mouth in challenge. She knew she had to move quickly. Loading her largest stone, she hurled it at the snake. It missed the narrow grey head but hit the trunk just behind it, so the snake struck at that spot.

"Run, Naaba!" she cried.

"Send one higher up the tree."

Her next stone was an arm's length above the snake's head, and once again, it lunged at the spot.

"Yes! Try another, even higher!"

The next was a good way above the snake, Asha worried it was too far away, but the snake moved with amazing speed up the tree and struck once again.

"Come on!" he yelled. "Get to the river!"

So they ran, hoping the gathering darkness would prevent the snake from following them. When they saw it move up the tree, they realized how fast it really was. It could easily have caught them, even as they ran for the river.

"You could have killed it," Naaba remarked, when they had built a fire.

"Perhaps," she said, wrapping up the yams to steam, "but I didn't. Perhaps it will repay the favor someday. It's an omen of some kind."

"I think it would be amazing to kill a snake like that," Naaba said quietly, not listening to her last sentence. "It has so much power."

"Dark power," she added.

"Yes, dark power." There was something he felt then that he didn't tell her: the man who killed such a killer would take to himself the power of death, and the fear of it.

That night, he dreamed he had killed the great snake and he carried its venom in a hollowed wood vial carved with serpent designs, which he wore on his chest, and his eyes were deep black orbs that never blinked.

* * *

Several days farther down the river, they came to a section that bowed out around a rocky promontory and the high bank behind it. The rocks rose in long irregular piles straight out of the water and protected the high ground behind it from the eroding effects of the river making it a natural lookout spot. They both noticed it as they worked their way along the riverbank, but it was Asha who saw the pattern. Carved on the side of the rock facing them was a diagram: a circle bisected by two straight lines, with a line of small circles running down two sides.

"How did someone carve that?"

"Why did someone carve that?"

"They must have run a rope from the top of the rocks," she said, answering her own question. "Even then, it must have been very dangerous for someone just hanging there, over the river."

"Why put up a signal no one can read?" Naaba continued with his own query. "If it's a warning, there should be a clearer clan sign. Maybe it's a message for the water spirits."

"In my experience, most signs people leave are meant for other people to see. They only say they're for the gods."

As they were talking, they were heading directly for the promontory, leaving the grassy riverbank behind as they followed the trail up the rocky hillside. The climb was difficult; as soon as they were away from the river, the footing changed, with larger, smoother rocks, some taller than a man. They searched for hand and footholds as they went along, stopping periodically to check their route from where they were to the top. Twice, Asha slipped on the smooth surface, but both times she caught herself before she fell. Later, she wondered why they hadn't simply headed inland and gotten to the top that way, but then she realized why: the pattern on the rock had pulled them to it. Naaba was pushing hard to reach the top, and when he finally pulled himself up to the ledge, he rolled over on his back to catch his breath. It felt very close to the sky there, and when he sat up to help Asha climb the last of the rocks, he was amazed by the view.

The two sat, speechless, at the top, looking at the world as the birds see it, the river winding in front of them and behind them, making a silver trail through the dense forest on both sides. Much farther off, they could see open patches where the villages were, each with its clearing and cluster of huts. They had grown up on flat land. Sitting up in the Community Tree in her village, Asha had seen the low, flat hills in the distance, but she'd never been there. She'd never thought what it must be like to stand on the top of them and look out at a world in which her village, the whole world as she had known it, was just another cluster of huts in the distance.

"Perhaps this is what the sign meant," she said, softly.

He put his hand up to block the sun as he watched a pair of hawks soar overhead. "It's the hawk's view of the world."

After they'd rested, Asha started to follow the ledge to the other side, but she was stopped by Naaba's hand on her arm. He was staring off to the right, inland. At the edge of the rocky outcrop, a stone the size of a man was standing upright, the only standing stone in the area. Carved on the stone was a diagram: a diamond divided into four sections by lines going top to bottom and side to side. The outside border had been filled in with white clay, as had the inside of the sideways "X" across the middle. The triangles that resulted from the bisecting lines were filled in white brown pigment or black, so it was a balance between light and dark sections.

They went up and studied the stone, running their fingers along the indentations and the thick clay pigments. "It takes power that's already there and concentrates it," Naaba said slowly. "This place by the river and this stone, they were already pulsing with energy, but the carving and the colors draw more energy to it, make it stronger."

Asha now went back to Naaba's early question, "Why would someone do this?" There were powerful places in every community: certain hills or lakes or trees that held special energy and spiritual power, but this was different somehow; it was a deliberate manipulation of that power.

"Let's see if we can find more," Naaba said, already heading off inland.

Asha hesitated. Her feet wanted to go back to the river, but she too was curious about the messages. Maybe Naaba was right about there being more of them. They seemed to say something to her, these designs, yet she didn't know exactly what, as if they spoke in something before words.

"But we'll come back to the river again later, won't we?"

"Of course. It's right there, waiting for us."

But they turned their backs to it and headed inland along what seemed to be a trail from the standing stone. Up on the high ground, it was hotter than it had been down by the river, and they each thought about turning back, but since the other didn't mention it, they kept going.

"Maybe there aren't any more," Naaba started, but Asha pointed to their left. A larger stone stood upright, a startling feature in the flat ground. On its face was carved a large diamond with two concentric circles inside it. The diamond was black, and the circles, which didn't quite meet in the center, were white.

"Male stone and female sign," Naaba said. "Why?"

Asha thought about a man in her village who had a problem with cockroaches in his hut, so he put a trail of honey dots from his hut to a trap he had set up. "A sweet death," the man had grinned. "Maybe it's a trap," Asha cried. "Maybe the stones aren't anything except a way to draw you in."

"If someone wanted to ambush us, it would be easier on the trail. All this work has to be for something more." He waved in the direction the trail headed. "Besides, aren't *you* curious?"

"Of course, but maybe that's the point."

"We'll be careful, then," he remarked over his shoulder as he walked off.

As they went, he had another thought, that these stones were part of a ceremony they didn't know or understand. In that case, they could be trespassing on sacred ground merely by being there. But why would the rock carving be set so that any traveler along the river would see it? If it were secret, like the shrines at springs or caves, it would be hidden from view, so only the properly initiated would know of it, and no ignorant passer-by would desecrate it. And how were all of these stones related?

Just as before, the distance between the standing rocks was great enough to keep the travelers waiting, but not great enough to make them give up the quest. The next stone was on the right side of the trail, hidden behind other rocks so it wasn't visible until they were almost upon it, where it had the maximum impact. The monolith towered over them, its bulk as well as its height making them feel small in comparison. Its carving had three parts: a circle with a black "X" across it, similar to the others, with the sections alternating white and red ochre against a black background, a line with ten dots on it above the circle, and another below it.

Behind the stone, the land sloped down and fanned out in an open space. Incredibly, it was filled with circles of standing stones, each about shoulder height and as big around as a person. Some circles had many stones, perhaps twenty to a circle. Others had as few as seven. Each had a stone rectangle in the center. Shocked, Asha stopped and stared. They seemed to be stone dancers moving, all of them in the same direction, endlessly, around and around, capturing her, capturing everything in their motion.

Naaba wandered among the circles, studying them.

"They are time," said a voice behind him, "time stopped but moving, endless but measured."

Startled, Naaba spun around to find a masked figure standing right behind him. Like the diagram on the stone, the mask was diamond-shaped, with the X sections alternating red and black. The large eyes were painted white, with slits across the center. Despite the heat, the man wore a red antelope hide tunic, covered with lines of bone fragments. Two long hippo teeth hung from a necklace, and a rib decorated with feathers was tucked into his head wrap

Naaba tried to read the situation, to guess how many others might be there or nearby, but the man, a shaman he assumed, was standing so close, he blocked the view of the rest of the area. When Naaba moved so he could see past the shaman, the shaman moved as well, the rows of bone fragments rattling with each step. "What are the circles for?" Naaba asked, hoping to figure out the situation. "How are they related to the stones on the path from the river? What are the symbols on the stones?"

"Which question did you want me to answer?" the shaman asked, slowly fanning the air with a large bird wing, not looking at Naaba.

Some irritation from a long time ago rose inside Naaba. "All of them."

Silence fell between them. Then the shaman jumped over to a stone in the larger circle. He moved so suddenly, so quickly, that Naaba started back. With a wave of the hand holding the wing, the shaman drew a circle in the air from east to north to west to south and back to east. "These are movement, like dancers in a circle. They are still, but between them, they mark everything moving, like the passage of the sun from the east through the north to the west, and then through the Underworld to be reborn in the east. The motion is always in that direction. They also mark the passage of the days and the arrival of the seasons." He looked past Naaba. "I know, for instance, when the rainy season will begin."

"There are many signs that the rainy season is beginning," Naaba shrugged.

"I know many days before the first sign," the shaman corrected. "I can tell people when to move their camps so they don't lose everything to the flooding. For this information, they pay me handsomely."

Naaba never had been impressed with people who bragged about their riches or their accomplishments. It seemed that people with real powers hardly ever mentioned the fact. "And what is this, in the middle of the circles?"

"A burial. It's the dead person who gives life to the circle, who starts its movement. And because the dead person is in the Underworld, it gives me a connection there as well," he said, waving the wing toward the middle of the circle.

"If you are counting days, why do you need so many circles? Why not have just one?"

"Because each circle and each burial adds more power. I use different circles for different calculations, moving counter stones around them to mark the moon cycles, the seasons, the reappearance of the great star after it goes to the Underworld."

"And why did you put the stones along the path and by the river?"

"To mark this place, of course, and to draw even more power to it. They also attract the curious," the shaman turned toward Naaba, but his focus never stayed on one spot for long, as if he had to check many things at once. "I meet many interesting people here, people who are curious about the stones and their markings, people who want my help knowing the day the rains will start, people who have other favors to ask of me. The stones are very helpful."

"But the giant stones, they're so heavy, you must have needed many men to raise them."

"Yes."

Naaba still couldn't see Asha. Wherever he looked, the shaman seemed to standing in front of him. "The designs on the stones, the circle and the diamond divided into four sections of light and dark – what do they mean?" he asked, turning back toward the trail, as if he was looking for the stone there.

The shaman answered as if he'd been asked the question many times. "They describe the round energy presence that was divided into four sections at the creation of the world, giving us the balance of elements, the four directions of being. Within the circle, the colors represent the balance of light and dark, wet and dry, day and night, male and female, life and death," he paused, "even good and evil. Opposites power the wheel of life."

"So people pay you for your knowledge?" Naaba asked, thinking they might have to bargain their way out of this place.

The shaman tilted his head to one side, as if considering the question. "Yes, everyone pays. They just pay in different ways, and for different things. The dots on the line in the diagram on the last stone you saw represent their money here: shells on a string."

"'Their money'? Isn't it your money as well? Isn't this your land?"

"I accept many forms of payment. I am of this land at this moment. At another moment, I will be of a different land." The mask turned to face Naaba, the large white eyes with slits across them studying him.

Naaba wasn't easy to intimidate. "It's one thing to take advantage of a special area; it's another to take that area's power to yourself."

"No, it's not different. It's the gift of the shaman. That's why the people come to me, pay me. They're looking for answers to their questions, for power beyond what they have."

"But knowing the weather will change doesn't mean you cause it to change, any more than you cause the sun to rise, or the moon to wax or wane."

"A distinction sometimes lost on the local people."

Alarmed, Naaba pushed past the shaman, looking for Asha.

"Don't worry about your friend," the shaman remarked. "She's fine. Beautiful woman, unusual eyes. She's just visiting with the women here," he added after a moment.

"What women? Where?"

The shaman pointed out past the circles. "Come, I'll show you. She's probably at dinner with the others by now. Surely you are hungry and thirsty after your long walk. It's the law of the bush, you know: please accept my hospitality."

Naaba could have run, right then. With his long legs, he could have easily outstripped the shaman. But he wanted to know where Asha was and what was going on. Besides, as soon as the shaman had mentioned it, he realized he *was* hungry and thirsty, especially thirsty, and bush tradition did require people to take care of guests. They had been travelling along the river, so they carried only the one water gourd with them. He hadn't had anything to drink since first light, and the climb up the rocks had been very hot. Following the shaman down the slope, he imagined a cool spring, with a dipper sitting beside it, the feel of the water in his dry mouth, the splash over his chest and hands as he drank. Asha would like that too.

But as they approached the long open area, covered by a thatched roof, he saw only men, many men, perhaps forty or more. They sat in circles around pots of food, eating, talking quietly to each other. No one looked up when Naaba passed, but those talking fell silent when the shaman came near.

A short, slight man approached, bowing to the shaman. "Lord Komo."

"Okung, this man is our guest. He needs food and drink."

"I'll bring it immediately."

The shaman waved Naaba to an empty spot in the corner. "You won't be able to see your friend until after dinner. The men and women eat separately." With that, he turned and walked away. Naaba watched the bone fragments moving to and fro on the back of the red hide, and felt a chill go down his spine. The servant brought him a bowl of soft-cooked cassava roots and a bottle calabash of what Naaba assumed was water, but after he took a long drink, he realized it was some sort of wine – plum, maybe, though he wasn't sure; the taste was new to him. But he was hungry and thirsty, and everything tasted good.

After a while, he realized the men were watching him. Then, when he looked again, their faces blurred, as if he were looking through a heavy rain, and there was a bright outline around each face. A big man stood up and approached him.

"Welcome to your new home," he said, as he gathered up Naaba's slumping form and carried it away.

CHAPTER 4
KOMO AND LORD KOMO

Back in his large hut, Komo ate alone, waiting until Okung had set the food down and left. He took the mask off slowly, reluctantly, and propped it up against the support beam so it seemed to watch him, the bulging white eyes studying him.

With the mask gazing at him, he felt naked and small, like a child being scolded by a parent. Yet he couldn't stop looking at it.

"I made you," he said to the mask. "I dried the wood in the sun, checking for cracks, but you had none. You were perfect. I knew you would never crack. Then I worked you, with the adz and the chisel. I knew exactly what to remove because I knew exactly what you looked like underneath that wood. All I had to do was release you from your prison. I glued river sand onto the sanding board with resin, and I smoothed the edges, made all the edges smooth. So smooth, they felt like real skin. And I mixed all the colors myself, making them perfect, for you. The charcoal black, the white clay that I dug out of the riverbank myself, the dyes I gathered, all so you could be so beautiful, and you are so beautiful. You are my face, my real face, not this," he clawed at his own face. "I don't know this face. I didn't make it. It made itself, and I don't like it.

"Now you're going with them, aren't you?" he said to the mask. "You're going over to them, on the other side. I can see them, sometimes, moving under the circles, going the opposite way, like a reflection in water. They're going around, the dead people, moving

31

the circle, but I'm keeping them away. The Morning and Evening Star, it's gone into the Underworld, so the dead people are in power, but they're not here, not yet. But I know they're coming to get me. I see them looking at me. That's why I have the owl wing, to keep them away.

"Look!" he cried to the mask, "I have treasure! All of this treasure," he said, jumping up and throwing open the baskets of fine goods given to him as payment: iridescent shells, collections of brilliant feathers from cranes, eagles, and parrots; leopard and eland skins, a pectoral made of sections from turtle shells, carved ivory pieces, a mahogany box, many strings of snail shells, a finely woven robe. "I'll give it to you!" he yelled, throwing the treasures on the mat in front of the mask.

He fell down in front of the mask, his face buried in the pile of treasures. Then, very slowly, he stood, took the mask, lifted it to his face and secured it. "Thank you," he said gravely, "for the offerings. They are very fine."

Then he slept, with the mask on. In his dream, he was three people: the masked Lord Komo, the young man Komo who had first learned about the stone circles, and the old man, the designer of the pattern, who had taught him. They were all talking at once and none of them could understand the others. Below them, the dead people circled in the opposite direction forever. One of them was pointing to him.

CHAPTER 5
PAYMENT

When Naaba awoke, it was night. His hands were bound by thick cords that went between and around his wrists. From the number of sharp stones sticking into him, he guessed he was lying in a pile of stone fragments, probably at the edge of one of the work areas. In addition, his head hurt terribly and he had a raging thirst, but there were other problems to deal with first. Sitting up slowly, he looked around for guards. With all the stone pieces, it was hard to read the shapes, especially with only starlight to help. After a while, he could make out several forms that seemed to be sleeping men. He had no idea where he was or how to find Asha, or even whether she was still on the site, or still alive. He shivered. How stupid he'd been, he thought, swept up like a fish in a river trap. If he could sort out his surroundings, he could find his way, but to where? He wished he could hold his pounding head, make it think clearly.

"Thirsty?" a deep voice behind him said.

Naaba jerked his head around to look at the speaker, and a searing pain shot through his head.

"Don't move fast," the voice said. "It just makes it worse." The big man who had carried him from the longhouse sat down in front of him. A flaming torch was stuck in the ground behind him, throwing his face into shadow. "Here," he said, offering a calabash, "This is water."

Naaba drank without stopping until the calabash was empty. He could easily have emptied four of them. The big man waited patiently. "I'm going to tell you the situation. You can be stupid and try to kill me or escape when you don't know where you are, or you can listen to me. Which will it be?"

His head pounding, Naaba tried to study the man. Tall and broad-shouldered, he had the strong arms, back, and legs of someone who did hard physical work. His large head and thick neck added to the impression of strength, but when he moved, Naaba could see the man's face was open, his expression calm and intelligent. Naaba nodded. "I'll listen."

"Good. Here's the situation. You have to make a payment for the privilege of visiting the stone circles. Do you have any treasure?"

"No," Naaba said as he tried to jump to his feet, but the big man swept his leg behind Naaba's knees. Without his arms for balance, Naaba crashed to the rocky ground.

"I told you to listen and not be stupid," the man said to the groaning form before him. "It'll just take longer to explain all this if you keep jumping around."

"I don't understand."

"What don't you understand? You wandered into a trap. Now you're caught in it, and you need to pay to get out." He helped Naaba sit back up. When he saw Naaba was calmer, he offered another calabash full of water. "When you walked in here, didn't you wonder who built all of this?"

Putting down the empty calabash, Naaba thought back to his first view of the stones. "I thought there was incredible power here."

"You were right about that, but the power comes from the hard work of people like you. And me. I wandered in here, just like you. But I stayed."

"You what?"

"If you'd stop thrashing around, I'll explain." He waited until Naaba sat back, uncomfortably, on the rocks. "I didn't think you had any treasure, since you were carrying almost nothing with you."

"What is he doing, that man, Komo?"

Sohko studied his mangled fingers, torn up from hard work. "That's Lord Komo, if you're talking to him. He says the energy that flows through all living things can be extracted, just as a hunter extracts the power from his prey when he kills it. More people, more creation, more power flowing through the city, it all keeps the stones dancing, the wheel of life turning."

Naaba thought of the black mamba and his desire to own that killing power. How different was he from this madman who collected people?

"If Komo is truly collecting energy, he'll kill us, so he can own our power."

"No, he won't. He needs your living energy. You're safe. So is your lady friend. Komo will not hurt her or allow anyone else to. Once you do your job, you'll be free to go. Or you can stay here, and make this your home."

"Why would I want to do that?"

"Because we're building something great here. We're making a trade center, here, at the point of the river. We already have people who bring honey and salt here for trade. Plus, in the city, we now have hunters, builders, musicians, storytellers, carvers, weapon makers, cloth and basket weavers, everything. We even have a way to keep track of everything on counter strings." He pulled a string out of his sash, showing Naaba. It had nineteen snail shells strung along one section, and two in another. Each section had a marker wood, with a v-notch cut in it, pushed into a place between shells. "You can count anything on it. Let's say I wanted to keep track of how many cone shells I had. I start counting from the bottom," he explained, pointing to the first shell. "For each one, I move the counter, until I get to the top. Then," he pointed to the top, "I move one shell, for twenty, and move the lower level counter back to the bottom. By the time I get both shells on the top moved, I have to start on a new string. If I trade some, I just change the counter backwards." He looked very satisfied with his counting string. "It counts by twenty, the same as the total number of fingers and toes."

Naaba looked unimpressed.

"This is going to be a great city, far greater than any little village."

"Thanks, but I'd rather be on the river."

"As you wish, then."

"And what is this payment? I thought bush hospitality required you to feed a guest."

"Yes, indeed," the big man smiled. "Your meal was free. But leaving is expensive."

The other shapes were stirring, and Sohko, the guard, spent time with each one, going through the same process. Then he called them together and explained their task would take two or three days of hard work. "*Hard* work," he repeated. Two of the men groaned. The others, including Naaba, would have fled into the unknown, in the dark, if they hadn't been bound.

Gradually, the other men went through all the same questions: Where were their companions? When would they be free to go? Why should they do any work at all?

"Would you rather spend three days tied up out here on the rock piles?" Sohko asked. "Look, we all paid. It's the cost. You can do your work and get through it, or you can whine and complain. It doesn't matter to me, but it will take longer if someone has to drag you along. You see, you'll be working with a partner on this job. Together, you'll be doing your part to make the city great."

"And what's all this for?" one of the men asked. "What are the circles for? Why did Komo build them? What are they telling him?"

Sohko's large face softened in a half-smile. "The strange thing is, from what I hear, Komo didn't even build these circles. An old man did, a wizard. He figured out how to count the days so that he knew when the rains were coming. Before that, people who were camped along the river were often caught in floods and mud slides at the start of the rainy season. Many died. So the old man realized he could warn people, before the first clouds appeared in the sky, when the rains would come. At least, his predictions were accurate enough for people to decide he was some kind of magician. They thought he actually made the rains come, even though he told them he was just counting days. But a young man named Komo came along, and he saw power sitting there in front of him. He begged the old man to teach him everything about the cycles he was counting. So he did."

"What happened to the old man?"

"He was the first burial in the circle. And since he really was special, Komo was right: his power added to the circle."

"Where is Asha?" Naaba said, tired of the talk of Komo and his circles of stone.

"She's working with the women's group," Sohko waved vaguely off to the west, "closer to the river. They do the shell work, dyeing, and weaving down there. She'll be done as soon as you are."

"And what's our job?"

"You'll be working in the tannery," Sohko explained, addressing the whole group. "Each pair will be working one hide. It should take two to three days, if you cooperate with your partner and get the work done right. If not, it'll take longer. You decide."

Two days, Naaba thought, maybe three. Then we'll go back to the river and the life we had there. Suddenly, it seemed very fine and far away.

CHAPTER 6
AT THE TANNERY

The following morning, Sohko cut their bonds and lead them away to the tannery, which was a long way from the village. The men realized right away why it was so far: it stank so fiercely, it made several of them sick.

Sohko sorted the six men into three pairs. "You'll get to be good friends," he laughed.

Under a mat covering was a pile of hides, just as they'd been cut off the carcass of the animals, mostly antelope. When Sohko took the mat off, a cloud of flies was drawn immediately to the hides, so he recovered them. "Each pair of you will work on one hide. Figure how to work together without killing each other. Otherwise, you will.

"Stake out your hide with the hair side down, in the open area, there. You'll find a pile of stakes and hammerstones next to the hides. Put the stakes close to the edge of the hide, but not so close the hide rips when you're working on it. About a hand's width should work. Then remove all the flesh with the dull knives that are also by the hides.

"Then you heat the antelope brains. They're already soaking in water, in the pots set in the ground, to keep them ready for you to use. Mash them, so you get a sort of brain soup, and put hot stones from the fire pit in the pot. Then heat the round river stones in the fire pit. When both the brain soup and the round stones are hot, rub the brains into the hide with the hot stones. When you've finished with the flesh side, unstake the hide, flip it over, and do the other side. Use all the brain soup. Then leave the hide in the sun for the rest of the day and soak it in the cistern overnight.

The next morning, you re-stake the hide. Use one of the rounded end sticks, over by the hides, to push the water out of the hide. Then work every bit of the hide with the blunt stick. You have to keep working it, or it'll stiffen. It'll take all day to do it right. Work both sides, then un-stake the hide and cut away the stake holes.

Next, pull the hide back and forth over one of those branches to stretch it and finish drying it. For the last part, rub it all over with smooth stones, then hang it over the tripods, right there, to smoke it. That'll keep it from stiffening up the first time it gets wet.

Some of you will need to make the hide lighter or darker. Then you'll finish it with fish oil and animal fat." He looked around the group. "Any questions?" He smiled. "Don't worry. I'll go back over it step by step. I've done lots of it."

It was a subdued group that ate the soft-cooked cassavas and bits of dried fish provided to them before they started work. Three of the men were obviously younger than Naaba, and they were scared. One said he was just recently married, but he and his wife had fled because a group of warriors had killed their chief and burned their village. "The attackers didn't even take much," he said. "They just destroyed the village and burned the forest around it, and then moved on." In the confusion, some of the villagers chose to join the attackers, but his wife was pregnant, so they set out on their own. When they saw the carving by the river, they assumed it was a trading post, and they headed inland, hoping to find supplies for the journey. Instead, he was here.

Another had a similar story. The man next to him looked around at the worried group and sneered. "You'll all die here, and they'll use your brains for the next batch of soup. What babies you are!"

Naaba tried to jump to his feet, but one of the other men put out his hand to stop him. "He's just baiting you. It's entertainment for him. Don't bother with him."

While most of the men were young, one was old enough to be their father. "It's strange," he said, "that I was hoping to create exactly what you are planning to build here: a trade center. It's the best place, the high spot on the river, safe from flooding. It would make a perfect gathering and trade area, especially for salt, wax, and honey, ivory, crocodile skins, that sort of thing. Unfortunately, like you, I was trapped when I followed the stones. The difference is that it's not my wife I miss; it's my grandchildren."

When Naaba told his story, the bitter man, Nassor, interrupted, "Very pretty, but it makes no difference. Trouble-maker, brother, lover, husband, grandfather, it doesn't matter. You'd have to be blind not to see what's happening. We work out our days. Somebody, some-place along the line, does something wrong, or Komo imagines some-thing's wrong. Then we all get more days, maybe ten, maybe thirty, who knows, whatever suits Komo at the time. We're just slaves now. We'll never get out of here alive. We're here for the same reason the fly is in the spider's web. It doesn't matter if the spider eats the fly today or saves it until tomorrow. The fly is never leaving."

He waited for a response, but none came. No one wanted to admit that fear by voicing it.

The last man said nothing until one of the others prompted him. "My name is Zola. I came here with my sister, Ayo, because I had heard of the place." He hesitated, moving pebbles into different patterns on the ground. "I love the circles of stones, and I believe in their power. Only, I don't believe they should be used to entrap peo-ple. They're amazing. You don't need to trap people. They'd come here just to feel the power of the turning circles of stone." Looking at the old man, he said, "It could easily be a great center of trade as well, but even then, the stones must be separate. They shouldn't be part of the world of trade. They're – above trade."

"They're a bunch of stones stuck in the ground," Nassor said. "The rest is just something people use to control other people."

"No," Zola answered, without anger, "they're knowledge, and knowledge connects us to the universe."

"I know my ankle is raw, but it doesn't connect me to the stars."

"But understanding the stars would."

Sohko broke in. "You don't have to see eye to eye here; you just have to work together. Understood? Everyone ready to get to work?"

There was a general murmur of assent, except for Nassor, who stood up, crossed his arms over his chest, and said, "Make me."

In a move so quick, Naaba missed it completely, Sohko hit Nassor in the chest and swung one leg behind his bent knees. The man fell with a scream.

"Other problems?" Sohko said, with a challenge lingering in his voice.

De-fleshing the hide was a gruesome job, pounding and scouring the skin to remove bits of flesh and fat, and the endless buzzing of flies was torment, but little by little, they could see progress. Mashing the cooked brains made the young man who was Naaba's partner sick, but once the rocks were heated, he worked hard rubbing the mixture into the hide. Then they unstaked the hide and flipped it over, working the other side. When it was done, they left it to heat up in the sun while they stoked up the fire and set up a new batch of brains to soak in the pots.

When Sohko called for a break, the men collapsed on the ground and drank every drop of water in the calabashes he offered. Even Nassor had worked hard, the sweat running down his back, and he said nothing more to the others, or to Sohko. At the end of the work day, they carried the hides to the cistern to soak overnight and fell asleep shortly after having something to eat. Exhausted by hard work in the blazing sun, they found sleep its own reward.

The next day they hauled the heavy water-soaked hides out of the cistern, re-staked them, and worked the water out of them with rounded-end sticks, pushing it from the center to the edges. Before it was completely dry, they started working the leather, pushing it, every bit of it, loosening the fibers so it would soften. It was slow going, and their muscles ached from going through the same motion over and over.

When Sohko called for a break, they could see the change. The hide that had been covered in dirt and gore was turning into a fine piece of leather, bit by bit. Even Nassor had nothing bad to say.

Sohko selected one hide to be dyed darker with crushed bark and one to be lightened with urine. Then all three would need to be worked again with oil and tallow and the blunt stick.

After the men had eaten, they stretched the hides by pulling them back and forth across smooth branches in the trees, then rubbed them with smooth river stones. Walking around, checking each hide, Sohko nodded. They looked fine.

As a final step, the men hung the hides high over the fire pits, so the smoke would help seal the leather. Then they rubbed the hides with oil.

While the teams had been tanning the hides, Sohko had been working on a piece of scrap leather, moving a pointed stone from one spot to another and tapping it with a hammerstone, holding it up, considering his work, and then continuing. When Naaba had finished his work, he went over and looked at Sohko's project. It was an image of a falcon on a rock, as if it had just landed there a moment ago, facing forward but looking backward, its large eye and hooked beak perfectly etched in the piece of leather no bigger than a man's hand.

"It's amazing," Naaba said.

"It's my clan sign," Sohko said, running his finger across the falcon. "It gives me strength."

That night should have been easy. Their work done, they knew they'd be heading back to the settlement, with the hides, the next morning, after they'd set up the area for the next group. But a nervous energy pervaded the camp, and no one slept well. After the moon was well up into the sky, two men started fighting over the drinking water. One was taking one gourd after another from the drinking water cistern and pouring it over himself.

"Stop it!" his teammate yelled, grabbing his arm. "You're wasting it! We need drinking water for the trip back."

The man shook off his grip and ran back to the water. "I have to get it off me, wash it off me. It's too much blood, bits of flesh and hair and skin. I can feel death on me," the man cried, splashing water all over. "I can't wash it off."

His teammate grabbed him and threw him on the ground. "You're going mad. You didn't kill anything. The hides were already dead. Hunters killed the animals."

"But their blood, it's all over me," the man cried, trying to grab the calabash.

"You're right, it is," the old man said, stepping between the two. "I feel it too."

"Then take it to you. Accept it, all of you," Zola said. "You're upset because you're trying to ignore it. Blood can't be ignored. Accept that this animal has marked you with its blood. You're connected now. If you make a beautiful thing from its hide, it takes on a new life. If you try to make the animal invisible, it will haunt you."

The man stood and stared at them. "They all haunt me. I see them at night, just skins and skulls, walking over the rocks."

Naaba sat up, listening to the argument, but his eye was drawn to the rocky horizon, now glowing with a fiery light. It was coming from direction of the settlement. "Sohko!" he called, but the leader was already climbing to higher ground, studying the flickering sky. Suddenly, he jumped in front of the men, shouting,

"Wake everyone! Take the hides you've completed, anything you think you can use as a weapon, two full calabashes, some branches and oil for a torch, and whatever else you value. We need to find our way back to the settlement, tonight! Hurry!"

The men rushed about, their argument forgotten, gathering whatever they could carry. The old man stumbled in his haste, cutting his leg on the rocks, and Naaba steadied him. "We won't leave without you," he said. "Don't worry."

The old man shuddered. "Thank you, but I'm more worried about what lies before us."

CHAPTER 7
DISCOVERIES AFTER THE FIRE

They ran in the dark, their torches lighting their path in bouncing circles around them. Only one man, the one farthest in the back, slipped away from the group. Nassor saw nothing worth fighting for among the people who had imprisoned him, nor among the men in his work group, so he headed off in the dark, on his own. The rest pounded up the trail, stumbling on the rocky outcrops as they went. After a while, their torches began to fade, but the red light over the settlement grew brighter and higher.

"Sohko, what if they've set the forest on fire?" Naaba called as they ran.

"We have to know what's happened first. Then we'll decide."

When they were quite close to the settlement, they heard the cry of an owl, and Sohko answered it. A short, slight man stepped out into the opening, his breathing short and ragged, his body covered in dirt and ash.

"Okung!" Sohko called. The shorter man was hardly able to stand as Sohko gripped his arm. "Get your breath. Then tell us what's happened."

"All the buildings are on fire. Everything." Okung tried to take a deep breath, but it came out in a series of coughs. "They came in the dark and killed the sentries. I heard one warning call, that's all. Then they were in the village, with their torches, setting fire to everything. Anyone who stood in their way was killed.

The men had white clay marks on their faces, like death. Long lances and sharp knives. They used burning pitch to set fire to the long house, the other houses, and then the forest."

"And Komo?"

"He's the one they were looking for. They went right to his hut, grabbed him, stripped him, killed him, and left him right there, in the middle of one of the circles." Okung shuddered. "Once Komo was dead, the people panicked, running into the forest, in all directions. The attackers set fire to the forest around the settlement. I heard one of the leaders order it."

Impatient, Naaba stepped forward. "Why did they attack? Where did they go? Where are the women and children?"

"I don't know!"

"Someone must know," Naaba pushed. "Did everyone run off into the forest?"

Nodding, Okung said, "Most of them. That's when the warriors set the forest on fire, behind them, pushing them along."

"That's just what happened to us, before!" one of the men cried. "They came in, killed the leader, and set fire to the village. When the people were panicked, running around not knowing what to do or where to go, the attackers offered them to chance to join the group. Most did. By killing a few people, the attackers gained many."

Sohko watched the fiery glow spreading higher into the sky. "We need to get to the river."

Okung shook his head. "It's worse. Everyone will go to the river, but according to Komo's calculations, the rainy season will start in a few days. That means -"

"That means," Sohko interrupted, "the floods will wipe away everything on or near the river."

In his mind, Naaba saw one person he knew would head to the river, no matter where they had put her. He saw her face shining as her feet sought out the water that worked its way through the earth, tiny rivulets bubbling through the rock and sand.

"We need to start with the settlement," Naaba said. "There may be someone there who knows where the others are."

"*If* they are," one of the men added.

Closer to the settlement, they ran into several of Komo's guards running, directionless, through the forest. When they saw Sohko, they immediately fell in with his group, even though he was heading back toward the burned settlement. Unfortunately, they knew nothing of the invaders, their reasons, or their plans. They had been sleeping when the attack started. One of them noticed, though, that the attackers knew immediately where to find Komo. Another pointed out that Komo had the largest hut in the settlement, so it wasn't hard to guess it belonged to the leader. But they all said it was a shock to realize Komo was just a man under his mask. "He wasn't even very tall, or strong," one man added.

Zola, the young man who loved the stones, stepped up. "Where is the mask now?"

Okung shrugged. "Back in the settlement, probably, unless the attackers took it. They didn't seem interested in it, though, or the stones, or much of anything. They just swept through the place, burning everything. It was as if they just wanted everyone out, the way you'd shoo flies away from your dinner."

"Then, if it is here, I'd like to claim the mask," Zola said. "I want to be part of the motion of the stones. I understand their power, or at least I'd like to."

The old man nodded slowly. "You'd be a good choice, but you need to be careful; it's easy to mistake their power for your own. That's what Komo did."

"No," Zola said, "Komo lied. The stones were just his prop, his show of power. The stones are the real power. If I'm allowed to tend them and learn from them, I will." He bowed before the group and then rose, waiting for their answer.

Naaba studied Zola's earnest young face and wondered if Komo had looked the same way at one time. Power was a dangerous drug, and very few were the same after they tasted it.

"We'll see what's left for you to work with," Sohko answered. "Okung can teach you how to count on the different circles, and which calculations are already in progress. He helped Komo every day," he added by way of explanation. "How strange it is that powerful people assume that those who serve them are ignorant, or uninterested. Okung never asked questions, but he absorbed everything."

"Then the mask is yours, by right," the young man answered gravely, facing Okung.

Okung shook his head slowly. "I don't want it, but I appreciate your gesture. You'll love your work with the stones, but I need to leave them behind."

Patches of the dry underbrush in the forest were still burning as the men picked their way through to the village. There, the burned thatched roofs of the buildings had collapsed, and some of the posts were still smoking; there was no sign of people anywhere. The men ran from one section to another, calling, looking for someone, anyone, some sign of life, but no one answered. The roof in Komo's quarters had collapsed so completely, it covered everything on the floor beneath it. When they sifted through it, they found baskets and boxes of gifts Komo had thrown down before the mask: strings of snail shells, woven cotton fabric, a leopard skin, beautifully carved spears, decorated bone knives, ivory, bags made of crocodile skin, collections of stunning blue and yellow feathers wrapped in raffia leaves.

"You're welcome to take what you can carry, either the hide or one of the treasures," Sohko called, "but the path is rough. If you can't carry it, don't take it."

The men took what they fancied and left the rest behind. Naaba tied the leopard skin around his shoulders, taking to himself the gifts of the great hunter it once belonged to, and tucked the carved bone knife into his sash. Okung helped him find his bundle of tools, which had been thrown off to the side by those looking for more attractive treasures.

"Where is everyone? Were they all taken prisoner?" one of the men cried.

"No." The voice came from the farthest circle of stones.

An old woman stepped into their circle of torchlight, her body twisted with age, but her face unafraid. "They took no prisoners. They didn't want prisoners. They wanted to kill the leader and scatter the people." She glanced around. "And they did.

"The men were taken by surprise, except for a warning call a sentry must have sent. The attackers fanned out around the village, driving out the people, setting fire to roofs with oil-soaked batons they brought with them. They killed only Komo and the guards who stood in their way. Most of the people ran off into the forest. The attackers set fire to the forest, but I think it was to make sure the people didn't return. They didn't attack the women; they didn't kill randomly. They took some treasures but left many others. It was strange."

"Are there others who stayed?" Sohko asked, glancing around the smoking ruins.

"Come," she answered, "I'll show you the others." Leading them back to the farthest circle of stones, she motioned for them to wait while she walked alone into the center of the circle, her ancient arms outstretched. When she gave a huffing snort, like an antelope warning signal, two small figures emerged from behind the stones: children wrapped in dark cloaks. Then two more, so covered that they were hard to distinguish in the darkness, then a toddler helped by an older girl, then three more, all swathed from head to foot in brown bark cloth. They stood, clustered around the old woman, hanging onto her sleeve or her long skirts, or each other, frightened by the night and the men with torches. But one turned and looked at the line of men, her head tilted slightly as she tried to see past the bobbing torches to the men's faces.

"Grandfather?" she said, her voice thin in the night air.

It was enough for the old man. He stepped forward and dropped to his knees, his arms spread wide, tears streaming down his face. "Deka!" he shouted as she ran to him, "Deka!" Then another child broke out of cluster and ran toward the old man. "Sule!" the old man cried as he pulled the children into his embrace.

"I knew the circle of stones would keep them safe," the old woman said to Sohko. "My husband built that circle, long ago, but its power has never been lessened by the time it measures."

Naaba bowed to the woman, but he was impatient to know more. "Thank you for saving the children, grandmother. Are the others here as well – the women and children?"

She shook her head. "I'm sorry. They're not here. Only the children without families. I think the women were taken to a different area, closer to the river. The others, the families who lived here, are scattered in the forest," she said. "With the fire behind them, they'll probably go to the river."

The river, Naaba thought. Everything was converging on the river. Only Zola, the man who loved the circles of stones, wanted to stay. Everyone else was either leaving or gone. And what of the great city they had envisioned, the center of trade and knowledge? The piles of treasure, the newly-tanned hides, the stores of dried food and salt, the half-finished projects and their tools, all these things were left behind after the fire.

But the stones continued in their endless stationary circle that marked the movements of the universe. They had the luxury of timelessness.

The following morning, as they prepared to leave, Okung explained the circles' counting mechanism to Zola and showed him how to align his position at the center with the different stars. At the end of his talk, he turned to Zola, putting his hand on the young man's arm.

"Are you certain you want to do this?"

"Absolutely."

"Perhaps I should stay to take care of you," the old woman offered.

"Thank you, grandmother," Zola bowed, "but don't worry. I'll be fine. I need to be here, alone. You and the children need to find a new home with other people."

"As you wish," she said, "but when they start pointing at you, you need to get to the river, right away."

Zola didn't understand, but he probably wouldn't have listened even if he had.

CHAPTER 8
THE STONEPILES BY THE RIVER

Where Naaba had been drawn in by fascination, Asha had been slowed by fear. When he went to see the stone circles, she pulled back, suspicious. She waited, torn by her desire to stay and her need to flee. When she knew, somehow, that there were people moving in behind her, she took off, running, jumping over the rocks like an impala, circling around her pursuers and heading back toward the river. The plump, round-faced woman who had gone out to meet Asha turned to the guard near her and threw up her hands.

"Too quick for me, that one," she sighed.

"Oh, she'll come around, Aminata," the guard smiled. "They all do."

Frightened, Asha ran all the way back to the tall piles of stone by the top of the river and then stopped. She didn't want to leave without Naaba, but she couldn't go back to the circles. So she sat in the shade of the stones for the rest of the day and considered her options. None looked good. At night, she climbed up into the rocks and hoped she wasn't disturbing a poisonous snake sleeping in the crevices. It was a terrible night, and dawn was little better. She had no idea where Naaba was, or where she should go. She could go back to the village, but if it was a trap, how would she escape being caught in it? How would she find Naaba without being captured herself? But the alternative was leaving him and going farther down the river alone. No, she decided, she wouldn't do that. So she found her way down to the river for water and then back up again, to her niche in the rock. Mindlessly, she watched tiny lizards hunt among the stones while the sun crossed the sky. She knew something had to happen; there was a growing pressure in the air around her that had to be released somehow. But for the moment, there was nothing for her to do but wait. At least, she could hear the river, she thought, but as she listened to it, she realized she could also hear something else: singing. The sound seemed to come and go, as if a group was singing a chorus but only one voice carried the verses. Asha moved down from the rocks and closer to the sound. They were women's voices. And that song they were singing, she knew that song, the long tale of the Monkey King and the great battles in the tree tops, pitting the tiny monkey against the monsters of the earth and air, always winning, but just barely, because he was so clever, and he had so many friends that helped. She found herself humming along with the chorus:

> *Monkey King!*
> *Monkey King!*
> *Small but clever,*
> *Undefeated,*
> *Sing now, with your friends!*

At the end of the chorus, there were five drumbeats in a row. That's the part the children used to stomp their feet to, back in her village, as they yelled, "Mon-key Mon-key King!" She felt a sudden pang, feeling the packed dirt under her feet long ago. She was so lost in reverie that she almost missed another sound, this one from behind her. Crawling back to the other side of the stones, she leaned over, listening to the sounds of men in boats on the river, calling from boat to boat, their voices carrying easily across the water and up the rocks. Slipping down to the next rock, she had a clear view of the river. Just beyond the landing, there were four war canoes, each carrying at least eight men. Several were looking up at the rock carving, pointing to it. As she watched, she shivered. With their faces were covered in white clay, the warriors looked like an army of death.

Without further thought, she ran toward the source of the song. By the time she reached the camp where the women were singing as they worked, she was straining to catch her breath. As she stumbled into the work area, a longhouse with a thatched roof, the women stopped singing and stared at her. Aminata, the heavy-set woman who had tried to catch Asha earlier, was surprised but pleased to see her. Sometimes, she'd found, you could catch more people with a good song than with drugs and threats. But Asha had more important things to deal with than Aminata's work plan. In broken sentences, she told these women she had never seen before about the war party on the river.

But they didn't respond. They only looked at her, one still holding up the rolled reed she was ready to insert into another, another keeping her place in the fibers she was weaving. Asha's wild appearance was a strange, unexplained interruption to their work.

"What?" Aminata managed to say.

Asha forced herself to calm down, to go over it all again, but she wanted to shake these women into action. They needed to get out of there. The path from the river would lead the warriors right to this camp.

"Are these men from this village?" Asha said, hoping to get them to understand.

They stared at her.

One woman said, "We're working off our stay here," showing her basketwork.

Frustrated, Asha spoke slowly, emphasizing each word, "Are you listening? There is a group of warriors on the river. They'll be landing soon. You can't stay here. Do you understand now?"

With a sigh, Aminata pushed herself to her feet, smoothed her wrap, retied the knot at the bottom of her thick braid, and faced the women. "Put away your work. Take only what you brought with you. Then follow me." With a glance at Asha, she added, "You too. We're safer together."

"Where's my brother?" the woman who was weaving cried. "Where is he?"

"Probably in the tannery," Aminata said, "on the far side of the village. He can't help you right now, and you can't reach him."

"We'll take care of you," the pregnant woman said, putting out her arm. "He'll find you later."

Asha thought she'd scream at Aminata's slow pace, but the other women didn't seem to mind, as they neatly put away their work, packed up their things, and headed away from camp. The weaver was keenly disappointed to leave her work behind. She had just worked out a new way to join the thin fibers from different plants. In the end, she took some of her work with her, tucking it into her wrap as she left. As they walked, they were aware that the pregnant woman tired easily, so they ambled through the forest, chatting with each other, following Aminata's shuffle. All of them expected to be back later, to finish their work.

Akin, the warriors' leader, had spotted the carving on the stone the day before and signaled a landing. He sent his two best advisors to scout the area and ordered the others to make camp away from the river, so they would remain out of sight of any sentries the settlement might post.

"No fires," he ordered. "We'll wait for darkness."

The two scouts stayed parallel to the main path, moving quietly, stopping when they saw or heard something, noting the monoliths, the stone circles, the location of the village, and the main hut, then returning to the camp without ever being noticed in the village. In camp, they sought out Akin and told him of their finds. He nodded at the information, but stopped them when they described the stone circles.

"This is strong magic," he said, troubled.

"Yes, sir, it is, but when everyone's gone, the forest will grow back, and no one will remember the magic stones. They'll be just another story."

"Perhaps, but we have to find a way to erase or cover the pattern on the rock over the river before we leave. Otherwise, it'll draw people back to this place. The monoliths too, can you pull them down?"

"If they were put up, there has to be a way to take them down."

Akin nodded. "True. And we need to make sure the families leave permanently. We'll light a fire in the forest behind them as they leave the village."

"You don't want to establish a river center here? It would be a logical spot."

"No, not here. We'll move the families downriver somewhere, as soon as we pick a leader for them. The warriors will join us." He paused, putting his hand to the rhino amulet that hung around his neck. "They'll see it's better to be part of a larger, stronger force. Besides, there won't be anything left of the old village to go back to."

CHAPTER 9
THE RIVER RISES

The families ran through the night, the fire always behind them, pushing them away from their village. They could hear people calling, yelling to others through the dark forest, and children crying, and separated loved ones screaming each other's names, but always the fire stood between them and the past, so eventually, they all moved toward the river. While they could have gone in any direction, they had fled instinctively toward the river, the escape route, and now the flames just added to their urgency.

As Aminata had expected, the attackers never even went down the trail to their camp, since the main trail was so much better marked and more traveled. But even if they had, they would have found no one. She had known exactly where to take the women so they'd be safe from the fire and could see down to the river where the people were gathering by torchlight. The first ones to arrive took the village's canoes and sped off down the river, even though the boats could have held many more. The next group was mostly young men and women who clambered down the rocks to the river edge and then stopped. It had been their only goal, to get to the river, but once they reached it, there was nowhere to go. The boats were gone. Behind them, more people came down the rocks, and they too milled around the riverbank. Some families were reunited there, and two of the women in Asha's group shouted when they sighted their husbands.

Asha stood high above the riverbank, watching the crowds, looking for Naaba, but she was distracted. It had started as just a brush of a feeling, a passing thought, but it kept growing, and now, even this high above the river, she was sure of it. As the two women were finding their way down the rocks, Asha turned to Aminata.

"We have to get all these people away from the river," she said softly, "or they'll drown."

The woman's round face was unconcerned. "Those people want to be next to the river. That's why they're there."

Asha reached for the woman's arm as she turned to go. "The river's rising. I can feel it."

"You're crazy," Aminata said. "The rains haven't even started yet."

If they could have seen far enough beyond the great trees, they would have seen the dark clouds massed to the north and east. The land was unusually dry, and the rainwater ran along it, filling up the flat pans and coursing along the dry creek beds, skipping across the earth, finding the lowest spot, moving ever faster as it was pushed by the racing waters behind it. Asha felt it coursing through the ground, the smallest trickle swelling, joining others, becoming transformed into a torrent.

"We need to get these people off the riverbank and on to higher ground," she repeated. "I don't know how to convince you, and certainly you know nothing about me," she pleaded, "but I'm telling you I know this for certain."

Turning, Aminata studied the strange woman with yellow eyes. "Even if I did believe you, there's no way to get those people to move. They think the river is going to save them."

"But they would listen to you."

"Thank you for the compliment. Yes, normally they would. But not tonight. They have no leader and no home. They're panicked. They're hanging on to the river as the only lifeline they know."

"Then you'd stand by and watch them drown?"

Aminata drew herself up and returned the younger woman's stare. "What they do is their choice."

"Even if you have the ability to save them?" Asha demanded.

"I'm supposed to trust some crazy woman who can feel water rising and risk my life with a group of people panicked from the loss of their home?"

"Yes."

The two women considered each other in the pre-dawn light. Neither one looked away. Then Asha held out her arm, and Aminata held out hers, and the two women connected, both their arms clasped on the others.

"You understand they may kill us both," Aminata laughed as she flipped her thick braid behind her.

As they worked their way down the rocky ledges, Akin and his men brought two war canoes to the riverbank and turned them sideways, holding them in the current with poles. Three men blew loud whistles over and over to silence the crowd. Akin stood in the closer canoe, torch held high.

"Your village is no more," Akin proclaimed when the villagers were quiet. "Your new village will be established downriver. There you will be able to build a new life as members of a great trade center." Pointing to the man next to him in the boat, he said, "This is Wekesa; he'll be your new leader, until you are established in your new village and select your own chief."

He looked at the ragged line of people on the shore. "The journey will take three days. It will be difficult, especially for the children and elders, but if you all help, it can be done. You will have a better life in your new settlement," he went on into the silence. "As part of our settlement chain, you will be protected by our forces, and you will have many opportunities to trade with other villages in our group. That means greater peace and prosperity for all of you."

There was a confused murmur among the crowd.

"What if we don't want to be part of your 'settlement chain'?" one young man asked.

"There will be nothing left here. Everything has been, or will be, destroyed. The new village will offer much more, though it will take time to build. If you'd rather try to survive on your own, you're free to go. But, if you decide, later, that you made the wrong choice, you cannot return. The decision is final. Also, understand that he who is not our friend is our enemy, and will be treated as such."

The murmurs grew louder, as people tried to understand, to decide what to believe.

"But this is our home," one woman wailed.

"No," Akin corrected, "it used to be your home. It is no more. We welcome new warriors to our ranks," he continued, "and administrators of our new centers. Wekesa will be training all those interested."

"Well, I'm not interested," the young man fired back. "I'll never go to your settlement. Who made you the one to decide what's best for us? What have you done except destroy what we had? We should destroy you!"

"That would be unwise," Akin answered slowly. Behind him, in the other boat, the archers were already on alert, reaching for arrows.

"He doesn't know what he's saying," the young man's father started, but the young man yelled, "Yes, I do! I know exactly what I'm doing: I'm fighting for our village. Why aren't *you* fighting for your village? Don't you care? Why would you believe these killers? They just destroyed our homes, killed our leader! And you're about to follow them downriver – to what?"

A young woman took his arm, "Let it go, Paki."

He spun around, taking her by the shoulders. "Leave with me, right now, or never see me again. These men are murderers, and they're pretending to be saviors. I'd rather die than go with them."

He turned to the others. "What's the matter with all of you? That village was my home. Our home. That was the only home I've ever known. Now someone else wants it, so we all have to go along with the new plan. Why? How did they get the right to change what we do, where we live, how we live?"

The people were tired and scared. No one stepped up to support him.

"Fine!" he yelled. "Go like turtles, hunkering down inside your shells, hoping the danger will pass. But I won't."

"Paki," the young woman pleaded, "let it go."

"Never. I challenge these jackals who threaten us and tell us to leave our homes in the dark. I challenge them because they're nothing but noise, sneaking up at night, murdering Komo, burning our homes. They're not leaders; they're shifters: wild dogs in human skin." He raised his spear and shook it. "I challenge you!" With that, he drew back his arm and launched his spear right at Akin, but it was barely out of his hand before the point of a poison-tipped arrow caught him in the throat, and he fell, his life-breath leaving him in a series of spasms, his body falling heavily on the riverbank.

The people were dumb with shock. His father finally gathered up the young man's body and carried it away while the girl screamed in grief. In the growing pre-dawn light, the people huddled, terrified, unable to go back and unwilling to go forward, clinging to the riverbank as their only haven.

Holding out his serpent-headed staff, Akin addressed the people. "I'm not here to kill people. I'm here to help you move to your new settlement. You must decide now. If you are coming with us, you'll need to follow Wekesa along the riverbank, to your new settlement."

It was at this moment, this least propitious moment, that Asha stepped forward. "You can *not* go along the riverbank trail," she cried. "The river is rising, and you will drown, you and everyone else near the river."

No one responded. After a moment, everyone continued shuffling toward the riverbank trail, where Wekesa was holding up a torch.

"The river is rising!" Asha cried, frustrated. "Don't you understand?"

This time no one even looked at her.

Aminata sighed and patted her thick braid, checking that the three blue parrot feathers were still attached to the tie by her neck. Then she stepped out onto the ledge.

"Are you people deaf, or are you too scared to listen?" Some people looked up, recognizing her. "If these men, who just attacked and burned our village," she paused for that last part to sink into the minds of her listeners, "really want us to have a safe new home in their network, they shouldn't mind taking us through the high ground trail, should they?" She waited for a response. There was none, but more people were looking up now, waiting to hear what she said. "If, on the other hand, they just want to see us all killed in the flood, then I could see why they'd want all of you to be on the riverbank."

In his boat, Akin saw trouble. Before he got to this village, his mission had been going very well, but as soon as he heard about the circles of stones, he knew this was going to be a difficult transition. This was clearly a powerful woman in the village, and killing her would start a battle. But what of the crazy woman who said the river was rising?

"I assure you," he called to the people, "the river is not rising. I'm on it, and I would surely know!"

There was a low murmur of assent, and the people started moving toward Wekesa once again. There was more light, now, and the people felt better about moving along the trail. But at this moment, a new group appeared. Naaba had watched the stand-off and knew Asha was right about the river, but there was no time to convince everyone, so he had a different plan. As Wekesa headed down the riverbank path, followed by the villagers, he found it blocked by an old woman and a group of children.

"Stand aside, old woman!" he called. "You and the children will be pushed off the trail by the crowd."

"No," she said quietly, "you stand aside. The trail goes that way." She pointed to the trail her group had just come down. "I think you can manage it. The children did."

Wekesa moved to push her aside, but suddenly a tall, thin man with a leopard skin tied around his shoulders and a big, powerful man stood next to her. "I don't think you want to do that," Sohko said slowly.

"I was wondering when you would arrive, Sohko," Aminata called. "Help these people onto the right trail, so this 'chief' doesn't make us all drown."

If he moved away from the river, Wekesa knew he'd lose the support of the warriors on the river. If he kept going, he'd have to fight these two, and they'd probably kill him before the others arrived to help.

With the growing light of the day, the people lost some of their terror, and those at the front of the line stepped boldly up the trail away from the river. Wekesa had to hurry in front of them or try to fight two different groups. Behind him, on the river, Akin motioned for the others to pull the canoes up onto the shore. The situation was still volatile, and Wekesa might need their support.

"As you wish, grandmother," Wekesa said, as he hurried to regain the lead.

On the riverbank trail, after the group had passed, the old woman hugged the children. "You were very brave," she said, "so brave that you saved the people of your village. But we have more to do today. Come; take my hand, so we can follow the others."

As the line straggled up the hill to the high trail, a thunderous sound, like a whole hillside collapsing, came up from behind them. As they turned to look, the river changed, in an instant, into a wall of brown water surging toward them from somewhere around the bend, tearing through the river chasm, dragging whole trees and boulders with it, taking down everything that stood in its way. As it coursed through the landing, it took both war canoes and dragged them along as well, while the warriors desperately climbed up and away from the river, pulling themselves up by tree branches and roots.

Aminata stood on the ledge above it all and nodded as she watched the last of the villagers reach the high banks.

Sohko stood at her side, his arm wrapped around her waist. "Getting in the middle of things again, I see."

"It wasn't my fault this time. She's the one who started it." Aminata pointed to Asha.

"That doesn't surprise me at all," Naaba said, as he joined the group.

As they walked, the clouds rolled in and the rains fell, great sheets of rain slicing through the air above the trees. For a little while, the dense cover of the forest kept them dry, but then the rain soaked through, and the drops rolled down the length of the leaves, one to another, until they splashed onto the forest floor. The villagers cut broad leaves and stuck sticks through them, which they held up as a rainbreak, but there was no getting away from the soaking rains that filled the shallow trough of the trail and turned it into a river that they had to slog through, step by step. When they stopped, later in the day, the villagers were exhausted, but they built temporary shelters between the roots of the giant fig trees. The children fell into a shivering sleep while the adults found some foods. It was the end of the first of three difficult days.

"Okung was right about the rains," Sohko commented.

"So was Asha," Naaba added.

CHAPTER 10
LAST SPARKS AMONG THE STONES

As soon as the others left, Zola sifted through everything in Komo's hut and around the stone circles, looking for the mask. He had used up almost all of the light of his torch in the search before he found it, discarded in the woods, as if someone had thought of taking it with him and then changed his mind. Taking it back to the hut, Zola lit a new torch, cleaned the mask and then put a new coat of white clay on the big eyes and in the grooves, running his hand over and over the surface of the mask, calling it to life once more. At dawn, he stood in the center of the circle, his arms out, turning slowly so that, with imaginary lines that ran across his body and through his fingertips, he linked the opposite stones, and once more the wheel of life turned, with him at its hub. As he turned, he realized there was another circle underneath him, a mirror version of his, but in the Underworld, and it was turning in the opposite direction, and there was another man turning it. He also wore the mask, and turned slowly, so he formed the connections in the other wheel. The first drops of rain fell heavily on the stones, but the other masked man never flinched. Only then did Zola realize the true power of the circles, not just as a link to the sky, but also as a conduit to the Underworld. It was the center of the world, and he was the pivot on which it turned.

At the edge of the settlement, a man pulled himself out of the rain-soaked bush, bent over and leaning heavily on a walking stick for support. His face and arm were bleeding, and one foot was swollen and turned oddly inward. Weak and unsteady, he stood in the heavy rain, staring at the strange image before him, seeing sometimes two men, sometimes one, sometimes four. But he was sure he knew who it was. It was the man responsible for all his pain, the man he now blamed for everything that had gone so wrong in his life. Dropping the crutch, he crawled close to the circle, pulling his knife from his wrap. As he watched, he thought the man in the circle seemed to be in some sort of trance, staring down as he turned slowly around and around with his arms outstretched, the rain filling the circle around him.

"Komo!" Nassor yelled, as he hurled his knife.

Zola never looked up. He had just realized that the man in the mask in the circle below him had turned and pointed right at him. So strange, he thought, just as the old woman had said.

Nassor's knife pierced his heart, and he fell right there, in the middle of the circle, his life blood seeping into the dirt along with the rain, and the other man in the mask bowed.

With a shout, Nassor acknowledged the kill. His hated enemy was dead. It wasn't until much later that he realized that it wasn't Komo he'd killed, but one of the men he'd worked with, and there was no one else there, no one to help him, or give him something to eat. As the infection from his foot spread through his body, he had the strange sense that someone he couldn't see was there, nearby, pointing to him. He looked around, but there was no one there, except for the dead man in the mask, or two of them, and the water filling the dancing circles and reflecting the stony sky.

Zola's spirit joined those of Komo and the brilliant man who had designed the circles, resting in the giant silk cotton tree, which, as the tallest tree in the forest, saw the birth and death of the sun each day, as well as its path across the sky. At night, it saw the turning of the stars in the heavens, the death and re-emergence of the morning and evening star, and, sometimes, the wonder of the rainbow, the wife of the great serpent god, after a storm.

Nassor's bones were scattered by the wild dogs, and his blood seeped into the roots that even today are too bitter for people to eat.

After the rainy season had passed, Ayo and some others who had moved to the new village snuck back to the old village, but they found it eerie with the buildings gone and the forest already reclaiming the space. One young man heard moaning sounds coming from the circles, and Ayo heard voices in the silk cotton tree. One was her brother's. When they returned to the new village, they told the others the old site was haunted with spirits. And so it was.

Once the trail was blocked and the giant stones toppled, no one came to the stone circles for a very long time. When people finally built a village there again, no one remembered what the stones marked.

CHAPTER 11
CHOICES

Because they had moved at the beginning of the rainy season, it took six moons before the new village was fully established. The site Wekesa had picked was ideal, with a stream flowing along one side of it and a good landing site at the main river, but still high enough to be safe from flooding. In the center of the village stood a giant silk cotton, which became the Community Tree, and at the far edge were three huge mahogany trees. One had a strange bow in a root that formed an open circle. Aminata left offerings there, so the spirits of the giants would protect them in their new home.

Everything was new, even the ideas. When the men set up a fermentation trench for wine, Ayo, the weaver, thought it might be interesting to try soaking different broad leaves, letting them rot until the wine was done. What was left was the strongest part of the leaf: the long fibers that formed the spine and major ribs. These she dyed with wood ash and berries, turning them a dark red, and then twisted together to form a strong, dark thread. Along with the other weavers, she experimented with all kinds of fibers, weaving narrow strips of rabbit skin, mixing a bamboo warp with a weft of wild cotton and antelope hair, making a basic weaving of raffia and coconut fibers and then decorating it with seed pods and feathers. Each piece was the first of its kind.

A basket weaver lined a basket with hot resin that soaked into the reeds and then dried to a dark, waterproof finish. Another lined one with grey clay from the riverbank that dried so hard in the sun that it shrank away from the basket beneath it, leaving a clay bowl still bearing the crisscross marks of the reeds.

When the new buildings were erected and the roofs thatched and the new fires officially lit, Wekesa called for a celebration. Despite his role in the destruction of the old village, he was a popular leader. People found his decisions fair and his judgment sound. Once they had moved, most of the villagers were happier than they had been in the old place. It seemed the air was lighter here and the future brighter. The pregnant woman had a healthy baby girl, and in the following moon, another woman had twin boys, a very auspicious sign. The group was already growing, numbering over a hundred.

Two teams of hunters went out looking for meat for the feast, in addition to the team that hunted for fish in the river. A separate team set up the roasting spits and prepared the meat, which needed to roast slowly for two days. Both men and women searched for wild yams, melons, manioc, cucumbers, plums, honey, grasshoppers, snakes, spicy ants, termites, caterpillars, and other foods. Then, of course, there were ongoing efforts. They needed all new bowls, baskets, fish traps, sleeping mats, arrow quivers, and all the other items they'd left behind. New boats, since the old ones had been taken before the flood. New tools, new cisterns, new latrines, new earth ovens, new everything. And they had to learn a whole new area. Where were the best wild fruits, clays, salt deposits? Where was the river dangerous? What trees torn out by the flood could they use for their buildings and boats? And all this information had to be gathered in a hurry. It was common knowledge that Wekesa would invite the young men to join his forces when he left. And there were others who wanted to go downriver with him as well, men and women who, once released from their old home, were curious about the rest of the world. So there was a current in the air, a sense of life speeded up, of impending change that colored everything of the moment in deeper hues.

Late in the afternoon the day before the festival, Naaba and Sohko were sitting under a shade tree, passing a large calabash of water back and forth until it was empty. They'd spent the day working different pieces of stone into arrowheads, scrapers, choppers, and knives, carefully heating each piece, then wedging it into a holding log so it wouldn't slip when they hit it with the chisel and hammerstone. Then it had to be turned and hit again, each time exactly right, scooping off one piece of the stone after another, until the final piece broke free of the stone right along the edge. Then it had to be cooled immediately in the water bowl. None had been perfect, but many were very good. Leaning back, Naaba considered the village that he'd watched spring to life here in the forest, the people busy with their preparations for the feast, the cloudless blue sky overhead. It was nice here, the most like home he'd ever known, with hard work and good friends. It had a promising future. And he knew he probably wouldn't stay to see it happen.

Sohko threw a piece of scrap stone at another, making it slide along the ground. "I'm going to ask Aminata to take the long vow," he said, still looking at the stones.

Naaba smiled. "Good. You two were made for each other, happy as two fruit bats in a fig tree."

"What about you and Asha? The same description fits you two."

"I don't think that's a great idea. You'll be happy here, both of you. You'll be chief and make wise decisions. Aminata will haul you back when you go down the wrong path, and you'll save her when her own good intentions get her in trouble."

"Is there something wrong with all that?"

70

"No, it's fine. It's good. It's just not me, that's all." Naaba twirled a scrap of stone between his fingers. "I started out as trouble. Part of me still is. And Asha -"

"Asha what?"

"She can't be tied down, even if the ties are invisible."

"Who's tying her?"

"It's complicated. You know."

"No, I don't know. It's simple. I'd like to spend the rest of my life with Aminata, and I'd like to village to know that and support it."

They sat for a moment, studying the chips of stone at their feet.

"Asha wouldn't want to be my wife, anyway," Naaba said finally, tossing the stone shard into the grass.

"How do you know? Did you ask her?"

"It would be bad, afterward, if she said no."

Sohko considered his friend for a moment, then stood up, clapped the stone chips off his hands and legs, and turned to leave. "Of course. Well, I have to get some things taken care for Wekesa."

"Have you asked her yet?" Naaba called after him.

"No," Sohko admitted, without turning around.

"Just give her that fine speech you gave me," Naaba called after him.

But Sohko's words sat on his mind, and he went over the whole thing several times, until he was convinced that he had been right all along: taking the long vow was a terrible idea and would ruin everything they had together. So, when he saw her later, with the white crane flower in her hair and her eyes glowing in the late afternoon sun, the first thing he said was, "You wouldn't like it at all, would you, if we took the long vow."

Asha looked at him; his expression was as wild as his hair as he stood before her. "That's one of the strangest things anyone's ever said to me."

"But still, it's correct, isn't it?"

71

"I'm not sure what 'it' means," she said slowly, her eyes searching his face. "What's going on?"

Naaba studied his long feet then met her gaze. "There are so many things that could go wrong. I could get angry; you could feel trapped; one of us could want to leave and the other to stay. Don't you see? That's what it means." He looked away but then turned back to her with a sudden intensity. "No, that's not all it means. It means the days and nights I've spent with you have been the finest I've ever known."

She waited for him to continue, but he only looked off into the forest again, and the air between them crackled.

"When you found me in the meadow," she said quietly, "I was asleep. I'd been asleep for many seasons. It was like being dead while still living. I went through the day and the night and the next day, but the only thing really awake was my feet. They wouldn't let me stop completely. They made me keep going, pushing me along, even though I knew I'd be beaten for it. Then you came along and you asked me if I wanted to be free, and I realized, at that moment, that it would be hard to be free, to be completely awake. Much harder than what I had gotten used to. But I knew if I said no, that I'd give up. Even my feet wouldn't be enough to keep me going. So I went with you, and I learned to live. It's that simple, really -" she stopped short, right in the middle of a breath, and looked at him.

He folded her into his arms, and they held onto each other with a fierce strength.

"So, then, what do you think?" he asked.

"About what?"

"This isn't going to be easy, is it?" he sighed into her hair.

"Probably not."

Sohko, on the other hand, thought the whole business was easy. When he found Aminata, she was working on a new sash, incorporating a line of Gabon nuts along the border. After watching her work for a moment, Sohko asked her to be his wife.

"Yes, of course," Aminata said.

* * *

Festival day was hot and humid, but everyone was turned out in their best. Wekesa wore an elaborate reed headdress, a pale wrap with sun and moon designs along the edge, and a new red and yellow sash that the weavers had given him. Sohko too had a new wrap and sash, decorated with Gabon nuts along the edges and the image of the falcon on the rock in the center. Aminata, resplendent in long crane feathers that curved down from the braided knot at the top of her head, wore a wrap she had over-sewn with raffia tassels and crane quills.

Ayo had retied Asha's hair, braiding in the hollow bird bones and a Bird of Paradise flower. "That's better," she declared, stepping back.

Only Naaba still looked like a wild man, with the leopard skin around his shoulders and his long hair matted and twisted in all directions.

The air was thick with the sound of celebration and the smell of cooking. The drummers started early, the leader calling out to the crowd, inviting them to be part of the celebration, the birth of the new village. "It's the people," the lead drummer called, "that give a village life, and the drums that call forth the celebration of that life." Slowly he started, with a steady pounding sound on the hollow log with the long slit cut in the top. It was insistent, urging, singing to the people, and they were pulled in, just as he wanted, leaving their worries and their arguments behind and taking up the celebration. Then he stepped back and motioned to two drummers behind him who shook large calabashes covered in netting. The animal teeth, shells, and bones tied to the netting rattled against the hollow gourds as the musicians shook them in rhythm, over their heads, down low, off to their sides, in a dance only they knew. But with a motion from the leader, they stopped still, and another two drummers started. Unlike the rapid, chittering sound of the calabashes, this was a galloping force, a pounding of antelope hoofs on dry grassland. Theirs was the slap of open hands and the pounding of rib bones against the hide tops, a source of fire, of energy. But it too was stopped by the leader, as he nodded to the last of the drummers, who played a series of curved wooden pieces, each of which produced a different tone. Tapping them with wooden sticks, he made the wood sing. Where the others were pounding and insistent, he was lyrical; where they traded in happiness and energy, his rhythm was full of dreams and longing.

Then it was the leader again, hands raised high, stopping everything for a single moment when everyone was poised and ready, making the people wait just that extra moment so they were hungry for the sound of the first drum. Only then did his hand fall and his drum start in a driving beat, demanding attention, grabbing control of the crowd. And when he had it, the others joined in, building in power and complexity as they went, working counter rhythms, reflecting the pounding heartbeats of their listeners, all different but all hooked together in that instant in a single rhythm.

When the drums had drawn people in, the leader raised his hand once again, and all the drums stopped. Then he dropped his hand, and the drummers started a five-beat pounding, all in unison, followed by a pause, then another series of five, then a pause, then again, and again. The call to gather went out clearly, but there were very few who weren't already in the village center. As the last of the villagers hurried to the edge of the circle, the drums shifted into a straight beat that picked up tempo ever so slightly as it went along. As it got faster, the people clapped along, driving it forward just as they were being pulled along. When it was furiously fast, the leader dropped his hand, and they stopped.

Into the sudden silence, Wekesa stepped up to the raised earthen platform in the center of the square, greeted by the cheers of the people, and stretched out his hands, the carved serpent staff in his right hand. Behind him, a row of warriors stood, never moving as their leader spoke.

"People of the new village!" he called, "Today we sing the beginning of a new age, a new time, a new path, for all of us. May it be filled with peace and beauty!

"I know that after today, we may go in different directions, but we will always be connected. You, all of you, are part of a new world, one that you can create, so it is exactly the way you want it to be. It will be larger than this village, or any one village. It will extend up and down the river, so that you will feel all of the people along it are related to you. But always, this village, this spot on the earth, will be precious to you. I know it is to me, though I've been here only a short while.

"A group of warriors will be arriving here shortly, and I'll leave with them, but before I go, I want to hand over control of this village to your new leader. I've spoken to almost every one of you, and you all had the same choice for your chief as I did: a strong man, a wise man and a good man, a man who will lead this village into a bright future. The man is," he paused, scanning the anxious faces, "Sohko!" With one voice, the crowd cheered, shouting his name, and Wekesa waited, nodding, then went on. "Also, I know several of you are interested in going with me down the river, and I welcome you. However, know that the world is not all like this village. The river becomes much deeper and wider, and it becomes salty, like the great sea beyond it. There are crocodiles, hippos, waterfalls and rapids, where the river turns into angry froth against the rocks and kills men in their canoes." He paused. "I would advise you to consider what you have as well as what you seek before you choose to follow the river. If, at that point, you still want to join us, good! We want you to join us! Keep in mind that, in addition to warriors, we'll need people to establish trade routes and keep records of transactions along this section of the river." He looked around at the strong faces in the crowd. "But enough of tomorrow's concerns! Right now, let's celebrate today and everything we have right here!"

As the crowd cheered once again, a group of men came up from the river and stood at the edge of the circle. Wekesa nodded to their leader and waved them forward to join the celebration.

"We have two other beginnings to celebrate today," Wekesa called. I call on everyone present to witness the long vows of Sohko and Aminata!" With a flurry of drumbeats, they stepped forward, and Wekesa clapped Sohko on the shoulder. "A fine day for you," he said, leaning in and turning to include Aminata, "in many ways. Much happiness and good fortune to you both."

"And Naaba and Asha!" he said, swinging back to face the crowd.

With a sweep of his staff, he drew Naaba and Asha out into the center as well, and the drums sounded once again. They stood, facing the crowd, with Wekesa up on the platform behind them, holding his arms out, drawing the crowd's attention to the two couples before him.

But as the drums stopped and Wekesa raised his staff for silence, a voice from the crowd called out, "She can't be his wife! I own her!"

CHAPTER 12
THE CHIEF DECIDES

There was a long moment where nothing happened. Everyone stood, suspended between where they thought they would be that day and where they actually were. The lead drummer motioned for the others to wait until he knew what to do. Even Wekesa looked confused. In this instant, when everything else was stopped, Guedado, the man who had spoken out, stepped forward and grabbed Asha by the arm. But as soon as he took hold of it, Naaba wrenched the man's arm back while he pressed his flattened hand sideways against Guedado's windpipe. He would have killed Guedado in that same motion, except that Sohko asked him to stop.

After a moment, Naaba released the man, who staggered backwards, his hand clutched to his throat, trying to breathe. The other warriors in Guedado's group stepped forward, but they didn't attack. They found little to like about Guedado, but they had to provide a show of support.

Wekesa stepped into the middle of the stand-off, positioning himself between Naaba and Guedado. "If there is a dispute, we'll settle it," he said, pointing his staff toward Sohko. "The new chief will decide what needs to be done, but everyone must abide by his decision." He looked at the two men, Asha, and the villagers. "There is no private revenge for a decision you don't like. Is that understood?" Naaba was the most reluctant, but he agreed after everyone else did. "Now," Wekesa said, "we'll hear from each one involved."

Guedado, still holding his throat, stepped forward. "There's nothing to say, except that I own her. Her father needed to pay some debts, and I gave him two crocodile skins in return for the girl. That's the story."

When he didn't add anything else, Asha stepped forward, feeling as if the air was swimming around her. She looked at Naaba, trying to find the place where they had been just a moment ago, but everything had changed. "That's not the whole story," she said, finally. "This man, Guedado, used to follow me around, scaring me, saying he wanted me, but I refused him. So he tried a different way. He knew my father had a weakness for gambling, betting on the toss of the five-string beads carved with two faces. Papa and his friends often played, betting their treasures, but few ever demanded payment. But Guedado lured my father into betting more and more, even our hut, our tools, our food, our baskets and calabashes, everything we had. Then he had nothing left, but he kept betting, thinking his luck would change. Finally, Papa lost more than all of his goods together could pay. Guedado then pretended to be generous, offering to forgive all of the debt, as long as he could have me. It broke my father's heart, but he did it: he sold me to pay his debt." It was hard to admit that, but it had happened; her own father had handed her over to this monster, despite her desperate pleas. "There was no payment of crocodile skins," she added, feeling sick, feeling the air thicken so much that she couldn't even see the others. It swirled around her, taking her down into a hole in the earth. But Aminata was there, next to her, holding onto Asha's arm, steadying her. "Don't let him win," she whispered.

With a deep breath, Asha continued. "He raped me and beat me. Yes, I left. I left because to stay was to die. And then this man," she said, turning to Naaba, "took me to the river and showed me how to be alive again, how to be happy." Tears rolled down her cheeks, and she could find no more words. "That's what I have to say."

"You would believe her?" Guedado yelled, looking to the warriors in his group. "The fool couldn't pay his debt, that's all. It's business."

"When I found Asha, she was bound, hand and foot!" Naaba shouted. "Is that the way you do business?"

Sohko stepped between the two men, addressing Wekesa, "You've asked me to make a decision here, so I will, but I think there are two issues at stake, not just one."

Wekesa nodded. "Go ahead."

"The first issue is Asha's freedom. Guedado, you apparently forgave a gambling debt that may or may not have been worth two crocodile skins in return for Asha. But today, you were given your life back, when it could easily have been taken, with justification. So, since I assume you feel your own life is worth far more than the skins of two crocodiles, I would say that debt has been repaid in full.

"The second question is whether or not Asha is able to take long vows today. Since you never made Asha your wife, she has every right to marry today, and she would be a great deal better off, if I may say so, with a good man like Naaba than a poor excuse for one, like you."

The crowd yelled in agreement, and when Guedado tried to yell his protest, the lead drummer started up his group in a frenzied galloping beat that drowned him out. At the end of it, Guedado tried once again, but Wekesa silenced him. "As agreed at the start of this procedure, there is no exception to the ruling."

Guedado looked from one to another in his group, trying to find support, but there was none.

Wekesa went on. "If I find you have caused either one of these people any trouble, I will call for your blood. Do you understand?"

Guedado seethed, but he nodded ever so slightly.

Wekesa waited.

"Yes," Guedado said, finally, "but there's no justice here! You're just taking care of people you like."

Wekesa looked from the glowering face of Guedado to the gathered crowd. "When will you all learn that we *have* to take care of each other? That's how we will all change for the better! When we stop taking care of each other, when we consider only ourselves, when we hurt each other, we'll die. And we'll die lonely and bitter, dragging ourselves through the mud as the crocodile closes in on us. But we could be so much more. So much more." He signaled the drummers to get ready. "Thank you, Sohko - a judgment well made! Now, now that we have taken care of the little problem, I would like to present these two couples to you, good people of this village!"

With the fall of his hand, the drums started again, with an insistent, energetic beat that helped to clear the air of the unhappiness, and the people were swept up into the festivities once again. Naaba and Asha witnessed their love for each other and their desire to spend their lives together. Naaba presented Asha with a leather pouch he had made, decorated with a turtle design and two crane feathers. Asha gave Naaba a sash she had woven, with Ayo's help, which had dark and light patterns like the ones they had seen on the great stones leading to Komo's circles. They were both genuinely happy for Sohko and Aminata, and they were grateful for all the good wishes people extended to them, but the truth was that both Naaba and Asha were shaken by the confrontation with Guedado. When the ceremony was over, Asha thanked everyone for their support, but she said she needed to take care of something, and she went off to the edge of the village, far from the celebration. Once she was alone, she slid to the ground, shaking with grief, sobs welling up from the deepest part of her. In her mind, she knew she'd never escape the stain of her past and the monster who'd escaped from her nightmares and appeared before her on the day she took the long vows.

Ayo came and sat beside her. "I made something for you, as a wedding gift," she said when Asha looked up. "It's not like anything else anyone has made, but I thought you might understand." Before

80

Asha could reply, Ayo unrolled a piece of bark cloth painted with odd pieces of designs, a bird's foot and a series of lines that might be an arm or a tree branch and a hooked beak and another branch and an eye and another branch and a wing and another branch and a bit of a person's face and another branch, or it might be a leg, all flowing into each other seamlessly, from one end of the cloth to the other. "It's the way we are, the way we see things, the way we feel things," Ayo said. "All bits of things that we see: the flash of a bird wing, the look in its eye, the speed of its flight, its cry as it flies, its shadow on the ground, its disappearance in the branches of the tree." She waited, but Asha only studied the cloth. "All of it, everything, is all pressed up against everything else: the bird's beak against the sky, its wing against the tree, the tree against the air, the air against you. You against another." She paused. "Sometimes it's good and sometimes it's not. The bird is pressed up against the insect it eats and the sky it flies across, but also against the hawk that catches it. Everything is pressed up against everything else. There is no place to go that it's not. Don't run from it. Be part of it. Be part of the design that's you. Don't let someone else erase it."

Picking up the strange cloth, Asha studied the designs. It was just as Ayo said: everything was pressed up against everything else. Perhaps this is what it means to be part of life, she thought, to be pressed up against everything around us, even the bad things. "It's so beautiful," she said, the tears coming again as she hugged Ayo, "it's incredible."

"Don't give up. You have friends here," Ayo said, as she stood up. "One of them is worried about you. Handsome, sort of tall; dark hair flying in every direction."

"I think I know him," Asha smiled, a little sadly.

* * *

"It's unfinished," Naaba complained to Sohko while they were being served the feast. "He's still here."

"It's never finished, even when we die. The stores that we involve ourselves in continue after us. What stories do you want those to be?"

"That's not the same question."

"Yes, it's exactly the same."

"Why is it so easy for you? Everything around you looks good."

Handing his friend the bowl of roast meat, Sohko said, "Because I choose it to be, not because it is. The truth is that pain hides from no one, including me. I don't deny the pain, but I don't let it rule me, either. If I did, I wouldn't be able to live through the day."

"It's just that things always seem clear to you, peaceful."

"Peace is a choice, not a gift," Sohko said, returning to his meal.

"You'll make a fine chief. You will."

But in his heart, Naaba felt only a sick restlessness, and the day's events grated on him, rubbing him raw, like a blister reopened with each step. When he found Asha, they held onto each other, hoping somehow they could weather this storm, but her past and his future made poor companions. In the middle of the night, he left her and wandered out into the jungle, looking for a way to settle everything into place. He listened to the noises of the river, a pair of owls calling back and forth, the bushbucks' startled snorts, the call of a leopard far in the distance. He thought about the leopard's gift to him so long ago, the way she had called him back to life when he was dead. How was that so different from Asha and what she had gone through? It wasn't different, except that she was Asha, and he wasn't, and it's easier to forgive yourself than others, even when the transgression is the same. It all seemed clouded now, as if something had changed in the course of the day, even though all these things had happened long before he met her. And what was she guilty of? It was just the fact that she was sold as a prostitute, and she was one. He sat in the dark, hugging his knees. She had told him a man had bought her. It's not as if he didn't know. But it was in front of everyone that the secret was revealed, in every sordid detail. Well, what of his past? What if someone had shown up today to tell everything he had done? Would she think less of him? Yes, probably. There was little there that would engender tender feelings. It was all so ugly, suddenly. But it wasn't really Asha's fault. Perhaps they could leave, head up or down river, find somewhere else, start again. But the past, he thought, will always be part of us, always right there, just beyond each remark, each caress, an old wound just waiting to be reopened.

Finally, exhausted, he stretched out on a long branch overhanging the river and fell asleep, but his dreams haunted him, taking him back always to Asha, tied up in Guedado's hut.

* * *

It had been so easy for the man, waiting in the dark, watching as the one he hated left the hut, listening to the sound of his footsteps as he moved farther and farther away into the bush. Then the man knew she would be alone and asleep and there would be no one around to defend her.

He had a wrong to right.

CHAPTER 13
AN END AND A BEGINNING

Asha wasn't asleep when Naaba left. She knew something terrible had happened between them, and she had no idea how to fix it. She rolled up Ayo's cloth and kept it under her arm, trying to remember Ayo's words, but everything blurred into sadness after a while. Then, suddenly, she was fully alert, as if every nerve ending had been awakened at once. In the dark, she lay on the mats, listening to every night sound and separating out just one of them: the sound of someone trying to walk without making any sound, but having no experience in it, so that the very slowness of the step called attention to itself. It wasn't Naaba's step.

She rolled slowly off the mat, winding her wrap around her, feeling for Naaba's knife but finding only his carved bone dagger, slipping it into her sash, stepping back against the wall of the hut. The quiet of the night was humming in her ears, every sound magnified, so that she heard him fumbling with the latch of the door cover, felt his touch telegraphed around the wall of the hut. If she waited until he entered, she could slip out behind him.

But when Guedado opened the door, he didn't enter. He lit his torch and held it up, scanning the interior until he found her. Without a word, he lunged at her as he threw down the torch. It fell against the woven reeds of the wall, the palm oil of the torch fueling the fire until it caught the reeds, small flames licking upward along the spines of the wall, feeling their way through the woven sides and up to the thatch on the roof. Asha darted sideways, but

Guedado stopped himself before he plowed into the wall. Spinning, he reached out to grab her, but he missed, and she raked his open hand with the dagger. With a scream he lunged again, grabbing her and knocking her down, as the wall of the hut caught fire. She remembered how strange it was, how furiously bright it was, as he fell on top of her, thrown off balance by the lunge. With a grunt, he tried to get his balance, to lift himself, but as he did, Asha drove the carved bone dagger up between his ribs. And the entire roof burst into flame.

By the time the villagers awoke to find the hut engulfed in flames, Guedado was dead and Asha was gone. At dawn, Naaba returned, only to find there was nothing left of the world he had celebrated just the day before.

CHAPTER 14
THE LUNGFISH

Even shivering in the dark, racked with an empty sickness, Asha could find her way to the river. The path that paralleled the feeder stream was so close to the water, she could hear it talking, telling stories that never ended. Above her, in the break in the trees, the stars pressed close to the earth, as if they were just beyond the tallest tree.

At the river, she sat on a flat rock, with the water lapping at her feet. She couldn't go back to her old village. She couldn't stay here. She had to go downriver, she knew, yet something held her to the rock. So she sat, wanting to stay, to change things back to where they were. But events couldn't be reversed any more than the river could flow backwards.

With a sigh, she stood up, thinking she would just follow the edge of the river until there was enough light to find a path, but almost immediately, she bumped into something hard. Feeling around, she realized it was one of the canoes the warriors had brought, large enough for ten men and their gear. Just beyond it was another. They'd launch them, later, looking for her, and they'd look first on the river. She considered fording the river and taking a different route on the other side, but she'd have no way of knowing where she was going and she'd be easy to track there.

Beyond the war canoes was a mahogany canoe that the boat builders had completed only a few days before the celebration and kept secret until its official display. The tree it was made from was so beautiful that the builders had left offerings, asking the spirit of the tree for permission to use the wood. The boat they made from it was perfect, its dark red interior smoothed and oiled, its exterior carefully shaped and carved with the sign of the new village. The boat was a thing of beauty made from a thing of beauty. As Asha ran her fingers along its smooth edges, she could picture it as it was carried through the square to the cheers of the people. She couldn't take that boat. Just beyond it was a simple dugout made from a tree the flashflood had left behind. She felt along the rough-hewn edge, removed the long pole from the bottom of the boat, untied the rope, and pushed the boat into the river, poling it away from the bank and into the current. But as the boat moved backward, it caught on a sandbar that reached almost to the surface of the water, pushed up by the currents that split around submerged tree trunks. Jumping out to free it, she found herself standing on a pile of rock and sand that the river had dropped in that spot as the currents had risen and the weight was too much for them to carry. The water was very shallow, just above her ankles, and the rocks were hard and cold on her feet. Holding onto the boat's stern with one hand, she pushed off, stepped in, and poled away into the dark river under the close stars.

When daylight came, exhaustion claimed her and she slept, huddled over in the middle of the canoe as it took her into the unknown. She dreamed of her grandmother, who used to tell her the story of The Lungfish, which was not a particularly pretty fish, but it could survive, even when it had no water. *Imagine,* her grandmother would say, *a fish without water. Most fish would die, but not the lungfish. It can make this big sack full of air, and secrete a slime covering that keeps it from drying out, so it can wait out the drought. Then, when the waters come again, it can go back to being a regular fish.*

But why is it so hard, even for the lungfish? Asha asked her grandmother, who was sitting right there in the boat with her.

Because it's a struggle, her grandmother said, with a small smile. *It's always a struggle.*

And what do you get if you win that struggle?

The right to love, and to work, and to dream, her grandmother said, drifting away with the bits of sunlight playing on the water; *you get to be part of all this.*

By the time Asha awoke, the day's sun was already past its zenith. The canoe had run up onto some partially submerged tree trunks. Stiff and aching, she grabbed the pole and pushed against the trees, but the tangle of old branches held the boat fast. Jamming the pole into the riverbed, she leaned against it, hoping to roll the boat back off the tree, but the current pushed it forward at the same time, and the boat stayed locked in place. Frustrated, she tied the mooring rope around her hand and slid out of the boat. Balancing on the tree trunk, she tried to push the boat back, but it didn't move. Carefully, she worked her way to the other side of the boat and then saw the big branch that was holding it. Somehow, the boat had pushed it down as it went forward and then the branch had sprung back up, like a trap, as soon as the boat cleared it. The branch was as big around as her leg; there was no way she could break it. The only way would be to push the boat farther forward, so it cleared the main trunk. Climbing back into the boat, she pushed the boat forward, but it couldn't clear the tree with her in it. Sliding out on the far side of the boat, she took the boat pole and wedged it under the canoe, lifting the bottom of the boat just enough for it to slide over the trunk. Once again, it stuck, farther back, and she lifted it again, working it forward. With her final push, the boat was free. But in that moment, it was taken by the river, pulled along by the currents swirling around the downed trees. With a jerk, Asha was pulled into the water, dragged by the canoe as it headed downriver. The rope wrapped around her hand snapped taut, pulling her arm forward, dragging her into the water. Grabbing the rope with her free hand, she wrenched it back toward her, getting barely enough slack to work the rope down and off her other hand. Then she let it go, and the boat floated away. As she gasped for air, she considered trying to swim after the boat, but it was already too far ahead.

The swim to shore took the little energy she had left, and she crawled up on the bank too tired to care about what dangers might lurk there. The sleep that engulfed her was the dark, dreamless exhaustion of those who have lost any sense of today, tomorrow, or yesterday. There is only now, and barely that.

Wild melon. That was the smell, sweet and heavy. And cucumbers pieces, delicate and crisp. Grasshoppers, toasted on sticks to crunchy perfection. Hibiscus and honey water, syrupy sweet and fragrant. The smells ran through her, full of sounds and colors and memories.

"Hungry?"

It was a bird talking. Specifically, it was a grey parrot with a red tail. Twisting its head sideways, it looked at Asha.

"Hungry?" It repeated, following the word with a series of clicks and whistles.

Asha pulled herself up to a sitting position and stared.

"Well?"

The second voice wasn't the bird's; it was a man's. Spinning around, Asha saw a man, or something like a man, sitting cross-legged on the shore. His head and neck were oddly swollen and lumpy, and one of his legs was half-gone. Beside him sat two wild dogs, but they seemed to be only momentarily still, as if they were stopped midway between lying down and flying at her throat. Their intense black eyes never left her. They were the still center of a body of moving colors. Beyond their large, rounded black ears, their coats were a swirl of tan, black and white, long hair and short, with a confusion of patches and dots of color that ran down their thin legs. Incongruously, not far away, a firefinch perched on the top of a basket, apparently unconcerned by the proximity of creatures with a stunningly powerful bite. But then, the parrot apparently wasn't worried either.

"I find it's best to answer when they talk," the man said. "I always do."

Looking back to the man, Asha wondered what could have happened that made the man's head so misshapen. But then the entire lumpy section moved. It moved as only a snake can move, slowly and seamlessly, its irregular dark mottled pattern curving around the man's head and neck and dropping down his back, only to raise its head around the far side.

"Ah," Asha began but could find nothing else to say.

"A fine start," the man said, raising his arm as the python came around, so it climbed once again back up around his neck and lifted its head, considering Asha, from the far side of the man's shoulder, the light-colored V down the center of its head clearly visible. "But the question was whether you were hungry."

"Well, I -"

"I'll assume that means yes. You look a little poorly."

Something about the remark, on top of everything else, struck Asha as very funny. "Probably. It's been a difficult day."

Shooing away the firefinch, the man lifted the lid off the basket and presented her with exactly what she had smelled: cucumbers, melon, toasted grasshoppers, and a calabash of hibiscus and honey water. Asha waited, but he waved her on. "Eat! Please," he said. "I've already eaten. It's all very good. The honeyfinders showed me where the honey was," he added, handing her the drink. "Do you know them?"

Unsure, Asha reached for the calabash and took a sip. The sweet liquid was exquisite, full of sunlight and flowers, like the happiest of memories, all golden and slow. "I've heard of them," she said. "They lead another animal, like a honey badger, to the beehive. The other animal gets the honey, but the birds eat the eggs and larvae. Everyone gets what they wanted."

"Well, they *tell* me where it is," the man corrected, pushing the basket toward her. "Try the cucumbers. Very good right now,

I think. Very good," he repeated, biting into one. Asha studied his face, almost obscured by the thick beard and mustache. As he ate, a cockroach wandered through his beard, looking for stray juicy bits.

"He's a nuisance, mostly," the man said, noticing her stare, "but he helps keep me tidy. If he's any trouble, he's just dinner for one of my friends here."

Taking a piece of cucumber, Asha thought she had slipped into a dream world where things were slightly different. Or perhaps the world was a bigger place than she had thought, and things could be a great many ways.

"Very fine, isn't it?"

"Very fine, yes."

"So then, we should introduce ourselves. These are my friends. I don't know their names, and I don't feel I have the right to replace whatever name they really have, so I call them all 'friend.' They all found me, you know. The dogs here, they saved me from the croc that had my leg. Don't know why they're not in a pack. It's tough for the dogs, you know, especially the females, like these. They have to compete for the males. Not much like people, in that way. But only the main female gets to have pups. These two were off on their own when they found me. I guess we helped each other out a little, sort of like the honeyfinders. Anyway, they've helped me out more than once." Holding up the basket to Asha, he added, "You need to eat something, and I need to talk to someone, so we could help each other out, if you'll let me."

Asha took a large melon piece and nodded.

"Anyway, so people come here sometimes. Actually, lately, it's pretty often. It's like a town full of people stopping by, one at a time. A man tried to steal the snake one time. He said it was worth a lot to some folks down the river, but I said the snake was meant to live here. That's why it lived here. He thought that was pretty stupid and tried to stuff the snake into a basket, but the two dogs didn't like the idea very much. When one of them growled at the man, he kicked at it, but his leg was still up there, in the air, when the other latched onto it the same way they latch onto their kill. As the man was shrieking at me to do something, the other dog jumped up and bit him hard in the rear. That's the way the pack does it, you know, one at the nose and one at the rear. Then the others come in and tear out the middle. Well, there weren't any others here, but those two did a pretty good job on that man. After a while, though, I was afraid they were going to kill him, and then I've have a mess to deal with, so I asked them to stop, and they did. The man looked at me as if I was a demon or something, and he ran back to his boat, screaming all sorts of things at me." He smiled. "Do you like those grasshoppers? I toasted them this morning. Anyway, so maybe he said something, but the next few people who stopped here were very nice, offering me presents and talking about how fine the snake was, but I got worried. Some people mean to be nice, but when they see treasure, they change. So I asked the snake to stay in the basket while the people were here. That worked really well until one man grabbed the lid off the basket to see what I had in there, and the snake rose up out of it. You can imagine how that went. And I had meant for it to be easier, but they got excited, saying I was hiding treasures here. They forgot about the dogs, see; that was the trouble. You left some pieces of melon there.   It won't be any good tomorrow, you know, so you might as well eat them. Oh, don't worry about me, I've had lots already. Where was I? Oh, right, the men who wanted to steal my treasures. The thing is my treasures can't be stolen. They're already free. I don't believe in putting animals in cages, especially birds. They need to be able to fly away if they want to. Maybe people are like that too," he said, with a glance at Asha, but she didn't respond. "Anyway, the dogs didn't like these men, and I can't say the snake thought much of them either. The trouble was, the snake had come out of the basket and worked its way around my neck and head, the way it does sometimes. When I got upset, and the snake got upset, it did what it was designed to do. It's a constrictor, you know; it crushes its prey. Well, as the men were standing there, pulling out their knives, the snake started to tighten its grip around my neck. I didn't want the men to know, but it was getting harder and harder to breathe. I tried stroking the snake, as a way to relax it, but one of the men started shouting at me, and the whole thing started all over again. Finally, I tried to unwind the snake, but I started with the tail, and as I lifted it away from the back of my neck, the snake tightened against the front of my neck, almost killing me. Fortunately, for me, one of the men grabbed at the snake's head, and it struck out at him, throwing itself away from me at the same time. The man jumped back, and I grabbed the snake behind its head and unwound it. I'd never have had the strength to do it if he hadn't accidentally helped. How's that for strange? There's water in that other calabash, if you want some. But mostly, it's great having my friends around. They never get mad at me or tell me to stop talking. I have no idea why they like it here, but it's nice that they do, don't you think?"

Asha nodded as she took a long drink.

"I didn't have many visitors at all for a long time. Now, recently, I've had lots, or at least I've seen lots of people. Not everyone stops to talk. But, you know, it's interesting: most of the boats have the black rhino symbol on them. Lots of those people going back and forth on the river. They have faces painted with white clay. Well, sometimes they do, and some of the people do. Others don't, but they have the same boats. Anyway, the other day, two boats pulled up on the bank." He snapped his fingers into the number gesture, "and they had a whole different symbol on them, and they dressed different, the people, I mean, not the boats. Friendly enough to me, I guess, though they didn't stay long. But they looked around at everything. So, did you get enough to eat? I could fix something else, if you're hungry."

"Thank you. It was all delicious, but I couldn't eat another thing."

"Good. That's what I like to hear. That's exactly what I like to hear. So, tell me about yourself. Traveling far? I'll bet you're heading downriver to meet someone, your lover, maybe. That would be nice." He paused and looked at Asha. "Or maybe you just left him behind you." When she looked down at her feet, he went on "Yes, well, I'm sorry for that. But, you know, the river takes a great many turns before it reaches the sea. You may find that things are different later on."

"Thank you," Asha said slowly, "but the problem is the past, which is always there."

"Not really," the man replied, brightening. "The past is most important when it's close. The farther away it gets, the smaller it gets, unless, of course, the person keeps renewing it, which keeps it in the present, so it's not really the past then at all, but the present, which is the most powerful thing in our lives. Right? I mean, take me, for example. I couldn't learn counting, so I was considered a failure. My people keep track of transactions on split sticks. For example, you mark how many shells you gave me in return for my parrot. No, I wouldn't sell the parrot. Well, take something else: a cucumber, perhaps, or a nice fresh fish. You and I agree on an exchange: six snail shells for the nice fresh fish. You say you can't pay me today, but you can pay me tomorrow, or the next day. But you want to take the fish with you because, you know, it wouldn't be very tasty three days later. To remember the deal, we make six marks on a stick. Then we split the stick in half down its length. You get half to remind you of your debt, and I get half to remind me what's owed. Then I have to file the stick so I remember what it means and that it goes with you, not someone else who bartered for a fish. That's the way my people do business, and they're very good at it. But, unfortunately, I'm not. I could make the marks on the stick, but then I'd forget what they meant: six what? For what? Who owes this? and so on. No matter how hard I tried, all of the marks just looked like the scratches birds make in the sand when they take a bath. After a while, I'd escape to the bush, trailing along after turtles or birds or watching spiders. My father sighed when he talked about me, and the other boys made fun of me. Oh well, I suppose I was very peculiar. Anyway, sort of for a joke, the other boys lead me out into the bush, blindfolded, and then left me there. They thought it was funny, in a hard sort of way, the way boys, and I suppose girls, can be to each other. Anyway, they left me there, and it was getting dark, and I knew I couldn't find my way home before night fell, and I thought I was going to die out there. But, you know, a funny thing happened. I didn't. I found a whole world that was incredible and exciting. After a few days, my father led a group searching for me. Of course, it was a little late to rescue me if I had been in trouble, but, in any case, he found me and said I was welcome to come home with him, but I knew when I listened to his words that I was also welcome to stay. So I told him it was very kind of him but I was very happy where I was. He nodded, wished me well, and left. I haven't seen him since, or anyone else from my village for that matter, though it's not all that far away. But they know I'm here, and I know they're there, and I guess that's enough, for all of us. Maybe someone will stop by, one of these days, but probably not. You know how busy life gets. There's always the sick grandparent or the new baby or the jealous lover. Not that I'm saying that to you, of course. I don't know your situation. You say the past is the problem, but, as I've learned from my past, it doesn't really matter, unless you think it matters. See, what I did was make something else, something new, and then the past doesn't matter so much. You could make something new, something new here. You could stay here, with me, and my friends, and they'd be your friends too."

"Hungry?" the parrot called, bobbing its head excitedly and whistling.

Standing, Asha said, "No, friend, I won't stay here. And it wouldn't be wise to try to force me to stay, even with your fearsome-looking allies. I killed the last man who tried to force himself on me."

Shaken, the man rambled on even faster than before. "Well, no reason to get upset. It was just a thought, you know, a beautiful woman like you, why it's just a compliment, that's all, you know. Anyway, I knew you wouldn't stay, but I thought I'd ask in case you were, you know, hoping I'd ask, and then I'd feel terrible if you'd been hoping I'd ask and I didn't, you know, but anyway, don't worry. No harm done, right? No harm done here. But if you're going to leave, you probably want your boat. Yes, I have the little boat. It was easy, really. All the things that get loose on the river end up snagged just around the bend in the shallows, so it's easy for me to pick them up. So I picked up your boat. Actually, I've picked up many things. I sort of trade them to people who stop here, although I can't say exactly that they're mine to trade, but whoever really owned them lost them, so I guess the river claimed them, and then I claimed them when the river dropped them off. Anyway, I have your boat, and I could give you a paddle, which will be a lot more useful than the pole later on, but it would be nice if you had something to trade for a fine paddle." When Asha hesitated, he went on, "I could add some other things: a firestone and a basket, even a carved wooden box."

Asha looked at him sadly as she lifted the string that held Naaba's gift over her head and handed it to him. "This is the only treasure I have, but you're welcome to it. I don't think the man who gave it to me would do so again, had he the choice."

Taking the leather pouch in his hand, the man drew in his breath. "It's beautiful." For once, he seemed to have run out of words, but he stood up, sending the animals in all directions, and motioned for her to follow him. "I'll show you where the boat is," he said, starting to get his old momentum back. "I tied it up for you, so it wouldn't drift away. The pole's in it, and I'll get you the paddle. Well, there are actually several paddles. One is quite beautiful, with carvings of birds and fish on it. I find things, you know, or they find me, I suppose that's just as accurate. I found a flute once, and I tried to learn how to play it, but it just came out air. I felt bad, then, that someone who knew how to play it had lost it, but there was no way to find that person, so I just kept it. I don't suppose you play?"

Asha shook her head. "No, but a young man in our village played very well. He said the trick was to aim the flow of air from your mouth, so it didn't all go into the hole; it went across it. Maybe you could try that. Also, put your fingers over some of the holes, but not all, until you can get a sound out of the flute. Then add different combinations of fingers over the holes."

"Thank you! I'll try it! Now, I'll have to remember where I put it. Anyway, I'll master it now, I'm sure. If you ever come back this way," he hesitated, "when you come back this way, you'll have to see how well I'm doing on the flute." As he headed off, the two dogs roamed on their own, trotting along effortlessly, but they always stayed in the same area as he was, even though they never looked at him.

"I'd like that."

"There," he pointed, "the boat's tied up there. And over here are the paddles. See, they're all in pretty good shape. Probably, you know, someone was trying to push off from a snag in the river and dropped the paddle. See, here's the carved one. Why don't you take this one? It suits you," he said, holding the paddle out to her.

Other than the hand grip and the flared top, the entire paddle was carved on both sides. Asha had never seen anything like it. Figures of flying birds, their wings outstretched in swirling clouds, filled the handle, while the blade was covered with images of fish, turtles, and a large creature she didn't recognize. "It's like nothing I've ever seen," Asha said, "the work of a master carver who knows the sky and the water."

"It's yours, then," the man beamed, putting his hand to the leather pouch he had hung around his neck.

A sharp pain shot through Asha as she saw it there, but she put her hand on the man's arm. "Thank you for your kindness. Take care of your friends. I hope we'll meet again someday."

Tears welled up in his eyes as he took both her arms. "Yes, I would like that. Now, push off into the center of the river. Both sides have rough snags. And about four days down the river, you'll need to walk the boat past the rough water. You know what I mean? Leave the boat in the water, but walk along the shore, pulling the boat along with a rope. You'll see a sort of path where others have gone. The boat's too heavy with anyone in it, but it'll slide over the rocks and snags if you pull it. Well, you should probably go before I talk you to death," he said, with a sad smile. "May you find what you're looking for on the river."

"And may the days be kind to you and your friends," she said with a nod of recognition. Then she turned to the little boat, untying it and polling away from the shore and into the current. With a wave, she was gone down the river.

He sat and watched, even after she had disappeared around the bend in the river, as if she might reappear at any moment. When the sun was very low, the parrot bit him on the ear, and the wild dogs came up, yipping at him, encouraging him to get up and move, so the man roused himself and headed slowly back to his camp, with the dogs trotting ahead, turning their heads to check that he was following.

It wasn't until much later in the day that Asha discovered the woven bag tucked into the bow space. In it were a firestone, a calabash, and a handful of kola nuts.

CHAPTER 15

AN INCIDENT ON THE RIVER

For days, Asha continued down the river, seeing no sign of a village or another traveler, not even a fisherman, only a few fire rings and makeshift shelters hunters had made of sticks and palm leaves. When she came to a stream emptying into the river, she stopped and walked upstream to drink and fill her calabash. There too she could find food, fruits mostly, and some succulent roots, but she didn't eat much. Mostly, she just drifted with the current, using the carved paddle to keep the boat in the middle of the river and the pole to stop it or push it off snags. The paddle was a wonder, so filled with designs, as if the artist had meant to compress all the world of the water and the air into one paddle. She wondered if there was a reason for each figure, or if the artist simply found them pleasing in that space. Beneath the eagle's wing was a flaming sun and beneath that the swirls of clouds and the tops of hills. From the middle of the center hill, a river flowed in a sinuous curve all the way to the bottom of the paddle, where it was surrounded by fish and turtles, snails and eels, cranes, and many animals she didn't know, all close to each other, "pressed up together" as Ayo had said of her blanket figures. She wished she had brought the blanket with her, it was so beautiful, but things hadn't worked out as planned that night.

With a start, Asha looked up. To her left, there was something splashing in the water, then a shout. Leaping up, Asha jabbed the pole into the riverbed, slowing and turning the boat toward the figure thrashing in the water.

"Can you grab the pole?" she yelled.

"Help!" the boy cried, seeing the boat.

"You need to grab onto the pole!" Asha tried again. "I'll pull you over to the boat."

"My sister! My sister's stuck!" the boy shouted.

Poling over to the boy, Asha called, "I'll help your sister, but someone must be in the boat. Can you get in the boat and steer it to the shore?"

"Yes," the boy said, without much confidence.

"Good. Grab the pole." Asha pulled the boy to the edge of the boat. "Can you get in?"

"Yes." It sounded even more tentative, but Asha didn't have time to delay.

"Where is she?" Asha called, as she slid into the water.

"There," the boy pointed. "Where I was. She got stuck –"

Before he could finish, Asha was under the water, looking. She had never been underwater with her eyes open before. The world looked very different, with the refracted light on the surface and the murky depths below, full of dead trees wrenched out by the floods, their roots sticking up, catching more branches and debris pushed to the edge of the river by the current, home to fish and pale crabs. Here, the girl was caught, her foot twisted into a tangle of branches that held her locked in. She can't possibly be alive, Asha thought, looking at the body being pulled forward by the current and the battered foot anchored in the branches, but it didn't matter. She couldn't be left there. After going back for another breath, Asha swam straight back down, pushing the branches, pulling them, wrenching them, but they held fast to their victim. In a fury, Asha wedged a branch in the hole next to the girl's foot and pressed down on it with all her strength. When she felt the root give slightly, she wrenched the girl backward, toward her, and the body slipped free.

Still angry, as if this had all been an unbearable insult to her, she hauled the girl to the surface, wrapping her arm around the girl's middle and dragging her toward the surface.

The boy had the boat on the shore, quite a way down the river, so Asha pulled the girl's body onto the closest land. On the shore, she felt sick with sadness, dragging herself through the sticky mud bank, vomiting. She could barely stand to look at the girl, but she took the child's arm to pull the body out of the water, and incredibly, she could feel life coursing through it. The girl was alive! But how could she call back that life? What was necessary to separate the girl from the river?

Down the river, the boy shouted, but Asha couldn't make out the words. Again, he shouted something, waving his arm at something near her, and Asha looked up to find a dark shape heading toward her, out of the river, like a moving log, with large bumps on the top, and yellow slits of eyes studying the two figures on the shore. The noise and thrashing in the water had called it out of its stupor. A large male, the crocodile had feasted earlier in the day on fish stranded in a shrinking flood pool, but it was always worth seeing what the river was providing.

A great anger welled up in Asha, anger for so many things that had happened, so many things that had never been resolved. She looked at this beast moving through the water toward them, and she made a decision. There would be no more wrongs without a fight. And fight she did. Grabbing a branch thrown up by the river, she stood between the croc and the girl, waiting. It swam toward the shore and then dropped under the water, disappearing in the shallows. It's impossible, Asha thought, for something that big to disappear. But the thought had hardly formed itself when the beast shot out of the water, rushing at her, its mouth agape. Asha stepped back reflexively but then pushed herself forward, swinging the log, running at the croc and smashing the log into the side of its head. Then she stepped back one step, until it had turned towards her, and smashed the log into its head once again. Deciding this prey wasn't worth the fight, the croc slid backwards into the water and disappeared. Unsure, Asha waited, breathless, for it to return. But there was no sign from the water, so she grabbed the girl's body around the waist and hauled her away down the beach, glancing over her shoulder occasionally, ready to fight it again if it chose.

But the croc did not reappear, and gradually Asha's anger turned to exhaustion that left her unable to move. She sank down in the dirt next to the girl. "I don't know!" she cried. "I don't know how to separate you from the river!" She reached over and pulled the girl's form toward her, but the pressure of Asha's arm under the girl's ribcage made her vomit out water. Startled, Asha tried it again, and the girl threw up more water. A third time brought up more. Each time was less than the time before, so Asha thought it might be like wringing out a cloth. The first time brought out the most water, but each time brought out more. She tried once more, and this time the girl made a strangled sound as the water left her. Only living people make sounds, she thought, as the tears rolled down her cheeks. Only living people make sounds. One last time, she tried, and the girl moaned as she tried to get rid of the last of the river inside her. But she was hurting. When she did open her eyes, she was dazed and couldn't talk. It seemed as if she might slip away again, so tentative was her connection to the living.

Asha yelled to the boy, "Tie up the boat! I need your help!"

As he hurried to do as she asked, she looked around frantically. The river. She had to give the river something in return, if the river gave this girl back her life. Yet she had nothing she could offer. The carved paddle was in the canoe, and she needed something right away. Something to appease the river, to thank it, to recognize its power in taking the girl and then giving her back. She reached into her wrap and pulled out Naaba's carved bone dagger. It wasn't really hers to give, but it was all she had. Surely its beauty would balance the violence it had caused. Stepping to the very edge of the bank, where the water lapped against the dirt and rock, she drove the dagger into the boundary, the edge of water, and she bowed. Only the top half of the hilt showed, its white top looking like a stone the river had left in that spot.

When she stood back up, she found the boy already there, shocked to see his sister alive but not responsive.

"It'll take time for her to return completely, if she can," Asha said. "You'll need to help her start all over again and to remember the life she had. Can you do that?"

The boy nodded.

"Good. Now," Asha started, but she couldn't go on. It was simply the end of the day's story for her. "Not now," she corrected. "I'm too tired now, but I'll take you home tomorrow. We'll be safe in the boat. Can you help us back to it?"

Nodding, the boy helped his sister back to Asha's boat, and they curled up as best they could in it for the night. Later on, the girl had no recollection of that night. But the boy remembered everything from that day and night, very clearly.

In the morning, Asha took the children back to where the boy said their father was camped. When no one appeared, and there was no sign of a camp on the shore, she was worried about leaving the children there, especially with the girl's future so clouded, so she waited, hoping someone would come along and welcome the children home.

"Do you know where your father is? Your sister needs attention. I can't just leave her here."

"Oh, I'm sure someone will be here."

"Well," Asha started, but she didn't get the chance to finish the sentence. From the bush, at least twenty warriors materialized, each with a spear, every one aimed at Asha.

"No!" the boy shouted, holding up his arms. "She helped us! She saved my sister!"

That remark brought a familiar figure out of the bush: Akin, the man who had planned the invasion of Komo's village. He ran straight into the river, jumping aboard the boat, lifting his son up into his arms. Then, seeing his daughter's vacant look, he fell to his knees in front of her, putting one hand on her head and another on her arm.

"She drowned, Papa," the son said. "She got caught in the trees underwater. This lady brought her back."

Akin turned and bowed to Asha. "My life for my debt." Then, seeing her golden eyes, he stopped. "I remember you. Aren't you the woman who knew the floodwaters were coming, back at Komo's village?"

Asha nodded, tired down to her bones, feeling oddly removed from the scene, as if it was something from a dream. Akin handed his son to the warriors waiting by the riverbank, but as he picked up his daughter, his eyes were drawn to the most unusual object lying, as if it had been forgotten, in the water sloshing around the bottom of the boat. This had to be a trick. No one would have abandoned such a treasure. Handing his daughter to one of his men, he turned back to the paddle, picking it up, studying it.

"Where did you get this?"

It took a moment for Asha to remember the paddle. "A friend gave it to me."

"A friend? Are you a friend of hers?"

"Hers? A man gave me the paddle, a sweet, crazy man with animal friends," Asha said, but somewhere in her tired mind she was aware that the story was not very believable.

"You'll need to come with me," Akin ordered. Turning to his aide, he whispered, "She's a witch, and she's in league with the other one. We need to get word to The Leader. And have someone look after my children." The aide bowed and left.

After Akin left her in a hut, guarded by an old woman, Asha sank into a deep sleep, from which no dreams came. But later, when the old moon was rising, she awakened suddenly, to feel the river calling to her. In the sleeping village, it was easy to slip out of the hut and past the old woman and the guards, out to the water's edge. Her boat was tied up at the landing. The paddle was gone, but the pole was still in it, and she pushed off quietly into the night with a shiver of sadness, letting the river take her on into the unknown once again.

She headed back to the river because it was the only place she felt she belonged, but the days wore on her, and she hardly noticed as she passed wonders and terrors on the river: the tiny monkeys playing in the trees just over the surface of the water, the howlers roaring in the morning over some imagined wrong, the parrots' flash of color and sound, the dark spotted civet standing on a rock, the duiker bringing her baby down to the river, a creature with long slender legs and tiny feet scrambling down the bank and the bending over, knees buckled, as it took a drink, the cheetah slowly lapping the water at dusk, the hippos standing almost completely submerged to escape the biting flies, the crocodile sunning itself on bank in the morning, the slanting rays of late light finding their way through the leaves to dance on the river. She went by all of this but cared about none of it. Everything was shades of gray except the blue sky reflected in the river.

Later on, she couldn't say why she stopped where she did. Perhaps she was just tired.

CHAPTER 16
A CONFERENCE WITH THE LEADER

Toward the rear of the open-fronted building was a carved wooden bench covered with two lion skins. On it the man known to many as The Black Rhino, but to his warriors as The Leader, was seated, cross-legged, holding a long spear in his right hand. The carefully oiled topknot with yellow parrot feathers and the exquisitely embroidered tunic and loinwrap did nothing to soften his image. He was a fighter. Behind him a servant with a large feather fan stood ready to cool the air or shoo away insects as his master wished, but The Leader's attention wasn't on the temperature; it was on certain strange new developments that were threatening his plan. Seated on mats on the floor were his three lieutenants, each wearing an open tunic dyed a different color, the badge of their rank. Akin, as first lieutenant, was the first to report. But even he waited for the signal to start.

"Yes," The Leader nodded, impatiently. "Tell us of this strange news you bring from downriver."

Akin held up the paddle he had taken from Asha. "This is her sign, the eagle with the sun under its wing. Her people call her The She-Eagle."

"Start at the beginning. It makes no sense, jumping into the middle."

"Yes, sir, but I don't know all of the beginning. When I was working on the sections far upriver, I heard that someone was doing the same thing on the great river to the south, the River Born of

Twins, attempting to organize the people along the river, to encourage travel and trade, and discourage skirmishes. But the leader was a woman, a powerful queen who drew people to her as the flame draws the moth."

"Perhaps with the same effect," The Leader commented.

"Not everyone liked the plan, but that was all right; no one was forced to join the alliance. It was all voluntary. A lot of people saw the advantages, though: allied villages could call on others when they were attacked. They had much greater success hunting and foraging because they were safer. There were gatherings, exchanges -"

"Yes, Akin, we're all familiar with the advantages of alliance."

"Of course, sir. Well, the queen's alliance became the power all along the river, from the twin hearts all the way to the great sea."

"But that river isn't very long," The Leader said, dismissively.

"Correct, sir, but she has also made contact with the villages on the sea, or at least one that we know of." He paused while he showed off the paddle again. "And, we found this on your river, sir. It seems to indicate that her forces, perhaps including the queen herself, have been on your river."

"Where did you find this?"

"A woman had it, sir, but she was alone, and the boat was very small." Akin left out the part about his children being on the boat with her. "I think she probably found the paddle somewhere along the shore."

"Probably? Didn't you question her?"

"Yes sir, but she was incoherent."

"Crazy?"

"Yes, sir. She talked about animal friends giving her the paddle."

"And where is she now?"

"Somewhere downriver, I would think, sir."

"You would think? You don't know? You might have had this queen in captivity and then let her go?"

"No, sir. The queen is supposed to be so powerful that her energy lights up the night. This woman was nothing, a poor wreck who'd lost her mind. She had nothing else with her, no valuables, just a firestone and a calabash in a bag."

"Perhaps," The Leader conceded, "but perhaps not." He paused, trying to sort out what this might mean, and no one stirred, not even to shift position on their mats. "We need to get to the sea and find out who this leader contacted. We need to make allies on the coast as well. Then, we need to see what this 'queen' has established on her river. Find out her strengths as well as her weaknesses. Eventually, we'll need to take over her empire as well, but if she wants to do the organizing for us, it will save us the effort later. In the meantime, leave the paddle. I'll study it."

"Yes, sir," Akin bowed. "Shall I take my force to the sea?"

The Leader studied the designs on the paddle and replied without looking up. "Take a small group, four men, and get to the coast. Then come back with the news as soon as you know. Between now and our next meeting, find out what the local politics are, who is competing for power, who has a debt or a grudge to settle. If you're contacted by the local chief, set up an exclusive arrangement: if they join us, we'll spare their village and burn the others. The usual bargain."

"Yes, sir," Akin said, waiting to be dismissed before he sat down.

"Use the face paint," The Leader added.

Knowing this would put his men in danger of attack as soon as they were sighted, Akin hesitated. It was a terrible idea for spies to advertise their presence in enemy territory.

"Is there a problem, Akin?"

"No, sir."

"Good. I'd hate to think there was, or that you had bungled the whole incident with the paddle and let the only person who knows anything about it escape down the river without telling you anything. That wouldn't be a good situation, would it?"

"No, sir."

The Leader waved Akin away. "Dismissed. Now, what is this about a group of people between the rivers?" he asked the second lieutenant, as Akin stepped quietly back to his place.

Aware that The Leader was already angered, the second speaker was careful to start at the beginning and explain what he knew as clearly as possible. In his exploration of the headwaters of their river, he had learned that there were small groups of San people, as well as other fiercely independent peoples, who were living in the hilly area between their river and the River Born of Twins. These people made only temporary camps as they followed the big game. When he had approached them about joining the alliance, they turned him down. And, since they had no permanent village, they couldn't be forced into submission the way the others were. They had no interest in trade, or accumulating trade goods or treasure. There was no point in trying to use one leader against another because they had no real chiefs, in terms of concentrated power. They shared power among everyone in the group, even the women. No one was anxious to have more power than others. Apparently, the queen had also approached them, but she didn't require anyone to join the alliance, so they turned her down as well, though they found her very likeable. "They call her Dwyka, the Lioness," he added, in a tone that carried a little too much admiration.

"I don't care what those fools call her!" The Leader shouted. "Forget them. We'll deal with them later, once we've consolidated the rest of the territory." But the news didn't sit well with him at all. People who couldn't be frightened into submission were always a threat. He needed everyone to be part of this plan. Otherwise, the plan wouldn't work, and all of this effort would be for nothing. It had to work, and it had to include everyone. How did this woman think she could build a unified society if half the people were wandering off on their own? It sounds very nice, asking people, but what do you do with the ones who don't join? What if they want to live there but not obey your laws? What if they want to benefit from your trade routes and centers but not be subject to your law? What do you use to control them? No, there could be only one way. His way.

He waved his spear. "Forget those people. They're too far removed to be a concern right now. Go back to the top part of the river, recruit more warriors, and head downriver with the warriors as soon as they're ready. Dismissed. Now, Sekon, what is this great find that has the people in such an uproar? Some kind of rock?"

The third speaker rose slowly, dragging a heavy bundle under his arm. "Yes, sir," he said, setting the bundle down on the floor in front of The Leader. "During the recent flooding, the river undercut a part of a high bank, causing a large section of the bank to fall into the river and be carried downstream. However, a strange rock piece was left exposed." He unwrapped the bundle and everyone strained to see what it held. On the floor was a rock holding the fossilized head and neck of a creature none of them had ever seen. The head was something like a snake head, except it was as long and narrow as a man's arm, with fearsome teeth on the upper and lower jaw, like a crocodile. The neck was long and narrow, like a snake.

Since no one made any comment, Sekon went on. "The strangest part is the rest of the creature, which is still in the rock. It has wings, sir. Very large wings, about the same length as the height of three men. There are claws on the wings, like bats have."

"It's a bat then? Or a snake?" The Leader said impatiently. "We've found strange large bones before that no one recognizes. It is an animal from the ancient times, that's all. Nothing for us to be concerned about."

"Well, sir, the people are concerned. They think it's the spirit of the Sky Serpent that made the land and then shed his skin, releasing the waters over the land. When you sent word that you wanted to see the stone animal, I told my men to chip it out of the stone, but in working on it, they broke it, right here," he pointed, "at the neck. There's more of the long neck and the huge wing still in the rock. The people were very angry with us. With me. They said no one had the right to break apart the spirit of the Great Serpent. They were terrified, thinking the Serpent would call down destruction on them for my action."

"What are you saying? What happened?"

"After I left with this rock, they killed the man who split the rock, sir, and the two others who were working with him, by hitting them with slabs of stone. The rest of the warriors fled to the next village. I found out about it only yesterday."

With a shout, The Leader leaped to his feet. No one looked at him. "You bring me nothing but problems, all of you! I ask you to establish and maintain a network of villages along the river. It doesn't seem so difficult. Done correctly and quickly, the change would seem inevitable to the people. But is that what you do? No. Oh, no. You bring me one problem after another: the woman on the River of Twins, the people who listen to no one and have no chiefs, the village revolting against us because of a winged crocodile/snake/bat you found in a rock. What is this? A waste of time! If we don't move forward, we'll lose our momentum, and people will go back to their tiny worlds, all battling against each other over petty wrongs someone fabricated or exaggerated to foment war. Is that what you want to happen? Is that your vision for the future?"

No one responded. "Well?" he thundered, "Is it?"

There was a general murmur "No," but no one spoke up.

"You're pathetic - every single one of you. I need you to help me, not to bring me problems. Do you understand that?" Turning to Sekon, he said, "Put the cursed rock back and leave an offering, explaining that you're very sorry you broke the stone. Then find the ones who killed our men and have them executed. Fix the problem and move on. Understood?"

Sekon nodded, but he knew it wouldn't be that simple. It would only cost more lives, and perhaps even then the winged serpent wouldn't be forgotten. Some problems couldn't be fixed easily and some things were bigger than The Leader. But, of course, he said none of these things.

The Leader waved them all away. "We'll meet closer to the coast, on the next full moon. I'll leave a signal for you to tell you the location. Understood?"

They nodded. Everyone understood the signals: always three sticks the same length, the length of a man's leg from groin to heel. They would be arranged somewhere on the shore, very close to the river. They'd look as if it was possible they landed there accidentally, except to someone looking for them. They would have one of six possible arrangements, each indicating a specific command. In this case, two would be upright and the third pointing out toward the river, indicating the place to stop. Once they had landed the boats, they had only to search for the sapling tied over to the ground. If they stood under it and looked for the next one, they could sight a straight line to The Leader's camp.

The aides bowed and filed out, silently, each to his mission, but they could read the worry in each other's faces. Something very dangerous was happening. They had gotten started in this because they believed in it. A united network of villages could stand together against any foe. They could take the energy they used to waste fighting each other and put it to better use, building something great. But it had become something a little different. Perhaps that's what happened. Only a very strong leader could hold small groups together long enough to cooperate in building something that was to their mutual advantage. But old rivalries die hard, and it would take very little to break up this alliance. Akin hadn't mentioned the fact that Sohko's new village had gone back to using circles of stones to keep their records. They said it was the easiest way to keep track of many things at once: the days, the moon cycles, the trade numbers for the village. Wekesa had told him, and they had agreed it seemed to be a good idea. But The Leader would see it as a threat, so Akin didn't mention it. They all had things they didn't mention; a conspiracy of silence. And The Leader became more isolated and angry, determined to bring people to their knees before him, all in the name of progress. But it didn't always work that way. Akin and the others bowed and left.

With the lieutenants gone, The Leader stood looking at the carved paddle Akin had left. "You won't find it any easier," he said to the absent owner of the paddle, the woman, somewhere out there on one of the rivers, who had shared his vision. "And if you do, I'll wait until you succeed; then I'll defeat you." The servant approached with the feather fan, but The Leader grabbed it out of the servant's hand and threw to the ground. "This is stupid," he yelled at the cringing servant, "if there's nothing behind it. It has to be strong. It has to be so strong it's unstoppable!" As the servant hurried away, The Leader picked up the beautiful fan of plumes and smashed it into the floor. He could feel the whole dream slipping away, like sand between his fingers. He had to come up with a plan, right now, a plan that would ensure the success of the dream, even if it cost everything else.

Once out of the building, the servant's demeanor changed completely. He straightened up, removed the tunic worn by The Leader's staff, rolled it up, and stuffed it into a rock crevice. Then, without a backward glance, he headed off into the bush. His name was Okung, and he had his own ideas about the future.

CHAPTER 17
THE SINGERS AND THE HUNTERS

The boat Naaba had taken was little more than half of a hollow log, the sort of boat the villagers used for fishing in the creeks, useful because it had such a shallow draft. But for a long journey on the river, it was terrible: heavy, hard to steer, and very tippy, constantly wanting to roll over. He learned to sit very still, right in the middle of the boat, so it was less likely to roll, but any unusual motion, even catching on a sandbar or a snag, was enough to make it tip dangerously.

At one point, he was distracted, watching a group of howler monkeys argue with each other, jumping and crashing through the treetops near the bank, roaring their threats. He wasn't aware of anything wrong until the boat lurched to a stop, caught on a tangle of snags in the middle of the river. Grabbing the pole, he pushed away from the branches sticking out of the water, but they were attached to a submerged giant that had the boat in its clutches. Slipping out of the boat, Naaba stood on the submerged trunk, slid the pole under the boat and wedged it off the trunk, pulling it toward him. With a rush it was free and moved right onto Naaba's foot, crushing his toes. With a shout, he pushed the boat back far enough to free his foot and winced as he stepped carefully back into the boat.

Once he was back on the river, his mood darkened, reflecting the dark clouds gathering behind him. It would be a wet night, he knew, a bad time to be on the river in a boat with a tendency to take on water and to roll over. Everything seemed to be conspiring to slow him down. There was nothing for it but to find a place to pull the boat in and set up camp until the storm passed.

Once he'd dragged the heavy boat onto shore and secured it, the clouds moved in, prematurely ending the day. It wasn't hard to gather some branches and broad leaves for a shelter, but his foot stung with every step, and the rolling thunder coming toward him made him hurry more than he should have. Knowing the rain would soak all the firewood and tinder, he tried to gather as much as he could, quickly. With a load of branches under his arm, he reached over with his good foot to shove another bunch of branches under his makeshift tarp. But the viper was curled there, rubbing sections of its rough-scaled skin together, making a sizzling sound that every child was taught to recognize and fear. But with his hurry and the noise of the storm, Naaba never noticed. A flash of lightning lit up the sky, followed by a loud crack of thunder. In that same moment, the viper sensed the heat of its victim and lashed out, striking Naaba's calf. Stumbling backwards, Naaba screamed and fell, dropping the branches in all directions, sending the viper darting off.

He knew, even in his confusion, that the viper's poison could kill. A child in his old village had died of the viper's bite. Another had his leg turn grey and rot away. And that was after the medicine man had tried to help. Naaba felt sick and his head was pounding. He should get back to his shelter, he thought, but he couldn't remember exactly where it was. It was easier to stay where he was, curled up on the ground, as the storm pounded him. He had a rush of confused thoughts. He remembered an old man in his village who fed a parrot with a broken beak but never told anyone. Naaba had hidden in a tree and watched the man one day. Why would he do that? And in Asha's village, the woman who hummed so beautifully as she wove, as if the melody was driving the design of the basket. Did she know the two were connected? His mind filled with unrelated questions. When people die, do they become part of the bush? If so, do they know they're a bitter melon or a kinkeliba tree? Does the rain wash away your skin?

Who are you when you don't have any skin? Would people say, "My, you don't seem to be yourself today"? Then even these thoughts faded, and there was only pain and darkness, as the storm soaked the earth and filled the rivers.

In the morning, Naaba was dimly aware that the sun was already high enough to cast long rays through the trees, and that he had company. Two children out on the river had seen him lying near the shore and had stopped to see what was wrong. The girl moved slowly as she got out of their boat, and followed the boy, but her walk was lurching, and she supported herself with a heavy stick.

"May-Maybe... he's...dead," she said, pushing her hair back from her face.

"Look at that swollen leg, and the bite marks. He got bitten," the boy said. "Viper, maybe, or adder."

"Papa wouldn't....want us...to - to be here," she hesitated, working on the words.

"Papa's not here," the boy answered dismissively. "Anyway, you're the one who wanted to come back over here."

"I – I did," she started, "but -"

"Let's take him home. At least somebody could help him there. Maybe," he added.

"I...don't know," she worried, but the boy was already walking up to Naaba.

"If nobody stopped to help anybody, you wouldn't be alive today."

With awkward steps, the girl walked up to Naaba's curled form. "He looks...awful."

"People with snake venom in their body don't look pretty. Now, help me figure out a way to get him in the boat."

The seeds and ground root of the velvet bean plant that the healer fixed for Naaba gave him dangerous visions, with images packed together so tightly he thought he would burst open, spilling all those pictures in too-bright colors over the ground. He awoke once, to find the stars dancing wildly around the sky like crazed celebrants at a festival, more and more of them, until they were squeezed together in a band across the sky and fanned out at the edges, like a great serpent with two enormous heads. Then, later, he worried that the river was changing its course and leaping through the air, dropping fish and turtles down on the ground below, and Asha was riding along in the river, heading somewhere far away, leaving only the empty trough where the river used to flow. The healer gave him draughts of aizen berries and leaves soaked in water, but she shrugged when the girl asked her how he was doing. "It's all I know. Sometimes these things are not so serious. But sometimes they are." Seeing the girl's face fall, the healer put her hand on the girl's shoulder. "He needs something beautiful. Maybe you could find that."

Something beautiful, the girl thought. It couldn't be a treasure, since he couldn't see very much. But he might be able to hear.

The following morning, it was a single flute that Naaba heard first, then a boy singing:

Golden land of the river
Heavy green of the forest
The cry of the birds in the canopy

Then there were other voices, six in all, and they sang in harmony, answering the boy.
The howler's roar
Sudden, dark and strange
The hiss of the adder
Death moving so fast

The herds of the eland and kudu, bushbuck and duiker
    Their feet like drumbeats on the grass
The chimpanzees climbing, the baboons crashing
    The stinging bees and cities of termites
The mass of the rhino, the hippo, the elephant
    The giants of the world, certain of their power
The stealth of the lion, the leopard, the cheetah
    So quiet among the antelope,
The patience of the aardvark, the anteater, the warthog
    Digging through the stings and bites,
The connections between the sunlight, the moonlight, the circles of stars
    The ancestors, the living, the yet-to-be-born
The wonder of the great fishes flashing in the water
    More fishes than there are leaves on the trees,
The delight of the porpoises swimming under the boats
    Leaping and diving, playing, laughing
The pain of death, with its long wail
    The agony of loss
The sound of the people
    The beat of the drums

All the voices came together, soaring in harmony:

    Golden land of the river, with the green forest all around it
    Golden land, golden land by the river
    Golden land.

And finally, it was just the one voice again, the one boy:

    Spirits of this golden land,
    Show us the golden land
    Show us
    Show us
    The golden land.
    Show us the golden land,
    Oh, spirits of this golden land.

Then, it was just the flute, playing the same haunting melody. Naaba shook as the fever loosed its grip on him and sweat poured down his skin, dropping down, soaking into the earth, finding its way through the sandy loam to the rocks below, the rocks that held up the world.

The healer nodded to the girl. "Well done."

Days later, Naaba was still weak, but he sat out in the sunlight, next to his fire, working pieces of stone into arrowheads, spearheads, and knives. It was tedious work, but he was good at it, and it was something he could do to repay the kindness of these people. Besides, it kept his mind occupied. When he tried to sort out where he should go or what he should be doing, he couldn't escape the feeling that he had run out of chances, that it didn't matter much which path he took; all of them wound up turning in circles.

He was a strange figure, sitting there, so thin that his shoulder blades and collar bones stuck out oddly; his hair longer and wilder than ever; his dark eyes sunken. But people stopped by to talk anyway. Some, like the girl, felt an odd kinship with him, two lives reclaimed. Others only wanted someone to talk to, and he was there.

One was a very slight, leathery-faced man who kept two vipers in a basket. When Naaba recoiled in fear, the man held up his hand. "They won't bother you. At least I don't think so. They're not all bad, you know. They're like fire. Yes, it can kill you, but it can also help you. It's the same with these two. That venom that almost killed you, I have it," he said, waiting for Naaba's response.

"Why would you want it? Why would you want anything to do with them?"

"Why do you make arrowheads? Don't they cause pain and suffering?"

Looking down at a particularly fine arrowhead he had been finishing, Naaba said, "I suppose so, if you're the antelope. Or the enemy."

"And what if you could make it so the antelope died instantly, instead of running off a long way, so you had to track it while it's bleeding and suffering? Maybe there were times you shot an animal and couldn't find it later at all. Maybe it got dark, or the animal ran faster than you could follow. This way, you shoot the game and it dies within moments. Isn't that better?"

"Yes, I suppose. But how do you use the venom without poisoning yourself?"

"Ah, the very important part. You can't touch it. If you have even a tiny cut on your hand, and everyone does, it would kill you. You need to use a stick. Mark the stick with a notch on one end, so you don't accidentally grab the wrong end. Use the notch end to apply the poison to your arrowhead or spearhead. Then you can put the notch end back in the vial of venom, or you can burn the stick, if you don't plan to use it again."

"You've done this?"

"Many times. It's how my people hunt. The venom's very dangerous to handle, but very effective in hunting big game. These snakes, just like the one that almost killed you, have kept many of my people well fed." He paused. "It's curious."

"How do you handle the arrow without accidentally poisoning yourself?"

"The same way I handle the snakes and extract their venom - very carefully. I respect these creatures. They're life and death. They ask nothing of anyone; they'd kill in an instant, even me; but they're also a great gift. I like them for all those reasons."

"I'm sure they know that. Maybe you could show me how you prepare the arrowhead sometime."

"I'd be happy to," he nodded, pleased, drawing out a hollow tube with holes along the top, like a flute, with plugs at both ends, and placing it on his lap. Then he slid the lid off the vipers' basket and spoke quietly to the snakes. One lifted its head, watching, but it didn't strike. The other one looked as if it was asleep.

"That's when she's most dangerous," the man said, in the same soothing voice. "She's aware of my every move, aren't you, my beautiful girl?" Moving slowly and quietly, he took the hollow tube from his lap and held it above the snake that seemed to be sleeping. Suddenly, the viper rose up and struck the tube. The man grabbed her behind her head and held her there so she couldn't move and strike somewhere else. As she bit the wooden tube, the venom dripped along it, ran through the holes and into the bottom, where it pooled into a concentrated juice of death.

"This is the challenging part," the man said, still soothing and calm. "You're not happy now, are you, my beautiful girl?" He held the snake to the tube, even though her body was thrashing angrily. "I'm sorry, but it's necessary. I'll get you a nice mouse tonight. Two, perhaps." At that, he lifted the viper away from the tube, ran his hand along the long body, calming her, and set her down in the basket, putting the tube in front of her head in case she struck again. But the viper knew the schedule. She was done now, and she'd be rewarded later. With a final hiss, she settled back down in the basket, and the man slid the lid on top of it.

"How did you know she would strike and not the other one?" Naaba asked, still uneasy about watching vipers work.

"I know them. Someday, they'll probably kill me, but in the meantime, I like dealing with them, being only a moment from death. It's interesting. Now, I need to see one of your arrowheads. Make sure you'll recognize it later. You don't want to grab this one by mistake."

Naaba handed him the best of the arrowheads, quite fine and narrow, with a very sharp point. The man leaned the tube against a stone, removed a notched stick from the top of the basket, and pulled the plug from the higher end of the tube. Inserting the notch side, he picked up the venom on the end and then rubbed it on the tip of the arrow. "Let it stand here for a while," the man said. Then put it in your quiver but wrap the arrow in leaves so you keep the poison from evaporating." He turned to Naaba. "I hope it helps you."

"Thank you. Do all the other hunters here use your poison?"

The man stood up, gathering up the basket of vipers. "None of them. They don't like the vipers. They only want the venom for their medicines. For hunting, they build pit traps and try to run the game into them. Sometimes it works," he shrugged. "I'll show you how to tie that onto the shaft tomorrow. It helps if you don't kill yourself in the process."

With a smile, Naaba thanked him again and watched him pack the venom tube into another tube and then shuffle away, the small figure with so much knowledge that no one wanted to learn. He thought of his dream of carrying the Black Mamba's venom in a wooden vial. It seemed very different now that the idea was stripped of its vanity.

When he was stronger, Naaba went out with a hunting party, looking for eland, bushbuck, or duiker. There were four of them: three seasoned hunters and one boy on his first long hunt. In general, the hunts went on as long as it took to find the game, perhaps a day, perhaps ten days, but the hunters wouldn't return without meat for the village. As they went, they fanned out, looking for tracks, scat, game paths, watering spots, antler rubs, places where the bucks had urinated and then dug up the spot, spreading the smell, any signs of the passing herds. They spoke only when necessary, though the boy, excited at finding some antelope droppings, shouted to the others before he remembered. The droppings were old and dry, but the trail looked promising, so they followed it deep into the bush, but they found nothing. In the heat of the day, they rested in the shade, half-dozing, and then went on. They saw monkeys and birds of all kinds, signs left by anteaters and small wildcats, but not a single antelope.

Around the small fire that night, they discussed where they'd head the next day, deciding to continue working south. If they still found nothing, they'd try the other way. There was little conversation. Blank days were a part of hunting, but they weren't the part the men liked to talk about. Eventually, they found places to sleep in the trees, braced against the trunk. The men were all used to this, but the boy slept fitfully, waking often and listening to the night.

With dawn, they started off again, heading south, following game trails, checking the damp ground around the waterholes for tracks, but the tracks they found were old, covered over by newer tracks of different animals coming down to drink. They could have hunted what was available, smaller game like hares, lizards and turtles, but they wanted something better – and bigger – to bring back to the village. So they kept looking.

Later in the morning, Naaba, in the lead, held up his hand for the others to stop. Turning, he put his finger to his nose, and the others nodded. The scent was unmistakable: the heavy, oppressive, sour smell of the giant forest hog. It wasn't the game they had set out to find, but it explained why the antelope had abandoned the area temporarily. Forest hogs were so ferocious, they could scare a hyena away simply by rushing at it, and their pervasive smell claimed the area they were in as theirs, as long as they wanted it. The boy, puzzled, turned to ask his father, but his father shook his head and put his finger to his lips.

Moving quietly through the bush, alert for any sound, the hunters climbed up a rise, where Naaba signaled them to hunker down, so they were hidden by the undergrowth. There, they had a clear view of the hogs in the distance, perhaps thirty of them, feeding in an open area. The leader was a big male, the size of a rhino, an ugly black-haired beast with a huge head and flaring tusks. Under his eyes were big warty growths that looked like a second set of eyes. As they watched, the leader lifted his head, reading the scents around him, and the hunters had a clear view of his upper canines, as long as a man's forearm, flaring upward and outward, that ground constantly against the lower canines, making them sharper than the finest stone knives. With a loud grunt, he called the group to move, but almost immediately he stopped them, lifted his head once again and swung around, suddenly tense, the bristles along the ridge of his neck and back rising.

From the far side of the clearing the challenge came, from another huge male, with different, lighter coloring, pounding across the clearing, grunting and screaming, his powerful hindquarters propelling him straight toward his target. In an instant, the leader answered the challenge, lowering his head and charging the attacker. Tearing through the underbrush and tall grasses they raced toward each other, throwing up dirt clods and torn branches, locked onto a collision path, never slowing as they approached each other, so that they met with a horrible crash, head to head, the terrible crack echoing through the forest. For a moment, they were both stunned by the impact, but it was only a moment. Then they ran again, crashing headfirst into each other with a force that could have easily broken down a mudbrick wall. The challenger stumbled as he stepped back, and the leader ran on him, grinding his teeth and grunting. Before the challenger could regain his strength, the leader slashed at him with his bared teeth, ripping open the tough hide along the boar's shoulder. With a yelp, the challenger turned and fled, his tail raised in defeat. The leader urinated on the spot where the fight had taken place, claiming the victory. But there was another smell in the air, and still agitated, the big boar led his group toward the hunters on the rise.

Motioning the others to follow, Naaba moved off at an angle away from the boar and his herd, but before long, he realized he was moving out of one danger right into another. The pig smell was strong all around them, heavy and sour, and their marks were everywhere. The second hunter touched Naaba's shoulder and held up two fingers. Nodding, Naaba stopped and studied the area. They were now in the territory of the second group, whose leader had been run off. But to where? Would he return to his own group? It would depend on how badly he was injured. Once they knew he was injured, the males in his own group might challenge him if he returned, or, if the group was leaderless, they'd challenge each other.

One of the other hunters pointed to the left and then waved his hand toward it. Agreeing, the group followed him to what he saw as a better path to take. As they moved through the bush, they could hear grunting and barking ahead of them, then behind them, then on both sides. The now leaderless second herd had moved toward the dominant herd, so that the hunters found themselves surrounded by the beasts. Several times, they saw the giants quite clearly. One stared at them, only twenty paces away, clacking its teeth. It was as big as all four of the hunters combined, black bristles standing up along its neck and back, its tiny eyes studying them. It would have charged the group except another male challenged it, and they clashed heads with a terrible smack that sounded as if it would break their skulls open. Through all this, the hunters kept moving, not fast, not threatening the pigs, but staying near trees that might give them an escape if they were charged. The boy, exhausted with fear, never said a word.

After a while, the sounds grew fainter and the intense smell lessened. Feeling sick with relief, the boy stopped and bent over, holding his stomach, while the others went ahead. In that moment, the injured boar charged out of the underbrush. Unbelievably fast, the beast churned up the ground as it ran forward, his head lowered, his eyes fixed on the boy.

"Run!" Naaba yelled. "Run toward us!"

The boy staggered, trying to get his balance, then turned and ran for the group.

The men shouted, hurling their spears at the boar. The spearheads glanced off the thick hide, but they were enough to slow the boar's charge. The boy had been an easier target than four of them together. It stopped in front of them, but it was still ready. It was so close they could see the bloody wound on its shoulder, the black bristles on its snout, the huge curling tusks, the warty growths under its eyes.

Naaba moved with the fluid motion of the leopard, finding the right arrow, uncovering it, fitting it into his bow.

When the boar charged, it was straight at the boy once again, exploding into motion, grunting, covering the ground so quickly, there was no possibility of escape. Naaba had only one chance; he shot the arrow at the open wound. With a thud, the arrow penetrated the boar's shoulder, but the huge animal's momentum was so great, it kept going, kept running, straight into the boy, sending him flying and knocking down his father who tried to protect him. Then, as the boar turned, the poison raced through his system, confusing him, making his legs buckle underneath him. With a roar, he rose to charge again but his balance was off and he lurched to one side, slipped, and crashed back to the ground, thrashing, butting at his own legs, his long teeth grinding together. Every motion pumped the venom deeper into his system. At the end, he threw back his head, as if to read the air once more, but the power inside him was shutting down with a fierce suddenness. The beast's last scream was cut short when the breath of life left him and he lay still on the crushed grass, his massive body powerless, absurd, tragic.

The boy lay crumpled on the ground, more terrified than hurt, though his ribs were very sore. His father, nursing a wrenched shoulder, ran to his side.

"You shall have the beast's liver, Son, because you were so brave," his father said, when he realized the boy was all right. "Then you'll carry the boar's strength with you, always."

The boy nodded, but he was very tired and every movement hurt, even breathing. His father took him aside, talked to him, and wrapped his ribs while the others gutted the boar.

"So, the arrow was poisoned," the other hunter remarked, not looking at Naaba.

"Yes, it was a gift," Naaba started, but the man waved him silent.

"It's not the way we hunt."

"You would have preferred the boy to die?"

"No, of course not," the man said, trying to soften his stance. The fact was that Naaba's arrow had saved them, all of them, probably, but that didn't change the hunter's view of how things should be done. "You're just not from around here," he said, after a pause.

"You're right," Naaba said, his temper rising. "How exactly would you have handled it if I weren't here?"

It was a fair question, but it brought out the worst. "We wouldn't have gotten into the situation in the first place," the hunter said, throwing down his knife.

"And what situation would you have gotten into?"

"We run game into traps. It's always worked. We don't need your poisons."

His temper up, Naaba would have left them, right there, in the bush, with two injured hunters, except that the boy's father stepped in. "I am in your debt," he said, holding his shoulder as he bowed to Naaba. "If you hadn't been here, and been able to make that shot, my son would be dead." He paused. "Probably, I would too."

The other hunter looked away.

Naaba put his hand on the man's good shoulder, and he returned the gesture.

"We have a lot to do," Naaba said, looking around the group, "before we go back to the village. We can either work together to get it done, or we can kill each other fighting. I've seen it done often enough."

Realizing he was suddenly the outsider in the group, and that it would mean his death being left behind, the fourth hunter bowed. "Of course, we are all together. I only was commenting that we have different methods of hunting here."

"Our aim is the same, no matter where we are from," the father said.

The fourth hunter didn't reply, but he understood. Together, they butchered the great beast, packing the meat down in the salt bags they had brought, but a bond was forged between three of them at that moment. That night, when they had roasted some of the meat on a spit over the fire, they talked of the hunt, going over each moment and its sensations, but the fourth hunter didn't say much. He had been considered a great hunter in his day. People had run to him in distress: *The people are hungry; please find us some meat*, and he had gone out alone and brought back enough to feed several families, and they had greeted him as a hero. Who was this man, this half-wild man, to challenge him? Naaba needed poison arrows to hunt. Real hunters relied on their skill, not tricks.

The boy ate part of the boar's liver, as the father had promised, and he saw that day, and that night, as the beginning of his life.

In addition to the salted meat, the hunters took the boar's head with them, tied to long poles that two of them carried at a time. On the way back, they came across a herd of duikers, and they killed two, dressing them out and adding them to the litter they carried. By the time they returned to the village, they were greeted with shouts of welcome and praise, and the meat was set out to roast on spits. But the villagers also had news to share.

Akin and his warriors had come by, recruiting fighters to go with his group to the coast. Almost all of the young men had gone with him after he told them it was the most important war they would ever fight and that they would win high status for themselves if they fought bravely. Hearing this, the boy who had gone with the hunters pleaded with his father to let him go with the others.

"They're gone already," the villager said. "They left yesterday."

"I need to stay with your mother and your younger brother," the boy's father said gravely. "You'd be a great help to me here."

"I don't want to be here. I want to go where the others are." He had pictured his return to the village as the great hunter, but now, everyone who mattered was gone, and his victorious hunt was a hollow success. "I'll go on my own. I can find my way down the river."

His father shook his head sadly. There was so much he wanted to say, but no one can see through the eyes of youth and age at the same time. There were so many battles in life, and few were as glorious as they seemed in the descriptions given by those who were recruiting fighters for the next one. But he couldn't say this to the youth with the blazing eyes, the one standing with his arms crossed, glaring at his father.

"I'll take him to meet the others at the coast." Naaba's voice floated through the angry silence that had grown up between father and son, and they both looked at him curiously.

"But -" the boy's father began, searching for the words that would keep his son with him.

For an instant, the boy hesitated. It was one thing to want to go with his friends; it was another to leave his family behind, perhaps forever. Then he nodded to Naaba. "I'll be ready to leave at first light."

"Good," Naaba smiled. "I'll be ready sometime later in the day. I assume you have a boat, some weapons, and supplies."

"A boat," the boy began, but he stopped and turned to his father.

"Yes, of course," his father said, putting his arm around the boy's shoulders. "Take our boat. You can bring it back when you return." There were tears welling in his eyes, and his son put his arms around his father in a long hug. Naaba turned away. They'd have many things to talk about. Tomorrow, if the boy still wanted to go, they'd figure out a way.

"Thank you," the two called out to him as he walked away. In a way, it was strange, how he was always leaving a place just when he'd gotten settled there, but at least he was used to it. The boy, however, was about to get to know loneliness for the first time, and it was never an easy meeting.

As Naaba lay awake on his mat that night, he heard someone moving carefully through the village center, then whispered calls and another set of footsteps. The uneven footfalls of the second set he recognized immediately. I'll have others to pick up along the way, Naaba thought, as he drifted off to sleep.

But there were difficult goodbyes for the hunter and his son, and the sun was already past its height before Naaba pushed their boat off into the river, and Naaba saw no sign of the brother and sister until late in the day. They had come upon a stretch of river where jagged rocks piled up along the river bottom, carried along by the floods in the rainy season and then stopped there by the other boulders. On the surface, there were only a few rocks breaking the flow of the water, but underneath, the rest lay very close, and passage through was impossible. Not knowing any of this, the children had tried to find a way through but had gotten stuck in the rocks, far from the shore. Naaba and the hunter's son had been walking the boat along the shore when he saw them, stranded on the rocks.

He handed the ropes to the boy. "Can you manage the boat? I have to see to some friends. I'll need the paddles and pole. Wait for me around the bend, where the water clears."

Using the paddles as a float and the pole as a balancing beam, he half-swam, half-walked the rocks out to the children.

"Naaba!" the boy shouted, with a desperate wave. His sister didn't say anything; she only stared straight ahead, not moving. Being stranded on the river had sent her back to the most terrible moment of her life. She thought she was once again sinking in the river, the water filling her lungs, the green murky world of the river bottom claiming her.

"I'll have to take her first," Naaba said, lifting the girl. "Will you be all right until I get back?"

The boy nodded, but he hated to see Naaba go away. Setting the girl on the paddles, Naaba slipped and slid across the rocks, trying not to pull her down with him when he fell between the rocks, but he found his way to the shore. She still hadn't moved, but when he went to lift her onto the shore, she locked her arms around his neck and didn't want to let go, even when she was safe on the shore.

"I'll be right back," Naaba said. "I promise. Can you wait for me here?"

The girl nodded slightly, and he set her down on a flat rock. In his hurry to get back to her brother, he slipped several times on the rocks, cutting himself on the rough edges, but he kept going, anxious for both of them. The boy was crying when Naaba got to him. "It's my fault. I'm sorry. I didn't know it would be so hard for her. I didn't, but I should have."

"We'll take care of your sister. Right now, I need you to help me out, so we can get out of the river before something very unfriendly figures out that I'm the one bleeding. Hang on to the paddles. Try to keep your feet up. Some of the rocks have sharp edges."

Several slips and cuts later, the two hauled themselves out of the water, to find the hunter's son standing next to the girl, talking to her. It seemed to have helped bring her back, somewhat. At least, she had turned to look at him.

"You're Deka," he said to the girl, amazed. "And you're Sule," he said, turning to her brother. "Akin's children."

"Yes, we are."

Naaba's mind flashed back to that night, when the village was burning and the old man found his grandchildren. "You were with the old woman, hiding in the circle of stones at Komo's village?"

"Yes, the same night my father burned it to the ground," the boy said bitterly. "My grandfather had taken us on a trip upriver, looking for good sites for a trading post. We were caught in Komo's trap, just as you were. Of course, Papa didn't know we were there, and my grandfather never told him. But I saw what my father did to the village. Later, when he took us with him down the river, we were always running away. That's how Deka drowned. We were playing, jumping in and out of the boat, out by the snags."

"Deka drowned?"

"Yes, but then the golden-eyed lady came along and brought her back from the river. That's why we stopped to help you. It was right around the same place, and we saw you there, on the shore, after the rain, so it seemed like a balance, you know, a kindness for a kindness."

Naaba caught his breath. "Golden-eyed lady?"

"Her name was Asha, but my father said she was a dangerous witch because she had a fancy decorated paddle, so he kept her prisoner, even after she had saved Deka, but she escaped down the river. Why, do you know her?"

CHAPTER 18
AN ENCOUNTER AT A VILLAGE FESTIVAL

Asha had stopped at the landing because she was tired but also because she was hungry, not for food, but for company. Back when she was always walking away from her home village, she couldn't have imagined there'd come a time when she'd miss the hum of a village, the pulse of life there, the different dramas all being played out at once, so that life spilled over and filled the whole village with its power. But now she missed it so much, she was walking into a village she knew nothing about, just so she could feel that energy all around her once again.

The path from the landing was well worn, and Asha paid little attention to her surroundings as she followed the track to the village. Behind her, the sun was old and tired. Ahead, she could hear the beating of many drums and shouts of a crowd, all pulsing to the same rhythm. Closer to the village, she could see torches already lit around the village center. The gathering, whatever it was, seemed to have claimed everyone in the village as a participant. No one was lingering outside the huts or staying with a fussy baby or sick relative. At least, no one Asha saw.

By the time she reached the center, the drums were dancing in a three beat pattern, the drummers playing with the rhythms, handing off the lead from one drummer to another, playing against each other and then with each other, driving the energy of the crowd. Standing at the edge of the crowd, behind the light of the torches, Asha watched as the chief and his entourage paraded in,

and jugglers and stilt-walkers entertained the group. Then, with
a flourish, the leader stopped the drummers and stood, poised, his
hand in the air, until a single young woman stepped out into the
center and stood, waiting. Wearing almost nothing, she was painted
rather than costumed. Her entire body was covered with light clay
that was marked with dark, swirling designs. Her hair, completely
soaked in clay, was drawn up into an ornamental headdress of inter-
twining loops. Her face was covered by a mask with almost no fea-
tures, only round tubes for the eyes and slits she could see through.

The drummers started, a slow, insistent beat, and the woman
stepped slowly, her arms at her sides, but everyone waited. Three
loud beats of all the drums together announced the arrival of the
second dancer, a young man in a decorated loinwrap, also painted
and masked, but he walked in, as the drums started up once again,
with his hands held high above his head. In them was a large rock
python, obviously, as it swung its head around, very much alive.

The crowd, mostly men, as far as Asha could tell, went wild,
screaming, and the drums moved from their slow, insistent beat to
something faster and more intense. As the man paraded the python,
the young woman sank to her knees, then bowed over, her head
to the ground, extended her legs out behind her and lifted them
straight up in the air, as she leaned on her arms. The woman's body
seemed to have no usual joints; she could move any part in any direction, and all in perfect control. The man with the snake walked up
and stood next to her, running the snake around his shoulders and
between his legs. Then he stood across the woman, but as he did,
she sank down and folded herself over so that her head was facing
the ground and her legs went all the way over her body backwards.
As the man wielded the snake over her, she grabbed hold of one of
her own legs and twisted her body around so that she could stand.
Once she was facing the man, she bent over backwards, putting her
head between her legs, and stood on her hands, spreading her legs.
But as soon as the snake handler advanced, she moved once again,

bringing her legs down behind her and writhing like the snake that threatened her. The crowd cheered, yelling and stamping their feet, and the drums picked up the tempo. The handler showed off his skill, wrapping the python around his neck, down his body, and around his leg. But the woman was never still, always moving like another snake, or sometimes more like a spider, when she moved her legs while her back was bent completely backwards and her face was against the ground. The perfect headdress never came undone; the mask never slipped, but she never stayed still. Her body was a study in fluid motion, always a step ahead of the dancer with the python.

The drums went on, never letting the intensity drop, and the two dancers kept up this dance of arousal and refusal until the crowd was in a frenzy. It's all just a show, Asha thought; it's meant to do exactly what it's doing. That's why the dancers are masked. They're meant to be anyone, or everyone. But she found it disappointing. She had wanted someone to talk to, not this. So she wandered off, the drums still pounding behind her.

There was almost no daylight left as she found her way back through the strangely silent huts lined up along the lane. Most had only a woven screen across the entrance, and most of those had been left open in the occupants' rush to join the festivities. But not this one. This one was closed, and a bar was driven through slots on both sides. A man, now very drunk, was sitting in front of the locked door, while another was leaving.

"Too bad you'll miss the party in the square. It'll be interesting."

The drunken guard looked up and shrugged. "He told me to make sure she stays here until The Leader arrives. That's all I know. But thanks for the drinks."

"Maybe they should make her part of the show!"

"Good idea!" the man laughed.

Asha waited until the friend had gone and the bored guard, fuzzy-headed from the palm wine, had nodded off. "You're wanted in the center," she said in the loudest voice she could muster. "They need help setting up for the main event."

Shaking himself awake, the man went to stand, but he fell heavily against the wall of the hut. "They told me not to leave her," he began, but Asha interrupted.

"I'll take over until you get back."

"Is it the chief? Did the chief ask to see me?"

Asha put her hands on her hips and tilted her head. "What do you think?"

"No, probably not."

"You know who sent me. Hurry, or I'll get in trouble too," Asha said, waving him on. She walked right past him, as if she already assumed he was going, never looking right at the man.

After he stumbled away, Asha pushed the bar off the door and threw it open. A woman, who seemed to be sleeping, or unconscious, was tied to the wall of the hut. "I have no idea who you are or what you've done," Asha announced, walking toward the woman, "but no one deserves to be tied to the wall. I know; I used to be." Without waiting for the woman to speak, Asha fumbled with the ropes, trying to untie them, but they held tight.

"Do you have a knife?" the captive woman asked quietly.

"No. I have nothing," Asha answered, "but I'll find a way."

"There's a knife over there, by the door. They left it just out of my reach. A little joke among the guards."

Once Asha found the knife, she freed the captive's hands and handed over the knife. In the gathering darkness, the woman would know better where to cut the ropes. She was amazingly quick with the knife, leaving the scattered pieces of rope on the floor mats where they fell.

"Are you coming, or would you like to be killed for your kindness to me?" the woman called in a fierce whisper as she headed for the door.

With the frenzied drumming in the background, they ran through the village and all the way to the river, hearing shouts behind them but knowing nowhere else to go. In the dark, they felt their way around the boats on the landing until Asha had found hers, but the other woman kept looking. "If we can find my boat, we can go faster. I'll know it by its feel."

Afraid of waiting any longer, Asha stood close to the river, as if it would give her the strength to stay while this strange woman searched around in the dark for a boat.

"It's here," the woman called, "but we need paddles. We'll grab some as we go. Come, help me get the boat into the water." It had been hidden in the bushes and it took some time for them to lift it free and push it into the water.

"I can hear them coming," Asha called as quietly as she could, but panic was rising inside her. They needed to be on the river.

"Push off. I'll jump in once you're out in the river."

As Asha pushed the boat into the water and climbed in, she heard thumping noises behind her on the shore and yells from their pursuers coming down the path to the landing. As the current pulled the boat away from the shore and out into the river, Asha looked back, frantic, but all she could see was the spreading light of the men's torches as they ran down to the landing. There was no trace of the woman.

"There!" one of the men yelled, pointing to Asha.

Another ran up but stopped at the river's edge. The boat was clearly moving away, but it was dark on the river, and he had been enjoying the party for some time.

"Get a boat and go after her!" the chief's voice boomed from behind them.

Moved into action, the men searched for their boats, but as they went from one to another, they came to the same conclusion. "I don't think we can, sir," one man ventured. "There are no paddles or poles, anywhere."

Around the bend, at the current picked up, Asha heard a banging on the front of the boat and started when she saw a hand appear on the gunnels. Then a paddle was lifted up and flipped over onto the floor of the boat, and another, and another. After a moment, the woman let the other paddles go down the river, grabbed the side of the boat with both hands, and vaulted in.

"That was interesting," she said as she put her paddle in the water, but then she picked it up again and turned to face Asha. "Do you often walk into strange towns and rescue people?"

"Almost never! I only stopped there because I'd been on the river for a long time and I wanted someone to talk to. I'm Asha."

"I have many names, but I think I like Dwyka the best. You wouldn't have found much company in that village. The only women there are 'professionals.' It's a camp for warriors waiting for a man they call The Leader. They're all heading downriver when he arrives, probably tomorrow. That's why they're having a party tonight. Do you mind travelling through the night? I'd like to get farther ahead of them before I relax."

"Good idea. I'm sure I didn't make any friends back there."

"Only one, I think," the woman said, returning to her paddling.

When it was daylight, they stopped to gather food, but they hurried back to the river when they were done. Their pursuers would be along soon. In the afternoon they came to a section where the river ran over underlying rock so hard that the river couldn't dig a channel through it, so the water spread out over the land in many small rivers, braiding together and moving apart in a maze of channels and mangrove swamps. But Asha always knew where the river was going, and how to get there. By nightfall, they were back on the wide river, watching the moon rise into the clear sky, while those chasing them were getting themselves lost in the maze.

* * *

If a hawk flying high over the land had looked down, the following morning, it would have seen many different groups of canoes spread out along the length of the river, and more still on the River Born of Twins to the south, all pulled along by the great waters beneath them, all rolling through ever-wider banks toward the place the rivers ended, where they were swallowed up by the sea.

* * *

PART II – ALONG THE SHORE AND OUT TO SEA

- on the western shore of the area currently known as Senegal and The Gambia, about 12,000 BC

CHAPTER 1
GAMES

Sheeah was sitting on the grassy edge of the beach south of the mouth of the great river, scanning the groups of people gathered on the beach while her oiled and scented hair was plaited into narrow braids. When her whole head of hair had been separated into neat rows, and all the rows plaited and decorated with snail shells and carved tigerwood nuts, they would be swept up into a knot on the top of her head. From there, the flashing rows would cascade down her back in a show of beauty and wealth. At least, that's how the process appeared in her mind. Her servant was doing most of the work, but Sheeah made a great show of tying off the braids that fell to the front. She reminded the servant to make the braids very, very thin and tight, so no one could fail to notice. The servant nodded but kept on making the braids exactly as she had been, knowing they'd look just fine the way they were and Sheeah would never be able to see the ones in the back anyway.

Sheeah was beautiful, or at least everyone said she was, with the luminous skin and high, flat forehead so admired by her people that mothers massaged their babies' heads to achieve it. As the only daughter of the chief, she had always been pampered, but after her mother died, her father had given Sheeah anything she wanted: fine woven wraps with embroidered designs, leather belts with beadwork, carved coral necklaces. He felt a beautiful girl should have beautiful things. But for Sheeah, abundance made her treasures seem common, so she always wanted something more, something rare and difficult to obtain.

There was a long line of suitors bringing her gifts and seeking her favor, but she didn't like any of them. One smelled of fish. One had ugly teeth. One talked about himself all the time. One didn't talk at all. One was too short. One was too old. One licked his lips every time he looked at her. One spit while he ate. And so on. It was important, her father had said, to arrange a suitable match that would ensure good allies. Irritating was what it was, she thought, but when she complained to her father, he told her to stop acting like a spoiled child. That wasn't really fair, in that he had helped spoil her, but she didn't point that out.

So she was frequently annoyed these days, but this particular day she was annoyed not because she didn't want something but because she couldn't get something, or more specifically someone, she wanted, and this was a new and equally unpleasant concept. But she wasn't easily discouraged. Sooner or later, she always got what she wanted.

In fact, the object of her desire wasn't far away. That's why she was sitting, rather uncomfortably, out on the beach grass, instead of on suitable mats in the shade of her own house. He had the build of an athlete, with his broad head and neck, wide shoulders, trim waist, and well- muscled arms and legs. Across his chest were lines of scars, the lasting legacy of a fierce battle he'd fought with a lion. Unfortunately, he didn't notice her, even with her extravagant hair and stunning dye-cloth wrap. He was, at that moment, rocked back on his heels, concentrating on a series of holes he had just poked in the sand with his finger. There were at least a dozen people clustered out on the golden beach, men and women as well as children, all watching, some hunkered down, some leaning on staffs, as he laid out his pattern: six holes in the first row, five holes in the second row, six holes in the third row, three holes in the fourth row, two holes in the fifth row, one hole in the last row, and an oblong black stone at the top. Murmurs went through the group. Usually, the patterns were more regular. In fact, the children had learned to count the rows and columns, to predict how many lines it would take to build the picture, but this layout was a surprise.

. . . . . .

. . . .

. . . . . .

. . .

. .

.

Afutu, the man who drew the dots in the sand, was known as a great hunter and athlete, but right now, he was a storyteller. According to the rules of the game, once he was telling his story, he couldn't stop until it was done. At the same time, he had to draw the pattern between the dots without stopping, without speeding up or slowing down, without ever lifting his finger from the sand except between lines, if the figure had more than one line, so that the story and the pattern ended at exactly the same time.

The group fell silent, waiting for him to start. "Back when the world was ruled by the animals," Afutu said as he leaned forward, drawing a bird's foot, "there were great wars between them." He drew a line up to the top. "The victors became the kings, and they grew very powerful, like the white shark in the ocean, the python in the trees, the crocodile in the shallows, the bat in the caves, the hippo in the wide rivers." The line looped back.

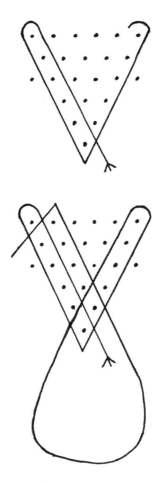

"But the greatest of these was the Eagle King, who grew so large that he filled the sky when he flew." His big hand moved steadily and surely over the sand, forming the large tail and the wing. "The Eagle King's amazing speed and keen sight made him impossible to conquer in the sky, but a very small creature, the Trickster Spider, knew his weakness. It was his vanity." He drew in the head, with the black stone as the eye.

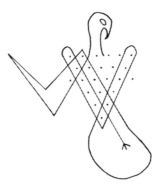

"So he asked the eagle if he could ride on its back up into the stars. Being a lowly spider, he said, he never got to leave the earth, but one as great and powerful as the eagle surely wouldn't mind carrying something as tiny as a spider. 'I suppose I could,' the eagle said, extending a wing, so the spider could climb onto his back. With that, the eagle soared off into the stars. But as he went, the Trickster Spider shot out his line of webs, across the sky, from star to star. 'Oh, please circle,' he called to the eagle. 'It's so beautiful up here!' So the great bird circled, and as he did, Trickster sent out his web in all directions, making a web from star to star that held Eagle King in the sky. 'Thank you, great Eagle King!' Spider called, as he dropped down along his webs to the earth, leaving the Eagle forever stuck there, in the sky. You can see him there in the stars when you look up at night," Afutu said, "still trying to find a way back out into the open sky," as he put the toes on the eagle's other foot.

The drawing was perfect, with no stops, no change of pace, no mistake, and the group cheered. Sheeah didn't understand the appeal of the whole game. To her, it was a bunch of people poking around in the dirt. Actually, she had tried to draw one of the designs once, but the effort had been so frustrating, she never tried again. Thinking they might be finished, she rose, giving her hair a little swing as she started toward the group. But they weren't finished; they were still bent over the sand. Sighing, she joined the group, standing across from Afutu, but he was watching the next player.

A thin young woman with wiry hair that kept escaping its ties was placing round black stones on the sand: one in the center and eight in an X-pattern radiating from the center. The stone drawings, unlike the dot drawings, went from stone to stone, instead of between them, and were made of many lines. But like Afutu, this storyteller, Dashona, had to finish the drawing at the same time she finished the story, and the pace had to remain constant in both the drawing and the telling.

"A long time ago," she started, "a wise man built a structure that made the villagers curious. They came around asking, 'What's this for?' and he would just smile or say something vague, like 'It's for finding treasures.' So, every night, when the wise man finished his work, the villagers would climb the walls into the center, but they would find nothing.

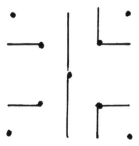

'What kind of treasures are these?' they'd ask the man. 'The best kind,' he said. 'A stolen prize leaves only bitterness in the mouth. These treasures must be earned.' So he kept building, making the walls higher and wider, and the villagers found it hard to climb them. They tried to walk through the maze, but they got lost and angry.

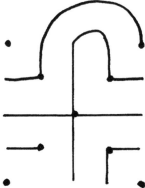

One woman panicked and screamed until others found her and led her out. So they gave up on the maze of treasures, until a child said, 'If we make a diagram and mark all the ways that worked as well as those that didn't work, we can find a way through. Just go in, remember where you went, then come out and mark it here, on the sand." Dashona's hand moved steadily around the diagram, filling in more parts of the maze.

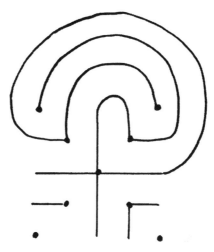

"So they did: men and women and children all walked through the maze, following others' findings, pushing their learning more each time. It took many days. Each wrong turn had to be marked, so others could avoid it; each successful path had to be marked so others could take it farther.

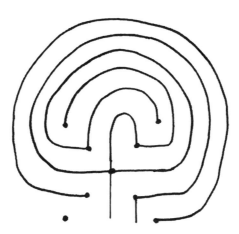

And, in the end, they went through together, in a long line, calling out advice when the leader got confused, so that they found a way all the way in, around, through, and out of the maze. 'But there was no treasure in there,' one man complained. 'Your treasure is your community,' the wise man said. 'A person is a person through persons, as the proverb says. When you understand the power of your connection with others, you own a treasure that cannot be stolen from you.' The man who had complained shrugged. 'True, but some fine shells or coral beads would have been nice.'"

With the last word, Dashona finished the diagram, and the crowd broke into enthusiastic cheers. Even Sheeah clapped; the diagram was well done, and it was a good story, even if it was an old one. But her face changed as she watched the group. Dashona's face was shining with intensity, and her smile was directed at the man looking at her: Afutu. That look was unmistakable, on both sides.

The morning was not working out as Sheeah had planned.

"Beautiful hair," a man in the group said to her, but she ignored him.

Two drummers announced the arrival of the chief's messenger. "Festival groups! Report to your Festival groups! Our guests will be arriving soon! Report to your Festival groups!" he cried as he moved around the village. It was impossible to ignore: the booming drums cut through every conversation, and the message could be heard over and over throughout the town. Reluctantly, the game people moved off, leaving their fine designs in the sand for the wind and waves to erase. It was a moment they would remember later.

Situated up the hill from the beach, the chief's home was a place of power, twice as large as any other dwelling in the village and made of the finest materials. The poles that supported the entryway were decorated with light and dark woven raffia, worked into dozens of different geometric designs: diamonds, bars, triangles, dots, squares, diagonal lines, so that it formed a dazzling display. The walkway was paved with mud bricks also arranged in patterns and fitted tightly together without mortar. Behind the entrance, the walls were all tightly woven, with openings left in the top, so that air and light could get through, but even these openings were laced across with designs, so that the whole structure seemed to dance with patterned energy. The thatched roof reached well down past the walls, giving shade on even the hottest day, and a cistern in the courtyard provided cooling water as well as irrigation for the green plants growing there.

But as much as the chief enjoyed the luxuries of his house, on this day he moved through it without noticing. His mind was on the festival. It simply had to be successful; it had to bring the three tribes together. And once everyone was feeling good, he had to sit down with the other chiefs and decide how to deal with the invaders from the east, who were no longer just rumors. His scouts had brought dire news just two days before: large groups were moving west. The threat came at a particularly bad time. The truth was the alliance of the three settlements was faltering. All of the tribes were growing larger, needing more room and hunting or foraging more often in what used to be considered others' land. There were frequent disagreements over boundaries and rights and power, usually just arguments, but sometimes the fights escalated. It would be easy for the three allies to split into enemies now; it would take only some petty mistake, some tactless move, some angry comment. They needed an alliance to cement the bond. Of course, Sheeah was the logical choice; she could marry the son of Berko, the leader of the northern settlement, and then it would be hard for Berko to turn against him. But Sheeah was being so strange, and he didn't have the necessary gifts to give Berko - unless Kofi, chief of the southern tribes, brought the new boat and the ivory he owed from his losing bets at the last festival.

But not one of these things was certain; the whole world, Tau thought, was balanced on a knife edge.

He dressed with care, selecting his best woven caftan marked with dark red, black, and yellow designs, but his mind kept going back to the festival. Somehow, over the course of the next few days, something had to happen to make these three groups unite against the invaders. They had to feel different from those people, better than them, stronger. Only then would they have the will to fight. Of course, the festival games would help, but they tended to increase factionalism, when what the groups really needed was unity. It had to be something more lasting than the thrill of entertainment, but he didn't know how to provide it, or even what it might be. So he paced up and down in his courtyard in his fine clothes and waited for inspiration, or at least the beat of the beetle's wing that would start the chain of events that would resolve the problem one way or another.

Late in the day, the groups from the northern territory started arriving, boat after boat being pulled up onto the sands at Black Oyster Cove, while greeters ran to meet them, giving them sweet tea drinks in calabashes decorated with trumpet flowers and showing them to their host families' huts. Most of these people already knew each other, but there were some children and some newly eligible young adults who needed to be properly introduced, as well as some sad news of people who had left this world since the last gathering.

Chief Tau greeted the elders personally, and he stepped right out into the water to welcome Chief Berko as soon as he landed. "I'm so pleased to see you," he said, putting his hand on Berko's shoulder. Berko was also dressed to show his power, his long bark cloth robe embroidered with repeating designs and set off by his conical hat covered with shells.

"And I you," Berko replied, returning the gesture. "We have much to talk about."

Tau looked at the others getting out of the boat. "Where is your oldest son?"

"Unfortunately, he can't be here. He took a wife not long after the last festival, and she's expecting a baby soon."

"Congratulations, of course! May they find great happiness together." But his disappointment was keen. The plan was already failing. Berko's other sons were far too young to consider marriage.

"Is something wrong? You look strained."

"It's nothing. It's only that I'd hoped he and Sheeah might wed someday."

Berko laughed. "Well, we certainly tried! They didn't like each other, remember? As much as it might have helped us, they weren't meant for each other."

"You're probably right," Tau smiled in return, but he felt a little sick inside. "Come in; make yourself comfortable. I'll get us something to drink."

"Don't worry about entertaining me. I have other matters to discuss, and it's better if we're alone to talk about them."

"As you wish," Tau waved him to a low carved wooden stool while he sat in the one opposite.

"You're aware of the invaders?" Berko started.

"My scouts reported two days ago that they had seen traces of a large group hunting near the river. That's all I know for sure. The rest is rumors."

"Perhaps you should listen to the rumors. The group is very large, and they're doing more than hunting. From what I've heard, they're so fierce, anyone they don't frighten away, they kill." He paused. "And they're headed for the coast."

"Where on the coast? Here?"

"Who knows? Perhaps here, or north to our coast, or down to the southern coast, or somewhere in between. No one can say, except their leader. Have you had any contact?"

"None. Not even a message."

"Nor have I. But I have my suspicions about Kofi."

"What?" Tau stammered. "Why?"

"He said he might be late for the festival because he had an important meeting," Berko said, pausing on the last word. "Now, who would he be meeting when everyone is already here?"

Stunned, Tau searched for a reply. He felt the world was unraveling like an old mat. How were they to have a festival if this news was true? What would he say to Kofi when he finally arrived? How were they to stand together when they were already faltering, and they hadn't yet faced the foe?

The messenger horn announced the arrival of new boats, and Berko stood up, ready to leave. "I'll leave you to welcome your guests."

"But you'll be staying here, and your family, of course."

"Thank you, but my wife so wants to stay with her friend that I agreed. I'll be very close by, and I'll talk to you tomorrow. We need to stand together on this."

Tau headed for the shore, but, instead of going up to meet his guest, he waited for Kofi to land and walk up the beach to him. It was a small rudeness, but it was noticed.

"Greetings," Kofi said, somewhat stiffly, holding up the bottom of his long black robe decorated with shells so it wouldn't get wet. This action also meant he couldn't, or didn't want to, extend his arm in greeting.

"Welcome," Tau said, but he didn't extend his arm either. "Is your family well?"

"Yes, thank you, and yours?"

"Well," Tau said, but he could hardly form the word. Nothing seemed to be going very well at all, especially if he now had to host a traitor. "You'll be my guest, I hope, and your family also?"

"Thank you, I will, but my wife and daughter were unable to attend. They are looking after my newest grandchild."

"Congratulations!" Tau said, as he searched the boats pulling onto the shore, wondering how many came from the southern settlements. "I hope you brought some players for the teams."

"Yes, of course," Kofi smiled. "I have to win back my losses to you from last festival. Unfortunately, I wasn't able to bring you the new boat I promised. Perhaps you can use it as a wager on the game. Then, if I win, I can come out even; if not, I'll owe you two boats!"

Tau tried to smile. *And I'll never see either one.* He knew he should have left it there, but the missing boat annoyed him. Kofi had some great boat builders in his village. Not only were their boats sea-worthy, they were beautiful, with high carved bows and sterns, and Tau had been looking forward to receiving this prize. So, instead of moving on to talk of more pleasant things, Tau turned on Kofi and said, "And what of the ivory? Did you forget that too?"

Kofi's look was dark. "I don't recall anything about ivory. Perhaps you'd like to explain what you are accusing me of with the question."

"You owe me an arm's worth of ivory, as well as the boat, from your bets last festival." There was silence between them. With a shock, Tau realized he was doing the very thing he had been afraid of, alienating his ally. "I was hoping to use it as a dowry for Sheeah," he said, trying to soften his tone.

Kofi hesitated, then relaxed slightly. "A beauty like Sheeah won't need a dowry. Any man would be lucky to have her."

It was meant as a compliment, and Tau smiled, but he was still annoyed, and the moment lingered a little too long before he responded. "True, but I'm afraid I've spoiled her. Now, I think a husband would require a large gift to put up with her." Somehow, he had wandered back into dangerous territory, and the silence returned.

They walked up the hill toward Tau's house, with no further conversation. At the entry, Tau stopped and turned. "I've treated you badly, Kofi. Please accept the hospitality of my home and enjoy the festival."

Kofi nodded and studied Tau. "You're worried about the invaders, aren't you?"

"Of course. Aren't you?"

"Yes. That's why I thought we would be stronger if we stood together rather than fighting."

Tau hesitated, but only for a moment. "Exactly right. Our only hope is to strengthen our alliance, so we can stand together. That's what I told Berko, as well."

Kofi drew in a sharp breath. "Berko. Yes, of course. Now I understand. But when you talked to Berko about strengthening our alliance, did he tell you he's been meeting with the invaders?"

"Berko?" Tau's head was spinning. Berko was lying? How would Kofi know? Was he spying on Berko? Was Kofi dealing with the enemy and then accusing Berko just to deflect the blame? Were they both making deals behind his back? It was like a shell game, where truth was the pearl that was always missing, no matter which shell he picked.

* * *

High on the cliffs that overlooked the shore, two men stood so only their painted faces showed above a rocky outcrop, their eyes trained on the beach below.

"Maybe he was wrong," one said. "There's nothing going on down there, no forces massing, no archers assembling, not even scouts posted. Just people gathering for a festival."

The other shook his head. "No, I don't think he was wrong. First it's a party. The rest will come later."

CHAPTER 2
A GAME WELL-PLAYED

The festival had the usual attractions: good food and drink, music, dancing, storytelling, games, and trade, but its most intense energy came from the presence of other people, new people. Even if they were known, they weren't known the way the locals were, and that was their appeal. There was a good deal of flirting, most of it harmless, some not, and the changing patterns of the drumbeats, and the smell of Freesia blossoms. The call to the competition was a double series of three beats. After a pause, the same pattern was taken up by the other drummers, so it was impossible to miss the signal. "The games are starting!" the drum leader called, and the drummers picked up their drums and headed out to the square, with a line of spectators trailing behind them.

Out in the square, the three chiefs sat at one end, under a special shelter newly thatched with palm. Next to them were their families and advisors, but the rest of the square was open to everyone, in any seating arrangement they wanted.

First to go were the children. Their games weren't divided into teams by settlement; they were open to all. The tug-o-war, for instance, was open to any child who was taller than the lower mark on Tau's staff and shorter than the higher mark. If the two teams had different numbers, they were simply adjusted. It didn't matter; many of the children wound up falling down anyway when the line rushed forward or fell back. It was mostly a way to get the children acquainted and the games started. The children's foot races were more serious, with prizes awarded for the first and second place winners, but still, none of these results counted toward the championship.

After the children's events were done, things turned more serious with the Feather Shoot, with its fine carved spear to be claimed by the winner. Contestants were divided into groups of two. Each man had only one throw in each round, one chance to throw his spear through a feather poked into a hole in a log. If both missed, both were eliminated. If both speared the feather, they both had to shoot again, until only one was the winner. If someone knocked the feather down but did not spear it, he was eliminated. The winners of each group faced winners from others in successive heats, until there was only one winner. With each round, the target was moved farther away.

"Afutu," Sheeah said, wrapping her arm around his while he was working on keeping score, "aren't you in the Feather Shoot?"

He carefully extracted his arm from her grasp and went back to setting score stones in different boxes. "They have plenty of contestants. I need to keep track of the winners for the championship."

"But I bet on our team, and we'll do better if you're on it." Her wide eyes were pleading.

"I'll play later, in the ball game."

"But we need you."

"The score boxes -"

She flashed her perfect smile. "I'll watch them. And don't worry; I won't let anyone touch them, even me."

So Afutu was put on a team with Emai, the man who always wound up as captain of the other side in the ball game. "Emai!" Afutu said with a smile. "A fine partner."

"I would have lasted longer with a different one," Emai said, clapping Afutu on the shoulder.

As they stood on the line, waiting for the feathers to be set in the target log, Emai turned and spoke softly. "I need to talk to you when we're done here."

"Can you come back to the score boxes to talk? I left Sheeah in charge of them, and I'd like to get back as soon as I can."

"I'll meet you afterwards."

With that, Emai stepped back, took two running steps up to the line and hurled his spear, which neatly pierced the feather. A cheer went up from the crowd.

Afutu wasn't nervous. He didn't really get nervous. When he had an important task, he just concentrated on it, so that everything else faded into the background. Even now, it was easy for him to narrow his range of vision so that it took in only the feather that was waiting for his spear. He moved backward, never releasing his lock on that spot, then ran up to the line and threw his spear. It went where it had to go, where it had been directed to go by every muscle in his body, right into the middle of the feather.

"A matched pair!" someone in the crowd shouted, and the chant was taken up by the crowd. They went again, and once again, both spears pierced the feathers.

"Move the target!" someone cried. "They'll be at this all day!" And, indeed, after three more rounds, that seemed like a good idea. Both men were sent to the next round, where the target would be moved farther out. Only ten, including Emai and Afutu, made it to the second round, where the target was moved twice as far away. Of that group, only five managed to pierce the target, including Emai and Afutu.

The target was then moved three times as far away, despite cries that no one could hit a target at that distance. The young man who had been the first to qualify was now trembling, but Afutu put a hand on his shoulder. "Breathe away your fear," he said, blowing out a breath through his mouth, "and take in good air. Let it fill you. Trust your skill and forget everything else."

The young man exhaled and drew in a ragged breath, then another, and stepped up to the line. His throw struck the feather and knocked it down, but it didn't pierce it. Still, it was a worthy effort, and the crowd cheered. The young man stepped aside, but it wasn't in defeat. He was quiet now, not blown about by winds of fear, and he nodded to Afutu as he turned to leave.

Next, an old man from the southern settlement stepped to the line. Thin and frail, he moved tentatively, as if he wasn't sure if his legs would support him. But his arms were still strong and his sight perfect. Instead of running up to the line, he took two walking steps and hurled his spear. The throw had exactly enough energy to reach the feather and pierce it, before the spear fell to the earth. The judges ran up to check and found the tip of the spear still poking through the feather, only barely, but it was through.

While the crowd was still cheering, the next contestant stepped up, his wild brown hair matching his rough brown wrap. In contrast to the old man, he seemed all energy, as if it would have been impossible for him to stand still. His moves were jerky and his feet hardly touched the ground as he ran to the line. At the last moment, he seemed to remember that he had to throw his spear, so he launched it wildly into the air. It flew high into the sky, as if, like its owner, it had forgotten to stop, but then it changed course and headed straight down toward the feather, pinning it to the ground. When he saw the spear land, the thrower leaped into the air, spinning as he went. He was Kojo, more a bundle of energy than a body held down to the earth, and the crowd loved him.

Then Emai moved up to the line. He seemed distracted, looking up at the hills to the south, but then he drew his focus back to the task of the moment, stepping back, running to the line, and hurling his spear in a graceful arc, right into the heart of the feather. It was perfect, and the crowd stomped. This was turning out to be a great contest.

Finally, Afutu approached the line, drawing a mental line from the feather to his center, seeing the path of the spear as it cut through the air. Then he stepped back, took two running steps and threw the spear, so it followed exactly that line, as if it had been already established and the spear had only to follow. It pierced the feather and pinned it to the ground. The crowd stomped again. Now, betting had become serious, in that all the contenders seemed to have a chance at winning.

The target was moved again, and the crowd moaned. No one would be able to hit a feather at that distance. Most men couldn't even throw a spear that far, let alone hit a target. But the four men were competitors, and they wouldn't back down from a challenge. The old man offered to go first, stepping to the line slowly, focusing on the target, then backing up. He took a deep breath and blew it out his mouth as he locked onto the target, walked up to the line, and threw his spear. It was a good throw, straight at the target, but it fell just short, hitting the dirt in front of the target log. The crowd clapped and he gave a brief nod before stepping away.

While they were clapping, Kojo exploded up the line without bothering to sight his target. Instead, he barreled up to the line, stopping just before it and launching his spear in another impossibly high arc. He quivered as he watched it, willing it forward, and indeed, it once again turned in the air and headed down to the feather, but this time, it knocked the feather down without piercing it. A groan went up from the crowd, and Kojo momentarily lost his vibrant energy. But with a shake of his wild mane of hair, he jumped up, his hands held over his head, as if he was diving straight into the air, then swept them down behind his back as he landed and brought one knee to the ground and bowed his head to the cheering crowd.

When Emai approached the line, he looked at Afutu and nodded. As always, it was down to the two of them. His approach looked slow, after Kojo's wild run, but the throw was perfect, the spear sailing through the air and straight into the feather.

Returning the nod, Afutu stepped up to the line, set up his mental path, stepped back, blew out his breath, and ran. The spear flew in a perfect arc, right through the feather and into the ground beyond the target.

"They'll be at it all day!" someone called from the crowd.

"Yes, make it harder!" another yelled.

In the chiefs' section, the betting was heavy, with Berko putting up most of his fortune on Emai to win. Tau felt obligated to bet on Afutu, since he was the local champion, but the chief's heart wasn't in the wager. He felt as if the air was heavy under their canopy. Out there in the open, where the people were cheering, it must be better.

"I have an idea," Berko said. "It'll make this contest more challenging, and end it faster. These two men still have a ball game to play."

"What's this plan?" Tau asked.

"They have to shoot a feather out of the air."

Kofi turned to him in disbelief. "A feather will just fall out of the air? Did you plan on sending a bird flying across the square?"

"No. We'll set up a basket on a pole. You already have a pole at each end of the square. We'll clear out the people at one end, put a feather in a basket, pull a rope attached to the basket and make the feather fall out."

"Even if we could do all that," Tau complained, "we'll kill someone, probably the one working the rope for the basket."

Berko shrugged. "Make it a long rope, so someone could pull it from far away. Or forget it and keep going this way."

The other two were silent for a moment. It was a strange challenge, but once Berko had suggested this ridiculous game, they couldn't back down.

"It would be even more interesting if you had a beautiful girl drop the feather," Kofi laughed, thinking that would end the discussion, but Berko carried it further.

"Yes, of course. We'll give the girl the basket and have her climb the pole."

"That's absurd!" Tau said. "You would get the girl, or some spectators, killed."

"Perhaps we could use Sheeah. That would make it very interesting, and you want the games to be interesting, don't you, Tau?"

Where had this first gotten so out of hand? They were laughing, now, as if they had made a very clever joke. Perhaps both of them were traitors, and this was their way of showing their power, taunting him for his weakness.

"You do what you like at your festival. This is mine."

"Of course." Berko dismissed the subject with a wave of his hand. "It was only a joke."

But the air was poisoned, and the taunt still stayed there.

"Each will have a feather," Tau said into the silence, "and each will throw it for the other."

"What? Have Emai hold the feather while Afutu shoots at him? Absolutely not."

"Not hold it. Throw it. Drop it." After a moment, Tau added, "Of course, if you're not interested in continuing the contest, you're welcome to forfeit."

The color rose in Berko's cheeks and his hand reached instinctively for his knife.

"Why don't we ask Afutu and Emai?" Kofi broke in. "They may have another idea."

The two competitors were called off the field. When asked, both said they would accept either challenge. "If we were to throw the feather, we could stand so the wind caught the feather before it was released," Afutu offered.

"Yes, with only one throw each," Emai added.

"What if you both miss?"

Emai spoke for both when he answered, "We won't."

So it was decided. But while the leaders were conferring about the size of the feathers and the distance from the spear thrower, the crowd grew bored and wandered off to watch the girls' ball game. Only a few remained to see how the contest between Emai and Afutu was resolved.

"May the better man win," Emai said, as they headed back out to the field.

"We're both good men, Emai, and a spear through a feather doesn't make either one of us any better or worse than the other."

Emai stopped and searched Afutu's face. "I wish we weren't always adversaries. We seem more like brothers, you and I. Listen, Afutu, take care. Stay alert."

"What do you mean?"

"I'll try to tell you later, when the game is done, though, truthfully, I don't know if either of us will live to see tomorrow."

Afutu stopped still. "What?"

"Don't stop. You need to keep going. Please."

They walked along for a moment without saying anything.

"It changes the game, doesn't it?" Afutu said finally.

"Not necessarily. If you knew the land would be swept out to sea tomorrow, would you play the game any differently today?"

Afutu shrugged. "Probably not. If I'm going to play, I'll try to play well."

"Then that's all we need to know. Let's look back on today and say the game was well-played."

"Who's going first?"

"You are," Emai smiled. "Then I can watch and learn."

The handful of spectators edged forward until the judges pushed them back to the sides of the square. Emai took one of the two large blue feathers and stood so the wind pulled it away from his body.

"Ready?" he called.

"Ready!" Afutu moved back behind the line and raised his spear. There'd be no time for a running approach, so he'd have to sight his line and throw from the spot. Emai lifted his arm, yelled "Now!" and released the feather into the wind. It moved in arcs, back and forth, as it fell, and Afutu measured the swing, taking an instant to understand its movement. Then he lifted his arm and let the spear fly. The path of the spear had to be exactly right. Too high or too low would mean the air currents would send the feather lurching up or down, away from the spear. But because the path of this spear *was* exactly right, the spearhead simply pushed the feather in front of it until its superior force sent it right through the shaft of the feather, carrying both to the ground at the end of the arc. It was an amazing sight. Even Afutu was pleased, smiling broadly as he retrieved his spear from the judge.

It took a moment for the spectators to realize that he had really done the impossible. Then they broke into shouts, chanting his name as they stomped the earth: "Ah-fu-tu! Ah-fu-tu! Ah-fu-tu!" People who had left the square earlier came running back, asking what had happened, joining in the shouting, until the judge raised his hand for silence and Emai stepped forward.

"Perhaps I should have gone first."

Holding the feather exactly as Emai had done, so the wind would take it away from his body, Afutu shouted "Ready?"

"Ready!"

"Now!" Afutu threw the feather into the wind, and it lurched through its arcs as its companion feather had. Emai also took his time estimating the feather's path, figuring the exact path his spear would need to take, then he hurled the spear. It was a fine throw, arcing straight for the feather, but just a hair's breadth short, just enough to send the feather spinning away from the spear. The spear actually hit the feather before landing, but it didn't pierce it. A groan went up from the crowd, and, though he tried to shrug it off, Emai was keenly disappointed. Still, he turned to Afutu and said, "Congratulations, you had a fine shot."

"As did you."

"Just not quite fine enough."

"Aren't you leading your team in the ball game?"

"We'll see. Many things could change between now and then. Berko won't be pleased at the loss." Emai hesitated. "I'll try to get away to talk to you. Will you be at the score boxes?"

"All day, except for the ball game."

"Until later then," Emai said, but his voice sounded odd.

In the strange ways of sports heroes, Afutu found most people had already forgotten about his incredible feat by the time he got back to the score boxes. They were busy talking about the girls' ball game and the amazing volley that kept the ball going back and forth between the sides, without going into the middle trench or out of bounds, for twelve points! It was a huge score for the southern settlement team that helped them win the game handily.

Sighing, Afutu checked his score boxes, square baskets really, each one standing for one of the events, in the order they were scored. Champions were decided on the cumulative wins, so the stones in the baskets recorded first place (and second in some events) by colored stone: black for the northern settlement (Berko's territory), yellow for the central settlement (Tau's territory), and red for the southern settlement (Kofi's territory). Each win was worth two points; when there was a second place awarded, it was worth one point. The team with the most points at the end of the games was declared champion. An assistant scorekeeper from a different settlement checked all of Afutu's work. He, or in this case she, also recorded the scores for any events Afutu was part of; she was in the process of recording the Feather Shoot results when he arrived.

"Congratulations!" she called. "Well done!"

Afutu nodded, acknowledging her compliment. "Did Sheeah manage all right while we were away?"

"Well, everything's still here, so I guess she did."

"She promised she wouldn't let anyone touch anything."

"She'd promise you anything."

He waved away the comment. "I'm just a man she hasn't caught, yet. Let's get the boxes for the foot races set up."

CHAPTER 3
AKIN AND THE LEADER

It wasn't hard for Akin to find the signal sticks The Leader had ordered left for him upriver from the shore. From there, the path was clear, showing recent heavy wear.

The encampment was huge, the largest force of warriors he had ever seen, yet he recognized none of these men, not even their captains. The Leader's encampment was heavily guarded, but once Akin was admitted to The Leader's area, there was no one else there. The man known and feared all along the river sat alone on a flat stone behind his hut. When Akin walked up, The Leader seemed preoccupied, jabbing a line of holes in the dirt with his staff and then another and then another. Akin stood, waiting to be recognized.

Instead, The Leader addressed him without ever looking up. "Are you happily married?"

Surprised, Akin stammered, "I suppose so, sir."

"And yet, you're here, not with your family. Why is that?"

"Because I feel that this is more important."

"Ah, yes." The Leader resumed poking rows of holes, sometimes connecting them with lines. "War is more important. It's one of the few things that bring people together. People are very strange, you know, Akin. They're capable of great things when they work together. What efforts do you know of that require people to work together?"

"Musical groups, I suppose," Akin ventured, unsure where this conversation was headed. "They have to give up some individual control in order to make a group effort possible. And dance, especially the very complicated group dances, where one group heads off into a circle and the others dart in between the members of the circle to form the star in the center. That couldn't happen without cooperation, without some sacrifice of individual control. If everyone went their own way, they'd bump into each other and fall down."

"That's all?"

"Well, no. Paddlers in a boat. Singers in a chorus. Boat builders. Roof thatchers." Akin warmed to the subject as he thought about it. "Any hunt requires cooperation. Someone must plan the attack; someone must flush the game; someone must dig the pit; others must be in position to throw their spears or shoot their arrows. Once the animal is killed, they must all work together to dress it out and carry it back to the village. Then others work together to butcher it, skin it, preserve it, cook it, and distribute it. No hunt would be successful without all of these people working together.

"Anything else?"

"Everything in the life of a village requires group effort. If there's a crisis in the family, everyone must help to overcome it. If the river floods and the people are in danger, it takes everyone in the village to put things back to normal. Even the smallest child and the frailest elder have some part in the transformation. If the village is attacked, all the villagers must work together to drive the attackers off."

"But what happens when things are back to normal, when the flood is gone, or the attack is over, or the hunt is completed?"

Akin shrugged. "People are complicated. Sometimes they want something for themselves that's not good for others. Sometimes they destroy what they've built. Or what others have built."

The Leader didn't reply immediately. He studied his lines of holes in the dirt. "They make stories out of these, you know, the people

169

on the coast. Stories from holes in the dirt. They play games on the golden sand, completely unaware." Jabbing the stick in the sand, he destroyed the clean rows of dots and the connectors. "While they are telling stories with dots in the dirt, their chiefs are busy plotting against each other, bargaining with me. Did you know that?"

"Sir." Actually, Akin knew all about it. He was the one who had reported the chiefs' interest to The Leader some days ago.

"Berko, in the north, and Kofi, in the south, both offered to join us against Tau's people, and against each other. Tau seems to be only one who still believes the coastal alliance will hold." He looked back at the lines of dots he had smudged. "But part of me envies them, those people on the beach, still happy to tell good stories and play their games to the best of their ability. It's very fine. They live beautifully. It's a different kind of warfare against the disappointing side of people." He threw down the stick and looked at Akin. "How are we going to change people?"

"Sir?"

"All of this, all of our effort, is for nothing if people are still going to be petty and weak, failing over and over again because they're lazy, or selfish, or mean."

"The gods made people the way they are, sir."

"No! I don't believe that. The gods made people to be great. It's just that some people fall short of what they should be. Blaming the gods is just a way to excuse personal failure. I don't believe that. The gods wouldn't have made something so unfinished. Nothing else is. There's no unfinished part of the heavens, or the rivers, or the forest. There are no unfinished crocodiles or monkeys or antelope. Why should there be unfinished people?"

Confused, Akin could think of no reply.

"Do you know what I see? I see people who can't wait to line up behind me. 'The Black Rhino will protect us,' they cry when danger approaches. 'He's strong and fierce. We need him as our leader.' But then, as soon as the danger passes, they talk among themselves: 'Oh, the Black Rhino is too strong. He shouldn't have punished those men. I disagree with his decision to take that village by force. The problem with him is that he's too fierce.' And what do these men do, these men who feel called upon to criticize me? They pick their toes and chase after other men's wives. Where are they in the heat of battle? Too tired or lazy to fight. But never too tired to criticize."

Carefully, he smoothed out the dirt where he had destroyed the lines and dots. "We need to start over again, and this is a perfect opportunity."

"Sir?" Akin had the strange sense that he had been standing here before, with this same prickly hot sensation, like stinging nettles all over.

"You know what a lion does when he takes over a new pride?"

"He kills all the cubs."

"Exactly. It's his way of establishing a new order. His order."

"You're planning on killing children?" Akin's voice seemed to come from somewhere far away.

"No. Don't worry, Akin. I'm not planning on killing children."

There was a strange silence between them.

"Then what *are* you planning to do, Sir?"

"Let the old order die at its own hand."

"Sir?"

"You know the great colonies of herons that nest in the trees?"

"Yes, of course, the rookeries."

"Over many years, their droppings kill the trees they're roosting in. It takes a long time, but one day, perhaps in a high wind, the branches collapse and the trees start falling. Then the herons have to move on to a new area. All of the roost trees die, but the soil is so rich from the droppings that after a while, new trees spring up where the old ones were. Fine, strong trees."

"I don't understand."

"We don't have to do anything on the shore. We just have to show up, like the wind, and watch the branches collapse. Then we can establish a new order, a place where people can realize the greatness they were meant to have. There won't be any more selfishness or meanness. We won't allow it. People will have to prove their worth, to earn the right to exist. If they fail, they lose that right. It's simple, really. Yet it's the path to glory. It's the single greatest thing we can do, to allow the forest to start over. And it will be a glorious forest: every tree strong and beautiful."

"Have you contacted Tau, talked to him?"

"No." The Leader looked back down at his clean patch of dirt and carefully punched a line of holes. "We'll let Tau and his people enjoy their last golden days on the beach."

The meeting apparently over, Akin bowed. The Leader didn't look up or reply, but only continued, preoccupied, drawing lines between the dots in the dirt. He had never even invited Akin to sit down. After a while, Akin turned and left.

CHAPTER 4
PREPARATIONS

Dwyka and Asha hunkered down among the tufts of beach grass on the hill, watching the bustling crowds on the beach. "I need to find someone, but the town's full of watching eyes. And we're not alone up here." Standing up, Dwyka dusted off her wrap. "We'll have to hide in plain sight. Let's go find something to carry."

For anyone trying to prepare a feast, the most welcome question is "How can I help?" and that's exactly what Asha asked a particularly harried woman who was unloading melons from baskets and setting them on a long table.

"Well, I was supposed to have four helpers," the woman said, looking up, her face flushed and sweating. "But they've all gone to watch the game. And then they'll be betting: kola nuts, gold flakes, shells, whatever they brought. Probably lose it all and forget about me until the game's over. The problem is, there won't be time to set up then. People'll come streaming over here, expecting to be fed. Just like that." She stretched her back as she stood up and gave Asha a long look. "You must be new here."

"Yes, it's the first time I've been to one of these gatherings."

"From the north, are you?"

"How did you guess?"

"Well, you talk funny, and your appearance, if you don't mind my saying so, could use some attention."

Dwyka stepped up. "I've been telling her that for a long time, but she doesn't listen to me. You know how it is. You can't tell a younger sister anything."

"True," the woman sighed. "Well, let's get to work, as long as you're here." After explaining how to set out the melons, she added, "You'll need to bring up the other loads from the boats. Those down there, with the turtle sign on the bow. They're ours."

There was a great deal of activity around the boats, mostly people doing exactly what they were, bringing up supplies for the feast. On their second trip down to the boats for more melons, Asha settled the basket on her head and was about to head back to the woman's table when she noticed several figures approaching them. "Dwyka," she started, but the other woman had already spotted them. Where the area had seemed empty just moments ago, it was now filled with people, most of them moving in her direction.

Lifting the basket to her head, Dwyka started toward the woman's table, but her senses were alert, reading the motion of each group. There were two men carrying a canoe upside down, over their heads, four men armed with clubs and spears walking toward them, a family group with several children, another group of warriors, someone with a basket of fish, a diviner in a bird costume, several dancers practicing, a pair of lovers walking along the sand, their arms wrapped around each other, a short, slight man walking toward them. This man Dwyka recognized immediately, but he didn't greet her. He seemed to be looking at something out in the water, so that he could approach without seeming to approach her.

"Two groups," he whispered as he passed, "both armed. Ball players' area, later."

She never responded or even looked at him. Asha was about to ask what was going on when she saw one of the groups of warriors move closer to them on the right and the other on the left. The group on the right moved in even closer, but as the group on the left prepared to close in, a voice cried out, "ASHA!" It had a pained intensity, that cry, and it stopped everyone in their tracks.

The man holding the front of the canoe switched his hands and stepped out from under it, off to the left. The tall, thin man in the back did the same to the other side. But the boat was hardly by his side when he dropped it in the sand and ran to her, folding her in his arms so that the basket toppled off her head and melons fell in a rolling pile behind her, and everyone on the beach stopped to watch. But for that moment, there were only the two of them, locked in an embrace so tight it seemed impossible that a moment ago they had lived in two separate, lonely worlds. Asha felt something release inside her, as if she could finally let go of a breath she had held for an amazingly long time, so long that she had gotten used to the hurt.

The sudden reunion had forced the warriors on the right to move away slightly, but Dwyka had moved away also, and the group on the left now moved closer to her.

With a sweep of her arm, Asha motioned Dwyka into their circle. "This is my older sister," she said, simply because she couldn't think of anything else. At that moment, Sule and Deka ran up, yelling "Asha! Asha!" and Aminata joined the circle as well, everyone hugging and shouting and crying and asking questions and explaining everything all at once so that no one understood any of it, except how wonderful it was that somehow they had all found each other.

"Well, I suppose we might as well make it the whole family," Sohko said, a broad smile spreading across his face. As he joined the group, he said quietly, "Are these friends of yours?"

"Hardly," Dwyka sighed.

"Hey! I don't know a single one of you, but you're standing around trampling my melons," the woman with the table to prepare yelled as she came huffing down the hill toward the group, completely unfazed by the groups of warriors standing nearby. "It's great you all got to see each other again, but I have people to feed, you know, and the melons won't walk up that hill themselves."

"Of course." Sohko scooped up several of the melons and handed them to the children while he picked up others. "We'll take care of that for you right away."

After the whole group had trundled right past the warriors and delivered the melons to the impatient woman, Naaba, Asha, and the rest of the group retired to the far end of the food stalls. Dwyka bowed to them. "Thank you all for saving me, and you, Asha, for saving me again. But now, I should go before I cause you more trouble. I'm delighted at your happiness."

"You should go with someone," Sohko offered. "You're more of a target alone."

"We'll all go," Aminata said. "Where do you need to be?"

"The Ball Court."

Deka and Sule looked at the woman and at each other. "You're the She-Eagle," Sule managed.

"Yes," the woman answered, somewhat reluctantly. "Some people call me that. And who might you be?"

"Deka and Sule," the boy answered. "We're Akin's children."

"Akin? The Black Rhino's Lieutenant?" She looked closely at the two children who were staring at her. "This is an interesting group."

"We ran away," Sule said, deciding to skip the rest of the story.

"Was that Okung you spoke to on the beach?" Sohko asked.

"A very interesting group," Dwyka added. "Yes, it was Okung, and I need to meet with him. It's difficult here, with so many warriors looking for me. If I could take you up on your kind offer, perhaps you could go with me to the Ball Court."

"We'll all go," Naaba offered. "We might as well all wade into the crocodile pool at the same time. It's the least I can do for Asha's 'older sister.'"

"Regardless of how things turn out here," Dwyka said, with a slow nod, "it's been a privilege meeting all of you. If you value each other, keep a sharp eye out and know how to escape quickly. After today, this village won't see another peaceful day for a long time." Her tone had changed, from friend to leader.

"It was your paddle that made Papa think Asha was part of your group," Sule said, "the one with the carvings on it. Asha had it in her boat."

"How small the world is, and how ironic. Perhaps we are sisters, after all. I wish you all the best of life. Take care of each other." She thought about telling them that she too had a real love once, but she had left him for reasons she couldn't seem to remember now, and that when she looked at these people, glowing with their happiness, she felt his loss like a wound that didn't heal. But she didn't say any of that. Instead, she headed off with them to the Ball Court and the future she had chosen for herself a long time ago.

On the way, they saw the diviner woman in the bird costume, leaning against a palm tree, her head propped back awkwardly.

"Are you sick?" Asha asked as they approached.

"It's just that I'm so tired, and everyone wants advice. If I could just rest for a while, I'd be fine."

"I think we could help you. My sister here has a great gift of foresight. She could wear your costume while you rest. Then, when you want it back, you could have it. Does that sound better?"

The woman immediately started lifting the big carved bird head off her shoulders and unfastening the huge wings from her arms. "Thank you. I tried to go off by myself to rest, so I wouldn't shame the costume, but there are so many people here, there was no place I could go. I only need a little while. Here, I'll help you fasten the wings," she added, wrapping the long ties around Dwyka's back. "The head is very heavy, but there's a tie and weight that help balance it. Just don't look down." The woman was so weary, she sat down on the tufts of beach grass with a sigh of relief as soon as Dwyka was fully dressed in the costume. "Oh," she added, "most of them want to know whether or not someone loves them or did love them or will love them. I just say yes to all those. It's not my place to see into the spirit of others." With that, she exhaled and closed her eyes. "Thank you."

"Thank *you*," Dwyka replied. "May your dreams be filled with brightness."

In the flamboyant costume, Dwyka certainly didn't blend in, but she became a part of the festival, not a lone woman trying to sneak through the village. As the group moved toward the Ball Court, people gathered around Dwyka, asking her questions, and, as the original diviner had said, most had to do with the vagaries of their love life. In their moments alone, the friends tried to explain what had happened since they had seen each other last, but it was all rushed, and many things needed to wait for another time to be discussed. Sohko explained that The Leader had sent word to him and almost everyone else from the river villages to go downriver to the coast, but he hadn't said what the plan was. Sohko hadn't even been contacted by anyone from The Leader's camp since he arrived, so, like many others, he and Aminata were just milling around, waiting to hear something, when they ran into Naaba and the children. The hunter's son had joined his friends, so it was just the five of them, now six, with Asha.

"You should take your family – and your friends - away from here," Dwyka said when she joined them. "Take Akin's children as well. It's not safe here. Tomorrow, it will be much worse." She looked around the group. "Listen to me. You've been wonderful to me, but everything from here on is a dance with death. Even now, you could be killed for helping me."

Sule pointed out the warriors moving toward them. "They're still following us."

"All right," Naaba said, "let's keep moving. The closer we get to the crowd, the harder it'll be for them to get around you. At some point, you're going to have to get out of that costume."

"We'll switch."

"No," Dwyka began, but Asha waved her concerns away.

"It'll be easy. We'll slip into one of the vendor stalls while the men stand out front talking to Aminata and the children. If anyone suspicious comes along, just warn us."

"By yelling 'Someone suspicious is coming along'?" Naaba broke in. "It won't work."

"I can yell at my brother," Deka offered. "I'll say he's taken my dancing woods. No, my tether stick. Or he's broken my bead string."

"All right," Asha said, already walking toward an empty vendor booth. Dwyka followed, and the others stood in front, trying to look as if they just stopped there to talk, but the children were the only ones enjoying themselves. It seemed like a game to them, and they played it well.

When the two women emerged, Dwyka put her arm on Asha's shoulder and Asha did the same. "Don't forget what I said. Move your boats far from this village beach. Hide the paddles in the sand. Make sure you have water and food. Get away from here – up or down the coast. If that's not safe, head out to sea for a while then back to the coast. He'll have forces guarding the northern part of the village, near the mouth of the river. Thank you, my friends. May your journey be filled with wonders and love." With that, she ducked into the crowd and disappeared.

"She didn't seem like a witch," Deka remarked.

Moving around a little awkwardly in the heavy bird costume, Asha dispensed general advice and vague fortunes until almost everyone had moved to the Ball Court, even the groups of warriors. Then she took the costume back to the woman still asleep on the sand. Muttering as she awoke, the woman thanked Asha for the chance to rest and started to put the costume back on.

"That's strange," she said, lifting the head. "There are two different breaths in the mask." When Asha didn't reply, she went on. "Each breath has its own mark, you know; it's the same from the first breath to the last, the wind of life. I can feel the differences, like different scents." After a pause, she added, "I could tell your fortune if you wanted."

"Thank you, but no."

"Probably best. It's always trouble, knowing. Besides, it's only a guess. Pretty accurate most of the time, you know, but still a guess." Adjusting the weight and harness with a practiced hand, she straightened the mask and wings. "An interesting evening we have ahead of us." Without further comment or farewell, she walked off toward the Ball Court, leaving Asha wondering how much of the diviner's act wasn't an act at all.

When she started back, she found Naaba standing alone, his left foot resting on the side of his right knee, waiting for her. Over his wrap he was wearing the belt she had given him. As they walked along together, he took the leather pouch he had made for her wedding gift out of the folds of his belt. "I was hoping you'd accept this," he said. "Your friend, the crazy man with the snake and the finch, said he was just keeping it safe for you. Of course, I thought about killing him when I saw it around his neck, and the two wild dogs thought about killing me, but it all worked out fine, after I spent most of a day listening to him talk." Stopping, he turned to her, his hand on her shoulder, his voice suddenly low. "Please. Please love me, even after all that I've done."

After running the leather between her fingers, Asha hesitated for a moment before she put the string around her neck and lifted her hair over it. "Only if I can ask the same of you." There was something else too, a tiny wedge of resentment, but she tried to ignore it. Instead, they headed up into the hills together, but neither could think of anything to say, so they worked their way up the sandy slope in silence.

At the top of the hill, they wound through the bush palms and flowering shrub, until they came to a natural ledge.

"I'd rather you were angry," Naaba said, sitting down.

Looking out to sea, Asha sighed. "Why is it always so complicated for us?"

He reached up to take her hand. "Because it's how we are."

She slid down next to him and they sat on the ledge above the shore, his arm wrapped around her, her head resting on his shoulder. They might have talked, might have stumbled through the past with words that re-lit its pain, but neither one wanted to. Instead, they watched the waves roll into the shore and draw back again.

At the same moment, they both sat up. Below them, on the beach, warriors were fanning out, pulling the boats down to the water and tying them together. Two men got in the front boat and towed the others behind, or at least tried to, but the waves caught the line of boats and pulled them back toward shore. With two more men helping in the boats, they managed to get them past the breakers, but then the current made them all drift north. Once they were past the beginning of the wide mouth of the river, the men all climbed into one boat and cut the lines to the others, leaving them to drift at will.

A group of pied crows flew up from the trees behind them, their white bellies flashing between their black wings, their raw voices piercing the quiet.

"Asha, we're going to have company up here in a moment." Quietly, they moved up into the taller trees, scaling the tallest they found, stepping from one branch to another until they were above the surrounding forest. From their perch they could see three different groups of men moving through the forest toward them. It was too late to move to a more hidden spot, so they had to hope the warriors wouldn't look up as they passed by. But they didn't pass by. When the middle group was quite close to the tree, the leader blew a signal whistle, and the group gathered around him.

"We have to wait until it's almost dark," the leader said. "We'll stop here, where the cover's better, and move down to the beach later."

"It's just collecting paddles," one said. "Why don't we just do it and get it over with?"

"Because we have orders. Do you understand that part?"

"Yes, sir," the warrior replied, but it was an automatic response.

As the men moved around, setting up their camp, Asha and Naaba found their way down the far side of the tree, hoping the men decided to stay close to their camp long enough for them to escape. They were almost away from the area, starting to breathe normally, when one of the men came up behind them. He was carrying a load of firewood, but he set it down when he saw them.

"Hey! Stop!" he yelled, in a voice loud enough to alert the others.

They had two choices: stop or run.

Asha put her hand on Naaba's arm and turned to the man with an impatient sigh. "I was sent to look for the Lieutenant's children. This is my husband. Who are you? Have you seen them?"

"No," he answered, uncertain. He might have heard something about Akin's children, but he couldn't remember what it was. "You need to get out of here. We're supposed to be pushing everyone toward the coast."

"You're pushing me?"

"You need to leave the area. The children aren't here. Go back where you came from. Now."

"Fine," Asha huffed, "but if you see the children, send word to Lieutenant Akin immediately."

"I learned a lot from Dwyka," she commented on their way down the hill.

CHAPTER 5
THE TRENCHBALL GAME

As many times as Afutu had played trenchball at these festivals, it never failed to give him a thrill, like lightning flashing through him, especially as he got ready. From their changing area, the players could already hear the drummers and dancers working the crowd. There would be circles of dancers, one inside the other, going in opposite directions, joining hands and raising them up and out, forming a moving star flower. When they were done, there would be stilt dancers having a mock fight, chasing each other up and down the court, waving poles with long leaves attached, pretending to hit each other. Sometimes, one would swing the pole so low, the other dancer had to step over it, or jump over it, which got the crowd cheering.

When the entertainers finished their acts, helpers would remove the stone slabs placed over the trench in the middle of the field that gave the sport its name. While people could easily step over it, players could never cross it during the game. The trench split the long field into two equal squares, each 26 paces long and wide, all of it dug into the earth and tamped down, so it was, at least at the start of play, absolutely smooth. The side walls were slanted outward, and the players could use them to angle a ball to a teammate on the other side of the trench.

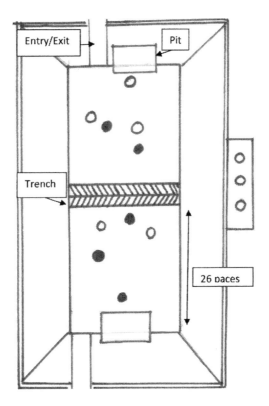

To score a point, a player had to hit the ball across the trench to a teammate, and the teammate had to return it to a member of his team. The more times the team could continue the volley across the trench, the more points they could accumulate, but in order for them to count, the team, at the end of the volley, had to sink the ball in the pit, a dug-out goal at the far end of the field that was guarded by a member of the opposite team. Game strategy involved how much to bet on continuing a volley, because everything could be lost if the attempt on the pit failed.

Any ball that fell into the trench was considered dead, with no points accruing to either team from the preceding play. A trenchball was a disgrace.

By the time Afutu was going over the signals his team would use during the game, then adjusting the broad padded belt around his middle and tying on his leather helmet and knee pads, Tau was addressing the crowd, officially welcoming everyone to the festival, recognizing his honored guests, Chief Kofi and Chief Berko. There was a good deal of partisan cheering as the players were announced: five starting players and four alternates for each team. Each team would have two players on each side of the trench, plus a guard for their goal, or pit. The players would be mixed, so that all three settlements were represented, but the host team captain would be from the host village. The players wore their village colors: black for the north, yellow for the middle, and red for the south, on their knee wraps, but their tunics were either light or dark, so that the two teams could be easily distinguished on the court. As starters for their team, Afutu, the captain, was joined by Kojo, who had also been in the Feather Shoot; Udo, another man from their village; Abran, a man from the north, and their goalie, a man from the south, who would be protecting the pit against the other team. All these men had played many times, even if they had sometimes been on opposite sides, and they were comfortable playing on a team together.

"To the game well-played!" Afutu called to his teammates.

"To the game well-played!" they called back in unison.

One of Tau's men stepped in to the hut. "The Chief has called for the teams," he announced, giving Afutu a nervous smile. "Please follow me."

They already knew their starting positions. After wishing each other good luck, they filed out, adjusting their pads and light-colored tunics, running past cheering fans yelling their names, down one of the two entrance ramps, so that Kojo, Udo, and the goalie went to the north side of the trench, while Afutu and Abran went to the south side. Afutu expected to see Emai appear as the captain of the opposite team, but it was a stranger who took the captain's spot, standing next to Afutu on the south side. This was strange; the captain usually played on the side with his goal, so he could help seal the points by sinking the ball in the pit. Another player Afutu didn't recognize joined them on the south side, while the other two dark team players and goalie went to the north. Afutu knew only one of the players on the dark team: a talented player named Naro, who had often been on the same team as Afutu in the past. He took a spot on the north side, between Udo and Kojo. The alternates waited, two at each end, until they were called to play.

Once they were all on the court, they stood, five men on each side of the trench, waiting. On the chief's platform, Tau stepped forward, and a long drum roll announced him to the crowd. In his raised right hand, Tau held the ball. It was always the same design: a wooden sphere surrounded with Silk Cotton stuffing and covered with leather hide carefully stitched together, so that the finished product was about the size of a coconut husk.

"You know the Trenchball rules," he called out,

"You cannot touch the ball with your hand; it cannot touch the ground while in play;

You can have no more than two body contacts with the ball before another player contacts it;

A volley must cross the trench and be returned to count as one point;

You can continue the volley as long as you are able; however, your team must sink the ball in your goal, the Pit, for the accumulated points in the volley to count;

You cannot have more than five players on the court at any time; you must switch out players off the court;

There is no stopping in the game, at any time, between the start and the finish, both marked by blasts on the conch;

20 points, or high point at darkness, determines the winner.

"Great honor to those who play well!" Tau called, and the drums started their steady beat, gradually increasing in speed until it was a frenzy of sound. Spectators crowded forward, claiming the few places still open on the top of the slanted walls and around the ends of the court, shouting to their teams. Though free to move around their side of the court at will, most players were most comfortable playing either close to the trench or farther back, so they found the spots they wanted, sometimes changing at the last moment, to confuse their opponents. In the middle of the chaos of sound and anticipation, Afutu studied the other players. The Captain was a big man, with a large head and thick body, not fast, probably, but strong. The others had obviously been told to shadow one of the light team players. Whenever one moved, the other did the same. Only Naro looked around, seeing who was playing in what spot, already knowing how each one played, considering how to best play his part.

The crowd started screaming as the drums reached a frenzied pace. Then, the drums stopped, the crowd fell silent, the conch sound rang out, and Tau threw down the ball. The game was begun.

"Two boats," Kofi said to Tau when he sat back down. "Two boats on the Dark Tunics to win."

"Accepted," Tau said, not mentioning the one that was already owed to him.

"A pectoral of gold," Berko said, stunning the other two into silence as he produced a disc of hammered gold representing the spiral of the sun. "It is the symbol of the sun, made from the sweat of the sun fallen to earth and hidden underground, forever brilliant and strong, giving the wearer the power of the sun itself." The two other chiefs stared at the object in his hand. "Anyone interested?"

Kojo caught the dropped ball on his shoulder and bounced it high off his knee toward Afutu, but Naro jumped in between, butting the ball with his head toward the slanted wall. Udo ran in, kicking the ball up toward his hip and sending it across to Afutu. With a twist of his body, Afutu caught the ball with his hip and sent it back across to Kojo. Naro tried to intercept, but Kojo bounced the ball off his shoulder to Udo, who sent it back across the trench to Abran. The dark team member guarding Abran tried to block him, but he was too slow, and Abran sent it back across to Kojo. Naro ran right into Kojo trying to get to the ball and knocked Kojo down, but Udo managed to get in and reach the ball with a raised knee, sending it back to Afutu. With a single movement, Afutu caught the ball with his shoulder then turned and slammed it with his hip, so it flew past the goalie and straight into the pit.

"Two points for the light tunics!" the scorekeeper yelled, though everyone already knew.

Afutu studied the captain of the dark team. He had done nothing during the whole volley except to walk around the court. If it was a ploy to confuse him, it was working. It made no sense. Why let points go unchallenged?

The ball was thrown to Naro, who sent it across the trench to the captain. Lumbering up to the ball, the captain butted it hard with his head, so hard that it flew past Kojo. The goalie popped it back into the air and Naro sent it back over the trench. His teammate rolled it up his leg and fired it back over with his raised knee, but Udo intercepted it and bounced it off the wall to Afutu. The other captain pounded toward Afutu, so he quickly sent the ball back over the trench to Kojo and stepped aside as the big man plowed through where Afutu stood an instant before. With a wild, high return, Kojo could only hope Abran could figure out how to return it, but the dark teammate ran into him, knocked him down, and sent the ball across to Naro. By the time Abran had gotten up, Naro had sent the ball back to the same man, who had bounced it off the wall back again. The man bounced it off to the captain who hit it with such force it flew straight into the pit.

"Two points for the dark tunics! The score is 2 – 2!" the scorekeeper yelled.

Afutu was stunned. This was an entirely different kind of game. They didn't play in a rhythm; they just pounded the ball through and made points.

"See?" Berko said to the other two. "Our teams are well-matched. That makes the wager more interesting, don't you think?"

"But I've already bet," Kofi said, "and I have nothing as grand as your golden medallion."

"You have an entire village, your whole settlement." Berko's words were careful, calculated. At the same moment, he once again extracted the golden sun disc and held it out to Kofi. "Here, hold it in your hand. Take a close look at it."

Kofi ran his finger over the disc and turned it so the sun was caught and reflected off it in all directions. "It's extraordinary."

"The price of leadership is greater than gold," Tau remarked, but Kofi didn't hear, or didn't choose to hear. He was running his fingers over the gold abstractedly.

"I'll take it back until you make up your mind," Berko said, reaching for the medallion.

"Perhaps we could come to an agreement."

"Oh, I'm sure we will," Berko smiled, putting the string around his neck and tucking the medallion into his robe, knowing Kofi's eyes never left the medallion until it disappeared.

On the court, the light tunic team was up by four points, having had a great volley, in which Udo, Kojo, Afutu, and Abran sent the ball back and forth at a dizzy speed, despite body blocks by the other team, and Abran made the goal. It helped that everyone was expecting Afutu to make all the major plays, so he got most of the attention, but all of his players were good, and they could easily take control of the play.

After his player had sent a ball into the trench, the dark team captain moved up to the trench and signaled the others. Naro moved up close to the trench on the north side, opposite the captain. Afutu sent Abran up slightly, so he was also closer to the trench. When the ball was tossed in, Naro caught it easily on his raised knee and tapped it over to the captain, who had it tapped back before Abran could move in. Afutu also moved up, but the captain and Naro had already completed another full circuit across the trench. When Afutu jumped in front of the captain, the captain leaped straight into him, sending him flying. By dragging his foot, Afutu was able to avoid being thrown across the ditch, but it made him fall badly, hitting his knee hard against the far side of the trench. By the time he had struggled back out again, Naro and the captain had gone through two more full exchanges. On Afutu's signal, Kojo ran into Naro, pushing him into the trench as well. The ball hit Kojo as he tackled Naro, spiraling upward. Udo barely managed to get under it, banking it off the wall toward Afutu. With his injured knee, Afutu could only hobble over to the ball, but he managed to send it sideways to Abran, who fired a shot right past Naro's block. It was so long, the goalie had to return it, turning his hip to send it banking off the wall. Abran was too close to the trench to get it, so Afutu ran for it, trying to ignore the pain shooting up from his knee. With his foot curled up, he knocked it carefully upward so he could throw his hip into it, aiming at Kojo, but Naro got in the way, knocking the ball to the ground.

"No points for either team! The score remains 6 – 2!" the scorekeeper called.

Berko leaned over toward Kofi. "The light tunics are playing well. Perhaps you should rethink your wager with Tau."

"How does one rethink a wager?" Tau frowned. "No amount of thought undoes an action one has already taken. The only thought one usually gives to the past is regret."

"You're right, my friend," Berko laughed. "And I've certainly done my share of things I regret. But there *is* a way to rethink a poor bet: by balancing it with a better wager. The answer to our problems isn't in the past; it's in the future."

"I should wager on the future?" Kofi interrupted. "Isn't every wager on the future?"

"A wager," Berko replied, enjoying being the center of attention "is a guess about the future based on the best information you have in the present. If you have placed a wager, and then you get new information, you should use that to balance your wager with another. That way you spread out your risk, you see."

"In other words, if I bet on both teams, I'm sure to win."

"Essentially, yes."

"But I'll also lose."

"True, but weigh the differences between what you'll win and what you'll lose." Berko didn't need to refer to the medallion. Kofi could still feel its smooth surface under his fingertips.

"Speak plainly, Berko. What do you want for the medallion?"

"Your village."

"That's absurd."

Instead of replying, Berko turned back to watch the game. Afutu's team had added another two points to the score, with a great rescue by Udo. Still, Naro was doing most of the work of the dark tunic team, flying from one side of the court to the other to block the ball while the others did little to help. As Chief Kofi watched from the platform, Kojo and Abran set up a nice volley, angling the ball off the wall between them. When Abran was body-blocked, Afutu managed to get under the wild ball, sending it back over to Udo, who sent it back to Abran. But just as Naro was getting ready to intercept the ball on the next pass over the trench, Abran turned and fired the ball into the pit behind him, taking the goalie by surprise.

"Two points for the light tunics! The score is 10 – 2!"

"What about you, Tau? Man enough for the big bet?"

"I don't wager my village. I hope no one else here would, either."

"But look, your team is up by eight points. It's obvious they're playing better. That's not really a bet. It's a certainty."

"No bet is certain. That's why it's a gamble," Tau said, his temper rising. "And no piece of gold is worth a village."

The servants fanning the chiefs with palm branches exchanged quick glances.

Berko sat back, smiling. "And yet, if you were to lose your village in a war, you would have nothing to show for its loss, would you?"

"What are you saying?"

"It was just a thought, that's all. Sometimes, a chief loses a village in a war with another chief. Then the winner gets everything, including the village, and the loser gets nothing. Isn't that right?"

Leaning across Tau, Kofi said, "I'll take your bet, Berko."

"Of course you will," Berko smiled. "You'd be a fool not to. I think the people are thirsty," he announced with a clap of his hands that sent a servant off to distribute borgon wine to the crowd.

It wasn't a huge gesture, but it sidestepped Tau's authority in his own village. Tau looked at the chief as if he had never truly seen him before. So, it is with little steps that we head into trouble, Tau thought, each one hardly worth notice, until later, when the progression seems so obvious. And what use was Kofi, so besotted with a single piece of gold that he would lose his whole village to obtain it? There had to be a way out, a way to reverse all of this, to make it work out the way he had hoped when he had planned the festival, but nothing presented itself as a solution. His mind was a grey nothing, filled with storm clouds.

On the court, Afutu and his team were tiring. It always seemed ugly to Afutu for a team to hold back for most of the game and then wake up and play hard in the last part, when the opponents were exhausted, but he had to admit it might be a winning strategy in this game. He could replace one of his players, but neither of the alternates played as well as the men he had on the court at the moment. It would be better if they tried to push through as many points as possible before the other team started playing hard. So he did, kicking up the energy level, sending volleys back and forth to Udo and Kojo, depending on Abran to step in when needed. Even their goalie had his share of saves. On the north side, Naro was playing close to the trench, so Afutu tried to send the ball deep, past Naro's range. Several times, it was so deep, the goalie had to keep it from landing in the pit, which would have killed the play. So Afutu's team wound up with another four points, while the dark tunics racked up only two, leaving the score 14-4.

As the wine bearers went through the crowd for the second time, the people got louder, screaming at the players, throwing calabashes at them. One man threw a stone, which caught Udo in the leg. Outraged, several men around the stone-thrower grabbed the offender and beat him. On the viewing platform, Berko laughed. "It's fun, isn't it?"

Tau glared at him. "What part would that be?"

"All of it. It's like building a huge city in the sand and then watching the waves come in over the top of it."

"Your wine helped bring in this wave."

"It's your city in the sand that I'm watching disappear." With another clap, he summoned a servant and whispered a message. With a bow, the servant left.

Shocked at Berko's rudeness, Tau wondered if Berko's transformation had started long before the festival. "What is the name of your son's wife?"

"What?" Berko replied, as if he didn't understand the question.

"You said your son took a wife shortly after the last festival and that they were now expecting their first child. I was wondering what her name is, the wife, that is."

"Her name is irrelevant."

"An odd name, especially for a daughter-in-law."

Berko didn't reply. Instead, he took a palm leaf from the servant's fan, stood up, and began waving it, back and forth, in sweeping motions. Soon, all around the court, the spectators were waving whatever they could find, including their own wraps. These makeshift flags obscured others' view, so there were arguments, then fights. With a laugh, Berko sat down once again.

On the court, the dark team substituted one of their alternates for one of the players on the south side. Like the captain, he was a big man, built for power, not speed. The two nodded briefly as he moved behind Afutu. Naro intercepted a ball Afutu had meant for Udo and lobbed it high in the air with his raised knee. Afutu backed up to get under it, but as he moved backward, the new player on the dark team ran toward him, head down, ramming Afutu with his head, hitting him in the lower back and throwing him forward into the dirt. Afutu tried to get up but couldn't. When Abran ran over to help, the dark captain lowered his head and rammed Abran, hitting him in the gut, leaving him crumpled on the dirt, not moving. Then he carefully readjusted his helmet, which had been reinforced with a thick, curved slab of wood in the crown.

Crawling over to Afutu, Abran tried to help the captain to his feet but found he couldn't straighten up, let alone pull Afutu to his feet. The game would continue, even with them down, and they'd

194

be trampled if they stayed on the court. "Call for the substitutes," Abran said, in a hoarse whisper. "Just wave them in." When Afutu had managed a pained wave, the substitutes picked up Afutu by his arms and hauled him to the side of the court. Abran crawled after, with one hand holding his stomach. Only the excitement of the game got him off the field. Once he was on the sidelines, he couldn't move at all. The new players stepped tentatively into the game, trying to figure out the play that had continued while they rescued Afutu and Abran. Immediately, a dark tunic player rammed one of the new players into the trench. The other stepped away from the front, unnerved.

"Is this how you win your bets, Berko?" Tau cried.

"You're just sorry you didn't think of it."

"No, I'm sorry I invited you into my village." With a wave to the servant, he ordered Afutu and Abran to be taken away from the sidelines. "You are poison."

"Too late now," Berko laughed. "Any moment now, I'll own the villages on both sides of yours. Not a very strong position to be in, is it?"

As if to reinforce Berko's prediction, the dark Captain and his teammates set up a long volley, tapping the ball back and forth across the trench. When one of the light team tried to block them, the dark player kicked him in the side of the knee, leaving him screaming in pain. The remaining player was so intimidated, he did little to try to intercept the ball as it went back and forth, back and forth, over and over again. When the Captain signaled his teammate to sink the ball in the pit, both of the dark players rushed the goal, bouncing the ball back and forth between them. When they were close to the goal, the player without the ball rammed the goalie, leaving him in a heap at the bottom of the pit, while the other sank the ball.

Sitting there, watching the slaughter on the court continue like a bad dream, Kofi thought about his father, the great chief who established the village on the coast. *I've never had his strength,* Kofi thought. *I never had to fight for anything. But right now, I can feel my father's presence, inside me, and I am ashamed of my own weakness.*

"Twenty points!" the announcer cried, "The Dark Team wins!"

The crowds sat unmoving. The wine that had fueled their shouts and fights now made them very sad, as if, collectively, they had watched fine, intricate carvings smashed to pieces.

"Well, it looks as if I won!" Berko said, clapping Kofi on the back.

With a start, Kofi jumped up, facing Berko. "You won nothing! There's no honor here, only disgrace." When Berko only shrugged, Kofi struck Berko right across the face. "I challenge you," Kofi said, with a new strength in his voice.

Stung by the blow, Berko stepped back, but he recovered quickly. "Absolutely. Since you've already lost everything, you might as well challenge me. A little late for principles, though, don't you think? Seeing as I've already won your village, I assume I could call on two groups of warriors to defend me, but I agree to your challenge. Tau, here, will check that we're doing everything right, won't you, Tau? That's what you like best. Making sure everyone is acting like a good little boy - or girl."

The two never left the platform. While Tau backed out of range, Berko removed his fine robe, tucked his knife in his wrap, and held out his spear. "Was that an idle threat, Kofi, or did you actually mean to fight me?"

It was an odd, new sensation Kofi felt as he set his long robe aside: as if the air had finally cleared after a lifetime of dim fog. Reaching around, he tucked his curved knife into the back of his wrap and took up his war club. Someone in the crowd yelled that the chiefs were fighting, and everyone took up the cry. The victory on the court went uncelebrated, and the players left the field without being cheered, or even noticed.

On the platform, Tau tried to talk to the two men, but the day had moved beyond his control. Ignoring him, the two squared off.

"Well, Tau, begin it!" Berko yelled.

"No! Don't you see what you're doing? You're weakening our force so the invaders can more easily overrun us. This is the destruction of our alliance, our strength."

"No," Kofi answered, "it's the answer to a traitor and a cheat."

"Well said, by the other traitor and cheat," Berko sneered. "Did Kofi tell you, Tau, that he has already bargained with the invaders? Oh, yes, he was perfectly willing to go along with them as they attacked us. And this is what you want for an ally? You'll need better than Kofi to hold your alliance together. He didn't bring his family because he knew the invaders would attack during the festival. You know how he knew that? Because they told him."

"And you'll need better than Berko, certainly," Kofi shot back. "He didn't bring his family either. You know how I know that? Because he had already made a bargain with the invaders by the time I talked to them."

"Please," Tau pleaded, "you can both stop now, and we can put together something better. You know this isn't a good idea."

With a nod of his head, Kofi acknowledged Tau's effort. "It's too late, my friend." That done, his old life finished, he turned to Berko. "Now!" he yelled.

With a roar, they ran at each other across the platform, the club and the spear meeting first, the club splintering the shaft of the spear. But Berko took up the splintered spear and drove it forward as Kofi drew back his club to swing it again. The sharp ends ripped through Kofi's skin, leaving jagged wounds. Kofi, though, couldn't feel the wounds. With a stunning clarity of mind, he saw his opportunity, and he took it, swinging the great club back and then forward in a perfect arc, meeting the side of Berko's head with a crushing blow. The force of it threw Berko over the edge of the platform and down to the court below. With a yell, Kofi spread his arms and leaped down after Berko, landing so hard his leg bone shattered under him, so that he had to stagger over, taking the dagger from the back of his wrap and driving it into Berko's chest. Then, in stages, he too sank down, until he collapsed next to the man who had been his friend and then, later, his enemy, and, in the end, simply another man seduced by power.

All around the arena, the crowds broke into fights, especially the southern villagers against the northern villagers. The players who had disabled Afutu and Abran were dragged out of the changing room and killed by the mob. On the platform, Tau sat, weeping. Sheeah crept up and sat next to him, putting her arm around his shoulder. For a moment, they sat and watched, in tears.

"Take Afutu, Udo, Kojo, and Abran somewhere down the coast in a boat. Get them out of here. If they stay, they'll be killed, and you too."

"I'll go, but only if you come too."

Tau shook his head. "I can't. I have to see this through. But I can only do what I need to do if I know you're safe somewhere far away from here. Please. Go. Take any others you think you need. I can't think straight. You'll have to work out what to do."

"But I don't want to leave you. I don't know how -"

"You'll figure it all out. You'll do fine."

She fell into his embrace.

"Hurry," the chief urged. "Take things you can trade easily. Try to get away before they stop you."

"They?"

Shaking his head, he reached for her hand, holding it in both of his. "There isn't time to explain. May the gods smile on you while you are on your journey." Below them, the fights had moved into the ball court, with men tripping and falling over the bodies of Kofi and Berko as they battled. Someone found the gold medallion on Berko, and new fights erupted over the prize, so it moved from one thief to another.

"Let's eat!" someone in the ball court yelled, and a large group followed him out into the feast area, but there was no one to direct or control the mob, and the people pushed their way to the stalls and grabbed food wherever they found it. More fights broke out. People threw the fine, decorated fruits and smoked meats into the dirt, poured out bowls of nutmeats and gourds of sorghum beer. The woman with the melons howled as men ran up to her stall, picked up the melons, and threw them at others, their sweet insides breaking open and spilling into the fray. The melons were beautiful and delicious, but it was the wrong day for a feast.

On the platform, Tau let go of his daughter's hand. "Go quickly and quietly," he said. "Take my spirit with you."

Sheeah ran, afraid to look back, afraid if she looked at her father, she wouldn't have the strength to leave at all.

CHAPTER 6
CHANGES IN PLANS

It wasn't hard for Akin to find The Leader's camp just upriver from the village. It would have been easy for anyone to find, but hardly anyone was looking for it. Most of the warriors were already in position or on their way to the shore. So Akin walked into a camp of only a dozen warriors, just enough to protect The Leader in case of attack. It was odd that The Leader was behind his forces; he was always at the head of the charge. More than once, it was his iron will that had given those who followed him the strength to carry the day. But Akin found him, seated alone in the back of the encampment, as he had been at their last conference. Walking up, Akin waited to be recognized before he spoke.

"Do you know what my people brought me?" he asked without looking up.

"No, sir."

Reaching for the cord around his neck, The Leader pulled the sun medallion out from under his tunic and held it out for Akin to see. "It's made of gold. The sweat of the sun made into the sun itself, so the wearer is the sun-bearer. What do you think of that?"

Akin could feel something not right in the air, but he couldn't identify it. "It's very beautiful, sir."

"It's more than beauty. It's power."

"Yes, sir."

"More power than men have."

"Sir?"

"It's the power of the sun god. It's the sweat of the sun coalesced into a new form, a phantom version of the sun, except it's real and resting on me now."

Akin waited.

"I had a vision of a road into the sky, Akin, and I wondered what it meant. It twisted about like the river, except it left the earth and wound right up into the clouds. For two days, I thought about this dream, trying to understand it. Then, just before you arrived, one of my men brought me this. He said men were fighting over it in the village, so he took it from them."

"They were willing to give it up?"

"Of course. They were dead when he asked them. Mere men shouldn't have something like this. It will only make them even stupider than they already are, fighting and hurting each other in order to claim, even if only for a moment, the right to be more than they are. But they can't have this. Do you know why?"

"No, sir."

"Because it would be taking to themselves the power of the gods, and they cannot do that."

"But -"

"But I can. No, I have to. I was given the right, I was given the *obligation,* by the gods themselves. That's why they showed me the path into the clouds. I must be the bridge between the earth and the heavens, between the mortals and the immortals. It's why I was sent here: to perfect the living so they can commune with the gods." Looking up, he seemed to see Akin for the first time. "It's very difficult, the task they've given me, the most difficult task I've ever had. I'm not always sure how to do it. But I know it can be done."

"Sir, about the coastal villages -"

"They're irrelevant. They'll destroy each other by tomorrow morning. I've sent groups out to collect the paddles and set the boats out to sea. Once I have their escape routes blocked, they'll

201

panic and kill each other. That's not the problem. The problem is much bigger than that."

"And what would that problem be?"

"How to make people worthy of talking to the gods." He studied the medallion. "Or even to the representative of the gods, the voice of the gods here on earth."

As Akin watched, The Leader seemed to shiver, and he drew his robe tighter around him. "I don't need you here," he snapped. "I need you on the coast. See that everything goes as planned. Talk to me when the battle is over." With a wave, he dismissed Akin.

As the lieutenant was leaving, an aide hurried in with a steaming bowl of éken tea.

"Fever," the aide whispered as he passed.

"Of course," Akin muttered as he left.

On the coast, Sohko, Aminata, and the children had moved the canoe far from the village center, hidden it in the beach grass, and buried the paddles. In the feast area, Sohko wandered among the fighters, gathering foods the group could take with them if they had to flee. Drinking water was another problem. He found two large calabashes, but they wouldn't be enough for six people. So he kept looking. Once in a while, someone threw something at him or pushed him, but all Sohko had to do was turn and face his attackers for them to abandon the challenge. When he returned to the group, he brought with him quite a load of supplies, including baskets, mats, fruits, nuts, dried fish, two more calabashes – and another person. It was the weaver, Ayo.

"It's so fine to see all of you," she began, the words tumbling out in a hurry. "I came downriver because, well, because it seemed to be where everyone was going, and I was pulled with the current along with everyone else. But after I got here, everything started to go wrong, and today, the bottom fell out of the world. I had a small booth where I was trading my weavings, but most of them were stolen, or just destroyed by the mob. Then Sohko appeared, and I was so relieved. I don't mean to throw myself on your mercy, but, I suppose, that's exactly what I'm doing. If you can find a way out of this madness, I can help. I can make things -"

"Don't worry," Aminata broke in. "Of course we'll all go together. That is, once we find Asha and Naaba. And there's another thing we need to take care of," she added, looking at the children. "You two can't leave without talking to your father." It was a statement, not a question.

"Why?" Sule said. "He wouldn't notice if we left. He never does."

"We'll find a way to contact him," Aminata said, putting her arm around the two children, ignoring Sule's tone, "even in the middle of this mess."

"I wouldn't take children into that chaos," Ayo said.

"You won't have to; you'll need to stay here, with the boat and the supplies, and hope you can spot Naaba and Asha, and us, before everything falls to pieces."

She nodded. She had little choice. As the four of them headed back toward the village, Ayo surveyed the scene. There were two barely- buried paddles, one canoe, several piles of supplies, and one very small woman to guard it all against a mob. It didn't look good.

* * *

Akin was trying to figure out how to manage a leader who was drifting away into his own world and a gathering of villages that was becoming a battle of gangs. When an aide appeared, telling him that a woman with yellow eyes had said she was looking for Akin's children, it was one problem too many.

"That woman is always trouble. Just kill her the next time you see her," he announced to the aide, who had no idea who Asha was. Akin waved the aide out. What he wanted was for all of this confusion to lift so he could see a clear path ahead, even a battle path, any path.

It was at that moment that Sohko, Aminata, Deka and Sule were announced. "Your children would like to talk to you, sir," the aide said. He knew Akin wasn't in a very good mood, but it would be hard for the lieutenant to deny his own children.

"What are you saying? My children are at home, in their village up the river!"

"Excuse me, sir, but they're here," the aide tried.

"They're traitors, trying to find a way to trick me."

"I think, that is, they look like children, sir."

"Two children found their way here, all by themselves? It's absurd."

The aide waited, then added, "There's a man with them, and a woman. The man's name is Sohko, and the woman is his wife."

"Sohko? The chief that Wekesa appointed?" Akin hesitated. It was true; he had ordered more warriors from the river villages to come downriver to the shore; he'd forgotten that. Were there many of these men, just wandering around the area, waiting for someone to tell them what to do? His head hurt, trying to figure out how this had gotten to be such a mess.

"Fine. Bring them all here."

After the aide had introduced the visitors, he left. It was a painful scene, with the children just standing there, looking at their father, and the father saying nothing. Even Sohko was waiting to be recognized before he spoke, but there was no recognition, only silence. It was Aminata who finally broke it.

"Let's see: You haven't seen your children in four moons; your children ran away from home and want to come with us; we wanted them to straighten things out here before we did anything, so we're not kidnapping your children; the world is coming apart underneath our feet; your children want you to care about them; and you're sitting there saying nothing."

It was so rude, so insulting that Akin didn't know how to react.

"And you're still not," Aminata added. "We don't have a very long time here. I don't know if you've looked around lately, but the people from the three villages are breaking into gangs, roaming through the village destroying everything in their path. Was there a point where you were going to do something about this?"

"Who are you to speak to me this way?"

Aminata flipped her thick braid behind her. "I'm trying to keep your children alive. That's more than I see you doing."

"What we'd like to do," Sohko broke in, "is to give you a chance to talk to your children and make some very important decisions. Aminata's right about the situation in the village. If we're going to leave, it will need to be soon."

Akin shook his head slowly. "You won't be able to leave. They'll take the paddles and push the boats out to sea."

Even Aminata could think of nothing to say.

"Why?" Sule spoke up. "Why would you do that?"

"It's The Leader's idea, to allow the people to destroy each other, to force them to by blocking their escape routes. He wants to start all over again and build a better society on the ashes of the old one."

"That's murder," Sohko said, stepping forward. "That's murder of many people who've done nothing wrong except to be here at this moment. That's madness."

It was the word that Akin had feared for so long that he hadn't said it or allowed others to. It wasn't madness. It couldn't be. If it were, it would mean everything up to this point had been wrong, and it hadn't. "It's a matter of interpretation," he began, but Sohko's dark expression stopped him.

"Father?" Deka said, stepping up. "Do you like us?"

The question stayed there, breaking through all of the other words, all of the worries and accusations and excuses, so that it filled all the spaces between the people in the room.

Akin looked at the girl as if he had never really seen her before. "Yes, of course. I love you. I love both of you. I always have. How could you have thought otherwise?" But as soon as he heard his last sentence, he knew the answer. "I'm not a very good father," he admitted. "I never was. To tell the truth, I found the demands of children annoying. So noisy. Petty. Or maybe *silly* is a better word. I always thought it was more important to do grand things: fight battles, establish The Leader's network, build his vision of the future. So that's what I did. I didn't really think about leaving you behind. You were the ordinary world; his was the extraordinary world. It was bigger and more exciting. So that's where I wanted to be." He looked at the two children before him. They'd be growing up soon, becoming adults, leading their own lives, making their own mistakes. "You'll find it hard to choose sometimes, later on. I don't say that to excuse my choices, only to remark that it's the truth."

Confused, the children waited.

Their father looked around the hut and sighed. "Here's where my choices led me. Not a very glorious end, is it?"

Aminata was about to say something, but Sohko put his hand on her arm, asking her to wait.

"Thank you," he nodded to Sohko and Aminata, "for bringing my children here today. I had forgotten about them." To Deka and Sule, he said, "I'm sorry. I know you don't believe me, but you're very important to me. It's just that I just didn't think about you, or I thought about you as part of the home I left behind. Every day is a choice, and all of mine took me away from you. And then, when I didn't see you, I forgot about you. Not completely, you know, but -" Part of him was surprised to hear himself say these things. "I thought you belonged to the world that was nice and normal, and a little boring. I could always go back to it, to you. At least that's what I told myself. But too many days went by, and I never went back. I suppose I chose not to. It seemed more important at the time to help The Leader. I thought his plans would change the world. And they did.

"Because of The Leader, no one attacked our village, ever. We had more food and new tools and fine things." When the children didn't respond, Akin went on, "Of course, you had nothing to compare it to. It's just the way things were. But they were only that way because of what he, and I, did. The problem was that I put you aside, for later, and now, it's probably too late. But my choice was never against you. It was just for something else." It seemed a poor excuse, even to him. "But I'm sorry that you were - or that you felt - undervalued."

"Undervalued?" Aminata blurted, astounded at the speech.

"I know. We can't repair the past. And your future lies elsewhere. But we have this moment, right now, where we are all together."

"Are we together?" Sule asked.

"You have to understand, I was called to do something very important, to remake the world."

"Your son asked you a question," Aminata snapped.

"Of course," Akin replied, suddenly aware of the children. "Of course I care very much about you. You're my children." He hesitated. "But I can't take care of you. You need to leave. It's very dangerous here. I suppose you know that."

The children nodded, still standing in the same spot. Rising, Akin walked over to them and hugged the children awkwardly. Aminata and Sohko turned to give them some time alone, but Akin stopped them. "Please don't leave. I need to ask you a difficult question: Will you take my children with you? I can't – It's just that, right now, I can't -"

"Yes," they answered at the same time.

"Then I'll do what I can to help you escape. If you have a boat, take it far away from the village beaches and bury your paddles."

"We've already done that," Sohko said.

"You have?"

"Yes, The She-Eagle warned us," Deka said brightly.

"The – Our enemy? You've spoken to her?"

"She's never done anything to us to deserve that title," Sohko noted. "As a matter of fact, she encouraged us to take your children somewhere safe."

Confused, Akin started to say something but stopped. His children – the witch queen – it all seemed very muddled. She was the one he had tried to capture. No, he *had* captured her, or at least his forces had, but she had escaped. Several times, as a matter of fact. "She's here – in the village?"

"Why do you want to know?" his son asked.

Akin hesitated, but he saw no point in lying. "To capture her."

"Then we don't know," Sohko answered. "Perhaps you'd like to say good-bye to your children now. We need to leave before your grand plan reduces the city to ashes."

"No great plan is without some destruction. The Leader wants to build a society of those who are worthy of our inherent greatness."

Aminata glared at him. "No one makes a society great by killing everyone."

"You don't understand," the lieutenant continued, but the group was leaving.

Deka turned at the door and gave a little wave. "Good-bye, Papa." Then she took Aminata's hand and the four went back into the chaos that was the village.

He waited until they had gone. Then he lifted his head and called his aide. "Tell the men to light the fires," he said, his eyes shining. Now his doubts were gone; the path was clear. "The Leader's great vision will be our guide."

CHAPTER 7
ENCOUNTERS ON THE BEACH

After Sheeah left her father, she ran back to her house, thinking she would take things to trade, as her father had advised. But once she was inside, she looked around with no idea what to take. It seemed crazy to leave everything she had ever known and run – to where? Nowhere would be as fine as this place. It's just that she hadn't realized it. So she stood, staring at one thing and another until the sounds of the fights got closer. They'd be coming up the hill, of course, looking for more things to steal, or destroy.

For a moment, she thought she wouldn't leave at all. She'd stay, and she'd help her father get through all this, and then tomorrow, it would all be sorted out and things would go back to the way they were. But deep inside, she knew it wouldn't happen that way. In a woven bag, she stuffed small treasures that her father had been given: carved ivory pieces, polished obsidian, fairy-blue flycatcher feathers, a mahogany box with a lion carved on the lid, two containers of salt and one of millet, her most beautiful wrap with four colors woven through it. At the last moment, she grabbed a long, carved ebony staff and two decorated calabashes.

As she ran back down the hill, she saw the crowds fighting below. Some were already working their way up the hill. Behind her, she smelled something burning.

At the players' gathering room, by the ball court, she found Afutu and Abran still lying where they were left when they were carried off the field. Udo and Kojo had disappeared into the crowd.

Dashona had come in to wait with Afutu, but he wasn't talking to anyone. He only lay there, turned to the wall. A woman in the corner was talking to a slight man in hushed tones. Outside, beyond the ball court, the fighting went on in small groups, now kindled by fear more than factionalism.

"We have to get you out of here," Sheeah announced to the group, but no one responded. "The city is being destroyed," she said, facing one after another.

They already knew that.

"My father said to get you out of here, so I will," she repeated. "If you won't help me, I'll drag you across the sand myself. I don't know where the others are, so it'll just be you two."

The comment was so unlike Sheeah that everyone looked up. It was Dashona who said the obvious. "Afutu and Abran are seriously hurt. They can't go anywhere, especially not walking across the sand." She tried to ignore the obvious slight of being excluded.

"Then we'll find some other way to get to the boats. But we're going."

The woman in the corner spoke softly to her companion and then said to Sheeah, "There should be several boats coming back into the main beach area very soon. Unfortunately, there are no paddles. If you can find some, you're welcome to use one of the boats for your friends."

Sheeah had run out of answers. Where did people keep paddles of any kind? She'd never had to think about the question.

"Thank you. I know where there are extra paddles," Dashona said, nodding to the woman, "and some people who will help us."

"Tell your friends to look for more boats coming in at the beach," the woman said. "Also, the only route still open is to the south."

With that, she and her companion left the room.

Sheeah found all of this confusing. "Who's she?"

"A friend, apparently," Dashona answered, "and we need one. I'll go get help. We can carry them to the boat," she said, with a wave toward the injured players.

Afutu started to protest, but no one listened.

"See if you can make a litter," Dashona called over her shoulder as she left.

Panicked, Sheeah looked around the room. She had never made anything, much less something that could hold a ball player, or two of them.

When Naaba and Asha found their way back down to the beach, the boat was gone, and Sohko, Aminata, and the children were nowhere in sight. Oddly, there was only one boat pulled up on the beach, where there had been many before. Naaba walked up to look at it but then stopped short. There was a reason it had been left behind. In the bottom of the boat was a twisted bundle that could only be a dead body.

As Asha walked up, Naaba took her arm to turn her away, but she pulled it away from him. "The man is alive."

"What? Wrapped up like that? It's impossible. He couldn't breathe." But even as he said it was impossible, he came to think he saw some movement in the bundle. It would be a terrible fate, to be wrapped up like the dead and left. The panic alone would kill most men. "Maybe you're right," he said, reaching down.

"I'll get in the boat with him," Asha said, stepping carefully over the side and lowering herself to the floor of the boat. "If he's alive but hurt, he may still panic and kill himself."

With Naaba working from above, and Asha carefully rolling the body side to side, they managed to unwind the long sheet that encased the man. For a while, Naaba worried they would uncover a murdered man who should have been left alone, but he kept coming back to the thought that the man might be alive. If so, leaving him was unthinkable.

The death wrap was very long, the kind usually reserved for chiefs, their family members, or chief advisors. Asha worked carefully, turning the body so she could roll the fabric halfway under the body and then turning it from the other side to complete the unwinding. She dreaded seeing the unwrapped body and yet had to. There was something about this man, perhaps, that kept people from simply throwing his body into the sea and stealing the boat. He must be very important. Yet, if he were a chief, his people would have rescued him, or at least claimed him, if he were dead. So she and Naaba worked, unwinding one layer at a time, until they saw the broad, padded belt around the man's middle, the mark of the ball player.

When they removed the last layer, Asha cried out. The man's mouth had been stuffed with clay, but his eyes were open, looking at her from somewhere terrible.

Naaba jumped into the boat, helping Asha to dig out the clay without choking the man, but his mouth and throat were so coated and dry, he couldn't make any sounds. At first, he couldn't even swallow. His tongue was stuck, pressed back into his mouth. But Asha rinsed out his mouth over and over, until he could drink a little on his own. Even then, when he tried to talk, the sounds were only the rasping, gagging noises he made while he vomited up more clay. His head was still foggy from the drug he'd been given, but he knew enough to realize he'd been released from a living grave. Tears streamed down his broad face as he looked at Asha and Naaba.

"Well," Asha started, but she had no idea how to finish.

Naaba put his arm around her. "We'll figure out a way to get him out of here with us. He's been through more than most people could bear."

"But how? Where's our boat? Where are Sohko and Aminata?"

Having no answers to any of these questions, Naaba stepped out of the boat and scanned the area. Their part of the beach was strangely deserted. Farther south, he thought he could see some activity, with people and boats on the beach. Up in the hills, he could see spots of fire growing.

"They're going to burn the people out, just as they've done before. But this time, they're making it harder to escape. It looks as if the only way out is to the south. I can see people down there on the beach."

"Maybe that's where Sohko and Aminata are!"

"We can't leave him here, and he certainly can't travel yet. He's not ready."

Actually, lines of pain were shooting up the man's body, all the way from the soles of his feet to his fingertips, every time he tried to move. 'Not ready for travel' was an understatement.

"Then we'll take him and his boat. It's simple."

"Except for the lack of paddles or poles."

Asha wasn't interested in troublesome facts. "We'll make something."

Naaba nodded. There was no point in bringing up any of the many problems associated with the plan. Instead, he looked for driftwood pieces that he might be able to fashion into makeshift paddles.

While he was working on one of these, Asha tapped him on the shoulder and pointed down the beach. A peculiar procession was headed straight toward them. At the front, walking backwards and waving her arms, directing the others, was a young woman dressed in a multi-colored wrap. Extravagantly decorated braids swung from the knot at the top of her head with each step she took. Behind her, three men and a woman were staggering under the load they carried on their shoulders: four boat poles strapped to a wooden tabletop on which two very big men lay, also strapped down. Every step they took through the loose sand seemed to be a struggle, but they kept moving, and the woman in front kept walking backward, watching them work. When they reached the boat where Naaba and Asha were, the woman stopped, so the whole group stopped, and they immediately set down their burden.

"This will be perfect," Sheeah announced, glancing around. "It's Emai's boat."

"What you mean is it's the only boat," Naaba commented.

"What I mean is, my father told me to get these men safely out of here, and I've been all over the beach, and this is the only boat I've seen," she snapped. "So it will be fine."

The litter bearers hadn't moved since they set down their cargo. In the boat, Emai struggled to sit up, hauling himself up by the side of the boat. When he saw Afutu and Abran on the stretcher, he gave a strangled cry and tried to hold up his hand.

"No one's in the best shape, I see," Sheeah commented. "Still, it should work."

With one foot against the side of the other knee, Naaba considered the scene and the woman giving orders. "How exactly should it work?"

"I don't know. It has to, that's all. There isn't any other choice." She seemed close to screaming, or breaking into tears.

"Okay, let's take apart your litter, so we can use the boat poles," Naaba said. "But you can't go by the northern river, so you'll have to go down the shore to the south. Is anyone here used to travelling on the sea?"

No one replied. Finally, one of the litter bearers said, "I've been on the sea, but always close to shore, just past the breakers. Past that is the open sea and I know nothing about it. But it should be easy. The water moves to the south along the shore."

"Good," Sheeah sighed. "We just need to go down the shore for a while."

"Maybe," Naaba said. "Maybe."

"Who are you, anyway?" Sheeah asked, getting her old confidence back.

"No one."

"Well, there's not enough room in the boat for all of us."

"Then I'll stay," Asha offered.

"What?" Naaba grabbed her arm.

"They need you to help with the boat, but we also need to find Sohko and his group, so you can go in the boat, and I'll go along the shore. We'll meet farther down the shore."

"Look, Asha! Look up on the hill! What do you see?"

Fueled by the winds, isolated spots of fire were joining together to form a line all along the high ground past the town and then curving down to the sand on the north side, just before the mouth of the great river. The only open route was to the south, but everyone knew that, including the warriors. That's where the fighting would be.

"Then what should we do?" Asha cried.

"We're all going together. It's the only way we stand a chance of making it through. We'll look for Sohko's group on the way."

"And if we can't find them?"

"There's no guarantee we'll find them, even if you walk right into the enemy's camp, and I suspect you wouldn't get much of a welcome. Please, Asha."

"We'll be fine in the boat, but we need to leave soon," Dashona interrupted, pointing inland. "That group heading toward us - I don't think they're here to help."

Naaba agreed. "Get the injured men into the boat first. We'll load what we can after they're settled."

Two of the men who had helped carry the litter handed over the extra paddles Dashona had found. "We can't stay," the older of the two said to Naaba. "We helped Sheeah because she needed us, but we have to stay with her father. Good luck, and take care of her," he tilted his head toward Sheeah. "The world shifted today. Tomorrow, it will look very different, especially for her." Quickly, he grasped Naaba's arm, then the two left, heading straight toward the group of warriors on the beach.

"Load the boats!" Naaba yelled. "They're giving us the chance to escape!"

The third man of the group of litter-bearers was a very strong man who said almost nothing, but he lifted the injured athletes into the boat as if they were toys. "My name is Naro," he said, when Naaba introduced himself. "I'm a ball player, like these. We were on different sides, but I know them."

"Then I'm glad you're here," Naaba said, as he wedged the supplies into the boat when everyone had found a place. "Let's push off!"

The dug-out canoe was better suited to ferrying supplies along the river than to turning in the waves. When Naro, Naaba, and Asha poled it away from the beach and into the surf, a wave immediately washed over the side.

"Well, bail it out!" Asha said, handing Sheeah a half-calabash.

"I've never done this before," Sheeah complained.

"No one here has done any of this before," Asha snapped. "Learn."

There was more bothering Asha than the complaints of a spoiled girl. As the boat headed out past the waves, she could feel the rivers in the sea. Under the boat, the waters curled in strange, irregular loops, and past them, a powerful surge was heading north and west, fast. There was no way three poles and two paddles would take the boat south on that water.

CHAPTER 8
THE TIGHTENING OF THE NOOSE

True to his word, Akin had sent two aides to help Sohko, Aminata, and the children find a safe way out of the village, but as soon as they stepped out of the compound, they realized there was no safe way. As The Leader had tightened the noose around the village, Dwyka had maintained an opening to the south. Her people had retrieved stolen boats and paddles and brought them to the southern beach, but panicked people on the shore trampled others in their hurry to escape, and many boats left with only one or two people aboard. When most of the boats were taken, the people fought among themselves, just as The Leader had predicted.

Dwyka sent forces to open a passage for people down the shore, so they could escape on foot. However, once he learned of her plan, that's where The Leader sent his forces as well. Right along the shore, where families were struggling to escape, warriors from both sides clashed, battling with clubs and spears. It was hard for the warriors to know which group was which, since some of the shore people fought with the invaders, and no one seemed to know what the goal was. It was just fighting. Sometimes, the people fleeing were able to slip by the fighters. Other times they weren't. In the confusion, families got separated; children were left screaming for their parents, and the wounded cried in pain where they were left. The best the aides could do was to see the group safely away from the compound. Then Sohko sent them back and headed

217

straight into the chaos. They looked like just another family trying to escape the fighting that went on all around them.

Deka shrieked as she took a tighter hold of Aminata's hand.

"If we're going to help," Sohko began, as he looked around.

"We'll have to split up," Aminata finished. "I'll take Deka with me. We'll try to get the women and children out of the battle zone."

"But," Deka gasped, "it's -"

"Just stay close to me."

"But Ayo! We left her at the boat!"

Deka was right. In the confusion of the meeting with Akin, they had forgotten they had left Ayo to guard the boat and the supplies. And the boat was right where everyone was rushing. What possible chance would she stand against a panicked mob and two opposing forces?

For a moment, they all stood, silenced by the shock. Then Sohko said, "We have to find where we left the boat, first."

"Stay with me, Deka," Aminata called as she started off, though the warning was unnecessary. "It's better if we help each other."

Sohko wrapped his arm around Sule's shoulders, and the boy was glad of it. At Sohko's suggestion, they headed up the hill away from the beach. That way they could avoid some of the fighting, but eventually, they'd have to walk right into the middle of it to reach the spot where they'd left the boat.

From the high ground, they searched the beach grass for any sign of the boat, but there was none. "Are you sure that's where it was?" Sule asked.

"Yes," Sohko answered slowly. "That's where it was."

"Wait, I think I see something."

"Come along, Sule, we'll search farther down the beach."

"No, wait. There's something there," the boy insisted. "Look."

"I *have* been looking," Aminata said, trying to keep the edge out of her voice.

"There. Look where we left the boat. It was in a little dip in the sand, right?"

"I don't see anything."

"That's my point. You should be seeing something. You should be seeing the dip where we hid the boat. But it's not there."

"Now I can't remember where it was," Aminata admitted.

"Follow the slope of the hill," Sule said. "See how it has a little dip, as if the seawater sometimes gets that far up the beach but then stops because the hill is there. But there's a little trough where it collects sometimes."

"Yes, so?"

"It's not there in one section."

Aminata squinted. "So the water never got to that part."

"No. I think it did. I think we left the boat right there."

"Right where there's nothing now? Did the wind spirits cover it up?"

"No," Sohko said. "But something else did. Do you see the spot Sule's talking about?"

"No," Aminata admitted, "it's all sand blur to me."

"That's the idea. That's exactly the idea."

"You're confusing me."

"I'm not; Ayo is."

"And it's working!" Deka shouted, starting to run down the beach.

"Wait!" Aminata yelled, finally understanding. "Even if you're right, running down there and exposing it will only get her killed – and the boat stolen."

Sule was right: Ayo had hidden the boat under a light-colored material that she'd covered with patches of sand and sea grasses. At the same moment Aminata finally spotted it, she saw four men moving very close to it as they fought, grunting as they swung their heavy clubs at each other. One connected with a sickening sound of breaking bone, and the injured warrior crumpled on the sand. The victor shouted his triumph and wheeled around, searching for his next opponent. The edge of his heel dug into the sand as he turned, catching the edge of the material and moving it. Surprised by the movement, he turned, but his distraction was his downfall. The victor in the other battle swung his war club, hitting the man on the side of the head and throwing him down into the sand. With a satisfied cry, the warrior moved on. The other didn't move.

Farther down the beach, Akin was organizing the troops, trying to stop the free-for-all and get the men to shut down the open access route. But the chaos The Leader had unleashed wasn't easy to control. Even with Akin's threats, random fights continued, often turning into gang brawls, and in the time the warriors were distracted, several groups escaped south. Many of the fighters were Dwyka's warriors, and their orders were simple: cause trouble, slow any attempt at organization, and allow people the chance to escape.

But Akin had many more men, and Dwyka's warriors began to falter, falling back farther and farther along the beach, even as Akin sent his warriors to pursue them. But as they were retreating, they heard their own drummers coming toward them. Ten of them stepped calmly onto the battlefield, playing double three-beat patterns that grew faster and faster, until they were a blur of sound that got everyone's attention. People stopped where they were on the battlefield and waited. When the drums reached their frantic climax and then stopped, Dwyka appeared. She was dressed in yellow and orange, with a large feathered headdress of white, yellow, red, and blue feathers radiating out around her head and cascading down her back. Resting on her forearm was a huge bird with a white head and neck, black wings, and a red-brown belly. It turned slowly, surveying the crowd with its steady gaze.

From the hill, Sule pointed to her. "Look! She really *is* the She-Eagle!"

The drummers pounded three sets of the double-three signal and stopped again. Dwyka stepped up onto a flat rock and raised her arm. The bird launched itself into the air with two beats of its enormous wings and soared overhead, its white head bent down to watch the crowd below. The people stared as if she was an apparition.

"Good people!" Dwyka cried. "Why are you killing each other? Look around! What are you about here? Why is this ground soaked with blood?"

There was no answer from the men.

"We're changing the world!" Akin yelled as he stepped forward. "We're ending the old age and bringing in the new one."

"The old age when people killed each other?" Dwyka asked.

"Yes! The new era will grow as a seed from the ashes of the old one!"

"And yet, you're still killing each other? How is this world different?"

"The people must be allowed to kill each other, so we can start over, with better people," Akin replied, but even as he said the words, he thought he might have picked better ones.

"Then these men have no value?" Dwyka challenged.

The men were listening now.

"Their value is to end this age," Akin said. "They're doing their part."

"And who will be fit to live in your new age?"

"Great people. Only great people. There will be no lesser men, no lazy men, no incomplete men. Only great men."

"And you will create these great men? Men much better than these?"

"Yes." It wasn't exactly right the way it was sounding, but Akin wasn't going to quibble about choice of words. The point was the same, no matter how you dressed it.

"You cannot create great men," Dwyka said. "Great men create themselves. Even though they have many choices, they choose to live with a strong, generous spirit. Most of these fine men will never be called heroes, except to their family and friends. They simply live well, doing their best, helping others, caring for their families, honoring the gods."

Confused, Akin shouted back, "Those aren't heroes! Heroes do great deeds, worthy of great honor! They live lives that are larger, brighter, more important than those of normal men. The Leader is a hero!"

There was no cheer at The Leader's name.

"You will know him as a hero, because you will tremble at his name!" Akin yelled. "If you don't, you are stupid and foolish, like this woman."

Still, there was no response from the crowd.

"Then watch!" Akin yelled, as he raised his right arm. "Learn the power of The Leader, the creator of the new world!" As he dropped his arm and yelled, his archers fired a volley of flaming pitch arrows into the massed warriors around Dwyka, the sticky, burning resin landing on their skin and hair, so they fell, screaming in pain. Others ran away.

But Dwyka still stood in the center, shaking her head. "You cannot terrify people into greatness, Akin. Not even your great Leader can do that."

One of those listening was indeed The Leader. Finally, he saw her, saw his enemy and his competitor. There was no room for indecision today. It had to happen today. The new world had to be born on this day, and no woman would stop that. He knew he was right. The gods had shown him the path winding up into the clouds. It was his path, his awesome, righteous path, the one he was called up to take. There could be no confusing talk, no loss of momentum. From behind Dwyka, he ran up without a word, raised his powerful arms, and swung his war club with all his strength, so that it split her head open, throwing her down with the power of the blow, while her life blood pulsed out, staining the feathers, flooding the ground.

Gasping, the warriors watched as The Leader stood, his arms raised, where the queen had stood only a moment ago. "The new age is beginning!" he cried. "Let it begin! Let the fires purge the old ways! Only blood will heal the burned soil and bring it back to life. This woman was weak! Her words were lies! But she has failed now. And everyone who stands in my way will also fail. No one is safe from fear! It is fear that will purge the evil of the old way! Do you understand?" His eyes were shining as he threw his head back. "What is man except danger and evil and beauty? What can control this monster of darkness and allow the greatness to shine forth? Only one thing: fear."

There was a low murmur from the crowd, but no one spoke up.

"The new era will be extraordinary because it will no longer be the captive of lesser men. It will be peopled by men who talk to gods! It will be the finest flower, the one born of fire." He surveyed the crowd of warriors and families gathered around him. "Now, you need to decide who will have a place in the new world. If you want to live in it, you will need to survive the night – any way you can." The last words were said with a chilly calm.

Even Akin was confused. "Sir? I don't understand."

Taking up his war club, he walked up to Akin as if he was going to talk to him, but instead, he swung the great club into the side of Akin's head, sending him crashing to the ground.

"Still confused?" The Leader said to the crumpled form before him that had, just a moment before, been his most valued lieutenant.

On the hill, Deka and Sule screamed, but Sohko and Aminata hurried them away, even as the shock made the children's legs collapse under them. Aminata hugged them tight. They would all have to find a way off the beach soon. They could not see what lay ahead that night on the shore.

As the sun was setting, the fights moved farther south, and Sohko moved down the beach, looking for the spot where the boat should be. The children didn't move or speak, even though Aminata held them close to her. They had vanished to some place deep inside.

"Ayo! Are you all right?" Sohko called, to what looked like another patch of sand.

"Sohko!" she cried. "I'm so glad to hear your voice! I thought I would die here."

Waving the others forward, Sohko sighed as he lifted the cover. "If you weren't so good at hiding, you would have. We have difficult work ahead of us. For the moment, the fighting is farther south, along the only open escape route. We'll need to get the boat into the water and away from here as soon as possible."

"What about Asha and Naaba?" Aminata asked, as she loaded up supplies.

"We'll look for them at first light. We should be able to stick close enough to the shore to search for them." He stopped, holding a basket of root vegetables suspended over the boat. "Aminata, I should finish the task here first."

When she reached out for his arm, he set the basket down, and the two of them walked off down the beach to talk. "I know how you feel, I do, but without you, we won't make it out alive. It's that simple."

He took her hand in his. "You may not, with or without me."

"It looks better with you."

A little smile flickered across his broad face. "It looks better with you too."

"Someone will take care of the situation here. She'll have allies -" She left the sentence unfinished. It was impossible to continue without wishing death on someone else, and she didn't believe in that. At least most of the time she didn't.

"I could go now, and be back before dawn."

"No. Please, no. We, all of us, but especially me - we need you to stay. That monster will face his death before the night's over. And when he does, he'll be surprised that he, the one chosen to remake the world, is actually just another piece of it. But the children don't need to see it, any more than they needed to see their father's death. It's too much, Sohko, even for me."

He wrapped his arm around her shoulders. "Then let's get away from here. We'll find Naaba and Asha in the morning and go somewhere, somewhere far away, and we'll build something new there. We could head south and go up the River Born of Twins, or we could find somewhere else."

"We'll know the place when we see it," Aminata managed. There were other things she needed to talk to him about, but they could wait. At least, for now, they were all together, and that was something to be grateful for.

At the boat, Ayo and the children had finished packing the supplies while they eavesdropped. When Sohko and Aminata returned, they all stood up at once, ready to haul the boat down to the beach.

Looking at them, Aminata smiled. "A fine family we are, in on each other's secrets."

"You're the best family," Deka said, simply. "You're our family."

"Everyone grab an edge," Sohko ordered. "We need to get this boat into the water if we're going to get anywhere."

As they pushed off into the sea in the dark, they could hear the fights that had already started down the beach. They rowed in silence, out past the surf, with no moon to guide them, only the sound of the waves on the shore. They had no idea where they were headed.

CHAPTER 9
DARKNESS ON THE WATER

For the first time in his life, Afutu felt helpless. He was so stiff, he couldn't move, even to bend over, so he sat, motionless, where Naro had put him, his body slumped over, his head wedged against the side of the boat. Pain was the only constant; everything else drifted. He couldn't remember the last part of the ballgame, or anything much since then. People had spoken to him, he remembered that, but he couldn't recall what they said, or what he replied, if anything. There had been people in the players' room, but he didn't know or care who they were. Things went on around him, but he felt no connection with them. And now, it continued in the same way. The pain left him exhausted, raw. With all his being, he wished he'd been left to die on the ballcourt.

Abran was lying, curled up, on the floor of the boat. Placed in any other position, he screamed, so Naaba arranged the extra poles on the bottom of the boat and put a mat over them for him. It was the best they could do with what they had.

When they stowed the supplies, Asha made a mental list of the food they'd brought, realizing it wouldn't last long. The pleasant surprise was a box of crystallized plum honey bits. Sheeah had brought them and would have liked to keep them for herself, but even she realized that wouldn't be a good idea, so she handed them over, reluctantly, when Asha was doing her inventory.

When darkness fell, they couldn't light a torch for fear of being spotted and pursued, so they sat in the dark, drifting where

226

the sea chose to take them. As a diversion, Asha broke out the plum honey candies and gave one bit to each person. It became a ritual at night, the tiny bit of lumpy sweetness that helped to lessen the terror of the night. It was a short respite.

Later, the wind picked up and a storm moved in, leaving them soaked and cold, trying to bail out the boat in the dark. The two injured men suffered the most, cramping up from the cold and wet, unable to move or dry off. By morning, they were past miserable.

Afutu asked to speak to Naaba, addressing him in a whisper. "I can't go on like this. I was meant to die back there. Please, sir, I know you don't know me, but I need you to do this for me. Please put me overboard."

"I know you hurt. We'll try to help you," Naaba said quietly, putting his hand on Afutu's head. "Not all requests can be granted, at least not now, and not by me."

Dashona was sitting a little farther up the boat, shivering, her arms wrapped around her bony knees, pulling her legs closer to her body for warmth. Sliding down next to her, Naaba said softly, "This man is hurting, inside and out. Both these men are. Can you help?"

It was the first time anyone had treated her as an important member of the group. If she could have leaped up, she would have. As it was, she straightened up so fast, she knocked over the basket sitting in front of her feet. "Yes. I can. I will." Her thin frame seemed even more angular as she moved back to sit near the injured men. "I will," she repeated. It was actually what she had wanted to do all along, but she had no right to, until she was asked.

Afutu refused to recognize her or to cooperate with her, so she asked Emai if he would help her with the men. His throat was still raw, and his body stiff with the rain, but he agreed. Between them, they had two sets of arms, one strong back, and one voice.

"Afutu needs to move. It's very hard for him to sit in the same place, all cramped up," she said. "I thought maybe we could put him on his back, on the bottom of the boat, so we can get his legs moving. I'll also need help with other things," she said, hesitating.

Emai nodded.

Between them, Emai and Dashona got the pads off Afutu and set them aside. They didn't try to move Abran, since he couldn't move without hurting, but Dashona rubbed his scalp and feet and arms. She encouraged them both to work on their breathing, inhaling deeply through the nose, holding the breath for a slow count of five, and then exhaling slowly through the mouth. She told a story about the man who collected the star fragments that fell sometimes from the night sky. After the man had caught them, he put them in a beautiful black box with carved ivory flowers on the top. When the sun had died and gone to the underworld, and the night was very long and dark, he would take out the box, climb the hill to the east, and throw the star fragments toward the brightening sky. The sun, which was still new and weak, would then eat them, getting enough energy from them to rise once again, shining brightly in the sky.

While she worked, Abran took her hand in his and held it against his chest.

Then she moved to Afutu, but he was like a stone, refusing to respond. So she worked his legs gently up and down, and she massaged his feet, his calves, then his shoulders and his neck, while she told a different story, a story of a young hippo. When he was born, his mother had to sneak him into the group; otherwise, the other hippos would kill the baby. So the mother hid him in the shallows, having him stand behind her. The days went by, and the youngster grew bigger, but he still wasn't strong enough to defend himself against the brutal attacks of his own kind, so his mother told him to stand in the grasses by the edge of the river. But he was young, and after a while he was bored, so he looked out to see what was going on. At the same moment his head poked out of the grasses, a crocodile was lying on the opposite bank, pretending

228

to be asleep. The hippo looked at the croc, thinking it was a log with closed eyes. A very large log, perhaps. He wanted to ask his mother about these logs with eyes, so he stepped out farther, looking for her. But she wasn't anywhere nearby. Stepping out into the river farther, he found it a little too deep for him, and he tried to run back to the shallows, but the water pulled at him, dragging him farther in. Frightened, he screamed. At the sound of his cry, several of the adult male hippos lifted their heads, looking for the source. One opened his huge mouth wide, showing the long, punishing teeth that had inflicted so many wounds on other hippos, and rushed at the baby. Too late, the mother realized the peril her son faced, and she could only watch as the big male rushed to attack.

But a strange thing happened. The big croc slid off the bank and moved across the river. As the hippo approached, it swung its powerful tail sideways and opened its jaws in challenge. The poor baby wasn't sure whether he would drown or be killed in the next few moments, but as the hippo slowed, measuring the croc as an opponent, the croc bumped the baby hippo with its broad head, pushing it toward the shallows. Then it turned back to the hippo.

Doubt flooded the challenger's mind. Something very different was happening here, and he slowed, allowing the water to fill the space between it and the croc. But yet another large male, excited by the aggressive display, challenged the challenger, and much flashing of punishing long teeth ensued before they actually closed on each other in a fight.

In the meantime, the baby retreated to the shallows, under cover of the tall grasses, and the crocodile returned to the opposite bank, where he stayed, with his eyes mostly closed, smiling to himself. And even later on, when the baby had grown, he and that particular crusty, difficult old crocodile remained great, though silent, friends."

By the end of the story, Emai had fallen hopelessly in love with her and Abran wasn't far behind. But, in the strange way of love, the only one she cared about was Afutu, and he never said anything or responded in any way. It wasn't that he ignored her intentionally. He simply didn't see her, or anyone else. There used to be a world he understood, but it'd been taken from him. For the moment, he wasn't even capable of considering who or what might have stolen it. He lived in a world ripped apart, and, as far as he could see, there was no one, and no art or device, capable of putting the pieces back together. He knew of ballplayers who had died, either right on the court or shortly after the game, from their injuries. They were heroes. What was a man who should have died but didn't?

There was another member of the group whose world had changed with shocking suddenness. She watched the therapy sessions and storytelling with a bitter taste in her mouth. While the others worked, she did nothing. During the day, she stared out at the unfamiliar shoreline as they passed by. It was a world unrelated to anything she knew. The land had lost its familiar parts: old spirit trees, special beaches, certain rocks, tiny coves. From a distance, there was only the sameness of the coast, with the rocks and beach and mangroves. The mighty forests beyond the coast looked small, the villages even smaller. Occasionally, when they saw people on the shore, the men and women seemed like miniatures, with tiny lives that went with their tiny villages. Perhaps there was a chief there. Perhaps he had a beautiful daughter whom everyone admired. Perhaps, if that daughter was lucky, she would never know what Sheeah had learned: that it all crumbles in the blink of an eye. What you thought was the whole world is really only a tiny part of it. What you thought was so important doesn't matter at all. You don't matter at all.

She wished she had stayed with her father, even if it meant dying with him. At least that was a world she understood. She missed her old world so much, it hurt, just like a wound.

As night fell, Dashona told stories to ease the passage into darkness. But then, when she was done, there was a long silent time in the dark before the sun was born once again. Day after day, they could see the land off to their right, but they couldn't get any closer to it. One day, they awoke to the sight of an enormous spit of land sticking out into the sea like the point of an arrow. They were close enough to see a village there, with smoke curling up from cook fires. Excited, they tried to paddle toward the spit, but, perversely, the current swept them farther away, arching north and west and then gradually south again. But this time they were far from shore, and their hope faded with their view of the land.

When the sky was clear at night, they tried to determine their direction, but they weren't experts in the positions of the stars. And, as Naaba commented to Asha, "It makes no difference if we know where we're going, if we don't know where we are or where we need to be."

CHAPTER 10

MOUNTAINS THROWN INTO THE SEA

In and around the islands currently known as the
Cape Verde Islands, especially Santo Antão

The passengers lived in their own world, pushed along by forces outside their control, like birds in a storm. There was so little talking on the boat that Emai didn't notice when his voice came back. Mostly, people drank the water they collected in the calabashes during storms, ate cold millet mush or raw fish they caught, and spent the day lost in a kind of stupor. At dusk, they waited for Asha to hand out the bits of crystallized plum honey and Dashona to tell a story. It was the only part of the day that registered in their mind. Thinking about anything else would have brought on panic, and then despair.

When the storms came again, they set out the rain collectors and huddled under the mats Asha set up. Only Afutu never moved. It didn't matter to him whether he was wet or dry. Abran, however, started to feel better. He was probably the only one on the boat with a reason to rejoice, but the injuries that had left him paralyzed with pain gradually healed. While he was still weak and terribly stiff, he was shocked to realize one morning that he could move around, at least a little, without hurting.

One morning, Asha was going through the increasingly small supply of food when she sensed something moving, somewhere off to the side of the boat. Looking out, she saw the back of the largest creature she had ever seen moving through the water. At first she thought it was a mountain rising and falling in the sea.

"Look!" she yelled. "Look1"

Dozing, Naaba jerked awake at her cry. "What? What is it?"

But the words were hardly out of his mouth before he knew exactly what she meant. He leaned on the edge of the boat, watching as the enormous creature, easily four times the length of their boat, moved through the deep water.

Emai, Dashona, and Naro joined the group, gasping as the creature's giant tailfin rose out of the water and slapped down, sending its vibration right through the little boat. Slowly, Abran moved over too, so the boat listed dangerously to one side, but no one could stop watching the amazing beast in the water.

"So big, it could only live out here," Dashona murmured. "The King of the Sea."

"So amazing, it has to have its own world," Emai added.

Dashona stared. She hadn't the heard the sound of his voice since they left the village.

"And look who came over to see the whale," Emai said, pointing to Abran, who was sitting up against the side of the boat so that he could see over the edge.

"It's amazing," Abran managed, for he too hadn't spoken in a long time.

The whale moved quite close to the boat, so close they could see the white bumpy growth on its nose and the grooves that ran along its back. They thought it would ram the boat with its huge head, sinking it immediately, but it didn't. Instead, it moved off a distance and slapped its tail hard on the surface before it dove down out of sight. They kept watching the water next to the boat, but now it seemed empty, as if part of its presence had been taken away.

Later, Naro spotted a whole pod of whales resting on the surface not far away and another rising to the surface, blowing out a long plume of steamy air. "There it is again!" he called. "That big one, see the white knob on its nose? It's the same one we saw next to the boat."

Off to one side of them, the whale Naro was pointing to leaped up out of the water, throwing itself into the air, its flukes extended, its body unbelievably large, hovering there for a moment, a sea giant flying like a dancer, the water rolling, splashing down the length of its body. Then it crashed back down into the sea, sending up rolls of sympathetic waves that spread into the sea around it.

"His courtship dance?" Naaba asked, holding on while the boat rocked precariously.

Asha smiled. "If it is, it's certainly impressive."

They watched the whales until the giants were too far away to see, though the watchers still imagined they were seeing a tail fluke rising as a whale dove, or a spout as it surfaced. At dusk, Emai called for a whale story.

Dashona hesitated. "I know only one. My father used to tell it."

"Then the choice is easy."

"Well, then, a long time ago, a giant lived all by himself along the coast, in a place just like the spit of land we saw, sticking out into the sea. He was so big that where he walked around, he left holes that later filled up with water. When he slept, he rolled over and back, so that the land was pressed down and smoothed out into a broad valley. That was fine, except he wanted something to rest his head on, so he pushed up some dirt as a pillow. That became the biggest hill along the coast.

"When he was hungry, he'd just walk into the sea and splash around. Then he'd walk along the shore, picking up all the fish that the waves had left stranded there.

"He had plenty to eat and drink, but it was a lonely sort of life, and he went walking down the beach, looking for company. He met the giant birds of the air, and the biggest crocodile in the river, but none seemed to want to be his friend. Saddened, he returned to his spit of land, sitting out on the rocks as the old sun sank very close to the sea. Then, off to his side, he saw a woman sitting on the rocks just down the way from him. She was incredibly beautiful, with blue skin and blue hair, and a dark blue wrap studded with tiny sparkling stones that caught the last of the sun's light.

"Climbing quickly over the rocks, he tried to reach her, but the sun slipped into the underworld and there was only the faint high glow that the clouds make. He thought he could see her, but when he got to that spot, there was no woman there.

"The following day, he climbed to the very spot where she'd been and he waited. Very close to the end of the day, the blue woman came walking down the rocks, smiling at him, her blue hair blowing in the breeze, the tiny stones on her wrap sparkling.

'I waited for you,' the giant said. 'I hoped you'd return.'

'I know,' she replied.

"They became lovers, and the giant thought he couldn't be any happier, so he asked the blue woman to be his wife and stay with him forever, and he gave her a string of two hundred smooth stones with holes in the center, which he had threaded along a vine.

"She said no.

"They quarreled, and the giant became angry. In his anger, he hurled the string of beads into the sea, where they splintered into spots of light on the water. The blue woman went with them, disappearing into the sea.

"Furious, the giant ripped out the mountains that used to be along the coast and hurled them far out into the sea. Then he broke down and cried so much, his tears turned the seawater salty. The next day, he swam out after her, looking for her everywhere the light splintered on the water. Day after day after day he swam, until his body changed. His arms grew into long flippers, and his legs became absorbed into his long body. Only his sad eyes remained the same. He became the great whale, swimming the waters of the world, searching for the woman he loved.

"You can see them both, even now, in the night sky, the great whale and the beautiful woman. Her wrap still sparkles with lights. Her beads are scattered all over, wherever the waves have taken them. They're very worn and small now, but you can still see them sometimes, the round stones with the hole in the center, lying there on the beach."

At the end of the story, when there was no response from the listeners, Dashona regretted telling the story. It always left her saddened.

"I'm sorry," she muttered. "It's the only whale story I know."

"It was a good story," Emai said, in his deep, hoarse voice, and then almost everyone chimed in, agreeing with him.

Days later, Naaba was watching the clouds, worried about the storm fronts that seemed to be coming at them from two different directions. He was about to point out the formations when something else appeared, something very dark and pointed, right between the grey sea and the grey clouds.

"Asha," he started, unsure of what to call these apparitions. "Asha, there's something on the water. I don't know what. It looks like a jagged backbone, but if it is, it's -" He ran out of words. If it was a creature, it was a monster.

Following his line of sight, Asha scanned the surface of the water, trying to see something, but there was only the sameness of the sea and sky. "There's nothing. Maybe it was a whale, or several."

"No. These had long points sticking out, like spears."

"Off to the side, behind us!" Naro cried, "It's an island!"

The word was enough to stir the group out of its lethargy and strain to see something through the mist rising from the sea.

"It was right there!" Naro insisted, pointing to the same region, but there was nothing to be seen.

"Right there!" Asha yelled as she pointed straight ahead of them. "It's right there! Look!"

It was there, appearing out of the mist, a towering wall of sheer rock rising straight up right in front of them. It was many times taller than any hill they had ever seen, with not a single tree or even tuft of grass on it, just solid dark stone thrusting up through the sea.

"We'll be killed!" Asha cried. "It's the spine of the sea dragon."

"I don't think so," Dashona muttered. "I think these are the mountains thrown into the sea, the ones in the story. My father said he had seen them, but no one believed him. I thought he was crazy."

Reaching for the long poles, Naaba yelled, "We need to try to slow the boat down, so we don't crash right into that wall. Emai, let's tie the poles together in a V and drag them behind us. We'll save the paddles for avoiding the rocks."

As they headed closer to the island, even with the mist, they could make out the dark rock walls even more impossibly high and steep than they had seemed from a distance. At the base, the water churned, crashing its way through more rock under the surface and then throwing itself futilely against the fortress of stone.

"We'll have to head away from the island. It'd be impossible to land the boat," Naro called. "I don't see any level shore or beach, though it's hard to see very far in this mist."

"I could help you land your boat."

Every head in the boat swung around. The voice came from a man in a skiff that was coming up right next to the boat. He was standing up, working a long paddle that was connected to the back of his boat. His lean frame was covered by a wrap of woven palm leaves, but his most striking feature was his hair, braided long down his back and woven into his beard braids in the front. A small braid came off each end of his mustache, which was also braided into his beard. He was a mass of braids, big and small, front and back.

Woven in and out of his braids were the long spiky leaves of the Dragon Tree, sticking out at odd angles, as if they'd just sprouted there.

"Sorry if I took you by surprise. The scouts noticed you out here, so I thought the least I could do is help you land in the right place."

"Scouts?" Naaba said, unable to think of anything else to say.

With a sweep of his hand, the man indicated the top of the impossible wall. "Yes. Lookouts, really. You can see one over there."

They squinted and saw nothing.

"You need to head farther up the island. You could follow me, or I could tie up my skiff and bring both boats in."

Something about his absolute confidence inspired them to hand over the boat to this strange man they had never seen before.

"What's the worst that could happen?" Naaba whispered. "He could get us lost in the middle of the sea."

"Or crash on the rocks," Asha added, "which we were about to do."

"Is there a village on the island?" Naro asked, as the stranger tied up his boat and climbed aboard, bringing his long paddle with him.

"Oh, yes. Two, really. The main one is inland. It's much nicer there."

"And the people will accept strangers?"

"Well, some will. But some are very difficult. Actually, some aren't very happy with me right now, so we might just avoid them. I'll show you where they live, but we won't stop to visit. It wouldn't end well."

"You know everyone in the village?"

The stranger looked puzzled. "Know everyone? Of course I do. I know everyone on the island, know their names and their families. Others too." He worked the paddle expertly, threading through rocks they couldn't even see until they were passing right next to them.

"It must have taken you a long time to learn the coast this well," Naaba commented.

"All the time there was. Since this is a big boat, I may need you to work the poles on some of these rocks ahead."

Breaking out the long poles, Naaba thought how strange it was that they hadn't been used since their escape from the mainland in the dark. It seemed like a long time ago.

With a wave, the man pointed up ahead. "There, now, we're starting to look a little better, right?" On their left, the huge stone slab grew shorter as they passed, and, around a rock outcrop, a small beach appeared. "It's not quite as simple as it looks," he remarked, as if responding to something someone said. "You'll need the poles."

Naaba wasn't thinking it looked simple at all, but he handed out the extra poles and kept one. "Just tell us when and where."

Unflustered, the man steered the boat right through the middle of a rock-strewn passage, calling out every so often "Push from the left," or "Push off from the right," as the rest of the group watched the beach slide up to meet the boat as if it had planned on this all along and was only waiting for them to show up.

With a cheer, Naaba jumped out of the front of the boat, dragging the line up the beach. Then he thought perhaps all this was premature. "Should we stay to guard the boat?"

The stranger waved away his concern. "No. There's no theft here. It's a small island. Where would the thief run to with the stolen goods? Even if someone stole your boat, and no one will, it would still be right here after it was stolen. This is the best beach on the whole island."

After introducing himself and the others on the boat, Naaba extended his arm. "Thank you for your help. We couldn't have made it here otherwise."

The man touched his arm awkwardly and then repeated the gesture. "We're delighted to have you as our guests. You were lucky to have ridden that current, you know. It's not usual. Sometimes it shoots off the mainland and curves around to here, but mostly it would take you south down the coast."

Dashona climbed out awkwardly, forgetting what solid ground felt like. "That's what we thought. Does it shift back?"

"Oh yes, most of the time, it comes from the north. At least, that's what it seems. I wouldn't know, of course." As Naro lifted Abran and Afutu out of the boat, the man nodded. "They'll need the black sands. Very helpful."

Sheeah stepped up to the stranger, studying him, then pointed her finger at him. "What's your name? Who are you? How do you know everyone on the island? Are you the chief?"

"I suppose you could say that." Then he turned to help unload the boat. "We'll camp here tonight. The real village is inland, but it's a good hike."

The group had nothing to offer him other than some old food that had been soaked with seawater several times, but he seemed delighted at the prospect of eating it. In no time, he had gathered wood and started a fire, though there seemed to be very few trees growing in the area. From his skiff, he hauled out a yellow-fin tuna as long as his outstretched arm.

"Well, we have a group to feed," he replied, though no one had found the voice to ask a question. Already established on the beach were a three-stone hearth and a split fork turning spit for grilling. On a flat rock, he started to clean the huge fish.

"Are your people going to join us?" Asha asked, feeling as if the land was rising and falling underneath her feet as she walked over.

"Not tonight, but we have many guests besides you folks. We'll have a fine time, here on the island, getting to know each other and enjoying a good meal."

"Can I help fix something? Will the other guests need something?"

"Thank you, but no, I think it's all taken care of. Just relax and get your land legs. You've had a difficult journey."

Sheeah hadn't moved, standing on the beach with her hands on her hips. "You never answered my question. What's your name?"

With a smile, the man turned to her, setting down his knife. "What difference would it make?"

"People have names. That's what other people call them."

"Then what would you like to call me?"

"The caller doesn't get to decide."

"Why not? It would be more interesting that way. Pick one for me."

Confused, Sheeah had to consider this. "I guess I'd call you Marlin, since you're at home in the sea."

"I like it," the man said, returning to his work on the fish.

"I have to help unload the boat," she said.

With the fire started and the tuna on the spit, the man washed his hands in the sea and came back to Afutu and Abran. "If you'll trust me, I'll bury you up to your shoulders in the black sand. It has healing powers. However, if you don't, I would understand."

"A strange request," Abran admitted, "but I'm willing to try anything. If it doesn't cure me, will it make me worse?"

"No, the worst you'll feel is warm. The black sand heats up during the day. And we'll all keep you company while we eat. If it becomes uncomfortable, we'll dig you out right away."

"Then I'll try."

Walking off down the beach, the man moved a flat stone away from a dug-out section and waved them down. With Naro's help, they got Abran settled on what seemed like a sand seat, then used giant clam shells as shovels to fill in the hole with the black volcanic sand. Abran sat there, buried up to his arms, feeling foolish. After they had filled in the hole, everyone hovered, watching him, or what was visible of him, waiting for some response.

He felt nothing at all.

He felt nothing at all. It took a moment to realize what that meant.

"I don't understand," he said.

Naro stepped forward, ready to start pulling the sand away from him. "What? What's happening?"

"I don't hurt. Nothing hurts. I feel as if I'm floating, but at the same time as if I'm as heavy as the rock wall."

The man smiled and turned to Afutu. "And what about you? Still worried?"

"It doesn't matter," Afutu said, after a long pause. He didn't believe sitting in black sand could make any difference, though obviously Abran thought it did. And what if it did? What if it made him a little better, so that he could struggle around with the help of two staffs and someone to help him back up when he fell?

Dashona walked over to him. "Yes, it does."

Asha and Naaba joined her. "Yes, it does."

Sohko, Aminata, and Emai stood up next to them. "Yes, it does."

Abran raised his arm. "Yes, it does."

Sheeah looked at the rest of the group and stepped slowly over to join them. "It has to."

When he agreed, the group picked him up and set him down in another hole in the sand, pushing the black sand into the hole after him. They pushed by handfuls and armloads and shoveled with flat shells, covering each other in the process, afraid to stop, afraid to hope too much, afraid not to. For his part, Afutu said nothing, afraid to disappoint them, unwilling even to meet their gaze. So they buried him in the black sand, just as they had Abran, and they sat down, cross-legged, on the sand, talking as if it was a party someone had organized, and they hadn't seen each other in many days. Asha helped Marlin, as they had come to call him, cut off pieces of the tuna and put them out in a bowl in the center of the group, along with mangoes and coconuts. They forgot how ragged they were and how close they'd come to giving up. It all seemed very pleasant, and if Afutu wasn't cured, at least he ate well.

While they were talking, Marlin jumped up, saying, "I must excuse myself. We have other guests arriving!" With that, he ran out to his skiff, poled away from the beach and through the rocks, and disappeared into the mist hanging over the water.

The group stared.

"Well," Naaba said.

"I knew there was something wrong there," Sheeah said. "There's just something strange about him."

"It's hard to be too critical of someone who saved us from crashing on the rocks, and then fed us," Asha commented.

"How can he even see out there? I can't see a thing."

"Maybe his scouts saw something."

"And where are they?"

"*I* don't know."

And so the exchange went, round and round, because no one knew any more than the others. But the dinner was excellent, and after a while, they talked about other things and forgot their host was out alone on the misty sea.

Sometime later, Afutu was about to say that he felt very heavy, especially his legs, as if they weighed as much as tree trunks, but while he was trying to figure out how to explain the sensation, Naro jumped up, pointing.

"A boat! He's brought back another boat! It looks like a family."

The rest stood, trying to see what he was seeing, and trying to follow his arm as he pointed to it, but the mist had moved in and they couldn't tell whether they were really seeing something or just guessing.

On the boat, three adults and two children clung wearily to the side of the boat, looking up at the sheer walls of rock that faced them. When one of the adults looked straight ahead and saw the group of people on the beach, she screamed, a piercing shriek that carried across the sands and up into the rocks.

As Marlin brought the boat onto the beach, Naaba and Asha, jerked into understanding at the same moment, ran across the rocks and sand without thinking of where they were putting their feet, only about the boat and the people in it. They yelled as they ran, but no one could understand what they were saying, with the noise of the surf on the rocks. Frightened, the children backed away from these specters, and the adults put their arms around them to protect them, but then the smaller one stopped still, her head tilted to one side.

"Asha?"

"Naaba?"

The passengers had hardly struggled out of the boat before Asha and Naaba swept the whole bunch up into their arms.

"It's wonderful to see you," Aminata cried. "Absolutely, unbelievably fine."

When they had recovered slightly, Asha dragged them over to meet the rest of the group. Marlin excused himself, saying he had people he needed to see before dark. After the two groups had a chance to settle down, exchange news, and eat something, Naaba asked Aminata why she'd screamed when she saw them.

"I didn't scream. Maybe it was a cry of surprise, but not a scream."

"Of course not," Naaba said, his head tilted to the side. "Actually, it wasn't even you we heard. It was one big monk seal down on the rocks arguing with another."

"All right," she sighed, "the truth is, I thought you were cannibals. To me, it looked like parts of people left on the beach," she pointed to Abran and Afutu, "and the rest on the spit."

Everyone laughed, but a cold chill went down Asha's spine, so strong that it left her shivering. "Sheeah's right!" she yelled at the group.

No one found this remark more surprising than Sheeah. "I was? About what?"

"Him. Marlin."

"Aren't you the one who said we couldn't really complain about someone who saved our lives," Naaba pointed out, "and then gave us a fine dinner?"

"I know. I did. But there's something very strange here. If this is the main beach on the island, why isn't anyone else here? Where are the other boats? Where are the scouts he mentioned? If a storm comes, we're in -"

Abran stirred. "Now that you mention it, I'm starting to feel trapped here, especially with sunset not far away. Could you get me out of here?"

There was an edge in his voice, a hint of panic that drove them all to action, digging away at the sand that seemed to have gotten much heavier now that they were trying to lift it out of the hole rather than pushing it in.

"Me too," Afutu added bluntly.

So they split into two groups, digging away at the two buried men, but it took a long time to free them. The old sun was already swallowed up by the mist on the sea by the time they were completely dug out. Then, Naro had to climb down on one side of Afutu and Emai on the other, so they could link hands under him and lift him out. Naro and Sohko knelt by the top of the hole, waiting to take Afutu under the arms to help him out. But in the transfer, Naro's hand slipped and Afutu lurched sideways. At that moment, Afutu swung his leg out to brace his fall but ended up landing in a heap on Emai.

"Sorry," Afutu said, automatically.

"Sorry?" Emai shouted. "For what? You just moved your own leg! Didn't you notice?"

"And I really hurt," Afutu admitted.

Dashona was sitting, watching all of this, her eyes flooding with tears.

"So, what was that about me being right?" Sheeah broke in.

Shaking his head, Naaba rocked back on his heels. "I don't know. All we've had is good fortune since we met him. It's hard for me to see him as anything but strange, and we've all been accused of being that. Well, some of us have. But I agree about the beach. It's a terrible place to be in a storm. If a surge came up, these two would have drowned before we could have gotten them out. We need to look farther inland for a place to stay, and we should do it now, while there's a little bit of light left."

The youngest members of the group had grown tired of sitting around while the adults talked about the old village and the old times, and who had a relative or friend in a village up the river or on the shore, and how they might know someone who knew someone who knew them, and so on. Aminata had introduced them as her own children, so there was no mention of Akin or the battles on the beach, and everyone had been very kind to them. But they had a new place to explore, and they were finally out of the boat, so they wandered off on their own, as they had always done, and no one paid any attention. By the time they returned, Naaba was organizing the effort to get off the beach.

"There are huts all set up for us," Deka said. "They have mats and water gourds and an outside hearth. There's even a torch burning in a holder outside the entrance."

Naaba stopped still. "Really?"

"Well, we saw three of them, but there are probably more. We thought people were living there, but when we went in, there was no one there, not in any of them."

"You just walked into strange huts?"

"Well, there's no way to see in. The walls are stone, not sticks, and the thatch comes right down over the edge of the stone. We couldn't know without going in."

It was a weak excuse for invading what might have been someone else's private space, but Aminata knew only curious children would have done it, and the group needed the information. "And how far are these huts?"

"Not too far. Just up there and over a ways."

"Let's secure the boats before we go," Sohko called. "If we do get a storm, and it's been looking like it for a while, we'll lose the boats if we leave them just sitting on the beach. And we should wrap up the rest of the tuna in palm leaves and bury it with the coals."

"Don't leave Afutu and Abran alone," Asha added, pushing sand over the wrapped fish in the fire pit. She couldn't even say why, but she felt the injured men were in the most danger.

While everyone would have loved some private space, Asha's fears were enough to get them to divide the group among the three huts. They were very tired, and the idea of sleeping on something that didn't roll and pitch with the waves was very appealing.

"Drink lots of water," Asha called, as they said good-night.

"But then we'll need to get up in the middle of the night."

"Exactly. The more water the better. We'd never stay awake to keep watch, but if we're getting up regularly, someone will be aware of what's happening."

"You're probably worried about nothing. There aren't even any snakes here."

"Maybe," she nodded. "Then I'll be glad to be wrong."

CHAPTER 11
DISCOVERIES ON THE ISLAND

The night was very dark. One by one they stumbled out of the huts to urinate and stumbled back to sleep again. Naaba was tempted to tell Asha how wrong she'd been when there was a yell and a scuffle outside. Fumbling in the dark, Naaba found the palm torch they'd used earlier and struck a spark to it. By the time he'd coaxed it back to a weak flame and headed outside, there was only Naro standing there at the edge of the flat area around the huts.

"Are you all right? What's going on?"

"I was attacked. A man in a mask jumped out, from behind the rocks, I guess. I had no idea what was happening until I saw his knife coming at me. I raised my arm to deflect the knife, and he slashed me." When Naro raised his arm, the cut was still bleeding, though it didn't seem very deep.

"And then what?"

"That's the strange part. We struggled for a while, but - he didn't try very hard. I mean, he was armed; he had the advantage of almost complete surprise. He could have killed me with that knife. As we struggled, there were several times he could have struck very effectively, but he didn't."

"Did he say anything?"

"Nothing."

"Strange. You want help washing out the cut?"

"It's nothing. I'll take care of it."

In the morning, as they were talking about the attack the night before, a woman hurried into the camp, dressed in a dark patterned wrap and a light headcloth decorated with floppy stalks of yellow flowers.

"I'm so sorry. Forgive me. I know you must be terribly upset. I heard about the unfortunate incident last night. The chief has gone to pursue the attacker. Unfortunately, the poor man is crazy. He sees all visitors as threats. Of course, once visitors brought the sickness with them, but that was long ago. Please accept my apologies for this terrible event."

"Who are you?" Sheeah asked. She felt people on this island had missed some important part of their upbringing that included giving their name to people they just met.

"I'm terribly sorry. I forget. Everyone here just calls me 'Auntie.'" When there was no response from the group, she added, "But you can call me Fula, or Auntie Fula. Does that sound good?"

"It's not up to the stranger to decide whether your name is good or not," Sheeah complained. "It's just a name. It's just given, that's all."

"Where's the chief now?" Naaba said, trying to change the topic.

"Up there, on the high cliffs." She pointed to the very top of what looked like a sheer cliff wall. "You can see the outpost up there. Maybe you can't see the people, but he's up there, by the building."

They all turned to stare at the top of the cliff. There did seem to be a building perched precariously on the edge of the precipice, but it was hard to tell what else was there.

"You'll want to get cleaned up," the woman said brightly. "I'll show you the most beautiful place. Just wonderful. And the waterfall comes flying down from very high up the cliff. Very refreshing, especially after a long journey."

As soon as the woman mentioned the waterfall, Asha's mood brightened. "Can we go there now?"

Auntie nodded. "I thought you'd like it. I'll take you there. It's not very far, but it's a difficult hike because of the cliffs. Perhaps some of you could wait here while others go. Then I'll take the others."

Afutu waved them off. "Go ahead. I'll wait here."

In the end, only Naaba, Asha, Sohko and Aminata went with Auntie on the first trip. The hike was more than difficult. For people used to fairly flat ground, it was grueling. The muscles in their legs and backs ached from the endless stepping up and down. Asha would have asked the woman to stop, but no one else was saying anything, so she kept going. At one point, they had to hang on with their hands while they searched for footholds in the rock. Sweat soaked their skin and wraps, stinging their eyes. No one had brought any water, and they were so thirsty, their mouth and tongue seemed to be stuck together.

"There we are!" the woman chimed as she stepped over a jumble of rocks. Behind the sweep of her arm they looked on a land of dreams: a large green canyon enclosed by walls of stone, and, at the far end, a stream of water plunging straight down from the rocks high above to a pool below, sending up a cloud of mist that fed the profusion of flowering plants around it. Everything was green and lush, a misty softness surrounded by hard stone. On the canyon floor, different kinds of palm trees crowded against red flowering bushes. Up the rock walls, plants clung to all but the steepest slopes. In the open, dry areas, groups of dragon trees sent up their straight trunks and their sudden profusion of branches, like many serpents released from one source. Everywhere there was the fluttering of wings as birds sought out the fruits and insects in the trees.

"It's beautiful," Aminata said, while the others were still searching for words.

"I'm glad you think so," Auntie smiled. "It's fun to see it through a stranger's eyes. You know, when you live somewhere, you begin to take it for granted. But then someone comes along and reminds you." As she stepped easily over the confusion of rocks on the canyon floor, she called back, "Let's show you the waterfall. You'll like that. Oh, I know you'll enjoy that. And then, if it's all right, I'll go back and get some of your friends. It'll take a while for them to get here, so you'll have lots of time to enjoy the falls."

"Are there people living out here?" Asha asked, picking her way through the rocks.

"No," she said. "Not usually. Sometimes, I suppose, you know, for a while. But I don't think there's anyone out here now."

The closer they got to the falls, the more the thunder of the water dominated everything in the area. Up close, it was overpowering: chutes of water dropping one behind the other, fanning out as mist along the way, then drawn back into the flow, crashing into the hard rock pool at the bottom and flying back up, so the bottom of the falls was lost in the cloud of mist.

Asha was ecstatic.

"Well, enjoy!" Auntie called, over the noise of the falls. "I'll see you in a little while."

Sohko and Aminata moved off to the canyon floor, where flat rock ledges made perfect seats in the river, leaving the waterfall to Asha and Naaba. A tiny part of Asha was concerned about the strange events of the past day, but it was only a little voice, and the rest of her was singing with delight. Climbing over the rock ledge, she left her wrap behind and stepped into the pool, letting the splash cover her, the mist fill her. The stream of water was plunging down straight above her, and she lifted her arms, putting her hands together high above her head, pointing them directly into the cascade, so it parted and flowed down her from fingertips to toes. Once the water claimed her, she moved with it, through it, her arms sliding through it, her hand reaching out for Naaba, the only other who understood this dance. They moved around the center of the falling water, entwined and separated, absolutely wordless as they danced in the roaring falls. It was a dance of beauty, power, and desire. And the water surrounded them with its endless flow and spray.

When she was with him, like this, the water filling her with its power, she felt if she tilted her head back and opened her mouth, a flowering vine would grow from it, with each leaf uncurling and spreading outward, and more leaves following, and more vines and tendrils and flowers, branching through the air and filling it until it reached the open sky. There hummingbirds would flit through the vines, searching out the red flowers crowned with gold.

Later, when Naaba was bent over the pool, washing the sand off his head, Asha ran her hand over the scars on his back, wondering how much of the past people carried with them all their lives. He straightened up and took her hand in his.

"Don't worry about the past. It's part of who we are, but so is the present. So is the future. Who in our whole group has a past without trouble?"

"Other people's trouble doesn't look as bad."

"Only because you don't know it."

"Perhaps you're right," she said.

After a while, they wandered back down the river, where Sohko and Aminata were waiting for them.

"She should have been back by now," Aminata fretted.

"Who? Oh, the woman – Auntie something," Asha said, before she realized how upset Aminata was. "I'm sorry. I didn't think, about -"

"We're going to head back down," Sohko broke in. "We're fairly certain we can find the same trail. That way, if they're on the way up, we'll meet them on the trail."

"We'll find the trail," Naaba said, but he thought about how many paths there were, and how easy it would be to get lost. There were many questions he didn't voice: Were they abandoned? Intentionally? If so, were they the target, or were the others? Had the group already been split into small groups that would be easier to conquer? Had they been taken to different places? Were the children off on their own again, or did they stay with the group?

The last question was the one haunting Sohko and Aminata, and they hurried along the trail with far greater speed than the rocky terrain allowed, especially for those not familiar with it. So they slid down the rocks and stubbed their feet and kept going anyway.

CHAPTER 12
FIGURES IN RED

The children had gone wandering. There was nothing to do until the woman got back to take another group up to the waterfall, so they picked up interesting shells, including some giant conch shells that were lying on the beach. But then their old restlessness returned, and they headed down to the little stream that found its way down the rocks into the sea, splashing through it and climbing up the far bank.

"There's a trail over here," Sule called. "Pretty well-used."

Deka stepped carefully from rock to rock, following him along the path. In some points, it looked as if steps had been cut into the rock to make it easier to climb. With each turn, they went higher, quickly leaving the beach below. Looking over the edge, Deka gave a little shriek.

"Quiet!" Sule hissed.

"Sorry," she said, backing away. "Things are very high and low here."

"I've found where the path branches into two, but the tracks on this one look fresher."

"It's really steep."

"Then there must be something at the end of it that would make it worth the climb."

"You're only saying that because you want to climb it."

Her brother was already heading up the rocks, which seemed to have footholds cut into them, so she hurried along. After it went

254

up a level, the trail turned and went through a slit in the rock face, a space just wide enough for a person to slide through. On the far side, the trail opened up slightly and started rising again, until every step was up.

"Whoever walks this trail must be very strong," Sule commented, not wanting to say his legs and back ached from the climb.

"Maybe it's not a person. Maybe it's a leopard or a baboon."

"I don't think they have them here. Besides, the tracks are human."

"Then maybe -"

Sule put his hand up to silence her. In front of him, just around a jagged rock, was a stone hut with a thatched roof, perched right on the edge of the sheer rock wall. There was only one way to get in the hut without falling down the rock face.

They stopped still, listening, waiting, but nothing happened. There was no sound, no movement around the hut. Sule picked up a small stone and threw it at the hut wall. It pinged off the stone and bounced down the cliff, but still there was no response. He tried again. Nothing.

"I don't understand," Deka said. "Did the people move someplace else? Are they hunting?"

"Someone's been here. The tracks didn't make themselves. Let's go see what's inside."

"Umm, okay."

The path threaded between pointed rocks up to a gap in the rock that was covered by a rock slab. Deka willed herself not to look down as she crossed it, but she knew what it must look like. On the far side, Sule was standing right in front of the door.

"Do you think -" Deka started, but her brother was already pulling open the woven stick door and stepping inside.

The interior was dark, even with the door open, but after a while, they could make out rows of large baskets, overflowing with what looked like palm branches, fruits, stone tools, feathers, pots of clays and dyes, weavings, knives, spears. All of the area around the walls was filled with baskets, and more were hung from the ceiling. On one side was a sleeping hammock, but even it seemed to be filled with more things.

The only clear space was in the very center of the room, where a stone slab made a natural table. Hunkering down next to it, Sule studied the figures on it: tiny replicas of people, fashioned out of clay, thirteen of them.

"Deka, look. They're us." There were eleven adults and two children, each carefully made, right down to the details of build and clothing. Two of the adults were being carried by the others. There were also two tiny boats. Each figure had been rubbed with something red and sticky, and red circles were drawn over and around some of the figures. Around the whole scene, there was a thick red circle. Off to the side there were two sets of spirals, one white and one red, going opposite ways.

Deka reached out to steady herself, but at her touch, Sule jumped up. Without bothering to close the door behind them, they ran.

CHAPTER 13

THE TRICKSTER

The seven on the beach had also grown tired of waiting, so they passed the time telling stories. Dashona cleared a patch of sand and placed thirteen stones down in a pattern:

O   O   O   O

O   O   O   O   O

O   O   O   O

With a long line, she started the drawing and the story. "In a village very close to mine, there was an old man who was very wealthy, but he never laughed, so he was mean to everyone. His poor servant was often beaten for failing to do something the master hadn't even asked him to do.

So this day, the master berated him for failing to bring some meat for him to eat. 'I'm hungry, you fool. Go look for some meat.'

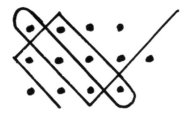

'Yes, sir,' the servant said, but instead of leaving, he sat down. 'What kind of meat would you like?'

Annoyed, the rich man answered, 'Antelope! Go get me an antelope!'

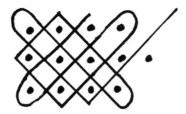

The servant nodded and said, 'You know, there's an antelope right here, in the stones. It's just hiding.'

'If there's an antelope here, I'll be glad to eat it,' the rich man scoffed, so the servant showed him where the antelope was hiding.

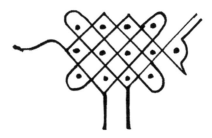

'You tricked me,' the rich man said, but he was laughing."

"The trickster!" came a voice from behind the group. "I know all about the trickster! I *am* the trickster!"

The group was struck dumb. The speaker was bouncing in place, so that the strange conglomeration of feathers, leaves, and shells he wore over his wrap floated and rattled constantly, making him the center of a blur. Over his headcloth were more feathers and leaves that fell part way over his face. On his cheeks and chin were swirling red tattoos. All parts seemed to be in motion, though of different kinds and in different directions, either up and down or side or side, or swaying.

Sheeah was hard to amaze. "Where's the woman who took our friends up to the waterfall?"

"Auntie? Oh, she'll be delayed, I'm afraid. But don't worry, your friends are fine."

"How do you know?" Sheeah demanded.

The trickster seemed a little annoyed. "Because I ran into her. Some sort of family problems. Her nephew is a troublemaker. You've probably met him already. Not all that dangerous, but just enough to be a problem. That's just how he is."

"Does he like attacking people with knives?" Naro asked.

"Well, yes, sometimes. And he throws stones at the birds sometimes. It's very sad, but every village has one, I suppose." When there was no reply, he went on. "So, would you like to hear my story while you wait for her to come back?" There was just a hint of hurt feelings in his tone, and when several people said they'd like very much to hear it, he seemed pleased. On the sand, he laid out an extravagant pattern of ninety stones lined up exactly:

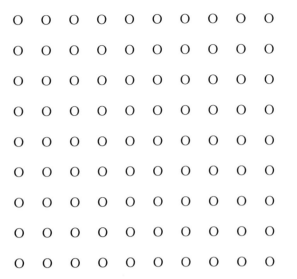

He looked up at them once, at the beginning of the story. After that, all the frantic motion in his body was stilled, and his finger flew between the stones, marking out his pattern, never stopping.

"In a village on the mainland, a poor girl went to the market to sell a basket of yams that she carried on her head. The basket was her pride and joy, beautifully decorated all around the outside with Dragon Trees. The fitted top had an intricate pattern with the sun at the center and a circle of birds around it.

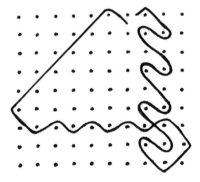

A rich man at the market saw the basket and wanted to buy it, but she didn't want to sell it, so he thought of a way to trick her into giving it to him. 'I'd like to buy your basketful of yams,' he said, holding out two strings of shells. It was a good price for the yams, so the girl agreed, taking the basket off her head in order to take out the yams.

'Oh, you can leave them in the basket,' the man said. 'You just sold me the basket, full of yams.'

"But that's not what I understood!' the girl cried.

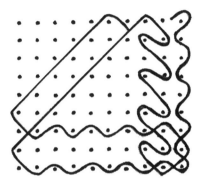

She went to the chief, but he sided with the rich man, so the poor girl went home without her beautiful basket. When her younger sister asked why she was crying, she explained about the rich man tricking her out of her basket.

The next market day, the younger sister went to the market with her beautiful basket. It was decorated with intertwined serpents around the outside and a fearsome hawk on the lid. Once again, the rich man was amazed, but when he offered to buy the basket, the girl said, 'I don't know much about counting, sir, but if you'll give me both hands full of shells, I'll sell it to you.' The man quickly agreed and held out the shell strings.

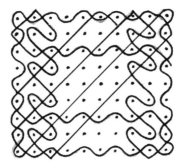

'Oh, no, sir,' the girl replied. 'You promised me two hands, full of shells.'

'Don't be absurd,' the rich man replied. 'I can't give you my hands!'

'Why? How much are they worth?' the girl asked. 'Let's ask the chief.'

The chief knew the girl had out-tricked the trickster, so he asked how much she wanted to allow the man to keep his hands.

'Only my sister's basket, and mine,' she said. 'He can keep the yams.'

'I don't want the yams!' the man cried. 'I only bought them to get the baskets.'

'Then give them back too,' the chief ordered, 'and count yourself lucky.'

So the man did."

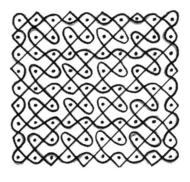

At the end of the story, the Trickster jumped up and bowed to the group as they clapped, but before anyone could comment on the story, Sohko and Aminata ran up from one side, with Naaba and Asha close behind.

"Where are they?" Aminata yelled. "What have you done with them?"

At the same time, Deka and Sule ran up from the other side.

"He's them!" Sule cried, but before he could explain, the Trickster had grabbed him by the arm and held what seemed to be a knife against the boy's side.

With a roar, Afutu was off the ground and lunging at the Trickster, even as one leg gave way underneath him. But he already had hold of the Trickster's arm and bent it backward as they both fell. Then he sprang for the man's throat, closing his huge hand on the man's throat.

"Wait!" Deka screamed. "It's only leaves! The knife! It's not real!"

Afutu released his grip slightly but refused to let the man get up, so he lay on the sand, gasping for life, his arm wrenched behind him.

"They're all him!" Sule said. "All the people. They're all him." He was out of breath, then, and faltered, his knees sagging under him.

Aminata gathered them both to her and hugged them.

Naaba stepped up to the crumpled form on the sand. "I think you have some explaining to do, and I suggest you do it quickly, while you still have some breath to talk with."

Dazed, the man sat up slowly, wincing as he moved his arm. The "knife" was folded over underneath him. It was the kind children make of folded palm leaves covered in clay.

"I wouldn't have hurt the boy," he managed, while he coughed and rubbed his throat.

"Start from where the story makes sense," Naaba ordered.

"Very little of it makes sense. Even to me or any of the others." When no one spoke, he cleared his throat and started again. "I was born here. My parents and two other families were blown here from the sea, just as you were, but they loved it here, especially this island, so they stayed. We – all the children – played all over the island, and in the water. When we were older, we visited other islands. It seemed as if it was our world, made just for us.

"Sometimes, we had visitors, desperate people who were lost on the sea. Of course, we took them in and helped them recover. Some went back to the mainland. Some went on, over the open sea. And some stayed. One of those was very sick when he arrived, and though we tried everything we knew, he died. Then the sickness spread through the village, worse than any illness we'd ever seen. First the babies died. After that, a few people tried to leave, but there was a terrible storm, and I don't think they survived.

"One by one, the people sickened and died, always in the same pattern. Except for me. Except for me. I wasn't even sick. I offered to care for the sick and dying, hoping I too would die, but I didn't. I dragged every corpse high up the cliff to a niche there, where the spirit would be free to fly back down to the green grassland in the canyon bottom, and I sang a death song for each one. But in the end, I was left here. All of them left me here. Alone.

"I used to be a person, but a person needs other persons to be, and I had none. When you're all alone, you see, there's no contrast, or balance, no reason, not even any morality. So I became, with every death, less and less. It was like waves breaking down a mound of sand on the beach: finally, there's nothing there that used to be.

"Many times, I stood on a ledge overlooking the canyon, thinking all I had to do was step off, and I could die. I stood there so often there's a path there, even now. But I didn't step off. I looked at the Dragon Tree, with its trunk that goes up more than half the tree and the hundred branches that sprout from it, and I decided that was my other, my guide.

"At first, it was a game. I'd dress up as the chatty, friendly woman who seems to be everyone's 'Auntie.' Or I'd lie around all day as the lazy man who never worked for his food but simply asked it of others. Then I became the storyteller, the ship-builder, the shaman, the trouble-maker, the musician, the cook, the warrior, the thinker, the judge, the trickster, even the chief. Male and female, old and young, bitter and enthusiastic. The more people I had, the more whole I felt. But after a while, it wasn't a game. I became these people. All of them. They're all me, just as all of the branches of the Dragon Tree are part of the whole. As a matter of fact, all my people wear part of the Dragon Tree: the spiky leaves, the droopy yellow flowers, the red resin."

"He has it all in his hut!" Sule said. "Baskets of stuff to make his costumes. "And," the boy added, "he has us. He has figures made out of clay, and they look just like us. There are eleven adults and two children. Two of the adults," he hesitated, "are injured. And there are circles of blood. Circles around some of the people, like Naaba and Asha, and Sohko and Aminata, and there are bigger circles, and everyone's smeared with blood. We saw it. It's all in his hut." Once Sule finished, he felt he had betrayed something he wasn't supposed to see, but it was his discovery, his and Deka's, and it was important.

"Well?" Naaba prompted the man.

"Yes, of course, the children are right. They assumed no boundaries and went where their curiosity took them, though perhaps an adult would have considered it prying. In any case, yes, it is as he described: a large flat stone with figures on it. But it's not human blood that forms the circles. It's the resin of the Dragon Tree. It's the same thing I've made the tattoos on my face from. It's the same thing that helped the injured men get better. I put it in the black sand, which is, in itself, very powerful. That's why your skin turned reddish after your stay in the sands. The Dragon Tree is my other; its blood is my blood. I rubbed its power on all of you, through your miniatures. I saw that everyone in this group was in pain, so I tried to increase positive power where it already was and draw it in where it wasn't. It was easy in some cases and harder in others.

"I sent Auntie to take some of you to the green canyon because I wanted you to see the waterfall, and I wanted Sohko and Aminata to have their baby delighted by the green canyon."

The group stared at him. Aminata frowned. It wasn't their way to announce a pregnancy so early. It could court bad luck to draw that much attention to it. They never even used the word until a woman was so pregnant everyone knew anyway.

"As for the storyteller, I've practiced that pattern many times, and you gave me the perfect opportunity to use it." When no one spoke, he continued, "When I first saw you, all of you, I thought we shared something. That's why I drew the Dragon's Blood circles around all of you. You only survived because of each other, yet each one of you carries a legacy of pain that cannot be eased, even with the kindness of those who care about you. You," he said to Afutu, "must have been a champion athlete. Yet what is an athlete who can no longer compete? You were robbed of your world, just as surely as I was robbed of mine. But you'll have to make a new one, my powerful friend, or you'll disappear."

Afutu didn't reply, and the air around the gathered people seemed very heavy, so the man changed his approach. "Actually, it was Sheeah who called me out first, and she never let up. She has a singular clarity of vision that I find amazing."

Sheeah stood, as if she had been waiting to be called upon to speak. "I don't have great clarity of vision, but I once thought I did. I thought I knew everything worth knowing. But I was mistaken. And now, now that I've lost everything, I don't know how to make something new. Everyone else here is better at that than I am. I left my father to die at the hands of traitors and mobs."

While the rest of the group was searching for something to say, the man replied, "I'd be happy to take you back to your village, if you'd like. I've been to the mainland, more than once, but I didn't stay. It had villages and people and life I didn't know, so I left. But I'll take you there, if that's where you want to go."

Since Sheeah seemed to be struck speechless, Deka spoke up. "What are the red and while circles on your stone table for?"

"The winds and the sea. The future. The birth of storms."

Not one to be pushed aside, Sheeah found her voice once again, and it was unusually strong. "I accept your offer. More than anything else in this world, I want to go back. If my father is dead, I can at least give him some proper commemoration. If he is alive," she faltered, "if he is alive, I'll fall at his feet and ask him to remember me with love, even though I abandoned him."

"He told you to rescue the ball players," Dashona said. "Remember?"

"It doesn't matter. I should have gone back. You people belong here, but I don't. I'm not looking for a future far from my past. I'm trying to get back to the past."

"You can't." Ayo shook her head. "There's no path back."

"I don't care. I'll find whatever's left. The shore will still be there, and the forest, and the hills. And part of my father is there, held in the memory of the land and the river." Slumping back down, she seemed smaller than they'd ever seen her.

"If you are going back to our village, Sheeah, I have a request," Dashona said. "My father told us stories about the mountains thrown into the sea, but no one believed him. I think now that he was telling the truth; I think he was here. In the chaos of the battle on the beach, I left without even saying good-bye to him. Perhaps, if you hear that he's still alive, you could tell him that I see now what he meant, about these islands, that they are full of strange magic, just as he said. But I can't go back." She stopped suddenly and said nothing else, even while the group waited for her to go on.

The silence was full of unspoken words. Finally, Emai spoke. "I'll go back, too."

In the middle of this confusion, Deka said, "Perhaps we should go back, too. You'll have your own family soon, and maybe our father -"

Sohko wrapped both children in his big arms. "You *are* our family. You'll always be our family. And if you leave us, you'd take my joy with you."

"And mine," Aminata added, joining the group.

"Well, the Trickster certainly managed to stir things up!" the man cried, but a dark look from Afutu stopped him.

The charged atmosphere lingered around the group, even after the decisions were made. It was one thing to want to leave; it was another to leave people who had become closer than family. Even Sheeah felt it. "I've never known people like these, people who'd help me out," she commented to Ayo, "even when there's nothing in it for them."

Ayo had her own concerns, but she didn't voice them. All her life, she'd felt she'd been blown by the wind to wherever it was she'd landed. There was no spot of ground she called home, so she was at home wherever she was, but it wasn't home the way Sheeah felt it, where the land held a memory of her that would comfort her. Ayo floated, and at the moment, she'd welcome being taken away to somewhere else. There was something very close here, as if the rock walls trapped her. If the gods were stirring up the winds, as the Trickster had said, it would be fine with her.

CHAPTER 14
A FAREWELL FEAST

Once the decisions were made, Ayo was the only one anxious to leave. The others found many things that needed to be said, or done, before they could part ways from people they'd come to care about deeply. And, there was the island to explore, with all its wonders. The day after all of the truths on the beach, "Auntie" reappeared, ready to take another group up to see the green canyon and the waterfall. Others chose to walk up the trails, or to go fishing, or to see the volcano's crater, or simply to spend the day with people they'd probably never see again. For the first time since she left home, Sheeah was the center of attention, and she loved it. The Trickster, the man of a hundred faces, had the most trouble with the impending departure, and he switched back and forth between different personalities frequently, but no one seemed to mind very much, except perhaps Afutu, who had taken a special dislike to the man, no matter which person he was at the moment.

It was Aminata who said there should be a feast to mark their farewell to the island. While the island didn't have the same wealth of fruits, vegetables, and game as the mainland, it had all the riches of the sea. Naro, a fine diver, happy in almost any kind of water, led a group out into the waters off shore, where they explored the extravagantly colored corals.

On the shore, Afutu sat off by himself, uninvolved in the preparations. After a while, Emai joined him, finding a relatively comfortable flat rock to sit on. "I'm glad someone's protecting the sand," he commented drily.

Afutu didn't reply, so they sat, watching the divers surfacing and diving down again. After finding spiny lobsters and giant conchs for the feast, they were headed back to the beach when someone called out something about sea turtles, and all the heads bobbed under the water once again. When they had all surfaced, there was a cry of "shark," and they all had to look again, even though Naro thought it was probably a good moment to head in to shore. When they did climb out at the beach, they were full of chatter about the wonders they'd seen. Asha, Ayo, and Dashona stepped unsteadily onto the beach, laughing and wringing the salt water out of their hair.

"I think Asha had an ancestor who was really a fish," Emai commented. "It's just that no one knew because she had legs when she was on land."

"Then she's lucky," Afutu said. "She'll always have a clear sense of what she loves." When Emai didn't answer, Afutu turned to face him. "Why are you going back?"

"It's hard to say. Dashona's part of it." He glanced at Afutu briefly and looked away. That part was hard to talk about. "But there's more. I want to go back to my village."

"Why? You think Sheeah's right, that the hills and trees remember you?" His tone was bitter. "Do you think those people care about you?"

"I don't know. I don't even know who survived the battle on the beach and the Rhino's insane plan to remake the world. But there's something there, some tattered shreds of something that once was, and I need to see for myself."

"Do you know who tried to leave you for dead?"

"Both of them. I was getting dressed for the ballgame. You know how that's always a special time. I always try to clear my mind, so it's just energy inside. I was standing there, with my eyes closed, when these two men approached me. They were great supporters of mine, always cheering for me at the games, coming around afterward, telling me how well I played. It was a little surprising to see them before a game, but I thought they'd come by to wish me good luck. When they started talking, I realized they'd lost a lot from their wagers on the Feather Shoot. After a while, I said I needed to get dressed for the ballgame, and they said they understood completely and started to leave. Then, just as an afterthought, it seemed, one offered me a small cup of ginger plum wine. 'Just a sip,' he said, 'to calm your nerves.' I don't like to drink before a game, but it was such a small cup, it seemed harmless, so I tossed it back in one swallow. I knew immediately that I'd made a mistake. My body refused to do anything I asked it to. My arms were useless - just heavy weights; my legs buckled under me. But even when I had I slumped down to the floor, I could hear them talking.

"'The big man's not so big now,' one said. The other kicked me in the gut. I'd never done anything to hurt either one of these men. I hardly knew them.

"When they stuffed my mouth, they laughed. In all the time I've spent going over those events in my mind, that's the one that still stuns me. Why would they hate me enough to try to kill me, and then laugh?"

Afutu pushed himself into a more comfortable position. "Because you're a champion, and they're not. When you walk through the village, everyone recognizes you. 'Oh, there's Emai, the champion,' the people cry as you walk by. But no one does that when those two men walk by, so they grow to hate you."

"But they always complimented me, cheered me on," Emai mused, "until they turned."

"Because you'd lost. When you were winning, if they were cheering for you, they were winning too. In some way, you made them more than they were. When you lost, you took that away."

"That's absurd. No one's more or less because someone else wins or loses a game."

"You're wrong. As soon as people invest their treasure, or their energy, in a player, or a team, they stand to win or lose, just as surely as the players."

"But I've lost before. No one wins every single contest. They never attacked me before. No one ever did."

"No," Afutu agreed. "They were used. It would be easy for someone like the Rhino, or Akin, to stir up trouble by using the locals. The resentment was right below the surface anyway. All he'd have to do is approach these men, tell them he had an important job for them that would bring them great honor and at the same time allow them to get back at someone they resented. Maybe there was even a small payment."

"Probably. Then they could be war heroes." Mindlessly, Emai dug holes in the black sand and piled up the extra sand. "You know, friend, I almost died then. And I know the exact moment."

"From lack of air?"

"No. From lack of will. It was the same choice you faced on the boat. I don't know how Asha and Naaba knew I was alive. If there was still a breath of life in me, it was very, very small. I felt I was sliding away, to somewhere else. Then, when they brought me back, it was only pain all around, and I wanted to go back to where it was easier."

Afutu said nothing, and they both sat silently on the black sand by the edge of the sea. Finally, Afutu said, "Then why would you go back to your village? What if those men are still there?"

"They probably are. They're too mean to die. But there's something else I want there, not revenge. Those men don't matter. They never did."

"Then what does?"

Emai started forming the piles of sand into winding shapes, twisting around the edges of the holes he'd dug. "The way I see things."

"Don't you see things the same way you always did?"

"No, I don't think I do. Take this beach. Do you see it the same way today as you did when you first landed?"

"No," Afutu admitted. "But things are different now."

"Yes, but the beach is the same. What you saw wasn't just the beach but the beach as seen through yourself."

"You can't see any other way. Your eyes are part of you, and how you feel is part of you, so of course you'll see something colored by your own feelings. Isn't that why people love the look of their village tree, or the path by the river, or the hill above town? Isn't that why Sheeah wants to go back, to see all those places she remembers?"

"Yes, of course, we all like to see familiar places, and things, and faces. But some of us need to see a different world."

Afutu's head snapped up as he glared at Emai. "Is this a lecture meant for me? Sort of like that jackal dispensing his advice like sweets to children – here's some for you, and here's some for you. Thanks, but I don't need it. I already know my world's gone."

"No, friend, your world is right here, just as the beach is. You just don't want to look at it. I want to go back, but not so I can look upon what used to be. I'll leave that search to Sheeah. But it's my land, and I want to see it as it is right now. I suspect it's hurting. Dreams gone wrong do terrible damage everywhere, and great dreams gone wrong destroy people's lives for generations. Next to that, my pain and my failure don't mean much."

"You never failed!" Afutu pounded his fist into the sand.

"To me, and to many others, my loss to you in the Feather Shoot was a failure. My lack of will to live was another. I admit these, but I'm trying to learn to see something much bigger, and much harder to judge." He formed a serpent head at one end of the twisting shape. "It's hard for athletes to see beyond themselves. We're trained to be focused on ourselves. We're always judging our own performance, always a little dissatisfied with some aspect of it.

273

So we push ourselves toward the impossible goal of perfection. As long as we're competing, and we're beating the others, and we're being told how fine we are, we can ignore the little voice in our heads that's telling us we're missing something."

"What are you getting at – that competing was never worthwhile? I don't believe it. You loved to play the game well. You even said so. Are you denying that?"

"Not at all. I did love to play the game well. But I don't think I'll play it again."

"I'd give everything I ever owned to be able to play again, even once."

"Why?"

"Because I'm nothing now."

"You're everything now that you were then. It's like the beach. You're just seeing it differently."

"Then I hate the beach," he said sullenly.

"And I thought Sheeah was spoiled," Emai sighed. "You believed all that nonsense people told you about how great you were because you could play ball. You simply were, with or without the ballgame. The people who fawned over you weren't your friends. Your friends are still here. You're still here. Look through bigger eyes."

But the conversation was ended, and Emai worked on his sand serpent, trying his best to ignore Afutu's angry silence. Then he got up and left.

After Emai left, Afutu closed his eyes so hard that red light shot across the inside of his eyelids. Behind him, hidden behind the rocks, the children waited, unsure what to do. They'd been playing among the stones when the conversation started. Not wanting to interrupt, they'd stayed where they were. But now, they'd heard things they knew the men wouldn't say except to each other. They could try to retreat, hoping Afutu wouldn't notice, or they could step forward and say something. As Sule glanced at his sister, she shrugged and pointed. They might as well get it over with.

"Afutu? Sir?" Sule started, walking up.

When there was no reply, Deka tried. "Thank you for defending my brother from the crazy Trickster. It must have been nice to know your legs are coming back." That struck her as strange, as if his legs had left for a little while and then decided to return. "I mean -" but nothing better presented itself, and the sentence hung in the air, unfinished.

"The truth is," Sule said, "that if you knew who we really are, you probably wouldn't have bothered trying to save me."

That made Afutu open his eyes. "Why? Who are you? I thought you were Sohko and Aminata's children."

"No," Sule said, quietly. "Our mother died when we were very young. Our father is Akin, the Black Rhino's first lieutenant."

"The one who organized the collapse of the alliance, the battle on the beach, the carnage," Afutu snapped. "Not much of a heritage."

"Actually," Deka spoke up, "he said the people would do in themselves. Then new people could take over and create a whole new world. It was the Rhino's vision, but Papa agreed with it, especially at the end. We tried to talk to him, but he didn't have time for us, so Sohko and Aminata took care of us. We just thought if you wanted someone to be mad at for what happened to you, that you could be mad at us. Then you wouldn't have to be mad at everyone." She hadn't really planned to say all that, and her brother was giving her a very strange look, but the words had flown out of her mouth and couldn't be returned.

"Go away," Afutu said, turning away from them.

"What were you thinking?" her brother hissed as they hurried back up into the rocks.

"I don't know," she cried. "He just seemed so sad. Sometimes, if you can blame someone, it's a little better."

"We're lucky he didn't kill us both."

"I don't think he would."

Away from the shore, Aminata was busy organizing the feast. The divers and shore walkers had brought back conch, crab, goose barnacles, squid, whelks, mussels and clams, as well as purple and green seaweed. From inland, they'd picked peppergrass and some tiny sour plums, red palm nuts, and coconuts, and Aminata now sat surrounded by the raw materials of the feast.

"Like some help?" Asha asked, as she walked up.

"I was terribly afraid no one would ask," Aminata laughed.

"I'll find you some more hands."

Almost everyone was given a task, from fire-building to water-hauling. The children gathered bundles of seaweed and grasses to use in steaming the shellfish and filled water gourds at the stream. The Trickster disappeared for a while and then returned, grinning and joking. Emai made torches from palm branches stripped of their leaves and stuffed with oil nuts.

Naaba was working stone, preparing gifts. The slow, careful work always helped him clear his mind, and he found this next step on their journey worrisome. He understood the forest, or at least something about it, but the endless expanse of open water was different, completely different. But there wasn't a lot of choice. Neither he nor Asha wanted to go back to the life they'd left behind.

Emai sat down next to him. "You've got a skilled hand with stone."

Naaba smiled briefly as he worked. "It keeps me from having to clean seaweed." When he'd struck a chip off one side, he stopped and looked at Emai. "Be careful with the Trickster. He's become all those people now, and some of them are dangerous."

"I know. I thought about that when Sheeah said she'd go with him."

"So you're going along to protect her?"

"No, though that might happen. I'm going because I want to." His tone was a little defensive, after his talk with Afutu.

"I could see that," Naaba agreed. But he didn't, really.

"Afutu thinks I'm crazy to go back," Emai went on. "But I belong there, even if it's a wreck now. That's my land. It's where I'm supposed to be."

"In a way, I envy that," Naaba said, picking his stone back up again, looking it over, and deciding where to make the next cut. "I was just thinking about how little I know about the sea. Out here, on a little island, it's different. It's reversed: the land's tiny and the sea is huge. People are just dots."

"You'll do fine," Emai said. "You're a natural explorer. It's just water this time instead of land. You'll have a life of discovery, while others are bored with the routine of life in their little village."

Surprised, Naaba set the stone aside. "Thank you. Your words give me courage."

"Then it was already there. I just reminded you of it. By the way, I never got the chance to thank you and Asha for saving my life. That was the darkest day of my life, and you two came along at the darkest moment of that day." He stopped and put his arm on Naaba's.

Letting the stones fall to the ground, Naaba returned the gesture. "I hope our paths cross again sometime," he said. "I feel as if I'm losing a friend I just met."

The feast was actually a day-long affair. The groups came and went, visiting as the food cooked, but there was a different energy in the air. Once they had all decided to leave the island, it suddenly became more precious, as did the opportunity to wander around it at will. Soon, they'd all be back in the boat and the cramped life it dictated. The children were sent to gather more seaweed, but they wound up playing along the shore, hitting coconuts with a stick. Others found private time, with or without a companion. Auntie showed up periodically, effusively complimenting Aminata on the preparations.

"She's like my strange uncle, who used to show up at the family gatherings and embarrass everyone," Aminata said to Ayo as they watched 'her' bringing in bunches of flowers.

"Strange Uncle is probably another one of his personalities. We just haven't met him yet," Ayo commented without looking up from the very thin mat she was working on.

The sun was getting old by the time Aminata declared the feast ready and set out the bowls of steaming shellfish in beds of seaweed. The conch had been pounded flat and wrapped around peppergrass, then briefly steamed. Whole steamed crabs and lobsters sat on the flat rock next to bowls of goose barnacles and whelks. Calling everyone over, she presided over the opening of the feast, offering a cup of fairly raw but intoxicating brew the Trickster had provided.

"This is to celebrate where we've come from and where we're going," she said, raising her cup. "Personally, I feel lucky to have met each one of you. 'It's the wealthy man, or woman, in my case, who has a fine travel companion' and I couldn't have chosen any finer."

"To the travelers and the journey!" Emai called.

"And to the maker of the feast!" Asha said.

"Can we eat now?" Sule asked his sister in a momentary pause in the toasts.

As they sat in a circle around the flat rock covered with dishes of food, conversation was set aside in favor of eating and passing bowls and eating and passing more bowls. Gradually, the fine foods vanished and in their place grew a large pile of empty bowls and shells. By the time Asha brought out the sour plums with honey, the diners claimed they couldn't possibly eat anything else, but somehow, all of the tiny plums disappeared.

By then, the old sun was close to the sea, and Naaba lit the torches.

"We'll need one behind the screen," Ayo said. "Can you set it up?"

In front of the torches, Ayo hung her thin mat, then set up a shorter thick mat for her to hide behind while she worked the leaf shapes against the screen.

"I hope this works," she whispered to Dashona. "If the torch is too close, it'll burn me and the mat. If it's too far away, we'll lose the shapes."

"It'll be fine," Dashona said, without much faith in the statement. The shadow screen seemed like a good idea when they went over it in the daylight, but soon Ayo wouldn't be able to see what she was putting up against the screen without getting her own head in the picture.

"Tell us a story, Dashona!" a voice called.

"A story worthy of the feast!"

She was going to say something about how difficult all this was, and how new they were to it, but she didn't. She was a storyteller, and she'd tell a story. She stepped up, next to the screen, standing to the side so everyone could see the screen, but so she could still know what was appearing on it.

"A long time ago," she started, "on this very island, a young woman was tired of doing her chores. She looked up at the high cliffs around her and wondered what it would be like to climb them." On the screen, Ayo held up a large piece shaped like a mountain, and a curling cloud on top of it. "She thought maybe, if she climbed all the way to the top of the mountain, it would pierce the clouds. From there, she could see right into the heavens, where the gods stored the star figures during the day. So she climbed up the mountainside." Ayo worked a small figure up the side of the mountain. "It was very hard climbing, and the girl slipped several times, barely catching herself on the sheer rock. When she got to the top, she had to climb on her hands and knees because the point was so sharp. At one point she saw a brilliant blue stone, and she tried to pick it up, but the movement was enough to upset her balance, and she fell off the point of the rock, sliding down one side. She would have perished, except an eagle had built a nest there, close to the sun, and the large platform of twigs caught her."

Ayo moved the mountain off the screen and put up the aerie, complete with young. "The girl had hardly caught her breath when she noticed there were eaglets in the nest, large, awkward babies with open mouths. Soon, the eagle would be returning to feed the babies, but there was no way for her to leave; the nest was built on the edge of a sheer cliff." At this moment, Ayo moved in the eagle she'd made of folded palm leaves, starting close to the screen and then pushing it back toward the torch, so it seemed to get bigger and bigger. "When the mother eagle returned, she picked up the girl in her enormous talons, carrying her away while the babies screamed. Far away the eagle took her, past the edge of the island, out over the sea." Ayo took down the aerie and had only the bird showing on the screen, getting smaller and smaller. "Then the eagle dropped her, and she fell into a rainbow that was stretched over the water. Dragging her feet, she slowed herself down, sending out splashes of magenta and blue and green as she went. But the rainbow took her all the way down into the sea." Ayo removed everything from the screen and waited.

"Farther and farther she sank, until she hit the bottom. There, she wandered around, astounded by the coursing sea, until a manta ray swam up to her. Its long sides were flapping slowly up and down, pushing it through the water, but when it reached her, it flipped her up on top of it and took off swimming again. The girl had to hang on to the front of the ray's wings to stay with it." Ayo twisted the ray shape slightly and moved it closer to the screen. "It took her to a palace, a black palace on the bottom of the sea. At first, the girl didn't even see it, but then a bit of light from the surface glinted off one of its decorated walls. They were carved with frightening shapes: huge cats and serpents and terrible fish with rows of long teeth. Terrified, the girl clung to the ray, but it shook her off and set her down.

"At that moment, the old sun died, and she looked up as it shattered into golden bits near the surface, then turned redder and darker as it fell. When it reached the bottom of the sea, it turned into a jaguar." Ayo held up the jaguar, but close to the screen, so it seemed very small, then gradually made it appear larger, as if it was getting closer. "As the girl watched, the jaguar walked into its palace, and every wall glistened with shining black light. Later, it came back out. Everywhere it went, the same glittering black light surrounded it, spreading out across the seafloor and the schools of fish as it passed. Mesmerized, the girl followed. After a long time, the jaguar leapt up to a strange rock formation, climbing up higher and higher. The girl struggled to follow, but she wasn't as agile on the rocks, and the jaguar got farther and farther ahead of her.

"Eventually, she came to a sea cave. She could just see the glittering dark light down the way, so she headed toward it in the darkness of the cave. The opening got smaller and smaller, as the floor rose. Then she knew she must be on land, for the water grew less and less. There was air now, though it was the still air of a cave. But always, ahead of her, was the strange dark light, so she knew the jaguar must be there.

"As she moved through the narrow opening of the cave, she felt the river at her feet, and she followed its course all the way to the opening of the cave, in the forest. Far ahead, she could see the jaguar as it prowled the land, the lord of the dark. But she was very tired, and she leaned against a tree to close her eyes just for a moment.

"When she awoke, she looked all around for the jaguar, but all she could see was a faint glow far ahead of her. She ran toward it, trying to catch up to it, but when she got closer, the jaguar turned once to look at her and then, with a mighty leap, hurled himself into the sky. There he burst into flame." Ayo put the sunburst over the figure of the jaguar.

"But the girl had seen what no human can see, the Jaguar in his Night Palace, so the gods changed her into a pied crow." Only the pied crow appeared on the screen. "Now you can see her, black head and tail, and white breast, because she belongs to both night and day. She wanted to tell the story of what she'd seen, but only one person heard it before her voice was changed to squawks that no one can understand. But she'll try to tell you anyway. You can hear her at dawn, still trying to explain, but no one pays any attention, except to yell at her to be quiet."

At the end of the story, no one said anything, and Dashona thought it had all been a terrible mistake, trying to add the shadows. The torch hadn't been bright enough, or the screen too thick. Or maybe the pictures ruined it for people. Or maybe the story itself wasn't the right choice. After all, she'd only told it once before and there were others that might have worked better.

At that point, Naro swept her up in his arms, and the whole group broke into loud cheers. Almost the whole group. Even in the torchlight, Afutu's dark look was clear.

Later, when different groups were sitting around the fire, talking, Emai approached Dashona, asking if she could spare a moment to talk to him. When they had walked a distance away from the fire, he sat on a flat rock and invited her to join him. He didn't bother going back over the past or bringing up his proposal to her. He didn't even feel uncomfortable, now, talking to her, but he loved her still.

"You need to keep working on Afutu," he said, taking her hand in his. "He's a good man underneath his anger, and your touch and your stories will heal him. But when he responds to you as a man, stop and back away; have nothing to do with him. Do you understand what I mean?"

"Yes, but I don't understand why."

"Because he has to earn your love. Otherwise, he'll never understand its value." It was more than Emai had planned to say, but it was the truth. "I wish you happiness," he said before he released her hand and bid her a good night.

As he walked away, Dashona shuddered. Suddenly, more than anything else, she wanted him to stop and turn around, or at least glance back at her, so she could run up to him, wrap her arms around him, and tell him that she'd been all wrong, that it was all clear now, that she finally saw what had been there all along.

"Emai!"

He didn't reply.

With a strangled cry, she fell forward, her head in her hands. "Why am I always so stupid?" she wailed. "A good man loves me, but do I care about him? Oh no, I wait for a stupid lump of self-centered misery who cares about nothing and no one except himself. Just a spoiled baby, crying because he can't play ball. He's got one leg that works, or would work, if he'd bother doing anything about it, but does he? Oh no, all he does is moan and get angry." She stood up, saying very loudly, "No, why should I choose happiness when I can have this ungrateful louse to ruin every day? What girl wouldn't want that? What girl wouldn't hope for a man who never even says hello to her or thanks her for saving his sorry life when all he wanted was to die? Isn't that what women want? To suffer?" With a scream, she pulled at her hair and staggered up the rocks. "After all, that's the way it should be, right? You give everything you have to someone who doesn't care, doesn't notice, and certainly doesn't respond. No, no, he just sits in his miserable little world day after day, feeling so sorry for himself that he poisons the air around him. 'Oh, poor me,' he thinks, 'I can't play ball anymore.' Well, you know what? Learn to live with it, because I, for one, am tired of it. I'm tired of - of nothing, of nothing at all." She walked along the path in the dark, stubbing her feet on the rocks. In front of her, the rock face shot straight up into the sky, and she climbed up it, putting her hands out in front of her, moving automatically, as her mind raced. "That's always how it goes for me, always nothing. I'm empty, and I sought the love of an empty man." She laughed strangely. "Then we could have empty children, and their skin would be so thin, it would be transparent, and there'd be nothing inside, so they'd be like shells of people, with the outside inside them, all stuffed with trees and water and sky, but no people in there." Higher and higher she climbed into the darkness. "Maybe there are stars up here," she muttered as she looked up. "I always wondered what they'd be like up close." In front of her, she felt a ledge open up, and she sat on the edge, her feet dangling into space. "I want a man," she announced to the night air, "and I'll seduce the first one I see. I know how. I have the power of touch. I don't care who it is, and I don't care what happens. It's all a joke anyway, no matter how hard you try. You might as well have something to show for it." She leaned over the edge and tried to see into the murky darkness in front of her. "Or I could just jump off here. That'd be a lot like a seduction: a momentary thrill, with me thinking that I know something or I'm in control of something." She collapsed into tears. "But I'm not. I'm not in control of anything. And I don't know anything at all."

"Then maybe we could start there," a voice said, far below her, "because I don't know anything either, and everything I used to know has been ripped out from underneath me."

CHAPTER 15
GIFTS

Farewell gifting is not a requirement; it's a luxury. Those who have much can give much. Those who don't may give a little something or nothing at all. However, there's always a sense of pride in giving an extraordinary gift. It might not be the most expensive, but it's the most impressive. Some gifting is done in private; some in front of the whole crowd. Sheeah liked the public version. Most of the treasures she had taken from her father's house had survived the trip, so she had a lot to give away. Oddly, she began with the Chief, holding out to him the mahogany box with the lion carved on the lid. "This is for you," she said, "but before you take it, I want you to tell me what you were called, first, long ago."

He looked at her, startled. "Chahuk," he said, after a moment.

"Chahuk," she repeated, as she handed him the box.

For the first time, the man of a hundred voices seemed to have none at his disposal. He ran his hand over the carving, opened the box and closed it again. Clearing his throat, he began, "And I have something for you, actually for all of you."

Slightly disappointed that the gift was for everyone rather than just for her, Sheeah said, "That's very nice. You can show us after I'm done." With that, she headed over to Afutu, offering him the carved ebony staff. She was going to say something, but the only thing she could think of was how it was just as well that they hadn't gotten together when she thought she wanted him more than anything else in the world, but she knew that wouldn't sound good at all, so she just smiled as she handed him the staff, and he nodded in return. For the children, she had small ivory pieces carved into an antelope and an elephant. For Asha and Aminata, the beautifully decorated calabashes. For Dashona, the four-color woven wrap. Again, she couldn't think of much to say, except that there seemed to be a very long, hard road ahead of her and Afutu, but that wasn't the sort of thing she could say, so she smiled, and Dashona smiled in return, for it really was a very beautiful weaving. To the men, she gave polished obsidian or agate pieces, and to Ayo, she gave the Fairy-blue Flycatcher feathers. "I thought you could make something beautiful out of them," she said, and it was the truth. To the whole group, she left the container of salt and the rest of the millet "for the journey ahead." It was a splendid gifting, all in all.

The children gave out interesting shells they had found on the beach, including strings of banded cone shells and several giant conch shells that Naro, Abran, and Emai knew how to prepare and play. Since each shell had a slightly different note, they made a sonorous harmony when the long notes sounded together.

Ayo had made sleeping mats for everyone, as well as some baskets. Aminata and Asha had dried seaweed and fish so it was easily transported, and put honey in lengths of palm branch sealed with beeswax. Afutu and Abran had made fishing spears to go with the barbed darts Naaba had made. Naro had gathered abalone shells, which he gave to everyone, and an abalone pearl, which he gave to Dashona.

Suddenly, Dashona realized she was the only one not involved in the gifting; it had completely escaped her mind. "I'm sorry. I – I haven't anything for anyone."

Sheeah waved away her concern. "Don't be ridiculous. You've been giving gifts to us every day."

"Are you done now? I also have some gifts. Two, actually." Chahuk was heading inland as he said it, motioning for the group to follow him. The footing was rough, with piles of rock underfoot. "They're boats," he added.

"Not very good country for boats," Sohko remarked, as he picked his way through the jumble of stone.

"Actually, it's the *best* country for the *storage* of boats," Chahuk replied. "On the coast, the boats would be damaged by waves and wind, or the violent storms we get sometimes. But here, as you can see, they're in very nice shape." He turned around a large standing stone, and pointed.

The group was speechless. No one had seen such beautiful boats before. Not even Kofi's famous boat builders made boats like these. The two boats, held up by support beams, were about 9 ½ arms long, gleaming deep red, inside and out, with a bowsprit that curved up slightly into a serpent's head, and a shorter one on the stern that ended with the serpent's tail. Where the serpent's tail met the boat, the handle of a large steering paddle was threaded through an arched opening. The bow was pointed, the stern flattened, except for rounded edges. A heavy wooden fin, an arm and a half deep, ran half the length of the bottom, connected by fitted wooden pegs. The interior of the boat had been burned out, then finished and supported by ribs. Both the bow and stern areas had holes drilled in them and pegs fitted through, to allow tarps to be attached, and the center had a cross beam with a square cut-out in the center. A line of serpent designs ran the length of the boat, just above the waterline.

"The mast can be set up in the center beam and rigged with a mat to catch the wind and make the boat go faster. Both fore and aft can be set up as storage compartments, when needed. Naturally, the paddle-hole covers along the side of the boat can be removed for easy paddling as conditions require. And the keel fin can be removed, if you're dealing with shallow water, but it's not easy."

"Mast? Wind?" Naaba started. Somehow, things had gone very quickly.

"So, do we get to go back to the mainland in one of these?" Sheeah asked, "You and Emai and I?"

"Oh, no, these are their boats. You'll be going in my boat. It's very nice; I'm sure you'll like it."

"I like these," she said quietly.

"Well, we'll need to move all three of them to the beach. It'll take everyone's help, even with the bracing and the rolling logs. I'll get the logs set up."

The stunned group tried to mobilize, but it was hard for them to stop looking at the boats.

Naro was running his hand along the inside of the hull with a touch as soft as a lover's. "It's all polished," he said, to no one in particular.

Once they had made their decision, Chahuk, Emai, and Sheeah were anxious to leave. After hurried and difficult goodbyes, they pushed their boat into the water. Sheeah waved as Emai rowed away from the island and Chahuk raised the center sail.

As they headed out past the rocks and into the open sea, Asha sighed. "It feels empty, as if most of the residents of the island just left."

Ayo gathered up her feathers and watched the boat grow smaller. "In a way, they did."

While the others went back to their preparations, Naro studied the boat as Chahuk swung the lower edge of the mat from one corner of the stern to the other. Since the wind was coming toward him, he couldn't put the mat full to the wind, or it would push the boat back toward the island. Instead, he went from side to side, in a zigzag, making the wind hit the mat obliquely, and rush past, pulling the boat forward at an angle. While Naro had often seen boaters add a mat to catch the wind when it was behind them, he had never seen someone trick the wind into helping, even when it wasn't.

"We need to take the boats out!" Naro shouted, but only Afutu and Abran were still on the beach.

"Let's start with one of them," Afutu said, setting his staff down on the sand. He had watched Chahuk too; like Naro, he thought it seemed so easy, so intuitive. A boater who could use the wind that way, no matter which way it blew, could go anywhere.

"Fine with me," Abran chimed in. "Pick one."

Afutu pointed to the closer of the two, and the others released it from its braces. Leaning on the edge of the boat as he hobbled out into the water, Afutu considered the gleaming red boat passing under his hand. "It's a good thing I didn't kill him," he mused.

Abran gave him a hand into the boat. "Let's wait to see if we survive taking it out before we congratulate the builder."

While Naro put up the mat, Abran and Afutu rowed away from the beach. The boat cut through the water easily, responding quickly. Once they were clear of the rocks, Naro tied the mat so the wind caught it squarely, pushing the boat along easily. The paddlers stopped, letting the wind take the boat across the water, faster than they could have possibly propelled it on their own. It was a fine feeling, skimming along, flying between the sea and sky, the spray coming off the bow, the water churning in their wake.

But after a while, Abran noticed how far they'd gotten from the island. "We may need to go back while we can," he said, pointing back to the beach.

"We'll just do what Chahuk did," Naro reassured him, as he pulled on the steering paddle to change direction. But he hadn't moved the mat, and the wind abeam filled the mat, suddenly pushing the boat over to port. Even with Abran and Afutu leaning off the starboard side, the boat hung, tilted up in the air, an instant away from capsizing.

"Untie it!" Afutu yelled.

"I'm trying! I tied it through the paddle hole, and the water's made the knot fast."

Grabbing his knife from his sash, Afutu cut the line, and Naro pulled the mat back to the line of the boat. In a rush, the boat fell back to its normal position in the water.

"The line's too short to tie at all now," Naro complained. "How'd Chahuk have it tied?"

Afutu shrugged. He hadn't paid attention to details like that.

"We're drifting farther away," Abran noted. "Let's start paddling." But the wind that had been so helpful before was now set on preventing them from getting where they wanted to go, even with all of them paddling.

"I'll try it again," Naro said, bringing the boat around to face the wind, "just like he did it, going back and forth." This time, he pulled the mat back to one corner of the stern, just as he'd watched Chahuk do, and the boat pulled forward at an angle.

"But it's the wrong way," Abran complained. "You're taking us away from the beach."

"We have to," Naro said. "It's the only way we can go into the wind. Now, we'll switch." He pulled the mat to the center as he changed the steering paddle to the other direction. Once the boat turned in the water, he moved the mat to the other corner of the stern, and once again, the boat was pulled forward. "See?"

Abran muttered a reply. The beach still didn't look any closer.

But they both had to admit, after a while, that Naro was on to something. It took a long time, certainly, especially compared to the easy flying they had done with the wind at their back, but it was possible. As they got closer to the island, the winds became more varied, and Naro had to experiment with the angle of the mat to keep the boat going where he wanted, but little by little, the island grew before them.

"I'll go past the beach, so we can ride the wind into shore," Naro called as he changed the mat. The others agreed; it seemed easier that way. But as Naro passed the beach and went to turn back toward the beach, the boat shot ahead, right into the rocks. Within moments, the boat's keel fin was wedged against a rock.

"Take the mat down," Afutu called. "The pressure's keeping the boat wedged."

When Naro pulled the mat so the wind slipped right past it, Afutu tried to push the boat away from the rock with the paddle, but the boat had turned sideways, locking the keel into the space between rocks. Even with all three men pushing away from the rock, they couldn't free the boat.

"Maybe we could back the boat out the same way we came in," Abran offered, leaning over to get a better view of the rocks. "Let's push backwards."

They tried, and the boat moved back slightly, but the current immediately pulled it right back where it was.

"There's got to be a way to put the mat so it would help," Naro said. "Since the wind's coming straight across us, I'll try moving the mat while you two push the boat backwards." He tried different positions with the mat, without much success.

"Abran's right. We have to go back the same way we came in. We know we can move the boat backward," Afutu said, trying to make out the shape of the rocks through the churning waters. "We just need to go little by little, whichever way we can get the boat to move. There must be a channel between the rocks; we had to get in here somehow. Once we're out of it, we should be able to head back to the open sea."

"But we need to get back to the beach!"

"No, we need to get back in the clear, and then come in exactly as we came out," Naro agreed, "if we can remember."

Bit by bit, they pushed the boat until it moved, then repositioned the poles to push again, over and over, until they had backed the keel fin out of the channel. Then all three rowed backwards, getting the boat clear of the rocks before they tried the mat once again. In the deeper water, they felt something hard bump the boat, first right on the bottom, then harder at the stern. Naro, trying to adjust the mat, staggered forward as the stern came up out of the water and fell back down.

"More rocks!" Abran yelled.

"I don't think so." Naro pointed to a dark grey shape sliding through the water off to his right, circling back toward the boat. As it approached, he pulled the steering paddle clear of the water. The broad, rounded snout, thick triangular dorsal fin, and stocky grey body, as long as two men, were unmistakable.

"It's a bull shark!" Afutu called.

At the same time they were watching the shark circle back on their right, a stingray came up from under the front of the boat to their left so quickly it touched the surface of the water. "Back up!" Afutu yelled, leaning back as he pulled on the paddle.

Abran already had the same idea, throwing all his strength into getting the boat to move backwards. Circling back, the bull shark read the motion of both the ray and the boat, and chose the ray, its original prey, charging right in front of the boat in its pursuit. Its huge dorsal fin broke the surface, as did the top of its grey back and the black tip of its long tail fin. It was easily as long as the boat, and massive. At the same moment, the men stopped paddling, holding their paddles out of the water, waiting. The ray disappeared into deeper water and the shark followed, both of them moving faster than the men thought possible, leaving the men still waiting, still watching the sea where the giant had been only moments before.

"Probably a female," Naro said, later. "They're bigger. We used to see them sometimes, in the river, at home."

"It could have sunk the boat with one bite," Abran said.

"Probably," Afutu agreed.

All at once, the release left them giddy. They'd come up against one of the most deadly creatures in the sea, and, incredibly, it had passed them by. It seemed funny somehow, really funny. Naro started it, when he tried to reply to Abran's comment, but he couldn't make any words happen; he just broke out laughing. Then no one could think of anything to say because they were all laughing, laughing so hard they had to struggle for breath. Afutu dropped his grip on his paddle and almost lost it to the waves before he retrieved it.

"Yes, but we're still way out here, and the beach is over there," Abran said, the first to regain his senses.

Naro nodded, trying to be serious. "You're right. We need to take this boat in, and we need to do it by paddling, so we can stay off the rocks. You first, Abran, up in the bow. Yell when you see rocks."

"There are rocks everywhere by the shore!"

"Then start with the ones right in front of us."

With only minor scrapes, they found their way back to the beach. As the boat touched the sand, Naro jumped out, then Abran, and together, they pulled the boat in and helped Afutu out, one under each of his arms as they stepped onto the sand. The only ones waiting there were the children. Together, they looked over the boat, which had fared very well, despite its adventures, with one exception.

"How are you going to explain that?" Sule asked, pointing to the keel fin. The lower half was shattered, hanging in ragged pieces that stuck into the sand.

"Rocks?" Abran ventured.

"With teeth?" Deka replied.

Afutu picked up his staff and leaned on it, regarding them. "Maybe we can repair it before anyone notices. Anyone else, I mean." It was an offer of a conspiracy of silence. They loved it.

"You know, you could compliment the builder, now," Abran said, as the group headed inland. "He built a good boat."

"He did," Afutu admitted.

When Sohko saw the group returning, he was glad to see everyone, but he assumed the men had gone fishing. "Well, didn't you catch any fish?"

"No," Naro said, "but we saw one."

While the others were enjoying their last days on the island, Ayo was increasingly restless. When the others were preparing foods and gathering supplies, she headed off on her own, climbing the trails that wound along the cliffs, passing the dragon trees that were growing at an angle, leaning against the rock, like so many travelers resting. There was a lookout, she remembered, or at least Chahuk had pointed to something that might have been one, somewhere on the cliff face. But nothing was easy to get to in this vertical country, and she found herself stopped several times by sheer drops.

When the sun was near its peak, she came upon what seemed to be a trail. There were still rough spots, and the views straight down from the trail's edge left her dizzy, but the hiking itself was much easier. She'd gone quite a way before she realized there was something attached to the rock face, above her. The trail switched back and forth, taking her closer with each step. It was impossible, but she was seeing a hut, and two, perhaps three people standing in front of it.

The last part of the trail was grueling, with each step an effort, straight up the cliff face, until she was facing the hut she had thought impossible. It was built on a rock slab and was just like any other hut, except this one clung to the side of a cliff. Its sides were made of stone, the roof and opening cover of palm thatch. Following the trail, she climbed up to a tiny ledge, with just enough room for her to find her way along the different angles of the rock. She told herself not to look down, but several times she did anyway. It wasn't that she was afraid of falling. It was stranger than that. She knew that if she looked down there long enough, she would have to jump, have to spread her arms wide, like a hawk, and soar through that space until she crashed far below on the rocks. So she turned to face the rock and stepped sideways along the ledge. That's how she bumped into them.

There were three of them, a man and a woman, and another man, life-size, carved out of the rock. They were so life-like, she gasped. Each one was an individual, with carefully detailed face and hair, and woven wraps decorated with figures of fish and birds, detailed even down to the fringe at the edge. The man and woman stood together, dressed elegantly, perhaps for a wedding or other ceremony. The man, whose head was turned so he was looking at the woman, wore a feather headdress and held a staff with an eagle head at the top. Next to him, the woman wore a feather fan tucked into the back of her hair. A row of thick braids framed her face. Her wrap was long, covered with an embroidered sash at the waist. Unlike the man, she looked straight ahead.

The third figure stood behind them, and he wore only a simple wrap. As soon as she saw him, Ayo knew who it was meant to be. It was Chahuk, in every detail: his face, his hair, his posture, even the way his left foot turned in slightly. His hair was pulled back and tied at the back of his neck with a string of cone shells. He was looking at the woman.

The figure of the woman was shining, and deep red.

Shocked, Ayo stood before them, staring, uncomfortable, as if she'd stumbled into a private meeting, full of private pain. It was hard to think of them as statues made of stone. Even in their stillness, they seemed alive, as if they'd been forever stopped at a single moment. Only Chahuk had survived, and he had tried to bring her back, covering her again and again with the red resin. Here, so far above the valley, the drama continued forever. Dropping down to her knees, she bowed, putting her head to the ground in front of them. "Know that you were loved," she whispered to the statue of the woman.

Just beyond the three was the hut. Thinking perhaps it was a burial site, she hesitated, but she wanted to see it. If it was a burial, she would leave immediately, she told herself. As she stepped in from the back entrance, the first thing she noticed was the ceiling. Most huts didn't have ceilings. In general, the roof supports went from the top of the circular wall to the point of the roof, leaving an open area on the side where heat could escape. This hut was very different. From one side to the other, at the top of the walls, the builder had put lines of branches, tying them in place with rope. Over these were several layers of stucco, the last of which was almost white. Even in the poor light, she could see everything on the ceiling. It was the night sky.

There were the familiar star figures, including the great bird rising near the center, and the serpent curling around it, the whale, the hunter, the antelope, everything she had been taught when she was a girl. There were others, too, stars with special marks on them and strange lines marking their changing path, and lines going from one figure to another, sewing them together across the sky.

The walls, also coated, were covered in dots, some red, some black, some in long series, some only a few. There were so many that they went all the way around the hut walls, top to bottom, closely fitted together, and then kept going, overlapping older dots, in a chaos of records. The hut was filled, overflowing, with information she couldn't understand. Was this all Chahuk's work? If so, was this something he did before or after his mind split into pieces? How was it related to the three figures on the trail?

She sat on the floor, studying the star patterns above her, until she knew it was time to go. There was a reason she'd been brought here: she was enriched by seeing all of this. No art, she thought, is wasted. No time spent on it is wasted. The fact that it exists, that someone brought it to life, is its reason for being and its gift to others. This man she had hardly known had given her the most extraordinary gift: his art, his vision, his knowledge, his desire, a glimpse of the world as he saw it. She took the medicine bag from her sash and, with a deep bow, placed it on the floor in the center of the hut.

"I wish you well," she said, as she rose. "I know you now, and you're not really a Trickster. You're so real it hurts, that's all."

CHAPTER 16
AT SEA

While everyone else was busy with final preparations for the departure, Naaba made the difficult climb to the waterfall once again, alone this time. After standing in the fall's pounding water, he sat in the pool, at the edge of the cloud of spray, leaning his head back, looking up the rock wall where the flowering plants grew, watered by the constant mist. The walls were, for the most part, unbroken, from the top of the falls to the bottom. Only one part seemed different, a section set in from the rest of the wall. Perhaps, long ago, a segment had fallen out of the rock wall, exposing this under-layer. Unlike the other surfaces, nothing grew there, not even moss. After staring at it, he got up and found his way over to it. It was relatively smooth and flat, and as he ran his hand over it, he knew exactly why he had come to this place.

From his bag, he pulled out his chisel and hammerstone. After putting his forehead to the stone, asking the spirits of the waterfall and the rock walls to help him, he started working. The design was a circle, with fourteen dots around its edge. On the left side of the circle, he chipped out three lines of dots: eight in the first line, five in the second, and a single dot in the third, to represent the eight people in one boat, the five in the other, and Chahuk. Between the second and third row, he put two wavy lines. On the right side of the circle, he put two different rows of dots: the first had three dots and a boat, for the group going back; the second had eleven and another boat, for the group going forward.

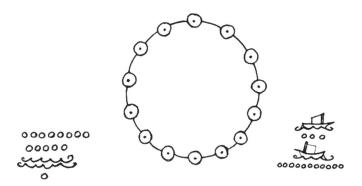

Then he lay down on the wet stone and stretched himself out, face down, his hands reaching out toward the stone, so that his fingertips just touched it.

While the sun was still young and the weather fine the next day, they finished loading boats, and, with a cheer, pushed them into the sea and climbed aboard. In the first boat were Naaba, Asha, Dashona, Afutu and Abran. To start, Afutu had the rudder and Abran the mat. In the second were Sohko, Aminata, Deka, Sule, Ayo, and Naro, with Naro on the rudder and Sohko working the mat. They had established a limited communication system with the conch shells, so they had only to stay within hailing distance of each other. Actually, they didn't want to be too far apart; the sight of the other boat was reassuring. After the vertical rock walls of the island, it was unnerving to see the vast expanse of the sea, the realm of the unpredictable water spirits, stretching out forever in front of them.

The first day, they discovered several problems with the boats. The higher sides were helpful in keeping out the spray, but once water did get in the boat, it was harder to bail out, so every time the bow dipped, the water rolled forward along the bottom of the boat, crashing in a miniature wave at the bow. The paddle holes allowed a better rowing angle than going over the high gunnels, but they

299

limited the range of motion and paddle placement. And, they let in water, negating the benefit of the higher sides. They could put the hole-covers on, but then it was an effort to take them back off and reinsert the paddles when they were needed.

But, as Naaba pointed out, compared to the tippy dug-out canoe they had arrived in, these boats were very fine, and that first day, when they skimmed easily across the surface of the sea, and dolphins swam alongside the boats, sometimes leaping up, twisting in the air, and splashing back down, the people aboard forgot there was a time when they didn't have the red boats to carry them.

At night, they took down the mats, lashed the boats together, and let them drift with the current. After watching the mat work all day, Naro thought they could go much faster if they added another mat. Why not put the second on top of the first, or sew two mats together to form one big one? When he asked about it, Sohko thought it was worth a try, and Ayo offered a smaller mat that he could try over the main mat.

The sun was hardly born when Naro climbed the mast to attach the new mat. From up there, he watched the boat sway back and forth in reverse, as if the sea was swinging rather than the mast, a view that made even his hardly stomach lurch, so he made himself look only straight ahead, at the mast, the mat, and the ropes. As soon as he had it attached, he found his way back down the mast and attached the main mat. He then had two more lines, one from each end of the top mat, in addition to the one running along the bottom of the main mat, but nowhere to tie them. As he'd learned the hard way, tying them through the paddling holes didn't allow a quick adjustment when needed. For the moment, he just coiled up the lines and left them on the bottom of the boat.

The winds were gentle, just puffs that came and went, so the other boat was still drifting with the current when Naro set up both mats on his. As soon as they were set, the combination made a big difference, even in the quiet breezes, and the boat pulled ahead.

First, it was just a little, but it increased as the wind picked up a little. Naro was elated, yelling to everyone aboard to see how the boat was gaining. Sule, anxious to see the upper mat, hurried back toward the stern, got his feet tangled in the ropes on the boat floor, and crashed forward. Only Sohko's quick grasp saved him from cracking his head on the side of the boat.

"Get these ropes off the floor. Somebody's going to get hurt!"

It wasn't the response Naro had expected. "Where should I put them? I can't tie them in the holes. I already tried that."

"I don't know. Figure it out. But they're not staying there."

Disappointed, Naro wound up the ropes tighter and tried to push them off to the side. In the meantime, the boat had continued to pull forward, even after Abran had raised the mat on the other boat. When he looked back, Naro was shocked at the distance that had grown between them.

"Maybe you could fix them up with the same thing," he said to Ayo.

"I'll make the mat. You figure out the rest," she commented. "Until then, you better take that one down, or we'll be too far ahead for them to catch up."

It seemed that no one was going to congratulate him on his discovery, so he took the mat down with a sigh and went back to working with the main mat, but he couldn't forget the feeling he got when he looked around and saw how far they'd pulled ahead. The new mat was a great addition, and it was staying.

In the other boat, the incident stirred Afutu's old competitive nature. He wanted to have the same mats as Naro had, so he could be in the race.

"Don't we have an extra mat here somewhere?" he yelled.

"Only sleeping mats," Asha said, knowing what he had in mind. "Can you use those?"

"I have no idea, but I'll give it a try."

"Why -" Abran didn't finish his sentence, so the word stayed there by itself.

"Why not?" Afutu answered the unasked question. "More mat means more wind made to work for us. What's wrong with that?"

"Nothing." Abran looked out to sea. "Nothing."

Ignoring him, Afutu addressed the others. "If we can travel the sea with less work, how could this be a bad thing? Let's hook up a top mat and see what happens. If we think it's not safe, we'll take it down right away."

That was hard to argue with, so Asha dug out one of the sleeping mats stuffed with silk cotton fibers, but she hesitated when she looked closely at it. "It's not exactly the same. It's a lot bigger and heavier."

"I'll put it up." The voice was Abran's, but it sounded very strange, as he started climbing the mast. "Hand it up to me."

Naaba helped Asha lift up the heavy mat and the rope so Abran could tie it to the mast. It was hard working up there, even when he didn't look down. There was no hole cut in the mat where he could run the rope through, so he ran it all the way around the mat, one line on each side of the mast, and tied it, then found his way back down.

"What do we do with the ropes?" Naaba called.

"Just hold them for a minute, until we see how this works," Abran said. He had no idea what to do with them.

With the addition of the new mat, which was easily as large as the main one, they expected the boat to fly over the water even faster than Naro's did. While they were waiting to get the new one adjusted, the boat had started to turn, going with the current rather than the wind. When the wind hit both mats, it put so much pressure on them that the boat couldn't stand it.

"It's going over!" Asha yelled, but everyone was locked into that moment, staring at the big mats fill with wind.

There was no warning lift. The boat simply heeled over in the wind, the weight of the mats in motion carrying the mast down. As the boat capsized, everyone was thrown out, and Abran ended up under the mats. In a panic, he tried to reach the surface, but he kept trying in the same spot, and each time he ran into the mat, thrashing and pushing against it until he felt a hand on his arm, drawing him away. Convinced it was a water spirit dragging him to his death, he pulled away, but then another hand grabbed his other arm and yanked it hard. Together, Asha and Naaba pulled him around the edge of the mat.

The new mat, rather than turning into a soggy dead weight, floated on the surface, carrying the mast with it, so they gathered around it, hanging on while they caught their breath.

In the other boat, it was Deka who saw the boat capsize. "Stop!" she shrieked at Naro. "You've got to stop!"

That was easier said than done. Naro had just put up the second mat, so he first had to wrestle that down, then try to remember how to turn around without getting his boat in the same spot as the other one. Then it seemed agonizingly slow going against the wind. By the time he got his boat back to the other, they had managed to untie the main mat, but they couldn't undo the knots Abran had tied on the new one. Reluctantly, Naaba cut the lines with his knife but kept the mat under the mast to help them right the boat. But even with Afutu pressing on the keel fin and the others lifting the mast, they couldn't manage it.

"Tie one of the lines around the mast and throw it to us!" Naro yelled.

Dashona tied a line around the notch the mat was usually tied into and threw it over the boat to Afutu, who tied a knot in the end and then hurled it over to Naro, but the throw was too short. Sohko jumped in to retrieve it before it sank and threw it the rest of the way.

"I'm going over to help," he said as he started swimming.

With the rope in his hand, Naro had to figure out how to pull the other ship upright without pulling his own over. If he tied it to the mast, even at the bottom, it could make his boat capsize. If he tied it to himself, the boat would easily pull him out into the sea.

"We'll hold a paddle," Sule offered. "Deka and I. Up in the air. Then you run the rope over it. If there's pressure, it will be down, not out, right?"

"Then I'm helping," Aminata said. "I'm not watching you two be pulled out to sea."

"I am too," Ayo added. "We'll all hold it, and we'll brace ourselves against both sides of the boat."

Two faced one way along the center of the boat and two faced the other, with Deka and Sule in the middle. Instead of one paddle, they held two, with two people holding each one. The children held theirs over their heads, but Ayo and Aminata held theirs tight across their bodies, hands tucked close to their shoulders. Unable to come up with any other idea, Naro ran the line across the paddles and started pulling. With a groan, the four felt the weight of the capsized boat falling on them. Naro pulled, hand over hand, ignoring the burns he got from the rope. It was only twisted palm fiber, and he hoped the whole thing didn't give way just as they were raising the mast. He just kept going, one hand over the other, throwing his weight backward as he pulled.

In the water, the group watched the impossible happen right in front of them. Little by little, the mast rose out of the water, turning the boat full of water with it. Afutu put all his weight on the keel, figuring it would either help or break it, and helping was worth the risk. With a rush, the boat swept upright, and Afutu was pulled under by the sudden roll of the boat. Naro was thrown right off the side of the other boat by the sudden release of weight on the rope, and the four paddle holders dropped to the floor of the boat in a heap.

Feeling his way back up the side of the boat, Afutu reached the surface and realized the boat was resting, filled with water, so its gunnels were just above the waterline. With an easy lunge, he was back in the boat, looking for something to use to start bailing. But all their supplies had been swept overboard when the boat capsized. Some, like the paddles, the other sleeping mats, the calabashes, the lengths of palm filled with honey, a few fruits, the coconuts, and the baskets, were floating nearby. The rest were gone.

Once he was sure that everyone was all right, Sohko organized the bailing and collecting efforts, as well the inventory of what they had and what shape it was in. Naro brought the other boat over and lashed the two together, so everyone at least had a place to get out of the water. But they were a poor group. Abran was the worst, dazed and mumbling to himself as he sat on the other boat. The others were soaked and shaken, saying little. Aminata fixed them up with fresh water and a place to breathe for a moment before they went back to work salvaging what they could. Using part of the mat rope that was still coiled on the floor of the boat, Dashona fashioned a clothes line from the mast to the serpent's head at the bow, so she could hang up some of the soaked mats and clothes to dry. When the wind made them flap, Naro saw a whole new possibility for the boat, but he had the good sense not to mention it at the moment.

The sun was getting old by the time they had completed the boat clean-up and rescued what they could. The warm temperature of the water helped, since they spent a good deal of time in it, retrieving things and hauling them back. And there was no sign of sharks or other predators. Even so, by the time they finished, they were exhausted. When Aminata brought out some dried fish, they thanked her and ate it without noticing.

It took a while for the realization to sink in that they'd lost things they had to have. Some things they could do without, like spare clothes, but others were essential. Their tools were gone completely, as was most of their food. Fortunately, there were two boats, and their friends would help them. But they understood suddenly and clearly how easily it could all be lost.

That night, Naro climbed into the other boat to talk. He needed to know why the second mat had worked one time and been such a disaster the next. Afutu explained what they'd done, how the sleeping mat was bigger and heavier than the one Naro had tried, almost as big as the main mat.

"So, you think the top mat has to be smaller and lighter, to keep the weight closer to the boat?" Naro asked, settling down to talk.

"Maybe. Maybe it put too much weight near the top of the mast. But I had another idea. The keel fin is good when we have one mat, but I think it's not enough to balance the pull of the mast when we have two, at least two big mats." Afutu held up his thumb and forefinger to the side of his knife about a thumb's width apart. "Let's say this is the keel fin, and the rest of this is the mast with the two mats. It's not enough to balance the push against the mast. If we had a longer keel fin, or a heavier boat, or both, I'm sure we could handle more mats."

"You two seem to be forgetting that you could have killed someone, or everyone, out there today." It was the first thing Abran had said since the accident.

"We were just experimenting," Naro said, shouldering some of the blame. "Now we're trying to learn from what happened."

It wasn't said with any rancor, but Abran bristled. "Fine. It must just be me, then. Maybe I'm the only one here who'd rather not be dumped into the sea and lose everything just so you two can show who's faster." With that, he got up and moved to the other boat, as far away from them as possible.

They were all tired that night, but no one could sleep. When Dashona sat up to look at the stars, the children asked her if she'd tell them a story. "Just a short one, if you're tired."

"I don't know. My thoughts are all scrambled up."

"Then tell a scrambled story."

"Or one about lost treasure," Asha offered.

"Or boats thrown over in the sea," another called.

"Or men who think they can control the wind," Abran said quietly.

The lost treasure idea reminded her of a story her grandmother used to tell. "A short one, then, a story about treasure. In a village not far from mine, there was a beautiful young woman and a handsome young man. Together, they'd stroll along the beach, picking up shells, but she always thought she'd find a better one, so she never kept any. In the rainy season, he'd pick flowers for her, telling her they were the children of the sun and the rain. She'd tuck them in her hair and laugh, but they were never very special to her. There were many flowers; she felt it was impossible to say which was the most beautiful unless she had seen them all. When he asked her to marry him, he brought her a hair comb he had carved from abalone shell. It was in the shape of a bird, full of bright iridescent colors, all flowing together. Its feet formed the prongs that stuck into her hair. But when she tried it, she was disappointed that it wasn't bigger so she could see it better. The young man was also disappointed. He had spent a long time on the comb.

"He tried once more to impress her, taking her to the top of the cliff so they could watch the sunset colors spread out against the sky. As the sun neared the sea, the colors splintered on the water and played out across the sky. When he kissed her, he said, 'Isn't that beautiful?'

"'Yes,' she answered, but there was a hesitation in it.

"'Yes, but what?'

"'Yes, but the sun dies every day. This isn't unusual. It's nice, certainly, but it's not one of a kind. I think a real treasure is one of a kind.'

"'Every day is one of a kind,' he answered. 'Every person is one of a kind.' With that, he stood up and left her to find her own way back to the village.

"Angry, she went over the conversation in her mind as she went home. Surely, he must see her point. There are many nice things, but they aren't special. They're just nice. A cool breeze on a hot day is nice, but it's not enough to make someone stand up and shout for joy. It's pleasant, that's all. A smile from a good-looking vendor at the market is nice. A plump, ripe melon is nice. But none of these would be worth remembering forever. Only something very special would be. She tried to remember very special things that she could use as examples the next time she saw him. That's after she told him how angry she was with him for leaving her alone on the cliff. Very special things. Well, a birth would be special, but she couldn't remember hers and she'd never been present at any others. A death? No, too morbid. A war victory? Too bloody. A complicated building? Just engineering. The shaman's healing medicines? She hadn't ever needed them herself, though she'd heard others say they were wonderful. No, other people's wonders didn't count.

"While she was trying to come up with ammunition for her debate, a messenger approached her, holding up his torch. 'I'm sorry to bring you sad news,' he said.

"'What?' she cried. 'What's happened?'

"'Your fiancé has had an accident. He slipped on his way down the cliff and – fell.'

"'Fell? Fell where? Is he all right?'

"'No, Miss,' the messenger said, 'he's dead.'

"'Dead?' the woman cried, unbelieving. 'He can't be. He was just here a little while ago. We were talking. We were watching the sun sink into the sea.'

"Unable to come up with anything to add, the messenger nodded. 'I can take you back to the village. I brought the torch so you could see your way.'

"She was about to say that she knew the way, that she'd walked these paths since she could remember, but she didn't. 'Thank you,' she said after a while. 'That's very kind.' As they neared the village, she said, 'I know now.'

"'Know what, Miss?'

"'What makes something very special. I had so many treasures I didn't recognize them. I'd give up everything I have if I could get back even one of the moments I had with him.'"

After Dashona finished, no one said anything. She thought it hadn't been the right story. Too sad, perhaps. Maybe something lighter, something funny would have been better.

"It was perfect," Asha reassured her. "It was exactly right."

Only Abran seemed immune to the charms of the storytelling. When he returned to his boat, he sat down with his back rammed up against the side of the boat, his arms wrapped around his knees. When Afutu tapped him on the shoulder, he flinched.

"What's going on?" Afutu said, trying to ease himself down next to him.

Abran's position didn't change. "Don't concern yourself with me."

"Too late for that, friend."

"I'm fine."

"No, you're not."

Abran lifted his head and turned. "And you're the expert on feeling fine, are you?"

"If I've done something to offend you, I'm sorry."

"Find someone else to work the mat. I don't want to."

"Okay, I will. But I still want to know what's happening to you."

"It's not —"

Afutu waited. His leg was hurting, but if he moved, Abran wouldn't finish the sentence, so he stayed right there, waiting.

"I can't do this anymore."

"Do what?"

"Anything. After I got hurt in the game, something happened. I felt as if rats were gnawing on my insides. I thought it was the injury, but it's no better now; they're always there. It's not the injury; it's fear. That's the truth of it. Today I almost drowned because I was so panicked. How's that for ironic? The big man so scared he can't swim around a mat."

"Well, look at me," Afutu said, "the big man, the champion, unable to walk across flat ground without help."

"But you're getting better. You're finding your way out of it. I can't see any way out." He looked up at the stars.

"It takes time."

With a sad laugh, Abran nodded. "And how much time would that be? And how can I be part of this journey when I'm not helping? Today, Asha had to save me, Asha and Naaba really, because I wouldn't listen to Asha alone. *I* used to save people."

"I once asked Naaba to put me overboard," Afutu said simply. "It's hard for us. It's really hard." When Abran started to object, he went on. "It was great to get into the boat by myself today. Of course, it was flooded at the time, but still, I didn't need anyone's help to get in, and I'd worried about that, especially with the extra-high sides on the boat. That's my world now. I can either deal with it or give up."

"But it's different for you."

"Only in some ways. It's a bad fight, for both of us."

Silent, Abran put out his hand and Afutu grasped it.

"Do you still want to give up your work with the mat?" Afutu said, as he levered himself out of his painful position.

"For a while, yes."

"Done. I'll ask Naaba. But the job is yours when you want it back."

"If," Abran corrected.

CHAPTER 17
THE EYE OF THE STORM GOD

Starting one night, a line of storms moved in, one after another, bringing brief bursts of thunder, lightning, and heavy rain. Each time, no matter how they set the mats, the rain poured in, flooding everything in the boat, so they spent most of the time between storms bailing the water out. For two days, they went through this cycle of storms and clearing. The next night, they saw the full moon shining through an opening in the clouds. The area around the moon was purple and blue, lit up by the bright moonlight, and around it was a circle of dark rainbow colors reflected in the clouds: deep yellow, orange, and blood red.

"It's the eye of the storm god," Ayo said, "a bad sign."

The following day, Asha felt something very strange. "Naaba, the water's going up and down."

"It's from the storm."

"No. I don't mean the water in the sea. I mean the water in the air."

He set down the twisted rope he'd been working on. "What do you mean?"

"There's something going on, something I've never felt before. The water from the sea is going up into the air. I feel as if the sky's pulling on the sea. Something's pulling on it. It's turning, and it's coming back down. It's growing."

Abran had been watching the water swirling behind the boat and the sky reflected in it. Of course, everyone heard everyone else's conversation on the boats, but mostly they tried not to listen. However, at the very moment Asha was describing her odd feeling, Abran was shocked by the connection between what he heard and what he saw. "That's what you're feeling, Asha," he called, pointing. "Look!"

Behind them, the skies were an odd blue-purple color, filled with ragged scatters of dark clouds, except for the formation to their north, where the cloud was very large and dense, with a round edge, and skirts of clouds hanging down from it. Strangely, they hung there, all the same length, stopping just above the water, like the fringes on a woman's fine wrap. But there was nothing of a celebration about them.

Asha shuddered. "We need to lash the boats together now," she called.

While Naro was ready to dismiss her fears, Sohko wasn't. "Asha knows when the water's changing," he announced. "Get the mats off. We'll lash the boats and try to head away from the storm."

"I don't know if that's going to work," Naaba said, once he saw the cloud. "That storm seems to be half the size of the sky."

"Well, we'll give it a try," Sohko said, and it wasn't a voice anyone chose to argue with.

In the time it took to prepare the boats, the storm system moved closer and grew bigger, until it was right behind them. They could see the bands of rain now, slashing the sea. They tried to head south, but the storm spread faster than they could take the boats away from it. For a while, they watched, spellbound, as it grew nearer. Then it was on them. With a rush, the wind rose, pushing the surface of the sea and the small boats on it. The water and the sky had formed a terrible new force, and it swung the world around at will.

They tied the mats to the forward area, hoping to minimize the effect of the waves crashing over the bow, but the wind came up so suddenly, it was hard to work without having the mats ripped away. In the end, they all tried to hold the mats down, even when they were tied. The noise of the wind was everywhere, fiercer and more insistent.

In a short while, the seas were driven to heights no one on the boats had ever seen before. They'd crest one gigantic wave only to be thrown out and down into the trough between waves. If they hit with the bow down, they risked being completely swamped by the next wave.

"It's too fast!" Naro called through the wind. "We're going too fast! We'll be buried in one of these waves and not come out!"

Afutu was sitting hunched over at the rudder, pelted by the rain and wind. "What should we do? We can't turn."

"We need something to slow us down, so we can stick to the top of the waves and not go flying through the air."

Ayo and Asha had the same thought at the same time. "Why not drag a mat in the water? It'll be the opposite of a mat in the wind. It'll catch the water instead of the wind."

"We're using them to keep the rain out!"

"What about the sleeping mats?"

"No, they'll float."

"They'd still be some sort of drag, and as they got soaked, the waves would pull them under a little. It's worth a try."

"We'd need a lot of line," Naro yelled against the storm, "and good knots that would hold against the pull."

Naaba reached under the forward tarp for the rope he'd made. "I'll tie them up for you. We'll use as many as we can."

Asha pulled out four of the mats. On the other boat, Aminata found another four. With the wind howling, they couldn't unroll them until they were ready to put them overboard, so they found their way, crawling over and around them, sewing in the rope, attaching one mat, then another, then another. Naaba made knots between the mats, hoping to keep them from bunching up. If they did, and they swung to one side, they'd turn the boat right into disaster. On the other boat, Aminata and Sohko worked, sewing the line through the mats and securing the knots at the end of each. When they were almost finished, a wave swept right over the bow as the boats dug too fast into an oncoming wave, soaking them.

"Let's set them!" Naro yelled.

Everyone grabbed a part of the line as Naaba dropped the mats off the stern. Sohko did the same, and their effect was immediate. Even with their buoyancy, the storm waves took them under the water, and the drag slowed the boats, pulling the bow of the boats up.

"Yes!" Naro cried. He was about to add, "It's working!" but a look ahead showed huge seas coming at them. "Tie yourselves together! We're in trouble!"

In a rush of trembling hands, they tried to work the rope, wrapping it around each other and tying each one with a knot. Then, because Naaba couldn't think of anywhere else to tie the line, he wrapped it around the center beam, where the empty mast stood. If the boat went down, it would take them all with it, but he felt that was a better risk than losing someone to one of the waves crashing over the bow.

"Hold the bow cover!" Naaba yelled. If we can keep the bow from flooding first, the boat won't dive." He didn't bother trying to explain the rest.

The people under the mat nodded. They were already trying to keep the mat secure, but their arms ached from fighting with the wind and getting flooded every time the water washed through from the stern.

In the stern, Abran never stopped bailing. He felt as if he was trying to empty the whole sea with a calabash, but he kept going anyway.

The boats plunged up and down in the monster seas. Even dragging the mats behind them, the boats flew off the top of each wave until the mats stopped them and they slammed back down into the water. Each time they hit the water, the people were thrown around and into each other, even though they tried to hold on tightly.

"Get the men out of the stern!" Naaba yelled to Sohko. "They've got to have a break. I'll take over for a while here."

Sohko agreed, sending Naro to the bow for some rest. It wasn't sleep, exactly, in that Naro woke with every crash down, but he was so tired, he dropped off to sleep for moments between waves. The waves came in sets of three, sometimes four. They learned the rhythm after a while. Three monsters in a row, then a lull, then three more. They lived in single, very protracted moments. Each wave became a lifetime: climbing up its front wall, crashing through the white surf at the top, flying over the other side until the mats caught, then swinging back down and crashing into the far wall. All they could do was try to keep the bow headed into the waves, so they didn't turn sideways. Their world was their boat, their boat on that wave while the wind shrieked. Nothing else existed.

They took turns steering, but the job was so punishing, they couldn't stay at it for long, especially when they were already so tired. Everyone, except the children, wound up taking a turn being lashed by the wind and rain, trying to see well enough to steer. At night, it was harder. They had only the feel of the waves to guide them. The mats helped too. If they were surfing sideways down the back of a wave, the mats were pulled out behind them, helping to turn them back.

Those who weren't steering were trying to hold onto the mats or bail. Those who could, slept fitfully, but there was always water sloshing through, and people being thrown around, and the few supplies they had left floating loose. Real sleep was impossible.

In the course of the night, they had no idea what was happening outside except for what they could feel through the boat, and the incessant screaming of the wind. When morning came, there was no sunrise, but the sky was lighter, and Asha and Ayo, who were steering at the time, had their first view of the storm at its height. That wasn't a good thing. The monstrous seas they'd dealt with during the night were at least unseen. When Asha saw the mountain of dark green water rising in front of the boat, it was all she could do not to scream. The sea was rising straight up into the sky. At the top, the water was curling and breaking over in a white froth. It was an animate thing, a vengeance made of water.

"It's the same," Ayo yelled against the noise of the sea.

Asha nodded, though she knew it wasn't at all the same. But she recognized there was a choice she had to make. She could either understand the power of this beast, or she could set it aside and think, as she had all night, only of this moment, the ascent of this wave. So she shut down her mind, calling it back from its wandering. The storm was like the beast that kills by mesmerizing its victim. She had to avoid looking directly at it.

So she did. By the time Abran came out to relieve her, she had grown used to the terror. Even it had a rhythm and a pattern. But Abran was shocked. Because the wind was still screaming, it was impossible to talk to him, so she sat with him, even after he had taken over. She sat facing him, so that she was between him and the rising waves. After they had gotten through the first set, he put his arm on hers; she nodded, and crawled back under the tarp.

When Aminata sent around the water calabash, it seemed odd that they were thirsty after being constantly pelted with rain, but they were, and it seemed a fine thing to have fresh water.

They lived in an alternate universe, one where time and space and the elements were very different from anything they knew. It was a world only the gods understood. Days came and went but they noticed only because it was dark sometimes and pitch-black others. They found they could concentrate only on very small tasks: the way a knot was tied, the position of their hand on the mat, the method of bailing. When Aminata passed around food, they ate very slowly, even though they'd eaten very little since the storm hit. It took a lot of effort to eat and everything tasted like sea spray.

One night, the wind rose to an even higher pitch, shrieking and tearing at them. To Asha, it sounded like a pack of wild dogs she'd heard once, near her village, closing in on their prey. One had already grabbed the nose of the antelope and the others were so close they could smell blood. Their cry was hair-raising, an ecstatic scream that grew with each dog that joined the kill.

The wind was so strong, the people had to crawl around the boat. The one time Ayo tried to walk, the wind lifted her right off her feet. If she hadn't been tied to the others, she would have been blown off the boat. The people bailing had to fight the wind to do their job. If they reached up to fling the water over the side, the wind took it right back to the front of the boat. If they leaned over the side, the wind tried to take them over too. Naaba and Naro, who were steering, were hunched over almost double as the wind and rain pounded them. As they crested yet another wave, the wind snapped Naro's boat's mast in half and threw it forward. It missed the main part of the boat but snapped off the serpent's head as it fell. On the far side of the wave, they went crashing right over the broken pieces as they flew down toward the trough, sending a crunching shock through the boats. When Afutu relieved Naaba and took up the steering paddle, he knew they had lost at least part of it, but there was no way to know how much, so he just kept going as if it was still there.

The time passed in sets of waves and changing shifts and bits of sleep. Everything was constantly soaked, everyone was exhausted, but the boats held.

By the time the storm passed and the waves gradually subsided, they hardly noticed. Once they could, they slept, not caring whether they were piled up like so many rocks in the water that sloshed around the bottom of the boat. They slept so soundly, they never moved. When they did wake, they could barely move. Every single part ached. Their hands were raw, their arms and legs covered in cuts and bruises and saltwater sores. Their heads pounded. Only then did it occur to them that they'd survived the storm. One boat had lost its mast, one had lost its steering paddle, the sleeping mats were shredded down to bunches of ragged strings hanging off the ropes, but everyone was alive and the boats were still afloat.

CHAPTER 18
THE DARK RAINBOW

After the storm, they offered gifts to the sea and sky for sparing them. Then they had to clean up the boats and see what supplies were salvageable. They wandered through the days, doing little bits and pieces, but mostly they were very tired.

One afternoon, after the children had helped Aminata, they asked Dashona for a story. "I don't have any stories right now," Dashona snapped. "If you want a story, make one up. I'm done. Do you understand? I've told stories every night, and I'm all used up. Out of stories. Empty. As a matter of fact, I don't know when I might know any stories in the future, so you might want to make up several. And while you're at it, make them entertaining, so everyone will be pleased with them. Oh, and by the way, that's impossible."

Confused, Deka and Sule just stared at her.

"You know what? I have a better idea," Dashona went on. "Ask Afutu. He used to tell stories, a long time ago. Maybe he can remember one. Ask him for a really sad story. He's good at those."

"I think we said something wrong," Deka whispered as they moved away.

"I think I will," Sule said.

"Will what?"

"Ask Afutu."

"Are you crazy?"

"Probably. But I don't think he'll throw me overboard."

"Don't be too sure."

"It's worth a try."

"Then I'm going too. Throwing both of us overboard would be harder for him."

"Not a lot."

When the children did get up the nerve to ask him, Afutu considered the question for a moment, then said, "If you can get Naro and Naaba to help, we'll all work on a story. Then, when it's ready, we'll tell everyone." Before they could answer, he added, "Oh, you'll need Ayo's help too. Maybe some others."

"It seems very complicated, just to tell a story," Deka complained. "When Dashona tells stories, all we have to do is listen to them."

"It's up to you," Afutu said, his face grave.

"Did the storm change the stories?" Deka asked, but her brother poked her arm.

"We'll go ask them," Sule said.

The group huddled at the stern with the broken steering paddle, talking quietly, throwing out ideas, making plans, changing everything and starting over. Naaba left and returned with something hidden under his arm. Then the talks continued, until Naaba left again. After a while, Abran and Sohko returned with him, bringing mats and rope. Then there were more plans, and snatches of songs, and overlapping comments.

"Do you have any idea what's going on back there?" Asha asked while Aminata was trying to repair one of the mats.

"Absolutely none, but I think curiosity is about to kill someone else here," she nodded toward Dashona.

It was more bitterness than curiosity. Dashona pretended to be watching the sea, ignoring all of the whispered preparations, but it hurt that they were planning something she wasn't part of. Everything hurt, even her own anger.

Later, after the group had eaten and passed around the water calabash, Ayo set up a mat and covered it with a dark wrap. Naro brought out several short lengths of rope; Deka carried some smooth round stones she'd found in the bottom of the boat.

Sule started. "We're not good at this, not like Dashona is, but we're going to try a story of our own, just like she told us. We had a lot of help," he added, looking around at the men, "but if it's not any good, it's our fault, not theirs. Anyway, it's got music, sometimes, and rope drawings, sometimes." Suddenly nervous, he handed off responsibility. "Afutu is going to start."

"We'll both start. You start the story. Naro and I will work the rope."

After a deep breath, the boy started: "A long time ago, when the world was brand new, a sky spirit, who often carried the clouds on his back, went searching for the rainbow." With lengths of rope, Afutu formed the serpent shape and Naro made the swirling clouds on its back. "'She's over Earth,' the falcon said, as it darted past, 'over there.' The sky spirit looked, but he didn't see her anywhere. Deciding that he had to get closer to Earth, he changed into the lightning serpent, flashing down through the sky. Usually, the lightning serpent makes the black stone where it touches the Earth, but this time, the lightning landed on the sea, so it raced through the water as a large black fish." Afutu pulled down the lightning design as Naro formed the fish. For its eye, it had one of Naaba's perfectly round obsidian points.

Finished, Sule turned to Afutu, who continued the tale. "The black fish, with its shining black scales, searched the coral heads and their rainbow of colors, thinking she might be there. The coral flowers pulsed and swayed, and the brilliant blue and yellow fish darted among the moving branches, but she wasn't there. A queen triggerfish of many colors swam by, and he asked it where he could find all the colors of the rainbow. 'Oh, the rainbow turns into fish when she touches the water,' the triggerfish said. 'Many fish, made of all different colors. Didn't you know that?'

Abran stepped into the quiet, his deep base voice swelling over the sound of the two small wood pieces he beat in tempo:

Many fish of many colors, at the bottom of the rainbow, scattered into the sea.

Sohko joined him, harmonizing.

Many fish of many colors, scattered in the sea -
How can I collect them again, all these fish of many colors?
Where do they go, the rainbow fish?
Tell me, please.
I would go anywhere to find them.

Afutu continued: "The black fish searched everywhere, but he found only schools of fish that were colored the same: all blue fish, or all yellow fish, or all red and white fish. He asked everyone he saw, even the sharks and the starfish, but they said nothing. Finally, he asked the smallest creatures he knew, the tiny blennies dancing on the seafloor. They pointed to the stingray, mostly buried in the sandy ocean bottom."

As he formed the stingray figure in rope, Naaba took up the story: "The stingray didn't want to talk. It hid in the sand because it didn't want to be bothered. When the black fish kept asking, it moved off from its sandy hiding spot, but the black fish pursued him, over the coral heads and out to the deep water. There, the black fish swam right in front of the ray, butting the ray in the head. 'You must tell me; it's very important,' he said, so the Stingray agreed to tell him where the fishes of many colors would be. 'Today's sun has died, so you'll have to wait for the moon to rise into the sky, the full moon, where the rabbit jumps. Go where the water strikes the rocks, always crashing into the rocks and sending up its spray. Look so you see the moonlight reflecting on the spray.'

'And I'll find the fishes of all colors there?' the black fish asked, but the ray had slipped away into the dark sea.

Afutu continued the story while Naaba and Naro formed the rope into new figures. "When the black fish found the rocks where the waves crashed, he waited until the full moon rose high enough for him to see its reflection on the spray. The spray caught the moonlight, reflected it, just like a rainbow, except it was dark, with dark versions of all the rainbow colors arching over the rocky shore, dark reds and purples, muted yellows and oranges, deep blues and greens, all shimmering in the mist. Then, as he watched, the rainbow changed into a beautiful woman. She was standing there, on the rocks, her skin and robe very dark, her hair incredibly long and black, blowing in the mist. She lifted her arms and threw her long black hair back, so that it arched up and over, filled with every color of the dark rainbow. It blew with the mist, moving all the colors with it."

Dark colors forming in the mist, calling me, Abran and Sohko sang:

> *Calling me, taking me,*
> *Beautiful lady, Dark Rainbow, stay with me.*
> *Stay with me, be with me,*
> *Dark Rainbow, stay with me tonight.*

"The black fish forgot about the rainbow he was looking for. He didn't notice that there were no brightly colored fish there. If he had bothered to look, he would have seen all the fish lose their colors when she touched them. But he didn't. He headed toward her, toward the Dark Rainbow."

> *Dark colors forming in the mist, calling me to join you,*
> *Beautiful lady, Dark Rainbow under the moon.*

"So he turned himself back into lightning, and he wrapped himself around her. But she changed under his embrace. She grew to fill the night sky, so that her face was as large as the moon at the center of the sky. When her mouth opened, it was filled not with sweet words but with the roar of the angry sea." Naro looped the rope around to form the face. Where her eyes would be were two round obsidian pieces. 'I take your lightning to me!' she cried. 'It will be part of me from now on. Only when I am in power will you be.' The sky spirit struggled to escape, but the tendrils of her long hair held him trapped. 'You're not who I thought you were. I thought you were the Rainbow,' he cried as he struggled, cutting at her long hair. The enormous Dark Rainbow face studied him, her obsidian eyes glinting. 'No, I am exactly who you saw. I am exactly what you wanted.'

Moving toward the mat, Deka held up the smooth stones. "On the beach," she began, "there were smooth stones that could roll on their sides and spin in place. Every time the moon was full, they had a dance, a very fine dance, with music provided by the humming insects and the bats. They formed two lines, rolled toward their partners, then twirled around, changed partners, flipped over, and so on, as the dance movements demanded. Then, the two lines bent at the top and bottom, forming a moving circle, and four stones rolled into the center. Three of them formed a triangle on the sand, spinning in place. The fourth rolled up on top of them and spun on its side, all around the triangle. It was a very beautiful dance, but after a while, the Dark Rainbow blocked the moonlight, and the dancing stones stopped, right there, in their circle on the sand. They needed an open sky to dance."

As Deka sat back, finished, Afutu continued: "The stones lay there, motionless, until the new sun was born from the sea. Then they rolled down into the sea and back out, shiny wet, and they climbed back into their triangle, reflecting the sun's light into the fading Dark Rainbow. 'It's too late!' the Dark Rainbow spirit called. 'From now on, he can only live when the clouds hide the sun, when the storms rake the land. He belongs to the dark now!' She sighed as she faded away. 'But I'll leave you these,' she said, and the two obsidian eyes rolled to the earth."

Sule held up the two round obsidian pieces in his open palm at the end of the story, and the first thing he thought was that he was sorry it was over, the story they'd made together.

Everyone congratulated the children, and their helpers, on the story. Naro asked Dashona what she thought of the story, and the children crowded around to hear her response.

"It's not like yours, not as good as yours," Sule added, trying to clarify.

Dashona put her hands on the children's heads. "It was very fine." There was more she could have said, if someone else had asked, but the children had worked hard to tell a good story. They all had. It wasn't their fault that their story, or, for that matter any story, no matter how fine, couldn't pull her out of the darkness she'd come to know since the storm had taken them. Before that, she'd never known that the gods simply toyed with the elements, tossing the giant waves before them like so many strings of beads. If this was the truth of the world, it was only a matter of days before the gods tried to kill them again, not for anything they'd done, but only because the gods found it entertaining. Even if they lived, and the gods let them pass, it was only a temporary reprieve. Ultimately, for these travelers in their little boats on the endless sea, there was only one story, and it was too grim to tell. So she smiled absently at Deka and Sule, forgot about Naro, and went back to staring at the dark sea disappearing under the boats.

Putting her arm around Dashona's shoulder, Asha said, "I don't have your gift, but I'd like to tell you about a tree in my old village. It had beautiful flowers that turned into delicious fruit, but every year, animals devoured the fruit and stripped off the stems and leaves. Mice chewed at the roots, and borers made holes in the trunk. But every year, even with all that, the tree still bloomed. Its beauty was its power."

"I can't find any beauty right now; it seems like a silly notion that people invented to make themselves feel better," she said without turning around, "but thank you for caring about me."

"We all care about you."

"What are we, out here, when we're measured against the sea and the stars? Nothing more than foam on the waves. One life more or less makes no difference."

"Your life makes a difference." Asha pinched the woman's arm sharply.

"Ow! What are you doing?"

"Showing you that your feelings matter; you matter; we all matter," Asha said, her temper rising.   "No one's going to dismiss any of us as unimportant. And if you think for a moment that we're going to be able to get along without you, you're very wrong. You can hurt, but we all share it. So think about that."

It wasn't that Asha didn't understand. She knew that it was a difficult balance, to acknowledge the power of the gods and yet maintain the importance of individual life. It was hard to know whether the gods had spared them on purpose or simply hadn't noticed the tiny specks on the sea being blown about by the storm. If the gods had spared them on purpose, what purpose did they have in mind? If they were simply playing with their creation for their own amusement, what would it profit people to worry about it? Asha sighed. Sometimes, it was better to simply do the best you could. It wasn't given to people to know the minds of the gods.

A pair of dolphins jumped out of the water in perfect unison, water spraying around them, as they rose in their arc, silvery and glistening, then turned back down, slicing through the waves. "We should learn from them," Asha said, as she got up.   "They live in joy. It must make the gods smile just to watch them."

Dashona nodded but she didn't care. The dolphins had their world; she had hers.

* * *

CHAPTER 19
MEMORIES OF THE LAND

In the area of the southern Caribbean currently known as
The Lesser and Greater Antilles, from The Grenadines
north and west all the way up to Cuba

"They're whales," Naaba remarked, squinting.

Sohko held up his hand to shade his eyes. "Then why don't they move?"

"Because they're so far away."

"Even far-away whales would move."

"They do move, but they're so far away, you can't tell."

"They're islands," Naro said, joining them. "Just rock outcrops or coral heads that break the surface. The water's pretty shallow around here."

"How long have you known that?"

"About the coral islands? Well, I saw one yesterday so close to the surface that the water swirled over the top."

"Why didn't you point it out?"

Naro shrugged. "We've gotten our hopes up before, for nothing. I wanted to see if there were more, or there were bigger ones, before I announced a sighting. A little button of rock or coral sticking out of the sea isn't going to be enough." He couldn't quite explain the rest, at least not to them. The sight of the land had sent him reeling back to the other land, his land, the day of the festival: Berko, the screams of the crowd, the weight of the ball on his shoulder and his leg. It was so clear, where everyone had stood, in the middle of the play, one instant before it happened. He'd watched Afutu fall, and Abran, the two heroes undone in a single moment. It was the land that kept calling up this memory. When he saw the rock stubbornly rising up through the water, managing to support a few mangroves, or provide a resting spot for a tropicbird, he saw his own history refusing to be buried. So he'd ignored the islands and said nothing. But now, others knew, and everything would change.

Sohko waved toward the shapes on the water. "I think those are more than buttons, unless buttons have trees growing on them."

Within moments, the news had spread and everyone had seen them, the fringed shapes rising out of the water in a line running north. Land! A string of islands, like beads on a giant's necklace. Land! Trees! And beaches, long stretches of white or dark sand where they could easily land the boats. They could imagine the rest: mangroves and sea almond trees by the water's edge, bright-colored flowers growing in masses on the hillside, a clear river flowing to the sea, parrots flashing in the treetops. There would be yams and mangoes ripe for the picking, figs, coconut palms, craboo trees, plenty to eat and drink, and room to explore.

The azure water was extraordinarily clear around them, so they could see right down to the coral fans swaying in the current and the schools of fish swimming around them. There were spotted eagle rays grazing along the grassy bottom and sea turtles swimming close to the boat. But even with these wonders, their gaze was drawn back to the land.

"I'd forgotten," Asha realized, out loud.

For most of them, the sight of the islands set off a desperate hunger to be on land again, and they began a frantic effort to steer toward the nearest ones, but the wind and current were against them, and they couldn't get any closer. The islands slid by, small and tantalizing, each with its own appeal, its own history that could have been written there if they'd been able to land. In their disappointment, they said little that night, and no one told a story. Even in the dark, they could picture the shallow waters around them, the corals and fish, the rays and sharks, and, most of all, the islands appearing like a line of dark forested whales moving just beyond their reach.

The following day, when they awoke, they were shocked to see the sun being born out of the split top of a mountain surrounded by the sea, right in front of them. The sign was unmistakable. With the tide in their favor, they were able to work their way toward the edge of the island and then, when the sun was past its height, around to the beach, a fine sweep of white sand behind which the hills rose in a confusion of giant tree ferns, palm trees, and flowering spice bushes. At the far end, another island rose abruptly, like the nose of a giant whale just coming to the surface.

As they neared the shore, they threw out the anchor stone and jumped into the clear water with a shout. But they were so used to being in the boat, they struggled to stay upright, even in the gentle waves. Even as they pulled themselves toward the shore, the sea held them back. One after another, they fell or dropped into the water, or splashed each other, or swam out among the corals. A moment before, the land had held them like the promise of a lover, but once they were within steps of it, they found it hard to leave the water. Afutu, especially, was reluctant to leave the boat. He'd come to define himself as a navigator. On the sea, his weak leg was irrelevant. On land, it was different.

"I'll stay with the boats while you look around," he said to the departing group.

Sohko swung around. "We'll take turns watching the boats. Do you have the conch?"

When Afutu nodded, Sohko waited for him to hold it up, then glanced around. Dashona was the first to step ashore, and Naro was close behind her. Aminata coughed quietly.

"Naro!" Sohko called. "We need you to help with the first watch."

In mid-stride, Naro stopped and turned on Sohko. "Oh? And *you* decided that? Who made you chief?"

Unfazed, Sohko spread his hands. "We'll all do our share. Is there a problem with that?"

Everyone stopped, exactly where they were, in the water or on the beach, listening. There was little Naro could do but agree. But the implied challenge was a sign that their world was changing. They'd needed each other when they were trying to survive on the open sea. Now that they were on land, it was different. The world looked idyllic here, but as soon as people stepped on it, it grew more complicated.

In the boats, Afutu and Naro said almost nothing until Naro felt the others were out of earshot. "So," he began, settling down in the other boat, across from Afutu, "did Sohko ask you to stay with the boats?"

"No, I offered."

"Noble of you. Of course, it's probably easier for you here, where you don't have to walk around. I only mean you're able to function normally in the boats."

"You probably mean exactly what you're saying, and more."

"What more would I mean?"

"It's only a guess. Perhaps I'm wrong."

Naro thumped his broad hand on the gunnels impatiently, looking out to the shore. "I'm really good with the boats, the best one in the group. I could take these boats right now, and sail away, leaving these stupid people to their own devices to live or die."

"When did they become 'stupid people' to you? I thought these were your friends."

"I don't have any friends. Neither do you. You're a poor excuse for what used to be an athlete. You're not much of a candidate for a husband, either. A husband should be able to protect his wife, but what can you do? Limp behind after an assailant?"

Afutu smiled oddly. "It's funny. You have everything I want: an able body, a quick mind, a talent for handling boats. You could be a ball player, if we ever found a court again. You can run and jump and swim; you can do everything. But all you want to do is torment me. If I was given my legs back, I wouldn't waste even a moment tormenting you. It's strange how it works out." When Naro didn't reply, Afutu went on. "If you feel that strongly about me, why'd you help me into the boat after the game? Why not leave me?"

"Sheeah asked me."

"And you were trying to impress her? Or you owed her a favor?"

"I guess you owe me your life," Naro snapped, pitching a calabash into the other end of the boat. "So you can repay the debt."

"What's going on with you?"

"You know. You just like playing the game, don't you? If not one game, then another, right?"

"Honestly, I have no idea what's going on here, except that you're very angry, particularly with me."

"Every woman I want, you steal."

"Every what?"

"You heard me. First Sheeah, then Dashona. As soon as you're around, I'm nothing. But all that's going to end. You owe me Dashona."

"She's not mine to give. She's her own person. Believe me, she really is."

"I sit here, day after day, watching her, but she doesn't even see me. But you can change that. Then we can be friends, after you've changed that." He was coiling and uncoiling the rope as he

331

talked, making it into knots and yanking them apart. "That's what you'd like, isn't it, for us to be friends?"

"She's not mine to give," Afutu repeated.

"Then everyone will pay."

"Why would you have come all this way, through so much, just to throw it all away?"

"Oh, I won't throw it away. I'll take it all with me. I'll just leave behind the unnecessary parts. Those would include you, 'friend.' And a lot of others."

"Something happened when we came to this island. What?"

"I would have been fine, with Dashona. I would've made her see who I am, except Sohko sent me here. But he'll regret that." Finishing a monkey's fist knot at the end of a rope, he twirled it around his head and hurled it just past Afutu, out into the water. "I suppose they might be able to survive here," he laughed, "at least for a while."

"Naro, something's taken your mind. I don't know when this happened, but you need to look around with a clear eye. We're in this together. You, me, Sohko, all of us. It's not a competition against each other. There are only losers in that game."

"What do you know of winning and losing? Nothing! You always won!"

"What is it that you want?"

"I already told you."

"No, I mean after today. What do you want in your life?"

Naro stared out at the sea without answering.

"The land brought back all this, didn't it? At sea, you were a happy man, but here, you're a fighter again and I'm your opponent. Dashona doesn't really matter to you; she's just the prize."

"I'm the best sailor in the group."

"Yes, you are," Afutu agreed, reaching for the knife tucked into his sash.

"And no one could catch me."

"What would you do, if you were free, on the water?"

"I'd keep going. I'd live on the sea so long that the wind and the waves were part of me, and the seas and great whales and spinning dolphins knew my name. I'd live on the sea until it killed me. Then I'd live in the bottom of the sea forever."

Afutu started cutting the line that had lashed the boats together since the storm. "Then you need to go, friend, because the land is full of darkness for you right now."

Naro stared. "What are you doing? You can't do that."

"It's either that, or you and I will have to fight until one of us is dead, and I have no wish to kill you, even if the feeling isn't mutual. I always thought of you as a friend, a good opponent, a competitor, but you have dark spirits chasing you now. I know them well, believe me. This anger isn't about me, or Dashona, or any of the others here. Leave them to sort out their own troubles. It's not their fault." With the last of the ties cut, the boats floated gradually apart. "Were you in on the arrangement at the game?" Afutu asked as Naro's boat, now free of the anchor stone, drifted with the waves.

"Yes." The answer was so low that Afutu wasn't certain for a moment that he'd heard it. "Berko talked to me himself, before the game. Promised me a fine reward, though I never got it." He stopped while he looked around for a paddle in the bow, then knelt and rocked back on his heels. "I thought it would make a difference with Sheeah, but she never noticed, even after I carried you to the boat. Not even when we got away from the battle, or when we stayed on the island. She never saw me."

"May you travel on better waters," Afutu called after the receding figure, but Naro didn't reply. As he picked up the paddle, he realized there were still many personal items in the boat: mats, baskets, boxes, even the children's carved animal figures that Sheeah had given them. For some reason, the little ivory antelope and elephant, especially, seemed wrong to take. He had no fight with the children. He simply couldn't stay. Packing it all in the

biggest basket, he tied it shut and threw it into the water, but he
didn't look back to see if Afutu picked it up. The past was killing
him. His only hope was the future.

* * *

The loss of Naro left them all weakened, easily threatened by
shadows. Ghosts of those who'd died violently haunted them. Deka
thought she saw The Leader standing on the mountain, smashing
her father's head open with a war club, the head spinning grotesquely
as the body crumpled in slow motion. Sule saw the boy, Paki, who'd
stood up against the invaders at the river. He was standing at the
edge of the forest, pointing to the poisoned arrow still piercing his
throat. Asha saw Dwyka falling in a rain of blood and brightly
colored feathers, even as her namesake soared into the heavens. Ayo
was sure she saw her brother's face hanging up high in one of the
trees. The mouth was moving, as if he was trying to talk to her, but
she couldn't hear anything.

One by one, they were drawn away, each to a separate memory and a separate pain, and the sunlight disappeared under the
curtain of the past.

All alone in the center of the island, Naaba wandered up into
the cloud forest high on the hill, the way he had long ago. The
air was cool and damp, with clouds trailing through the treetops.
Giants grew there, trees older than man could know. He stopped in
front of a locust tree that was so large it seemed to be its own village, its network of branches stretching out sideways into the forest,
its grizzled trunk rising straight up into the sky, its canopy so dense
it blocked the sunlight from the forest floor. It was easy to find
footholds in the creases of the trunk, and he climbed rapidly and
surely, his hands over his feet. When he stopped for a rest, he looked
down, surprised at how high he was, halfway between the earth and

the sky. Above him, parrots screeched at the intruder in their world then took off in a flash of red, blue, and green through the treetops.

The tree's night-blooming flowers were closed, but in the notch of a branch, lines of pale orchids cascaded from the parent plant, a mass of pinkish white glowing in the filtered green of the forest. Like jewels, crested hummingbirds flashed among the flowers then hovered, motionless, while their wings beat in a blur. His head lifted, Naaba drew in the smells of the forest, from the musty forest floor, to the strange smell of the tree that held him, to the tiny green frogs flattened against its trunk. Closing his eyes, he felt the length of the tree stretching down into the earth so far that it reached into the Underworld, spreading out once it was there, so it encircled the whole universe below, taking to itself all those who belonged to the Underworld and holding them in the arc of its roots. Then, turning around, it shot upward, piercing the surface of the earth, crossing into the realm of the living, ruled by the sun and the rain, enduring season after season as it grew. But it was unlike the other things of earth, and, over time, it reached up ever higher until it pressed up against the sky and sent shoots into the land of the spirits. It moved out of death, to life, to the edge of immortality, and back again. Like sentinels of the three worlds, they stand, these sacred trees, all over the world, each one the center of the universe. And Naaba, at this moment, was given the ability to understand them. As he turned around, he noticed the tree had a long scar made by a lightning strike, long ago. His back, still crisscrossed with scars, had touched the tree's scar: their separate pasts touching the present, the present healing the past. As he ran his fingers across the scar, beads of healing resin on the edges broke off into his hand. In return, because he had no other gift to give, he took out his knife and drew a line of dots like the tree's scar along his arm, and let the drops of blood fall on the great tree. As the red drops darkened and seeped into the bark, Naaba wept for all they had lost, and all those who had suffered, whether he knew them or not, whether he agreed with them or not. Then, exhausted, he slept, cradled by the branches of the giant.

At the same moment that Naaba's blood was taken up by the great tree, Asha found her way to the river, pushing through the thorny underbrush, stepping and slipping across the wet rocks until she stood stock still in the middle of the stream, feeling the cool water surge through her, clearing out the darkness. As she stood there, with the water all around her and through her, she felt something else: a fluttering, like the wings of a bird, under her heart.

* * *

One by one, the others were able to see the sunlight once again, and they sought out the company of their friends, finding their familiar faces very fine, and reassuring.

CHAPTER 20
DECISIONS

"We've got some decisions to make," Sohko announced to the group sitting in a circle on the beach, "like where we want to go, whether we want to build a second boat, whether we all want to go together or not. A lot of choices." When no one spoke up, he added, "I thought we'd hear from everyone about what they'd like, and then try to figure out how to do whatever we can agree on. We'll start with you," he said, handing the speech stick to Afutu, the first person to his right.

"First of all, I think we should make Sohko chief because he's so good at it," Afutu smiled. "Then, we should build a second boat. There'd be more room, and we'd have a backup if the other one is lost or damaged. It would be a help to me if we made one with a handle or ledge on the outside, so I can get in on my own. Maybe it's only vanity, but it might make a difference at some point." He passed the stick to Aminata.

"We have some valuable resources here on the island: calabashes, medicinal plants, foods, building materials. While you're building the second boat, we should gather supplies to take with us." When she was finished, she handed the stick to Deka.

"I don't think we're supposed to talk," she whispered to Sule.

He shrugged. "They gave it to you. Say something."

"I think we need a game to play on the boat, something that doesn't have lots of little pieces that get lost." Embarrassed at the

337

silence that followed that suggestion, she handed off the stick to her brother.

"I think we should all go somewhere together," Sule said gravely, "because it's bad when ... people go away."

"Well, I think that too," Deka added.

"Quiet. You don't have the stick," her brother said, handing the stick to Ayo.

"This chain of islands was shown to us for a reason," she said. "It points like an arrow, for us to follow. But before we go, we need to make new mats and baskets, plus a new fish funnel. Almost everything was damaged in the storm, and, as Aminata said, we have lots of material here. If you have other ideas about the boat mats, we could try to make something different." She wanted to go on, wanted to talk about new ideas she had, but this wasn't the time, so she passed the stick to Abran.

Hesitating, Abran studied the stick for a moment, then said, "I agree with everything that's been said. I'm happy to help build the new boat. Chahuk built a great boat, but we might want to make a few changes in the new one. It's worth considering, anyway. Also, I think we need to keep a record of some kind, perhaps on a stick like this, marking the days and what happened. I don't know how, exactly; maybe, Naaba, you could figure out something."

Taking the stick from Abran, Dashona also paused before answering. "To tell you the truth, I've found it extraordinary being part of this group, even though I may not have always acted that way. I can't imagine what I'd need, other than your friendship." With that, she handed off the stick to Asha.

"I agree with Dashona, and the others," Asha said, "but on a purely practical level, we need to figure out a better water collection system. If we stay on islands without fresh water, we'll need a back-up supply. Maybe we could build something into the new boat to help. Also, we need to decide on more conch signals, so we can talk to each other across the water." With that, she handed the stick to Naaba.

"I'll be happy to help with the building projects. We need better drills and chisels, since we lost most of our old tools in the storm. But, most importantly, I agree with the others. This circle is my family." Then he handed the stick back to Sohko.

"Well, that's the plan then," Sohko began.

"No," Naaba interrupted. "You didn't say what you want."

"I don't have to. It's all been said. That's why I let you all go first." He looked around the circle with a nod. "We'll take a complete moon to build the new boat and try it out, gather supplies and medicines, build new mats, make tools, design a game, figure out a way to record days and events, work on signals and a water collection system, and finish all the other jobs, then head on, following the islands. Is that the will of the group?"

"It is!"

"Then it's decided."

So Sohko became recognized as chief, partly because Afutu offered him the honor, and partly because everyone already saw him that way.

* * *

While the rest of the group made their plans, Naro headed away from them as fast as he could make the boat carry him, stopping only long enough to add a new mast, then a second mat, and a third. When he was finished, the wind took it skimming over the water like a seabird, a creature of the air only barely attached to the water. Always, he wanted to go faster, to lean tighter into the turns, to feel the boat yield to his commands. But he couldn't outrun his anger, and he blamed Afutu for it. Somehow, Afutu had won again, though he wasn't sure exactly how the competition had played out. At the time, it seemed he'd beaten Afutu, scared him into giving away the boat. But later, when he thought of it, it seemed Afutu had tricked him into leaving. As he went over it, he decided it was all Dashona's fault. Afutu had conned him in order to protect her, or to keep her for himself. Or she'd asked Afutu to get rid of him. In other moments, he thought it was his own fault, though he couldn't quite decide where things had gone wrong. When Berko approached him, asking him to do something special, should he have refused his chief? But it kept coming back to the strange feeling he'd had when they were telling the story the children wanted to put on, and he and Afutu were working the knots and rope figures, and it seemed so easy, like friends. Why hadn't it stayed that way? And now, why had Afutu sent him away, left him to die on the sea, all alone? It was Afutu's fault. And Dashona's, the witch always tempting him then refusing him. After the story was over, she hadn't even looked at him. It was like he was just air and she looked right through him. But it was good when they were working on the story, and he was good with knots. He was the best with knots, and the boats. So what if they didn't want him? He had his own boat, and the sea, and the wind above it. He'd be part of their world instead. Still, somehow, Afutu had gotten rid of him, thrown him out of the group. What gave him that right? What was he, just a twisted wreck, since the game. Always, it came back to the game. That was a stupid name for something that was really about life and death. And he'd known. "You've got to play better than ever," Berko had said, "so Afutu and the others don't notice the new players. But I know you can do that. You always play well." It'd been hard to ignore the compliment, and he'd agreed without really understanding what was coming. Well, not fully understanding. He knew about the substitutes and the helmets. But it was a game, and it was about winning, right? Who plays a game to lose? So he'd won. But somehow, he'd lost. And something very important remained unanswered, and it gnawed at him.

He tightened up the mats and pushed the boat faster.

CHAPTER 21
THE ISLAND OF BIRDS

When the wind was up, Naro would push the boat along a route parallel to the island chain, on the leeward side. But when the wind dropped, he'd make painfully slow progress, no matter how he arranged the mats. At night, he'd take the mats down and tie the steering paddle to what he thought was a safe course, then try to sleep. But the stars were too bright, and sometimes he thought he heard them singing. To block out the sound, he wrapped cloth around his head, but he knew it was still there. When there was a bright moon, he'd put up the main mat and keep an eye out for rocks, just to have something to do. Sometimes he'd dream his parents, or sisters, were on board, sleeping behind one of the large baskets. Then, confused, he'd think they were home, but he didn't remember where that was. He thought about a girl he'd loved, the first girl he'd loved. But he was popular, and there were lots of girls interested, and he let her go. He wondered if she'd settled down with someone else, if she ever thought about him late at night, when she lay in her husband's arms. What if he could find her, right now, sitting on the beach of some deserted island, under the bending palms? Would she smile and invite him into her arms, saying she'd been waiting for him all this time, knowing he'd be passing by? No, probably not. Why isn't there a warning when important things are happening, a loud drum beat, perhaps, that would let people know that this moment is very special, that it shouldn't be lost in the everyday flood of unimportant events. Perhaps that smile from that person in the marketplace isn't just a harmless flirtation; it's the beginning of a lifelong relationship. But how would you know?

When he filleted a fish one day, a gull flew up and perched on the bowsprit. With a nod, Naro threw it the remains of the fish. After swallowing its prize, the gull took off, laughing its "ha-ha-ha" cry. The next day, there were three gulls and a shearwater perched on the bow. The day after, a dozen gulls and terns perched on the gunnels, and a storm petrel ran along the water next to the boat, patting its little feet on the surface until it rose into the air. Naro found them entertaining, for a while, but after a few days, they got bolder. They didn't wait for him to throw the fish to them; they dove at it, pecking at it, grabbing it out of his hands as soon as he pulled it out of the sea. Then they flew over his head, squabbling, flying at each other with their screaming calls, sending out streams of droppings that landed all over the boat.

In the middle of the bird's noisy competition one day, he was surprised to see another boat, quite a ways ahead of him. At far as Naro could tell, with all the birds flying around, there was only one person in the boat, someone who was waving both arms broadly. A greeting? A plea for help? Naro tried to see it more clearly, but the birds whirled right into his line of sight, and the boat was too far away for him to catch anyway. Still, it was interesting to see another person. He hadn't even considered that there might be other people here. Maybe there was a whole settlement. He strained to catch a glimpse of the boat again after the birds moved off, but by then it was gone, and the unanswered questions bothered him.

A few days later, the birds came back in even greater numbers, lining up along the gunnels. Annoyed, he swung a knotted rope at them when they flew in close. They soared just out of reach, twisting and turning above him, laughing at him. He started throwing things at them: the extra calabash, pieces of wood, whatever he could find. When that didn't deter them, he picked up a rock from the bottom of the boat and hurled it right at them. A single tern fell out of the sky and thudded down at his feet, its white body, black cap, and grey wings crumpled together. When he picked it up, it seemed to be too light to be real, as if its weight had disappeared with its life.

"It's your fault!" he screamed at the other birds, waving his arms at them. "Go away!"

In his distraction, he wasn't thinking about the boat, and by the time he noticed the rocky outcrops breaking the surface, he was heading straight for them. Grabbing the steering paddle, he tried to turn the boat, but he was going too fast to correct his course in time. The bow caught first, throwing him face-first into the baskets on the floor of the boat. Just as he lurched to his feet, the keel caught on a different rock, throwing him sideways. He grabbed hold of the gunnels, trying to steady himself while he found a pole, but there was none in the boat. As the bottom scraped along the rocks, he found the spare paddle, turned it upside down and tried to push off the rocks. But the boat's speed had pushed it right over the top of the outcrop. There was nothing to do but push it off the other side. With a pained shout, he pushed the boat along, listening to the terrible sound of the rock tearing at the bottom as it went over. By the time he was free of the rocks, the boat was leaking in four different places. Unfortunately, he'd thrown his extra calabash overboard, so he had only his water gourd to use for bailing. Tilting his head back, he drank all the water left in it, and looked around, sorting out the possibilities. There were only two islands close enough for him to reach before the boat was swamped. He headed for the larger one, tying the steering paddle on a direct course for it, and bailing as fast as he could.

When he looked up to check his course, the birds were gone.

* * *

Jumping out in the shallows, Naro hauled the half-submerged boat onto the beach, turned it over on its side, and inspected it. The news wasn't good. In addition to the holes punched along the front and bottom, the keel was cracked. He slumped down to the sand and closed his eyes.

When he awoke, blinking in the hot sun, he was thirsty. He searched the boat, looking for more water, but he'd pitched one calabash at the birds and emptied the other. With all this vegetation, he thought, there had to be water nearby. In his search, he found coconut palms, loofah, soursop, papaya, and tiny limes, but no lake or river, not even a pothole filled with rainwater. He sucked what moisture he could from the fruits and drank a little of the coconut milk, but it didn't quench his thirst.

"It's not what I want," he complained to the air around him.

"And what is it, exactly, that you want?"

Jerking his head toward the sound, he saw a woman sitting off to his left, on a bluff overlooking a different beach, on the far side of the island. She was wearing a blue wrap and yellow pearls in her jet black hair, with more around her neck and the waist of her wrap. Her face seemed vaguely familiar, as if he'd known her long ago but couldn't remember. "I -"

"That's what I thought," she sighed, as she went back to her work. On her lap was a round piece of wood she was working on, carefully inlaying mother of pearl and abalone pieces that she had set out in palm leaves next to her. *"Oh, poor me,"* she said, whining in imitation. *"Why doesn't everything go the way I want it to, all the time?"*

He was still staring at her.

"Well, that doesn't add much."

"Who? What?"

"There you go, just about to hit your stride in the conversation. Let me guess. *Who are you? Why are you here? What are you doing on this tiny island far away from everywhere?* Am I close?"

Naro nodded.

"Well, they aren't the easiest questions to answer, for anyone, I suppose. I could ask the same of you, but I think you would make up some story about how someone double-crossed you and you wound up here by accident. Am I right?"

He nodded again.

"Right, except it wasn't, was it?"

"Not entirely," he admitted. "Actually, a lot of birds added to the problem, at least the latest problem. See, I was -"

"Oh, I know about the birds," she said calmly.

"No, I mean there were these laughing gulls, and some terns -"

"And a few frigate birds. I know." She held up the round wooden piece she'd been working on. The center was inlaid with highly polished black coral pieces fitted together to form a gleaming round mirror that flashed like a second sun in her hands. Around the edges, she'd chiseled out spaces for the mother-of-pearl pieces that she glued in with resin. They were carefully cut shapes of different birds, all flying around the border of the plate. It was an incredible piece of work.

He stared at the flashing plate. "But no one -"

"No one knows about the birds? Don't be silly. The birds do." She laughed with a sound just like the gulls.

Drawing away, he tried to find his old reality, but it seemed to have abandoned him. "I have to go now," he said.

"Of course you do," she nodded, "because you have a boat that can't go anywhere at all and no water and probably not much food." She waited. "I could show you the only fresh water on the island, if you were interested. Or not – whatever you want."

"Everything seems different here."

"That could be," she said, not looking up from her work.

He waited for some semblance of normality to return, but it didn't. "Fresh water would be good, if you were going that way anyway."

"And if I'm not?"

Naro searched the area around them, thinking perhaps she was sitting right next to a spring, or a well, but there was nothing. "I'm thirsty." It was blunt, but it was true.

Still she waited, looking at him.

He looked back, suddenly angry with her toying with him. "Where is the water?"

She worked slowly, cutting a wing piece and fitting it perfectly into its place.

Tired of her taunts, he thought about leaping across the space between them, grabbing her by her neck and shaking the truth out of her.

"Not a good idea," she said.

"What?"

"That."

"Then stop taunting me! What is it you want?"

"What is it YOU want?"

"Water!"

"Then ask for it!"

"May I have some water?" he said, clenching his jaw. "Please."

"Probably. Let's go see." Carefully, she wrapped up her work and set it under an arching palm, then started off toward the center of the island. "Are you coming?" she called back.

Driven by thirst and curiosity, he followed. She moved surprisingly quickly through the heavy growth. Occasionally, she'd call out something, like "Watch that tree with the little green fruits; it'll burn your skin," but she never pointed to the tree she was talking about, so he wasn't sure which one she meant.

As they moved inland, the biting flies found him, making his mood even darker. "Is there really any water here, or is this your idea of fun?"

She ignored him, pressing farther into the dense brush, slipping through spots that held him fast in tangled vines, so he had to cut his way through. By the time he freed himself, she was far ahead, calling back something he couldn't understand.

"What?"

By the time the word left his mouth, he knew what she'd tried to warn him about. Right in front of him, a great hole opened up in the earth. He slid to a stop at the edge of the rounded lip of rock. Like the rim of an enormous bowl, it fanned out in a circle, though some parts were hidden by brush. Far below, the sides of the bowl dropped down and down until they disappeared from view. The cool moist air fed the plants crowding around the edge, but the sheer walls were bare rock, marked only with dark stains running top to bottom.

"It's -" he stammered, "it's -"

"Yes," she laughed as she started off again, "it is."

"But how -"

"I'll show you. There's a series of ledges you can follow." Stepping easily from one rock bump to another, she moved down the side of the bowl at an angle.

After one unnerving glance down, Naro tried to move exactly as she did, stepping quickly from one tiny rock nub to the next, with barely enough room for a toehold on each. The walls glistened with moisture, but when he put his hand out to steady himself, he cut his hands on the rough bumps. Still, he went on, his legs aching, stepping from one stone to the next, angling his way down toward the water. The farther he went, the cooler and darker it got, since the sunlight couldn't reach down that far, especially off to the side away from the shafts of sunlight.

"You're almost there," she called, from quite a distance. "You can even jump from there, if you want."

He wasn't about to jump into unknown water in the half-dark, so he kept stepping from ridge to ridge, but after a while there wasn't enough light for him to see the bumps he was aiming for. Eventually, he slipped and fell. It seemed to take a long time to reach the water, like a fall in a dream. When he did land, the cold water was a shock, but it was pure, fresh water, and it tasted very fine. He gulped down as much as he could hold, then looked around for the girl. It'd be good to spend a little time here, the two of them together. "Pretty good. The water's good," he said, waiting for her to reply. "Are you there?" he added, but there was no answer other than his own echo bouncing off the walls and coming back to him. "Where'd you go?" The echoes came back, but no response. "Hey! Hello!" he yelled, peering into the dim light, but he couldn't see any form breaking the surface of the water or climbing the ledges that stuck out of the wall. "Where are you? Can you hear me? Answer me!" The words rippled sharply over the water, back and forth. "I've had enough of your games! Maybe you think this is really funny, but I don't. What are you about, anyway? Why bring me out here and leave me? Where are you? *Where are you?* Show me where you are!" Long moments went by, with only his overlapping echoes shouting at each other. When they died away, he listened, motionless in the water, but he heard absolutely nothing - no sound from anywhere in the water or along the walls. "Witch!" he yelled, swinging around, stabbing at the water. "You witch! You tricked me! You made me come here! You did this to me. You think you've beaten me, but you haven't. You'll see. You think you've left me here to die, but I'll find a way out. I will! Witch!" The shouts reverberated across the water and off the rock walls, but even with his temper rising, he couldn't force an answer from the air.

High above him, where the rock rim met the sunshine, a tern perched, its head cocked sideways, listening to the cacophony of sounds rising from the deep rock reservoir below.

* * *

The truth was, for the first time in a long time, Naro was worried. When he thought about the long climb back up, with only the tiny ledges for purchase, it seemed impossible. If he had ropes to guide him, it'd still be difficult, but at least he wouldn't face plunging back down into the reservoir with every wrong move. But he didn't have ropes. Or an ally on the surface to help.

After he'd exhausted his anger shouting and flailing around in the water, he took stock of the situation. On the plus side, he wasn't hurt; he knew how to get out, if he could manage it; he had lots of fresh water and had filled the calabash, though he couldn't think of a way to carry it up with him; for part of the day, the sunlight would illuminate the wall. On the minus side, he was hungry and tired and had wasted most of his energy being angry. For tools, he had his knife. That was it.

Reaching the side of the pool, he tried to pull himself up on the closest ledge, but the edge was rough and his hands were wet. He kept trying until his hands were scraped raw, but he still couldn't get a solid grip. He'd tucked the calabash under his arm while he was trying to climb, but it got in the way and he needed both arms free to climb. Unwilling to abandon it, he untied his sash and cut it into strips, tying one around the narrowest part of the neck of the calabash and crisscrossing it around his back and across his chest. He wrapped his hands with the others, leaving only his fingers free.

One ledge at a time, he reached up, finding a place to grip and pulling himself out of the water, but progress was slow. The same ledges he stepped down so quickly had to be traversed slowly, one at a time, on the way up. He'd gone only a quarter of the way when the light began to fade. There was no way he could hold himself against the rock wall all night, but as he scanned the area, he noticed one of the ledges had a hole in it, near the rock face. There was the chance it wouldn't hold, but he'd have to take it. Tying together the strips he'd wrapped around his hands, he made a loop that ran through the hole in the rock, forming a makeshift sling to sit in, balanced under the ledge. If it gave way, he'd fall all the way back down. If it held, he'd be able to keep going when he had enough light. He didn't sleep well, but he didn't crash back down into the reservoir, either. He thought about Asha, and how she'd love a place like this. Water, especially water underground, seemed magical to her. He didn't know what this water was or what it meant. The whole island was very strange.

The new sun threw its light into the cave at an angle, so it illuminated the wall opposite him while his side was still in deep shadow, but Naro was anxious to get going. Stepping out of the sling, he almost fell when he missed his toehold, saving himself by grabbing the loop of cloth and pulling himself back up again. Once he'd gotten himself calmed down, he reached for the first of the new day's grips. It went a little faster this time since he had a process: hand, foot, pause, other hand, other foot, pause, and so on. When he found a ledge large enough to sit on, he took a break, drank a little water, and started up again.

Later in the day, his legs and arms were so sore, he stopped for a break on a larger ledge but fell asleep as soon as he'd wedged his back against the rock wall. Later, he woke with a start. The cave was inky dark. He couldn't see his own feet dangling over the edge, or the ledges below him. But when he looked straight up, he could see the stars filling the night sky. It was the first sign of the surface he'd seen in days, and for the first time in his life, he found them incredibly beautiful.

When he got started climbing the next day, he realized how weak he'd become. His legs cramped painfully; his arms trembled when he extended them. The last part of the bowl had the biggest ledges, but the sides curved in under the rim, so he'd have to reach up for handholds behind his head and pull himself up and out, with no purchase for his feet, but he made himself go one ledge at a time. Finally, he could see treetops and blue sky through the opening. He just had to find a way to get around the lip of the bowl. Across the way, he saw a wider ledge just under the rim. It must have been the way he came down, but it meant finding his way sideways around a good section of the bowl. There wasn't any choice; he didn't have the strength left to pull himself up onto the rim without a foothold. Bit by bit, he worked his way around the wall to the opening at the rim, pushed himself up and crawled over the rim. Sunlight hit him full in the face as he stood up with a shout, his head thrown back, his fist raised in triumph. Then his trembling legs collapsed under him.

Once he was on the rim, he couldn't remember what path he'd taken to get there. Everything looked the same, heavily over-grown. He thought his boat was on the western shore, so he started through the dense brush in that direction, plowing through heavy vines and thick mats of thorny underbrush. When he came to a clearing, he tried to get his bearings, but he didn't recognize any of the landmarks he'd noted on the way up. At one point, he thought the trees looked familiar. Seeing small round green fruits on a tree, he remembered the woman's warning about the leaves. "Probably another trick," he said, as he grabbed a branch, but the leaves stung like warrior ants, and he jumped backwards and headed in the opposite direction.

Pouring some of his water on the burning skin, he yelled, "The truth is all twisted around lies here, like a nest of snakes!"

When he found his way to the shore, he realized it wasn't the beach where he'd left his boat. Somewhere in the interior, he'd lost track of the direction. Rather than risk getting lost again, he spent a whole day walking the perimeter, going from beaches to fields of rocks that tumbled straight out into the sea, to tidal flats where the mangroves' maze of roots made them impossible to traverse, so he had to swim around the edges. Past the mangroves, he came to an entire hillside full of birds. Whole colonies of birds, more than he'd ever seen before, more than he could count. It was a bird village, or collection of villages, of different species: cormorants, gulls, terns and others. They fluttered and squawked through disagreements, arguing over tiny patches of grass. After a while, he sat down on a rock, watching as more groups wheeled in from the sea and settled into the already crowded hillside. By the time the old sun was head-ing for the sea, the hillside was covered with birds. He could hear them squabbling and calling right up until the night took the land.

"The island's full of spirits," he declared, surveying the area in the last of the light, "spirits and ghosts." Another thought occurred

351

to him, but he didn't say it out loud. Perhaps every world is only a dream, so this world was only one of many, and people moved from one to the next with no more control than they had in a dream, but they reassured themselves that the one they were in at the moment was the real world and everything else was a dream. He found it a disturbing idea. He wondered about the woman with the yellow pearls and the beautiful woodwork. He'd never seen work that fine. She said she knew about the birds. The birds on his boat? These birds? The colonies of birds on the hillside? Was this whole island theirs? But why would they torment him in the first place? To see what he did? If he was being judged for the killing of the tern, why wasn't he killed? It would have been easy to arrange.

He sat up in the dark, listening to the flutter of bats hunting along the shore. Looking up, he saw the great bird in the center of the night sky, raising its wings as it struggled ever higher into infinity, and the serpent stretched out around it. They sang to him, these two, when he was on the boat; he remembered that now. *They, the forever ones, sang to me, and I tried to ignore them.* He hadn't noticed something as big as the sky. *No drum beats to make me pay attention. No drum beats when I needed them.* He walked out onto the beach and sat down with his neck craned back so he could watch the great bird swing in its arc through the center of the night sky, the combination of the powerful bird and the sinuous serpent coiling around it, forever, the masters of the sky, pulling the circle of the heavens around with them as they moved, making the heavens pulse with sound. He listened. And they sang to him.

* * *

352

CHAPTER 22
THE MAN IN THE BOAT

The following morning, he found his boat on the beach, lean-ing over on its side, just as he'd left it. Without a word, even to himself, he started gathering wood chips and soaking them, then pounding them to mushy pulp and squeezing out the water, leaving them to dry in the sun while he gathered resin bits from a Wood of Life tree and heated them on the rocks. Once they were soft and sticky, he stirred in the wood pulp and a little palm oil, mixing it together until it formed a gluey mass that he could push down into the cracks. These patches had to cure, so he used the time looking for a piece of wood he could use to repair the keel.

Occasionally, as he worked, he thought he heard a sound, per-haps the woman laughing, but when he looked, there was nothing there, not even a bird. When he took a break, he looked for her inlaid wooden plate, but there was no sign of it under the palms. Even after he'd finished repairing the keel, he glanced around before pushing the boat back into the water, but he never saw her. Eventu-ally, the repairs completed, he took it out for a trial run. Since the patches seemed to be holding, he headed back to his original course, leaving the island behind with a last long look.

A fresh breeze rose, and he set the mats to catch the wind. In the clear water next to the boat, a stingray swam, its giant wings moving easily up and down. Naro sucked in the clean air and nod-ded as the salt spray doused him.

Days later, dozing in the heat of the day, he was jolted awake by the sense something was out there, on the water, something he needed to see. Scanning all around him, he found it right there, a clear silhouette on the horizon in front of him. It looked like the same boat and the same man, waving, just as he'd seen before.

"That's impossible," he declared, tightening the mat and heading for the man in the boat.

The closer Naro got, the more vigorously the man waved, paying little attention to his own boat, or the direction it was taking. When he was close enough to hail the man, Naro cried, "Are you hurt? Do you need help?"

But the man only waved more, adding a little jump now and then, as Naro approached. When he was close enough to see the man, Naro paused. Wearing only a loincloth and a necklace of small bones, the man grinned at Naro, flashing an irregular row of brown-stained teeth. His boat seemed to be empty, except for him.

"I thought I saw you before," Naro started, "several days ago."

The man simply smiled and waved, as if Naro was still far away.

"My name is Naro."

"Nervel. Nergel." The man snorted and held out his closed fist.

"Where are you going?" Naro tried again, though he knew it probably wouldn't get any better response.

"Nervel-Nargo!" He opened his hand, to offer Naro some nut kernels. Naro was still too far away to see what kind they were, probably the same ones that gave the man's teeth their peculiar color.

"Do you have a home around here? Where do you live?"

The man nodded, with big head motions up and down.

"Point which way your home is," Naro said.

Still nodding way up and down, the man pointed to the east, to a large island with a mountainous center. One area of the forested slope seemed to have come unstuck, sliding down the mountain, pulling all the trees down with it. Even from a distance, Naro could tell something was very wrong.

"Are your people there? Are they hurt?"

The man collapsed on his boat, shouting things Naro couldn't understand.

"Do you want to go back there?"

Dragging himself to his feet, the man stood, nodding wretchedly while he wept.

"Then we'll go," Naro said. "Can you steer there?"

He shook his head, rocking back and forth. "NO, no, no, no."

Tying the man's boat behind his, Naro headed for the island. The closer they got, the clearer the devastation became. One whole side of the mountain had become detached and crashed down the slope, dragging everything with it. Huge trees lay buried in the mud, their roots sticking up into the air. The mudslide had carried boulders the size of huts down the mountainside, dragging, crushing, burying everything in their path. Some had pushed their way right down to the sea. Mud, rock, and debris covered half the side of the island Naro was facing.

"Point to where your village is, or where it was," Naro said.

The man held up a trembling arm, pointing straight toward the monstrous pile of mud and rock.

"I'm going to leave my boat here, in the water," Naro said, dropping the anchor stone. "I'll tie yours up too. You'll have to jump out here."

"No, no no no."

"Come on," Naro called, as he started up the beach. "Just jump down."

Behind him, there was a rapid series of unintelligible sounds, then the sound of a splash and more sounds. Naro, scanning the area around the mudslide, thought he saw people standing in the shade of the palms at the edge of the beach.

"Hello!" he called, then turned to the man. "Are these your people?"

But the man wasn't behind him. He was in Naro's boat, lifting the anchor rope and sliding his own boat pole into the water.

"What are you doing?" Naro called, sprinting back toward the boat. "Stop! No!"

The boat was still in the shallows when Naro crashed through the water and vaulted aboard, grabbing the pole away from the man, but the man was surprisingly strong. As they fought, Naro tried to grab the pole, but the man hit him hard in the chest with it, wagging his twisted, deformed tongue at Naro and shouting mangled sounds that carried their intention well enough despite belonging to no one's language except his. With a strong backhand, he caught Naro across the face. As Naro staggered back, the man swung the end of the pole against the side of Naro's head, then dropped the pole, kicked Naro in the groin, and pushed him over the side with a powerful shove to both shoulders. As he dropped into the sea, back-first, Naro felt the world spin around him. Spluttering, gagging on the salt water he'd inhaled, he fought to stand and breathe. He could hear the man in the boat shouting at him, long streams of crazed, spitting sounds punctuated by high laughs as he waved his arms up and down, up and down. Then the man grabbed the pole and pushed away rapidly, wagging his grizzly tongue at the former master of the boat.

Stunned by his quick defeat, Naro staggered toward the shore, turning around to watch the man, still shouting and waving, head out to sea with the boat he'd stolen so easily.

"Don't feel too bad," came a voice from the beach. "Everybody makes the same mistake. They assume if he can't talk, he can't fight. Nasty, clever one, he is. Had his eye on your boat for a while, I think. Been searching for you for days."

Turning around, Naro saw a thick-set man in a decorated wrap studying him with a half-smile.

"Everyone lies here. Don't believe anything you hear," a woman right behind him said.

"But, you know that's a problem, my dear, for if everything is a lie, that would include your statement. So what is our guest to think, that only you lie? That only I lie? That everyone except you lies? But he hasn't met anyone else, other than the man in the boat, and it's difficult to tell if he's lying, for one can never understand what he says." The man smiled.

The woman shrugged and sat down in the shade.

Looking at the enormous landslide, Naro wondered whether their village had been buried. Maybe they were in shock. "Is your village nearby? Did it survive the landslide?"

"I don't know," the man said, with a smirk at the woman. "Can't argue with that, can you?"

"You don't know where your village is, or you don't know if it survived?" Naro pushed.

"Okay, here's the story. There was a hurricane a while ago, and it soaked the earth. Then, days later, the earth started shaking, as it an evil monster was stuck inside and wanted to break free. Everything shook; we all fell down, then it stopped. A while later, the monster started up again, worse this time, and the earth split open up on the hill. I was standing on the hill when the ground started sliding, tilting right under my feet. The trees started leaning like drunkards. When the third shock hit, the earth broke loose, the whole top layer, and it slid away, taking everything with it. The big trees cracked and split, boulders crashed together, then it all came together in a roaring blur, all the way down to the sea."

"How did you survive?"

"He survived because he wasn't anywhere near here when it happened," the woman snarled.

"Where were you?"

The man smiled. "Out at sea, like you, having my boat stolen."

"That would be nice, if it were true," the woman added.

"You're becoming annoying, my dear."

"I'm not your dear. I'm not anyone's dear."

"It's easy to see why, isn't it?" he said, turning to Naro.

"But the man on the boat, did he live here?"

"Who knows? Maybe."

"Did you look through the rubble?"

"No. We've just been waiting here, for our boat to come back, and now it has," he said easily. "I suppose you could do the same thing, though you had a much nicer boat than ours, and it might be a while until he finds an even finer one to replace it."

"Are there others here?"

"People? I don't know."

"Yes."

"Which is it?"

They both shrugged. "It's hard to tell. Maybe."

Naro considered the two of them. The man was probably about his age, the woman slightly younger. She had the same quick, nervous movements as he did, emphasized by the jagged lines she had tattooed along her arms and across her forehead. Her eyes seemed to dart from place to place, even when she was talking, as if something was always distracting her. She wore an undecorated wrap overlaid with strings of shells and small bones. His wrap was woven in triangle patterns and tied with a long sash.

"What kind of bones are those?" Naro said, pointing to her decorations.

"Toes," she smiled coquettishly, as if he'd given her a personal compliment. "Animal toes."

"All very valuable, I assure you," the man laughed.

"Well, we can't stay," the woman broke in. We have places to be."

It surprised Naro that they didn't even offer to help him. They seemed so strange, so foreign. "Where did you come from? Where are your people?"

The woman tilted her head sideways and squinted at him. "You don't have anywhere, either, do you? Searching for someplace to be? Well, we came across the sea, stopped at some islands, and lived in the big land to the south. Everyone was sick there, so we left. I wouldn't recommend stopping there. They're crazy there. They eat people just to get some strength. How's that?"

"None of that is true," the man said with a slow shake of the head. "They were going to kill her for practicing witchcraft, so we left. The man in the boat tried to attack her, so she made the earth open up and bury his village. He got scared and left, in our boat."

"Nice try," the woman sighed. "Not true, of course, but interesting. This is my friend's husband, a fabulous cheat, a golden-tongued bastard. I love him."

"I'm flattered, my dear. Would that it were true. Oh well, it was fun momentarily, wasn't it?"

"When we weren't trying to kill each other, yes," she laughed, running her fingers along his arm. Swiveling her head around like an owl, she eyed Naro.

"So where do you come from? What are you doing out here all alone, a good-looking man like you in a place like this?"

"The last woman I met left me in an underground lake." The whole tale was too long to tell.

They both roared. "Very good!" the woman sang as she clapped her hands. "I like it! I'll have to figure out how to do that. It might come in handy."

"As if you can do anything but put on a show," the man scowled. "You haven't done any real magic in so long, you probably don't remember."

The woman turned on him in a flash of anger. "I know everything," she said, raking her long nails into the skin of his arm. "That's why I'm crazy."

He didn't even flinch as the red marks spread down his arm. "No, my dear, you're crazy. That's why you think you know everything." With a laugh, he draped his bleeding arm over her shoulders.

Cooing, she turned into his embrace, "Sorry about your husband."

"It was your husband, not mine."

"That would be fun, wouldn't it?"

Naro left them and walked along the edge of the mudslide, looking for any sign of the village the thief had pointed to. Any huts near the shore would have been buried completely, but if they'd been built farther up the hill, there might be something left. In any case, he couldn't stay on the shore with those two people.

It was strangely quiet along the edge of the slide, and rough. He slipped often as he climbed, threading his way around the boulders and uprooted trees. The mud was only temporarily stopped. At one point, as he stepped across it, it gave way under his feet so suddenly, he thought he'd be dragged under and taken all the way down the mountain with it, but it slowed at an upturned tree, where he was able to grab hold and find his way back out. Up the hill, it was more of the same, piles of mud, stone, and debris, all the way to the top of the mountain, except for an open spot near the opposite side of the flow, perhaps a cave or a rock ledge that divided the flow around it. If people had taken shelter there, they'd still be alive.

Rather than risk going across the mud again, he worked his way all the way to the top of the slide, then down toward the section he'd seen. As he picked his way through the rocks and trees, he looked around. The site had a spectacular view all the way down the island and out to the ocean. In the distance, the water was so clear he could see the land rising up from the depths of the sea then breaking the surface of the water and becoming islands. The islands he could see were far larger than anything they'd seen, real lands rather than mere rocky spots on the sea, exactly what he was looking for.

Easing himself down the rock ledge, he reached the broadest point, with the rock overhang he'd seen from below. The covered area was large enough for a dozen men to stand in. Obviously, there had been people staying here at one time. Near the back wall, a large turtle shell turned upside down held forest medicines: amaranth seeds, bay rum leaves, bits of mahogany resin, locust bark, white cedar twigs, all carefully separated into different areas of the shell. Near the open edge were the remains of a campfire. The charred logs were still warm.

"Is anyone here? I'm here to help you, not hurt you."

He was glancing down the hillside when he heard a movement on the ledge behind him. Before he could turn around, someone grabbed his hair and yanked his head back, pressing a knife blade against his throat.

A woman hissed words he didn't understand, but he caught their meaning quickly. "But the mudslide," Naro sputtered. "I can help you get out of here, move somewhere safer."

Without releasing his hair or lowering her knife, she snarled again, louder this time. "But I thought -"

With a jerk, she released his head and backed up until she was standing against the rock wall. Once there, she shouted at him again, waving her knife. Shocked, Naro backed across the ledge away from her and climbed down into the tangled debris of the mudslide. From there, he headed back to the shore. The man and woman he had met earlier were gone, along with their boat.

Very late that night, the man who had stolen Naro's boat returned to the island. Naro, hidden in the bushes beyond the beach, listened to the man drop the anchor stone and wade ashore, grumbling. He made camp near the shore, not bothering with a fire but heading directly for his hammock strung between two trees. When Naro could hear the man's irregular snoring, he stepped across the beach and into the water, climbed aboard his boat, raised the anchor stone and poled away in the pitch dark. Out in deeper water, he threw everything belonging to the man overboard with a shout, imagining him back on the shore jerking awake, stumbling out of his hammock in the dark, screaming his garbled curses. It was very satisfying.

The following day, Naro set all three mats and headed north and west as fast as he could. He had seen the big islands that lay ahead of him. All he had to do was get there, and away from this place.

At night, he looked for the stars, but the clouds had moved in, bringing a rainstorm, and he was left listening to the sounds of the raindrops hitting the tarp and the boat moving through the choppy sea. Right then, he missed the others in his group, even Afutu. He missed their company, their physical presence, the sound of their voices. It would have been good to listen to a story, or to have them listen to his.

* * *

CHAPTER 23
A CHANGE OF DIRECTION

When the rain stopped, the wind stayed strong, and Naro was pushed up and down wind-blown waves in the dark, without even the stars to guide him. Several times, he felt something hit the bottom of the boat, but he couldn't feel any leak or breakage, so he tried to sleep. There was nothing he could do about it anyway. It's hard to steer away from danger when you don't know where it is.

In the morning, he awoke to find himself in very shallow water, with coral heads all around and a long reef visible right under the water to the east. Threading his way between the coral islands, he thought he was in the clear when the keel caught an outcrop with a thump. He wedged the pole up against the hard coral and pushed, but he was fighting the current. He had to maneuver the boat bit by bit until he was clear, then hope the wind didn't push him sideways back into it.

He looked up ahead to find the next outcrop, so he could steer well clear of it, but when he found it, it wasn't at all what he'd expected. It wasn't coral, but rock, worn smooth by the waves crashing over the top. Sea grasses and beach peas swayed in the wind. It was probably a fine resting spot for weary seabirds. But at that moment, it held two people. One was waving broadly at him, shouting something.

"It couldn't be," Naro muttered, thinking the crazy couple had lost their boat again, or the man with the mutilated tongue had somehow found him and had waited here, in the middle of nowhere, expecting him to fall for the same trick twice. But this wasn't the same man or the same woman. She wasn't waving, just staring. Naro saw no sign of a boat anywhere around them, though it was possible that they'd hidden one on the far side of the island, or managed to camouflage it with sea grasses, but it didn't seem likely. Between the rocky island they stood on and the big island in the distance, there was only the wide expanse of the sea.

He paddled up to them, aware he couldn't take the boat too close to the rocks. "Are you hurt?"

"No," the man yelled back, "but we lost our boat. Can you take us to the big island?" He pointed to the east, but Naro already knew where the island was. It was the biggest shape on the horizon.

Nodding, Naro moved as close as he could to the island, then extended the pole. "You'll have to swim. I can't bring the boat any farther in."

The woman had no desire to step into the water, but the man pushed her forward. "Just stay with the pole. He'll pull you to the boat. I'll be right behind you."

She was very slight, with a large, untidy headcloth and a dirty wrap, and she stepped into the water as if she expected a monster to leap out and devour her. When a couple of fish nibbled at her ankles, she screamed.

"You have to keep moving. You'll die out here," the man said, bluntly.

"I'll die out there," the woman replied, pointing to the deeper water. "That's where it lives. It's waiting for me."

The man gave her a solid push. "Go forward. This is your chance, and mine. Grab the pole and swim."

When she did take a tentative step, she couldn't get any purchase on the seaweed-covered rocks. Each step was more off-balance, despite her failing arms. Twisting, she fell hard on one hip on the edge of the rock and slid into the water. Jumping in behind her, the man pushed her along until she was forced to swim, but she seemed to have no strength left.

Extending the pole, Naro pulled her close to the boat. "You'll have to vault in. Grab hold of the oar hole and swing your knee up."

She slumped over the pole. "It's too high."

Swimming up behind her, the man pinched her shoulder sharply. "Then we'll leave you here, and when he comes back, you'll have to face him on your own."

Wide-eyed, she turned on him. "You'd leave me?"

"You've got to make your own way in this world. Nobody owes you anything."

"You promised!"

"Will you move?"

At the boat, she reached up, half-heartedly, but not high enough to get a handhold. "I can't reach."

With a shove, the man pushed her aside, reached past her and hauled himself up into the boat. "You've got one chance. Reach up and grab the hole. Now swing your leg up."

She'd been sure he'd help her, but now she thought he might actually leave her behind, so she reached for the hole and tried to swing her leg up, but the side of the boat was higher than she expected, and the swing fell short. She was going to say "I can't" when she felt something catch her leg. Panicked, she screamed and let go of the oar-hole, but Naro, who already had hold of her leg, grabbed her arm as well, and hauled her into the boat in one pull that left her in an awkward heap at the bottom of the boat.

"Well, I'm certainly glad that's done," the man said, as if he'd had some part in it. "My name is Lo," he said with a strange little bow. "Thank you for helping us."

"What happened to you?"

"We were attacked by vicious black and white whales," the man explained.

The woman struggled to her feet. "He tried to kill one of the calves."

"I thought it would be good eating. They were just lying there, the females and calves, as if they were asleep. I thought it was perfect."

"They're huge!" Naro said, "even the babies. How would you get it on the boat even if you did kill it?"

"Well, I hadn't really thought about that. You know, you can't see how big they are when they're in the water. There's just the fin and part of the back visible."

"Of course you can," Naro said, unable to believe the man was really that stupid. "They're one of the biggest creatures in the sea, and certainly one of the meanest. And you attacked one of their young?" That seemed more unbelievable than finding two people stranded on a rocky spit in the middle of the sea.

When the man didn't answer, the woman spoke up. "Yes, he did. Then the bulls showed up. The biggest of them rammed the boat, then came around and rammed it again. Then he brought the others. They took turns ramming the boat, then disappearing for a while, then ramming it again, sometimes from both sides. We tried to paddle away, but when I put my paddle in the water, one of them bit it in half. When I raised it, it ended right below my hand. They were all working together. They hated us, and the boat."

"That's reading human feelings into the beast," the man protested. "They're only dumb brutes."

"You need to understand the sea," Naro interrupted. "It's not very tolerant of ignorance." It was more than he'd planned to say, but the man was annoying. "And who are you?" he asked the woman, in part to change the subject.

"My name is Lilla. I used to be from a village across the sea."

Naro waited, but she seemed unwilling to go on. The powerlessness that had defined her on the island returned, and she sat on the bottom of the boat with her arms wrapped around her knees.

"There was a problem," Lo added, without more explanation.

It wasn't hard to guess the nature of the problem, but Naro didn't pursue it. He decided he'd take these people to the big island and let them find their own troubled future. "Excuse me," he said as he set the three mats to catch the wind while the two passengers stared at him.

"This is a fine thing!" Lo cried as they picked up speed. "A very fine thing! You should sell these boats on the mainland. You could be the richest man in the village."

"No, thanks. I'm searching for something else," Naro replied.

"You've got to take opportunity when it's offered to you. Don't sit around dreaming of what might be somewhere, sometime. Grab what you can while you can. That's my motto. You'd be a fool to hide a treasure like this. Show it! I would. That's certain."

With a start, Naro realized the man would steal the boat without a second thought, probably the way he'd stolen this girl, and he'd see nothing wrong with it. Once again, Naro had picked up a problem when he was trying to do someone a favor. But what was the alternative – to leave them there, on that rocky point?

"So where were you before you ran into the killer whales?"

The man had to pull himself out of his mental plans for the boat once he'd learned how to use the mats. "One of the smaller islands. I don't know. They all looked the same to me. It had a hilly, forested inland, one nice beach, and a lot of mangrove swamp. Deadly mosquitoes and bad water."

"There were sick people there," Lilla added, finding her voice once again.

"Oh?"

"A whole group of them. Some were so sick they couldn't get off the beach. A couple of children, some men and women. They all looked terrible."

A strange feeling ran through Naro that went all the way down from his scalp to his feet. "What did they look like?"

"I don't know. Like people. The men were all big, except for one skinny one. Nobody did much. They just sat there, or lay there, on the beach. They had two nice boats, though, one red one," she paused, "like this one. And a yellow one," she added.

Lo watched Naro's rapt attention to the story of the sick people on the island and didn't like what he saw. "It was only a couple of people. And the boat was very dark. Brown, I think."

Ignoring him, Naro was already taking down the second and third mats while he turned the boat around. As he finished rolling them up and securing them, he turned around to find the man had pulled a knife on him.

"You need to keep going, just the way you were," Lo threatened.

With a single blow, Naro knocked the knife out of the man's hand, sending it flying into the water, then pushed the man to the bottom of the boat and held him there, his knee on the man's chest and his hand across the man's throat.

"You're a poor excuse for a guest: stupid, selfish, and arrogant. By rights, I should drop you off right here, or take you back to your miserable little rock so you can wait for the next generous soul to help you out. Would that suit you?"

"You can't go back there. Those people are sick. Believe me; I've seen whole villages wiped out. It's not a good idea. What good would it do, if you got sick too?"

"Then you could steal my boat," Naro said, as he sat back, releasing the man but not moving out of his way so he could get back up. "Maybe. With your skill, you'd probably run it into the first coral head you found, and rip the bottom out of it, or harass a whale until it flipped the boat over."

"It's not wrong to look out for myself. Everyone does."

"It's wrong if it hurts other people. I suspect you do that regularly."

"And I guess you're the most popular man in town. That's why you're out here all by yourself," the man retorted.

Naro thought briefly about killing the annoying man right there and pitching his body into the sea. Momentarily, at least, it would be very satisfying. "I'm going to help my friends. You can come with me and help, or you can stay. Right here. Decide right now, and mean what you say."

"I almost never mean what I say," the man started, but something in Naro's tone frightened him. "Fine. Apparently there's only one choice."

"Lilla?" Naro asked. It was more than courtesy. Lo could easily use her to do his dirty work and claim she'd never promised to help.

"I'll go back and help you," she answered. "I wish I could go all the way back to my village. At least I'd have my people. Now, I have only this -"

Stepping aside, Naro watched Lo as he scrambled to his feet.

"I find people overrated," Lo said, dismissing Lilla's insult, "especially in the villages. There, the people in power are always making up rules. Mostly the rules are established to make sure the people in power stay in power. And then there's war: the ultimate game for those in power. You criticize me for being selfish. What is war but the ultimate expression of selfishness? 'There should be more for me because I'm the chief, or the king. It doesn't matter what you want, only what I want. I matter more because I'm the chief.' Why? I like it better out here, on my own. If I do something stupid, it's my fault. At home, if the chief does something stupid, he doesn't suffer; I do."

Naro found this line of reasoning confusing, so he changed the subject. "This is my boat. What I say goes. If you do something stupid, like attack me again, I'll throw you overboard. Both of you, if necessary. Is that understood?"

They both nodded.

"Good. Now, tell me how to get to this island. If you lie, we'll just spend that much more time looking for it, but eventually, we *will* find it."

They stared at him, as if they noticed him for the first time. "It's that way," Lo pointed to the south, "but you'll never get there. The wind goes the other way."

"Sit up in the bow," Naro ordered.

Lo stopped partway and turned back. "Those islands are home to spirits, some of them really bad. They poison the air and the water. The best thing you can do is leave them alone."

With a brief nod, Naro swung the mat and angled the boat across the wind. That much he knew was true; the islands *were* home to spirits. But he had to go there.

CHAPTER 24
WIND ON THE WATER

The distance that would have taken less than a day with the wind behind him took two days of real effort to retrace. Along the way, he never saw the Island of Birds. Perhaps it wasn't real. But it had been real to him when he was there: the woman who laughed like the gulls, the cold water, the rough-edged ledges under his hands, the multitude of birds on the hillside, the sounds of the stars. If all of this was a creation of the spirits, why was it shown to him?

One person, he thought, might know the answers. She'd always been halfway between worlds. Sohko said her brother had been so fascinated by the circles of stones that he'd stayed behind when everyone else left the burned-out village. Later, she thought she heard his voice in the tree where ghosts live. Perhaps that's what she put in her cloth designs, that sense of things that are between worlds. She was an artist and a visionary. He needed that now.

"I'm telling you," Lo said, interrupting Naro's thoughts, "there's nothing good there. I've seen sickness wipe out every single person in a village, so there's no one left to bury the dead. There's no point in adding your body to the pile."

"Stop talking."

With a shrug, Lo turned back toward the bow. "I'd like to learn how you do that, making the boat go into the wind."

Naro didn't reply. Lo would figure it out while he was on the boat, and then he'd make, borrow, or steal a boat, perhaps this boat, in order to perfect and then sell the skill. Naro understood that, but at this moment, he needed to think something through, and the annoying man was simply getting in his way. "Just let me know when we're getting close to the island."

Lo pointed to a wide swath of golden beach with green hills rising behind it. "It's right there."

"I don't see anyone on the beach."

"Maybe they're dead."

When Naro spun on him, Lo held up his hands in defense. "I'm only guessing. I don't know."

"Then don't say anything if you have nothing to add."

Lilla was scanning the beach area. "They're back under the palms," she pointed. "I'll help. I can make medicines."

When they came close to the beach, Naro dropped the anchor stone, and Lilla was the first to jump into the water.

"I'll mind the boat," Lo offered.

"I'm sure you would. As soon as we were all on the beach, you and the boat would be heading away from here as fast as you could manage. But it's not going to work that way. You can either jump out, or be pushed out."

Lo considered the situation, but only for a moment, then vaulted neatly over the side. Before he got to the beach, though, he was already studying the other two boats and weighing his chances. Neither of them was guarded.

"Forget it, Lo. I need you to help carry water. It's the least you can do, in return for my saving your life." It was seldom necessary to remind someone of a life debt, but Lo felt few obligations to anyone but himself.

The man dragged himself along behind Naro, but he refused to go near the people lying on the makeshift beds of dried palm branches, walking way around them instead and standing on the far side, waiting. Lilla, though, was already approaching them, talking to them as if they were old friends, though they didn't respond. She looked nothing like the hopeless figure Naro had rescued earlier. By training, she was a healer. Unlike the open sea, this was the world she knew and loved.

Sohko, Aminata, and the children were in the worst shape. Ayo was sitting with them, fanning them to keep the insects away. When Lilla asked what had happened, Ayo tried to remember, but she had trouble thinking clearly. They'd eaten a large grouper they'd caught, and everyone got sick, or almost everyone, with diarrhea, vomiting, cramps. Ayo hadn't eaten it because she'd already felt sick. When she saw how sick everyone else was, she'd gotten water from the stream and encouraged them to drink it, but the water was bad too. It was as if everything on the island was trying to kill them. Some of them had strange feelings that their skin was burning or they were walking on knife points. Sohko's vision was so blurry he tripped and fell head-first over a rock. Some complained of terrible headaches. Then, one by one, they collapsed on the sand, all of them, unable or unwilling to move. She'd tried to do something, but nothing made any difference. Day after day, they lay there half-dead.

Lilla nodded. "Where did you get the water?"

"Right there." Ayo pointed to the nearby stream.

"We'll get better water for you." She nodded at Lo. "Go way up the hill to the source of the stream and draw the water."

"You should tell them that you were only an apprentice at home, the errand girl, not the master healer. You should warn them that almost everyone in your village was killed by the fever, despite your medicine."

When Lo had gone, grumbling, along the trail, Naro turned back to the girl. "How will the water be different up higher? Isn't the river the same?"

"Perhaps something poisoned it along the way. There's something bad here; some evil spirit that's poisoning their bodies. It's like wind over the water; it can take any form, enter any being."

Lined up in the shifting shadows of the palms, all of the stricken people lay, unable to move, unwilling to fight. Naaba was so thin his ribs stuck out. Afutu's eyes were glassy. It was easy to understand why Lo was frightened; Naro was too. "What can we do?"

"I need to find some medicines," she said. "Are you willing to risk your life to save your friends? Are you willing to visit a land of spirits, not knowing what they might do to you?"

"Yes."

She turned to Ayo. "Are you?"

"Absolutely."

With a nod, she picked up a palm leaf, folded it into a bowl, and walked off into the forest. Naro went down the line of people, talking to each of them, hoping they could hear him, hoping he could offer something more than empty words. By the time he got to Afutu, tears were coursing down his cheeks.

"I am so sorry, friend. I'll do whatever I can to help. You've always been strong. You need to fight now, for your life. Please."

There was no response, not even the blink of an eye. Beside Afutu, Dashona lay as if dead, her skin cold to the touch. Seeing her there, next to Afutu, Naro couldn't remember ever wanting her. With her ashen skin and hair coated with sand, she was only a sad figure, pathetic, like the others.

"They've been like this for days," Ayo said, her voice breaking. "Sometimes, they'll drink some water if I hold it up to their lips, but no one talks or sits up. It's as if the life was sucked out of them, and only the shells remain. They look like the people I love, but – they're not. I wish I'd been taken with them. It's worse to be here and watch them."

They sat together, fanning the sick, saying nothing, until Lilla returned with long strips of red-brown virola bark, a handful of bay rum leaves, and pieces of locust sap. Sitting down next to them, she scraped off the inner bark, with its blood-red resin, worked it into a ball with her fingers and then split it in half.

Handing one piece to each, she said, "Chew this. It will give you clarity of vision. I'll make a tea for the others, but you two need to find the source of the problem and correct it. Find the wind in the sea in the rock."

As she chewed the bitter resin, Ayo wondered if the woman was crazy and whether that made any difference. "How will we know it? Isn't it everywhere?"

They waited, but Lilla didn't explain. Instead, she started pounding the bay rum leaves and cutting the virola bark into thin strips. When it was cut up, she piled extra stones in the firepit and lit a fire to heat them. Looking up, she frowned at them.

"What are you doing standing here?"

By the time Ayo and Naro had gone from the beach to the interior, Ayo felt her feet weren't touching the ground and the world looked very strange. A trogon perched quite close above her head, its brilliant black and white wings and wedged tails vibrating intensely against the giant ferns behind it. Its underbody was split: the top part white, the bottom red. It turned its head and stared as if it was about to speak to her. Behind it, an enormous bird-like creature with red eyes and wings of smoke was waiting, the tips of its wings curling away into the air. On the ground, a figure something like a man stood facing the smoke-winged creature, as if squaring off in battle. The smoke wings floated among the branches of the trees, the tips fanning out ever wider, blocking the sunlight. Diving forward, it struck at its opponent with its hooked beak, but the red figure slashed at it. It was strange that she could see right through the red figure, even as it moved. Only its outline burned red. The battle went on, but it made no sound, as if she was watching something happening far away, but it was right there, behind the branch the trogon had perched on only a moment ago. The woods grew darker as the smoke wings spread through the forest canopy. She wasn't sure if she could see the other figure; there were flashes of an arm raised or a sword swinging, but it was only a faint trail of sparks in the distance.

"Naro," she started, but she couldn't think of anything else to say.

He was watching the rocks ripple, wondering why it hadn't been obvious to him before that the rocks used to flow. "Where would air and rock and water meet?"

"Everywhere. We're on an island made of rock and worn by the wind and the waves."

"No, a special place, where the rock used to move."

Ayo watched the forest colors flashing, pulsing, the two figures battling in the distance. "It's all moving."

"What is the wind on the water?"

"I suppose it's free, unchecked. Nothing stops it."

"And what would happen if it was blocked?"

"Motion would stop. The wind has to move the water. If it stopped, the weather would stop too. There would be endless rains, or drought."

Naro nodded. "Yes. Or complete stagnation. Or an illness that saps the will to live."

"But it can't be. I wasn't affected."

"Perhaps you were protected for a reason." He told her the story of the birds, the underground well, and the singing stars. "I think they were all connected. I was meant to listen to the stars when they sang to me. We're meant to be connected to the spirit world. When we forget it, we're... reminded."

"But why punish good people?"

Naro shrugged. "I don't know. I'm not sure we're meant to know. But you and I were meant to be part of things. Intensely."

As the battle raged in the dark woods, the rocks rolled like barkcloth hung out in the breeze under Ayo's feet. "Your moving stone is going toward the water," she remarked.

In the tree above her, the trogon nodded very slowly, the deep blue of his cap moving up and down against the throbbing greens. "My brother was a seer, you know, a visionary. He understood how the worlds are connected, the world we see, the world we don't see, the world of the spirits, the world of the dead. It all fit together for him. I think he found what he was looking for, but I lost the only one who cared about me.

"We left our village because there was trouble when I wove a cape for a bride. She saw the face of death in the design, and two moons after the wedding, she died in her sleep. Her husband's family said I'd cursed her. They would have killed me, but my brother got me out, and we found our way through the bush at night, not caring whether the wild animals killed us.

"When I lost him, at Komo's village, the world fell apart. I saw it in pieces, like a broken pot. Sohko and Aminata saved me the night the village burned and again the night of the battle at the beach, but the world has never fit together for me since then. Sometimes I feel there's nothing holding me to this earth. With only a tiny breeze, I could float up into the sky, dissolving into the air as I went, like curls of smoke from a fire."

It seemed very natural, and quite fine, that she was able to say these things that she'd kept tied up inside her for so long. It seemed to be a natural part of the extraordinary world that she was walking through, with him by her side. Everything seemed to present itself in terms of something else, so much that she wasn't sure whether she was seeing the thing she thought she was or the things it reminded her of.

After a while, Naro replied, "I saw a pearl once that was encased in a knot of black coral. The pearl was even more beautiful than it would have been on its own because it shone through the cage it was placed in. Darkness made it brighter."

"Do you think there is a constant battle between good and evil?"

Naro looked at her. "In people?"

"Well, yes, I think it's true of individuals, but is there also a battle between good and evil in the whole world?"

"What is good? Or evil? Is disease evil?"

"I think suffering is a sign of evil," she said, trying to decide what she felt. There had to be a difference. Isn't that why the forces were fighting in the forest?

"Is death evil?" he pursued. "Isn't it as important as life? There can be no life without death, and no death without life. They are two sides of the same mask."

"But in the woods, I saw them fighting, a huge bird with smoke wings, and a figure outlined in fire."

He paused. "I saw them too, but I didn't want to acknowledge them. I think we're part of their battle. So are the people on the beach."

"What do you mean? How? What are they?"

"You know what they are."

"They're battling for control over our friends," she whirled around to face him, "aren't they? Shouldn't we be back at the beach trying to help them? What are we doing here? What are we looking for? I don't understand!"

He knew how she felt, but he had no answers. He'd given up his anger when he was abandoned in the underground well. It was a poor weapon at any time and useless in matters of the spirits. "Their battle never ends. Sometimes one side wins for a while; sometimes the other. There's never a victory, only a balance."

"Then it doesn't matter what we do? What anyone does? I can't believe that! Why were you picked to be sent down the well, to see the birds?"

"I don't know. We can't understand the gods."

Angry, Ayo turned on him. "That's not an answer. You know it's not. If you really thought that it didn't matter what we did, or what anyone else did, you wouldn't be here."

Looking back through the woods, he shrugged. "We're on a fools' quest, drugged by people who want to steal my boat. What does it matter? What more could I be doing at the beach? I don't know how to heal those people. Neither do you. So we were sent here, with a riddle to solve. Perhaps it means something. Perhaps it's simply a joke. Perhaps there's no difference between the two."

Ayo grabbed his arm and swung him around. "No! That's not enough to live on. You can't say nothing matters. That's a grey life, a thin, meager life, almost indistinguishable from death. It's not enough!"

"And how would you know? Your life is as shattered as mine; you said it yourself. We can't undo the past, so we carry it with us, like a stone tied to our feet, every step of the journey."

She slumped. "No, I don't believe that. Our past isn't who we are."

"Of course it is. That's why people ask your name and your village, so they can figure out who you are by what you were."

"But it's only part. One thing is not forever."

"But the sun that brings the flowers also watches them die. It's not for us to keep the flower alive, even if we love it."

"Then why are we here?" she cried. "Why? Why give us something so wonderful if it has no meaning?"

Naro shook his head. "I don't know."

Standing, Ayo put her hands on her hips. "You said the pearl was even more brilliant because it was surrounded by darkness. But it was shining. It was beautiful." When he didn't reply, she went on. "It's not enough to live, just thin and grey. Beautiful, shining life is fat! Fat and singing! And red and yellow and green and blue and purple, deep shining colors, and brilliant white, and moonless night black. A life of fat colors says to the gods, 'Thank you for this glorious gift. It is unbelievably fine.'"

"And what happens to that fat life when tragedy overtakes it, or shame?"

"I don't know," she admitted. "Perhaps it becomes a dream kept alive by moments of beauty, or kindness." She lapsed into silence as they moved through the forest with no idea where they were headed or what they were supposed to find. "Wind in water in the rock," she muttered.

Naro was watching the rock moving, sliding, clumping under his feet, like drying mud spilling over a riverbank. In front of them, he could see a clearing in the forest, and beyond it, the deep blue of the sea. The rock slowed as he stepped into the clearing. Then it stopped. Round ridges of stone piled up where the rock stopped, all gathered in circles around a center spot where a large round stone lay, all alone. He stood, staring at the spot. Some motion was stopped right there.

"It feels strange," Ayo said, standing out in the clearing, "hollow under my feet."

As Naro stepped onto the stone, he could hear something inside it. "Listen. There's something moving under the stone." There was a deep, rumbling sound, and burbling noises.

"Help me," Naro called back to her as he ran toward the round, flat rock and grabbed one edge. "We have to move it."

As they struggled to move the stone, Naro realized there was a hole underneath it, the top vent of a hollow tube that ran all the way from the rocks below them out to the sea. As they stood back, the wind and water rolled through the tube and crashed up through the hole, sending the spray high over their heads, soaking them as it fell back to the rock. They waited, not moving, and moments later, it happened again, the great roaring under the rock, the spout of wind and water flying through the hole, the spray covering them, then the water falling back through the hole and pulled back to the sea.

"What color is it?" he called to her across the hole.

Weeping suddenly, covered with salt spray, she cried, "It's all colors! It's loud!" The wave rushed through the tube once more, crashing up into the air and falling back down, soaking them. "It's beating its wings furiously. It's the sound of the drums. It's fiery heat and deep water cool. It's dance. It's love."

"And what is death?"

"Emptiness," she said, as the water washed back into the tube. "It's total stillness, the end of the song, the end of the dance, the moment after the last beat of the bird's wing."

* * *

CHAPTER 25
THE JOURNEY REJOINED

When Ayo and Naro got back to the beach, Lo and Lilla were gone, as was the boat. But they had, in their own way, kept their promises. Lo had delivered clean, fresh water, and Lilla had made the tea that awoke the memory of life and longing in those who had forgotten. Then she had gone away with Lo not because he forced her but because she was in love with him. It was that simple, if that kind of love is ever simple.

But even when those who had been stricken with the spirit illness recovered, some small splinter of darkness remained with them. It showed up in flashes of selfishness or anger or resentment, especially of Ayo and Naro because they'd been spared, or because they'd helped restore balance. There wasn't any logic behind the resentment, and it was hardly mentioned, but it was there.

They welcomed Naro back, of course, but it wasn't quite the same as before he left. Plus Lo had stolen the boat, as Naro had known he would. It was hard to explain to the group that it was worth the loss of the very fine red boat to have them back. They'd never seen these people Naro described, and his story seemed unbelievable, even when Ayo corroborated it.

"We had fish poisoning," Aminata stated, to set the record straight.

There wasn't any way Ayo could remind them that for days they'd been like dead people, sprawled on the brittle palm leaves without hope or future. They had no memory of being there. But the same conflict that left a shard of darkness in them left the opposite mark on Ayo and Naro. After living so long in the dark, they felt a strange lightness welling up in them, as if bright lights wanted to shine through their skin like torches in the night.

People noticed. After watching Ayo blush when Naro reached past her, accidentally touching her, Aminata took her aside. "Is there something you'd like to tell me?"

A tingling sensation ran up Ayo's back all the way to her head. "Yes. I think I have torch lights burning inside me."

Aminata tilted her head to the side, studying Ayo, so intense and breathless. "No. You're in love."

The news didn't sit well with the group. For one thing, they were plagued by little problems: headaches, muscle cramps, a toothache, numbness in their fingertips, and the pain made them less generous. But there was more. Dashona, especially, was jealous. She knew Naro had been looking at her on the boat. She'd never acknowledged his glances or encouraged them, but now that his gaze was focused on someone else, she felt she'd been robbed of her chance at love. In her honest moments, she knew she didn't love Naro, but that did little to still her frustration. Aminata was pregnant. Asha was pregnant too. She hadn't told anyone, but they knew. But Dashona was still alone, and she felt it was a punishment. Every time she looked at Naro and Ayo, so locked onto each other that they seemed to be in their own world, her anger grew.

People took to sending Naro and Ayo off to find cashews or sea almonds, or to take the boat out fishing, so the others could breathe easier. They didn't talk about it much. But everyone knew, even the children. When they were all sitting in the shade one day, eating craboo fruits, Sohko broached the subject indirectly.

"We need to decide on a course and prepare to leave."

"Good idea!" Naaba called. "How soon?"

The others shouted their agreement, and a conspiracy of silence was born. They made their plans while Naro and Ayo were away. They worked on the boats, gathered medicines and supplies, dried fish, seaweed, and mangoes, roasted cashews, made and repaired tools, wove new rope, collected coconuts, and the more they worked, the better they felt, so that the desire to leave drove them and fueled them.

But Ayo and Naro were unaware of any of this. They spent every day off on their own, exploring the forest or the sea, or each other. Naro became a skilled free diver, bringing up pearl oysters, including two with yellow pearls inside, and black coral from the seabed. One day when they were supposed to be fishing, they cut and polished the black coral pieces, then searched for exactly the right piece of wood for the inlay work. For the polishing, Naro dove down to pick up the finest sand from the bottom, then the medium and heavier grains closer to the shore, plus the smooth stones from the river. These he separated into different piles, each one carefully wrapped in a palm leaf, together with a length of wood and sticky resin.

After Naro had roughed out the shape of the plate in the wood, Ayo finished it, sanding the surface and oiling it until it shone. From the thin layers of iridescent mother of pearl, she cut out the shapes of the birds then cut a space for each one individually in the wood. It was the most exacting work she'd ever done, and she found it exhilarating. Everything seemed to be glowing for her, and she worked intensely, afraid to lose it. But then, while she was working, he'd run his hand across her back, or re-tie her hair, and she'd throw her head back, forgetting the work completely. They were blind to everything else except each other. They knew there was something not quite right at camp, but the easiest way to deal with it was to ignore it. It wasn't really important, anyway.

Of all the people in the group at camp, only Asha stood up for Ayo. She reminded everyone how important Naro and Ayo had been on their trip across the sea, how much they'd helped. The others nodded, but their feelings didn't change. Ayo would have been fine; Ayo and Naro weren't.

When the lovers didn't return one morning, no one minded. They were busy making arrangements about who would go in what boat.

"You can't just leave them here," Asha complained. "They're part of us."

Sohko looked around at the group busy with its work. "Then they should be here."

"They're not welcome here," Asha retorted. "You know that. That's why they're gone."

"We've agreed to leave," Sohko said, fixing her with his wise gaze. "If they'd like to come with us, they'd better show up, and help us get ready."

But they were far away, exploring a brand new world.

"You can't leave them here! The island is haunted," she pleaded. "At least leave them a boat."

He nodded. "A fair solution. We'll leave them a boat."

But heated debate followed that proclamation. Afutu refused to leave the yellow boat, and Abran was used to handling the red one. Besides, it was the only one left of Chahuk's gifts.

"Then we'll make another," Sohko announced.

It took several more days, but they made a modest boat for the two missing members of the group. Then they made ready to leave.

Asha was frantic. "You're going to leave without even saying goodbye?"

"We don't even know where they are," Naaba tried to explain.

"It's cruel," she shot back at him. "That's all it is, but somehow, if everyone agrees to something cruel, it becomes okay. How can we abandon our friends and say it's okay?"

"I'll try to find them," Naaba offered.

"Then I'll come with you," she agreed.

Dashona sighed impatiently. "That's just a waste of our time. We could be gone on the tide today."

"Why? What's the hurry?"

Dashona looked away. She couldn't put it all into words.

"These are *not* our enemies. They didn't threaten us, or kill anyone. They helped us when we were sick, yet you're anxious to abandon them."

"Fine," Dashona said, "but I agreed to leave this place. I wish I were already somewhere else. It's full of -" she struggled, "full of pain." Without a backward glance, she walked off.

Shaken, Asha turned to Naaba. "Will you still go with me?"

He took her hand. "Always. Let's go find them. We need to settle this one way or the other, and soon."

"That was us, you know, at one time," Asha said when they'd left the camp behind, "the outsiders, with only each other."

"We still have each other, and I'd still be glad if I set you free today. Although," he admitted, "I had no idea what I was getting into at the time."

"Nor did I."

"We can't set their path, Asha."

"No, but we can say goodbye to our friends. They'll be back. We need them, and they need us. It'll just take some time."

When Naaba and Asha found the lovers, they were sitting out on a flat rock overlooking the sea, Naro sitting across from Ayo, watching her work. Having set all of the black coral pieces in the center, she had started placing the mother-of-pearl bird designs around the outside. Even unfinished, it was a stunningly beautiful piece of work.

"Asha! Naaba!" Ayo cried when she saw them approaching. Naro stood up and extended his arm to Naaba. "Welcome!" he cried, his eyes shining. "I was hoping I could talk to you." He seemed over-excited, like a child with a fever. "It's so strange and fine, here. We're building the mirror plate that the bird woman showed me."

Naaba gripped the man's arm. "You're slipping away, friend. Come back with us. The group's getting ready to leave, with or without you."

Asha had slipped her arm around Ayo, who was trembling, as if on the verge of tears. "Naaba's right. You two should come back with us, rejoin the group. You've been away a long time."

Ayo turned to her. "Have we? I have no sense of time. We're somewhere else, Asha. It's not just that we have each other," she smiled, "though, to tell the truth, I've never felt this way before, about anyone. It's more. We've been touched by the spirits here. There has to be a reason they called us here, a purpose for us. And I've been searching for that since I lost my brother, perhaps even before that. I know now how my brother could have been happy staying all alone in the circles of stone. He wasn't really alone at all. He was connected to something else, to everything else. That's how I feel, Asha, not just when I'm with him but all the time. There's something here we're supposed to be part of, something so strong I think sometimes it'll overpower me. But I can't leave it. Can you understand any of this?"

It was hard for Asha to say she understood, but in some way she did. Didn't she follow the river underground, even when it meant being beaten? What made her do that? Wasn't she being called, just as Ayo was now? "Yes," she nodded, "though I'll miss you terribly. You were my friend when I had no one else."

Ayo hugged her. "We'll always be friends, and we'll meet again, but right now, I need to be here, and I suspect the group would be better off without us."

"They've forgotten your kindness, that's all," Asha remarked, shortening the real story.

"It's all right. I knew. Still, I'm glad you came to say good-bye." Her face was glowing, even as tears welled up in her eyes. Setting her work down on a palm leaf, she stood up, brushing wood-chips off her wrap. "Come see what Naro is working on."

Farther down the outcrop were a several large flat stones standing almost perpendicular to the rocky ground. Naro and Naaba were deep in conversation, pointing to different sections of the rock.

"This is so much easier!" Naaba said, as the women joined them. "Once I see it, I realize of course, it's better this way."

"What is?" Asha asked. The marks on the stone meant nothing to her.

"When I tried to record numbers, I made a mark for each one," Naaba began drawing in the dirt with his stick, "like this: lll for 3, llll for 4, llllllllll for 10 – but it's hard to make sense of all those marks. Then sometimes, to make it easier to read, I'd make four slashes and put the fifth one across them, like all the fingers on one hand:

"But Naro simplified the slashes to dots, so 1 is ., 2 is .., 3 is ..., 4 is ...., and 5 is simply the crossbar, since that's all that's needed to identify it. So he can use the bar for 5, two bars for 10, three bars for 15." Asha was trying to keep up with the counts on her fingers. "Now the perfect count is twenty, that being the number of fingers and toes on a person, right?"

"That's also the arrangement on Sohko's counting beads."

"Exactly," Naro broke in. "That's what I used as a model. It goes by twenty. Once the counter reaches twenty, the top bead is moved to start over. Since I'm trying to do this on stone, I used a shell rather than a bead, so it didn't look like a dot. So the shell is twenty." He pointed to the standing stone, which was covered with carved symbols and lines. At first, it just swam before Asha, like pebbles and shells dropped up on the shore by the waves. But then, she saw the bars and the dots, figures of people, birds, boats, a man and a woman, an island.

"It's a story," Asha realized. "It's your story."

Naro beamed. "Yes, it is. It's our story."

They listened to Naro's explanation of the marks carefully chipped into the stone, realizing that any story could be recorded this way, as long as people agreed on the symbols.

"It's inspired," Naaba said, running his finger over the stone.

"I hope you'll use it, then," Naro said, "on your journey. It belongs to everyone."

"It's hard to leave you behind." Naaba put his hand on Naro's arm. "Are you sure that's your choice?"

"Don't worry about us. We'll be fine here. And when it's time to go, we will."

"Then I hope we meet again, along the way."

"I do too," Naro answered. "I'm sorry to leave the group, but it's time. And I have something different I have to do now. I was given a second life, and I will *not* waste it."

Naro stood close to Ayo as they watched the others slip back into the forest. "Are you sorry we're not going with them?"

"I am, but only because Asha is my friend. They're all my friends, and I'll miss them. But I know we belong exactly where we are."

* * *

The people who pushed the boats into the sea and headed north and west were unusually quiet. They had wanted to go, it's true, and Asha had told them that Naro and Ayo were happy to stay on the island by themselves, and the group had left them a boat to use when they were ready to leave. Still, even if they were annoyed with those two, the fact is the group was less without them, and they knew it. They'd start to say something about how Ayo could make a different kind of bowl or basket, or a new mat for the boat, and then stop in the middle of the sentence.

Dashona thought she'd be glad to see them gone, but she wasn't. Ayo was an artist. Dashona was a storyteller. They understood each other. But with Ayo gone, Dashona couldn't think of any stories worth telling. When the others pressed her for a story, she told a dark tale in which the heroes were torn apart by monsters that scattered their victims' body parts across the landscape. Their bones stuck out as rocky ridges, their limbs became hills, their blood turned into rivers. At the end of it, the children were screaming. On her own, later, Dashona dissolved into silent tears. More than any of the others, she was held in the grip of something terrible. When Asha tried to talk to her, she turned her head away and said nothing.

As the days and nights went on, she got worse, not eating or talking, just staring out to the horizon. In the beginning, she hoped there was something there, up ahead somewhere, that would make her feel better, but after a while she realized the view didn't change how she felt. It didn't matter whether it was here or there, this island or that one, whether it was hot sun or cold rain; it was all the same. She listened to the sounds of the waves touching the boat, the creak of the cross boards, the snoring of the sleepers, each one living in a land of dreams peopled by their own phantasms. Above her head, the stars pressed down so close, they were just over her head, all the furious stories that went on forever: the runaways always running, the scorpion always ready to sting, the antelope always charging, all of them never stopping, never done, swinging endlessly around the heavens, only to do the same thing the following night. Below her, the star reflections, wild doubles, danced erratically, calling to her in chirps and squeaks as they slid over the wave tops and fell into the troughs. But clouds moved in, and the stars were gradually blotted out, so there was only the dark sea and the dark sky reaching down to it. Dashona wondered if something as great as the sea could cry, and if anyone would notice.

The wind pushed the boat along faster. Too tired to keep her eyes open, and too exhausted to find her way back to her sleeping spot, Dashona leaned on the gunnels, her head propped in her hands, and closed her eyes, drifting into a half-sleep. She had no way of knowing that under the water, a large coral reef spread along the ocean floor, rising in some points all the way to the surface. When the starboard bow crashed into it, she was thrown overboard before she was even fully awake. Falling face-first into the water in a depression in the reef, she struggled in the dark, panicked, not knowing which way was up. Under her hands, the coral pulsed and swayed, keeping its secrets close. But no matter how she turned, or how fast, she found only coral. There was no clear up and down, and everything was dark.

With a jerk, she felt herself caught and pulled by her hair. Something had her, was dragging her along. In the confused recesses of her mind, she thought a shark had grabbed her, but when she tried to scream, she only got a mouthful of seawater. But it wasn't a shark that pulled her to the surface and shook her. There was a broad face right in front of hers, yelling something at her and shaking her again and yelling something else, and then there were lights from torches, and the face seemed to be melting, and she realized Afutu had hold of her, had found her in the dark.

"I don't want to die," she cried, gasping. "I don't. I want to be here. I want to be here. Here. Right here." She couldn't say everything because it was all coming over her at once, and she couldn't get enough air inside her.

"I know," he said, holding her close to him. "But right now, we need to get you back in the boat."

Everyone was hanging over the edge to help, so that Sohko had to remind them that capsizing the boat wouldn't help. Even so, many hands reached out to help her and then Afutu onto the boat, and Dashona was coughing and hugging everyone as if she hadn't seen them in a long time, which, in a way, was true.

* * *

They took turns bailing the water leaking into the boat. At dawn, when they could see the damage, they realized they'd need some time ashore, so they could patch the cracks. But it was a changed group that headed toward the very long land spread out on the horizon in front of them. They were lighter, as if the wind had finally blown the dark pieces out of their spirits.

CHAPTER 26
PIECES OF A PUZZLE

The land grew as they approached, stretching out before them to the north and west, its convoluted coastline cut with deep bays. Each section had its own character: rocky cliffs dropping straight into the sea, wide sand beaches, dark forests rolling easily to the water, twisted mazes of mangroves, gentle bays sheltered behind coral reefs. Sohko and Naaba watched the changing land with different thoughts. For Sohko, it represented everything they needed: a place for them to rest and repair the boat, to replenish supplies and regain their strength. It seemed to be perfect, perhaps for a long stay, maybe even a permanent home. For Naaba, it was a fine place, but not the place he was looking for. Lately, he'd been thinking about the leopard from long ago, and the other great beasts of the land: the lion, the eland, the hippo, the rhino, the ape. These islands were beautiful, and they had all the gifts of the sea, but he missed the land, where it was so big there seemed to be no end and the forest so powerful it ruled the land. When they'd left, he hadn't thought about any of these things. It was war, and they'd escaped in order to live. Now, from a different perspective, it seemed he'd left behind many things he'd loved but hadn't noticed.

But Sohko was right: it was a fine place for them to stay while they made repairs to the boat. Their experience on the other island had been rough on them; they needed some time to put themselves back together. They picked one of the sheltered beaches, a place of clear blue water and white sand bordered by tall coconut palms.

Leaving one of the boats moored in the bay, they dragged the other onto the beach and flipped it over on its side. Once they'd surveyed the damage and decided how to fix it, however, they had little interest in the project. Instead, they wandered off, exploring the new land, collecting sprouted coconut, ground nuts, mangos and guavas, climbing up interesting rocks, finding fresh water pools in the forest. Some walked the beach shallows, collecting conch and mussels. The children wandered up into the hills beyond it. Without any discussion, they had all agreed: there was no need to rush to fix the boat.

Late in the day, they returned to the beach. Aminata organized a fine meal, with shellfish, snake, turtle, dragon fruit, and coconuts, as well as lots of fresh water and a drink made from sea moss. It was a treat to have plenty of room and good food and nothing that had to be done immediately.

Naaba made the children the game that Deka had asked for: wooden pieces carved in various shapes so that they could fit together in all different ways.

Each piece was unique, but it could be attached to any of the others. At first, Deka put them together in a long line, but Sule tried putting them together in forms, big irregular shapes at first, then something that looked surprisingly like a crocodile with its mouth open. That got both of them to experiment with different combinations, seeing what they looked like. There was a face with wild hair that they said was a portrait of Naaba, a lumpy shape they said was a storm cloud, a monster beetle, a fish with wings, and so on.

When the group had finished eating and were sitting around the fire on the beach, the children challenged Dashona to make up a story that went along with the changing shapes. Unlike the shapes, the story had to make sense and flow without stopping, even when they were rearranging the pieces into a different shape. Deka and Sule took turns arranging pieces into shapes – whatever they wanted.

It started like other stories: "In a village near mine," but from there on, it was like no story they'd ever heard, "there was once a ... gourd plant that, at first, seemed like any other gourd plant, but when the gourd was ripe and the villagers opened it up, they found a - bird - inside. It was very...lumpy and had trouble flying, which is not surprising, since its mother was a gourd, but the people felt bad for it, so they tried to teach it to fly. They stood around flapping their arms but the bird didn't understand, so it just perched there, watching, with its head tilted sideways. The people thought they should ask something else, something not human, to help. And, for some reason, they asked a rock, no, no, it was a cloud, to teach the bird to fly, but even though the cloud knew how to fly, it didn't know how to talk, so it hovered in the sky for a while, and moved off. Then they asked a giant conch shell, but it only talked about how beautiful it was and what fine music it could play. The people were getting discouraged. They hadn't realized how hard it was to teach a bird to fly. Then one person with very strange hair -"

"You know who that is!" Deka called.

"- had a good idea. He said they should ask a bird to teach the bird how to fly. But the bird they found was so fat and had such tiny, stick-up wings that it couldn't fly either. It ... jumped up and down very well, though. The people were about to give up when a lizard appeared, no, a crocodile. A hungry crocodile, with its mouth open, ready to eat both birds. The fat bird jumped very high, then landed, then jumped even higher, then landed up in a tree. The hungry crocodile turned and looked around, thinking there must be something good to eat in the area. The gourd bird tried to jump, but it was only a little hop. He tried to run, but he had very short, thick legs, and they didn't move well. Looking behind him, the gourd bird saw the hungry crocodile following, switching his heavy tail back and forth.

"Just then, the cloud reappeared. It had figured out how to talk and told the bird to spread his wings and flap them up and down

395

very fast. The gourd bird tried to flap his wings, but they were tiny and couldn't lift him up very high, even though he flapped them so fast he looked like a bee. When the hungry crocodile saw all this, he moved in to eat the bird, but the bird, at the last moment, ran inside the giant conch shell. The crocodile snapped up the conch shell, but it got stuck, so he couldn't close his mouth. While the crocodile was struggling to close his mouth, the bird ran out very fast... as you can imagine you would run away from a crocodile with its mouth stuck open, with a conch shell inside it, and then the gourd bird flapped its wings the way the cloud told him to, and he flew! He flew right up into ... the lumpy cloud. And that's where he is today."

By the end of the story, Dashona was laughing so hard, she could barely make the words come out.

"One of your best stories," Sule declared.

* * *

The first few days passed in easy exploration, frequently not much farther than the line of palms at the edge of the beach, where they set up their hammocks and spent a good part of the day napping while the sea breeze cooled them. But eventually the old hunger to see what was around the bend returned. Some headed inland, others along the coast, to see what the land had to show them.

"Nobody goes off alone," Sohko announced early one day. "If you're taking one of the boats, let others know." That was the extent of the rules.

Sitting on one of the flat rocks near the shore, Naaba was carving new fishhooks out of pieces of bone, but he was restless. "Let's take the boat and see what's farther up the coast."

Abran nodded. "Too much time on land, right?"

"I've learned to walk again without staggering around. It must be time to get back on the water." He rolled up his carvings in a palm leaf protector and set them aside. "Asha?"

"Absolutely."

"Can we come too?" Deka asked. "It's fun here, but I want to see something else."

With an exaggerated sigh, Naaba put his hand on her head. "I'm afraid you're turning into a wanderer."

"Just like you!"

Naaba started toward the boat. "Bring some food and water. Let's see what looks interesting along the coast and catch some fish for dinner."

The breezes drew them north and west, along the coast. Stretching his long legs out in front of him at the stern, Naaba worked the steering paddle and Abran set the mats. When they were free of the reef, they sat studying the shore, trying to sort out what might lie behind the forested coastline.

"There," Asha announced, pointing to a deep cut in the shore, "I want to go in there."

"Then we shall," Naaba said, turning the rudder. "And what is there?"

"River in the mountain." She couldn't say more than that because she didn't know, but something called her there, where the saltwater ran in from the ocean and the sweetwater ran down from the mountain, and they met, inside the rock.

Abran took down the mats and rolled them, then studied the shore. "It's a very narrow passage."

In front of them, there was no beach. The land rose in red, yellow and black rock cliffs, huge slabs of rock upended in rows. Where Asha was pointing, there was an opening between the rock faces, wider at the water then closing almost completely overhead. Irregular masses of rock stuck out from the rock walls like half-formed heads of guardian spirits, with bulbous noses and tiny eyes. All along them, streaks of mineral colors ran from top to bottom, red, orange, yellow, black, and touches of green. Past the narrow triangular opening, they could see light beyond, and green vines hanging down from the far rocks all the way to the water. They were drawn in as if a power had hold of them.

As they paddled through the opening, they craned their necks to look straight up at the strange monsters in the rock that shifted shapes as they changed angles. In the shade of the rock, it was suddenly cool and damp, but on the other side, it opened up into a magical sunlit spot, with tiny white flowers trailing on long stalks from plants tucked into niches in the rock. High above them, red flowers decorated the top of the cliffs.

"There's something in the water!" Sule pointed to a pair of pale shapes at the far end of the pool.

"Manatees," Abran said, leaning over to watch them.

"Are they like hippos?"

"They're a lot friendlier, and they don't leave the water. They eat sea grasses."

Past the pool was an even narrower opening where a river came from inside the rock and emptied into the pool. Abran didn't even see it until Asha pointed it out; a screen of vines and hanging plants covered the top half of the opening. When they tried to go through it, the vines caught on the mast, so Naaba had to climb up the mast and cut them.

"It's strange that the vines all end well short of the water. If we didn't have a mast on the boat, we could have gone through without touching them."

On the other side of the narrow opening in the rock, the river took them inside the mountain. Just past the narrow passage, it opened up into a huge room formed by rock, with a high vaulted ceiling above them and the river held in a deep channel in the middle of the floor.

"The walls -" Naaba began, trying to find the words, "they're sparkling."

Even in the light from the entrance to the cave, they could see what Naaba meant. Strange yellow and white pointed formations lined the sides, mostly from the ceiling down, but some from the floor up. At some points along the walls, the rock seemed to flow in streams, as if it had just stopped when they appeared. The streaming rock was glittering with moving lights, as if it was alive.

"Light a torch," Abran called, leaning over the edge.

When Naaba held up the torch, the wall danced with light, the sparkling lights pulsing with the flicker of the torch flame.

Asha pointed ahead of them. "Look, over there."

A large formation, as big around as a person, was shining brighter than the lights on the wall. Made of white crystals, it rose from the floor of the cave into a confusion of spikes, each with multiple straight, smooth edges that caught the light and refracted it into other colors, sending it flashing back at the people in the boat. Ahead of them, the formations changed again, to long, pure white structures that in some cases dripped all the way from the ceiling to the floor of the cave. They were very narrow, like individual spears piercing the roof, but they often joined others to make bridges between them, so they looked like long ladders leading to the roof of the cave. On the ground, the formations were shorter and squatter, with rounded tops, like a row of very short people.

"I want to see them, up close!" Deka shouted. "Please!"

Everyone agreed. Looking from the boat wasn't enough. They had to stand right in front of these strange formations, touch them, know that they were real. It wasn't hard to stop the boat. Naaba had been poling it up-river anyway. Throwing the pole to Abran, he jumped into the water and scrambled up the side of the channel, taking the rope with him.

"I can tie it up, but there's no easy way to get out – or back in," he warned.

It didn't matter. Sule and Deka were off the boat and finding their way across the water as soon as Naaba was ashore. Abran went right after them, making sure they made it up the side of the channel. Only Asha hesitated.

"There's something about this place -"

"Throw me the torch," Naaba called. "Make it two of them."

By the time she'd thrown the second, they had the first one lit. Naaba held it up, moving from one section to another, lighting up an amazing world, every bit decorated wildly, some parts sparkling, others dull, some brilliant white, others streaked with yellow, orange and red, dark brown, others that glowed green. It was all the colors of a dream. She vaulted over the side of the boat and pulled herself up the channel side. Some things must be seen, even if they come with warnings.

Off to one side, the rock dripped down in shiny pink points, some connecting with inverse pink points on the floor. Running sideways between some of the ceiling sections were thin pieces like spider webs of stone, gleaming white. Trailing her fingers along the sparkling, dripping rock, she realized it didn't just look wet; it was. It really was streaming. Water was finding its way through this rock somehow and down to the river. Abran was stopped still in front of one of the biggest formations, full of long, sparkling crystals.

"I've never seen anything like it. Look at it throwing light everywhere."

Naaba walked over, holding up the torch. Over his head was a strange formation of drooping blobs of rock, as if they were going to be the thin spear formations dropping from the ceiling but changed their mind. As he looked up, he watched the smoke from the torch rise. Exactly where the smoke from the torch was hitting the ceiling, the color of the formation changed, from bright white at the outside to brown overhead.

"See what you can find on the cave floor." He said it casually, or thought he did, but Asha was already on alert.

"What? What are you looking for?"

"I found some really strange squiggly brown rock, like worms all tangled up," Deka pointed.

"I found something else," Abran said, waving them over. In the sandy deposit between two rocks, there was a mark, probably a footprint, though not a complete one.

As they huddled around it, trying to see in the flickering torch light, Naaba said, "There are smoke marks on the ceiling back there."

"There's something else here," Asha said slowly. On a rock ledge behind her were three human skulls, painted with swirling lines of red and black dots around the eye sockets, across the cheeks and around the edge of the chin. "I don't see any other bones. I don't think it's a burial."

"What is it then?"

She shook her head. Something had a wrong feeling. It wasn't the river, and the cave was a thing of wonder. But the skulls, lined up on the ledge, stared back at her, their painted dots pulsing in the torch light.

Naaba was already working his way into the side passages that opened off the main cave, studying the different formations, especially the pillars of flashing crystals. One very large piece, as big as a man, had large, perfect crystals shooting off in the center column in different directions. As he ran his hand along them, he realized several had been broken off. Above him, the ceiling was darkened with smoke, and off to one side, a different stone, a flat panel, caught his eye. Tucked back behind a wall of streaming rock, it was darker and drier than the rest of the rocks, but what caught Naaba's eye was the mass of figures and designs painted on it, in bright white, yellow, red, brown and black.

On the end nearest him was a writhing sea serpent with a boat in its jaws. And there were figures of people, men and women, each marked with lines of different colored dots that ran down their arms and along their shoulders, and circles of dots in their elaborate head wraps. They wore decorated body wraps as well, some with carefully marked red and black designs similar to the ones they'd seen at Komo's village. Some carried baskets on their heads; some played a drum or blew a conch shell. One man, the first one in the line, wore a fringed red cloth across his body and carried a serpent staff. Above the line of figures were a series of dots in different colors and wavy lines, all in white.

"Asha!" he called, without turning away from the painted figures, but she was already coming up behind him, staring at the panel.

"It's a story," she said, studying the figures, "like Ayo and Naro's, but more complicated."

"I'd guess there was a group of people, including a chief, or leader, who came here after a storm at sea. Just like us," he added, "but the dots mean something too, a count, just like Naro's system on the rock."

"That's only part of the story," Asha said, pointing deeper into the dark recesses off to the side. "I can see more figures."

When Abran and the children joined them, they all stared at the panel. Farther along into the side cave, Asha was already trying to sort out the next panel.

"Bring a torch," she called, straining to sort out the mass of figures on the stone in front of her. As Naaba held up the light, the wall danced with figures, so many figures that they were overlapping, as if there was so much to say and only this small space to say it, so the artist used the rock over and over again, like the sand that people used to draw figures in back home and then smoothed over, but there was no erasing here, so everything remained, in a confusion of figures. On the very top of the stone were three large spiral designs in different colors, forming a semi-circle around a four-pointed star shape with lines drawn around it. At the left edge, Asha could make out a procession of some kind. The leader was taller than the others and wore a sort of cape, all cross-hatched by the artist, and a headdress of long yellow feathers that curved down behind his back. Behind him were three men and two women, the last woman farther away than the others, but it was hard for Asha to learn much about them since other figures obscured part of them. Below them were animal figures that looked like a crocodile, a manatee, a barracuda, an agouti, and several macaws. Farther along the wall next to the procession there were two men standing with crossed spears, with people standing on both sides of them, more rows of dots, and a spiral with the outside end extending out. Over the top of these figures were others, painted more quickly, with less attention to detail. They were all battle scenes: men fighting with clubs and knives, men throwing spears, men falling to the ground, a woman being pushed into the river, two women fighting with knives. Bodies on the ground. The most recent had red dots and white dots and black lines going everywhere around the figures, forming outlines around them and then connecting them to other figures on the panel, so it seemed to throb with life and death.

Asha stood in front of the panel, weeping. "Why? Why, in this place of wonder is there so much pain?"

"People carry a dark seed inside them," Naaba said. "It doesn't take much to make it grow." Then, seeing the children looking at him with sad eyes, he added, "But it doesn't have to be that way. They can choose."

"Did the stars make them change?" Sule asked, pointing to the spirals at the top of the panel.

"Perhaps that's what they thought." He didn't put much stock in starry omens, though he knew others did.

"Someone was living here, at least at one time," Abran announced as he joined the group. "There's a camp down the next side cave, or at least what's left of one."

The camp he showed them was small, but had a fire ring with three hearthstones, a sleeping mat, a few baskets, water gourds, and painting supplies laid out carefully: shells containing powdered bird droppings, white clay, red and yellow ochre, orchid bulbs cut open to reveal the sticky fluid inside, solidified animal fat, rows of sticks with animal hair attached and some with pointed ends. But there was no sign of a recent fire, or any foods left in the baskets.

"Can we go now?" Deka asked, taking Asha's hand.

Turning toward the parts of the caverns they hadn't yet explored, Naaba started to say something, but Abran caught his eye and shook his head.

"Right," Naaba said, turning back toward the boat. "Let's head back. We'd run out of torch light soon anyway." He was trying to keep the tone light, but the mention of no light in these dark recesses gave everyone the shivers.

As they retraced their steps through the fantastic dripping rocks, Asha looked at them differently. They seemed threatening and alien, as if they'd been changed somehow, tainted by the troubles of the people who'd come here. Probably those people were captivated, at first, by the sparkling stones. But something happened, and after that, it didn't matter that the stones were a wonder of light and color. In a crass simplification, they had reduced everything, even beauty, to a desire to kill. She thought about moths that had taken over the forest one season, eating the leaves of the trees so voraciously that the branches were stripped bare, leaving the trees standing like skeletons where the forest had been. Nothing stopped the moths until all the leaves were gone. Then the moths died too, falling right out of the trees, their bodies covering the ground.

"Don't take anything from the cave back with you," she said to the children. "It's full of dark energy."

Heading back to the boat, they said nothing. It seemed a long time ago that they'd been sitting on the beach, bored, tired of sunshine and comfort. For all of them, the painted panels brought back all too clearly the chaos of war, and its pain.

As Asha and the children jumped in the channel and swam to the boat, Naaba untied the mooring line. Bending over to help him, Abran said softly, "They're there, bodies, laid out in a row."

"I thought that might be what you saw. But the artist or whoever laid them out – there might be someone still alive. At least it's a possibility."

Abran nodded. "But I wouldn't take the children in there."

"We could come back, tomorrow or the next day."

"I'm not sure what we're meant to do here, but we need to get them home now. Too many memories." Once he was in the boat, he caught the rope Naaba threw to him, and held the boat steady with the pole until Naaba had climbed in.

* * *

CHAPTER 27
THE WOMAN ON THE CLIFF

Aminata had started off thinking about baked eels, or prawns, or maybe steamed lobster for the main meal of the day, but as soon as she started working on an idea, it turned to mist and disappeared. Beside her, Dashona was trying to weave baskets out of palm leaves, as she'd seen Ayo do so many times, but they turned out more like tubes than traditional baskets. After the fifth try, she set the half-finished basket on the sand and closed her eyes.

When she opened them, Afutu was standing in front of her, leaning on his staff. "Ready for something different?"

"Anything," she sighed. "I'm so bad at this."

"Good. Sohko is bored but doesn't want to work on the boat. How do you two feel about a stroll up the hills?"

"A fine idea," Aminata said. "I can't make a single thought stay put in my head. Let's bring a basket or two, in case we find something interesting."

As they headed inland, they climbed gradually away from the beach and into the forest that cloaked the side of the mountain. With the forest came the mosquitoes, in clouds.

"Let's get out in the open air, where the breeze will blow these away," Aminata pleaded, swatting at the offenders.

It was an easy choice. Above them, the cliffs rose to a high promontory with a clear view all the way out to the sea, so they fought their way through the dense brush to get there. The forest was filled with the songs of birds, but the dense growth made them hard to see, except for the macaws, large and loud, the rulers of the canopy. But in looking up, Aminata spotted papayas in a cluster far up the trunk of the tree.

"Oh, papayas," she said, casually. "They'd be so nice to have, you know."

Sohko laughed. "Are you asking me to get them for you?"

"Well, if you'd like," she smiled. "That would be nice. They're good for so many things, you know, especially the seeds, and the fruit is so tasty."

"I'll take that as a yes," he said as he started up the tree, aware that they were all watching him. "You can keep going. I'll find you, I'm sure," he called down.

"No, we wouldn't want to miss this," Afutu said, resting against his staff. "It's educational."

With a groan, Sohko continued his climb up the tree trunk. Too many days in boats had left his leg muscles weaker than they used to be. Eventually, out of breath, he reached the hanging fruits, a little too green for his taste, but they'd ripen up.

"Ready? They're going to fall on your head," he called down.

"We'll be looking for them," Afutu called back.

"I'll send one right at you."

"I know you will."

Cutting the fruits loose with his knife, Sohko lobbed them down to those watching below. Afutu caught his. "Good work," he said, gathering up the rest, wrapping them in dried papaya leaves, and packing them in one of the baskets. "We'll leave them here and pick them up on our way down. No point in carrying them up and then back."

The rest of the hike was easy to see but hard to do, up the side of the rocky cliff, and they said little as they followed Sohko up. Afutu was last, mostly because he didn't want anyone to know how hard it was for him, so he was the last one to see what everyone else had already seen by the time he got to the top. In front of them was a flat ledge with a view of the whole side of the island and the wide sea fanning out in lacy edges as it met the shore. But that wasn't what they were all looking at. At the other end of the ledge from them, incredibly, a man and a woman were locked in a fight to the death, grappling and twisting, both covered with bloody smears. The woman was screaming.

The first to respond, Sohko yelled out "Stop!"

They looked up, the two of them, at exactly the same moment, and the man tried to wave them away, but the woman, in the moment he was distracted, slit his throat with a single ripping cut. The blood gushed from him, covering her as she held him by the hair, her head bent toward him, studying him before she pushed him off the ledge. She was shaking as she turned toward them, her head thrown back, her arm raised, the bloody knife poised. Her face was covered with yellow, red, and black dots, now smeared with blood and sweat.

"Wait!" Sohko called. "We mean you no harm."

For a long moment, she studied them, all of them, her gaze falling from one to the next. Then she dropped the knife and collapsed on the ground, wracked with sobs. Everyone ran forward, except Dashona, who simply couldn't make her feet move toward the woman. All she could think of was the cut of the knife, the life blood pulsing, and the body lying twisted and broken somewhere in the deep forested hillside below. She kept seeing his face, looking right at her, his long hair flowing loose beneath a knotted headband with a pointed stick thrust into it. She couldn't remember seeing a knife in his hand as he waved them away.

"Thank you," the woman gasped. "Thank you for saving me." Pulling herself to her feet, she made an attempt to retie the hair that had been fallen from the knot at the top of her head. Then, with her eye locked onto Afutu, she smoothed her wrap, running her bloody hands down the front of it, and tucked her knife away in her sash. "I was afraid for my life," she said, sliding one arm through

Afutu's and resting the other on his chest. Dashona thought the wrong person had won the fight on the ledge.

"It was terrible," the woman was saying. "He ambushed me here, on the ledge." She took a long drink from the calabash Aminata offered. "They killed all of us, except me. They killed all of my people."

"Who?" Dashona interrupted. "Why?"

The woman gave Dashona a long look and ignored her. "I suppose you're the chief," she said, still pressed up against Afutu.

"No, Sohko is," Afutu said, but he made no effort to remove her arm from his.

She slid her hand across his chest. "Then the wrong man was chosen."

Aminata wasn't a woman of hasty decisions or flights of wild emotions, but she found this woman annoying. "If you have something to say to us, you can say it to all of us, without seducing one of the group and insulting another."

The woman sprang back as if she'd been stung. "Oh, I'm so sorry. I didn't know you had two husbands. My mistake."

"Sit down," Sohko said, "everyone." The woman was the last to sit, and even then, it wasn't really sitting, but only leaning against the rock. Her streaked face, with its wild colors all run together, was defiant.

"Now, tell us what happened."

"Oh, yes, sir," she mocked, then winked at Afutu. "We were all from the same village in the big land to the south," she started in a sing-song voice, "but we hated it there, so we left to find a better land. After the sea dragon tried to kill us, we found this land, and we liked it, so we stayed. But after a while, something happened, and the two leaders started fighting with each other for control of the group. Everyone chose a side, and all we did was fight, all of us. In the beginning, it was just little skirmishes, but then it was bigger battles, and not just the men; it was everyone. We had a child in the group," she paused, "my child, but he was killed when he fell into one of their traps. I was so angry I killed the men who built the trap. Then I went after the others, one by one. At first, it bothered me to kill them, but after a while, it didn't." She looked from one to the next, holding each one in her gaze. "They deserved to die. A death for a death: that's the code."

"And who was the man on the ledge?" Sohko asked when she stopped.

"The last of them. The last of the hated ones. Your appearance gave me the opportunity I needed to – avoid his attack."

When she seemed reluctant to add anything else, Aminata followed up with another question. "Are there others in your group?"

The woman looked at Aminata. "Is there more water? I'm really thirsty."

"There might be, after you answer my question."

In a flash, the woman was on her feet, her knife in her hand. "Who are you?"

Aminata never moved. "I think a more appropriate question would be 'Who are you?'"

"Who am I? You don't know? I'm Noya."

"And who," Dashona interrupted, "did you just kill?"

"Just another one," she laughed, "one of many! He needed to die. He talked too much, just like you." She moved so quickly, Dashona was taken by surprise when the woman's knife slashed across her arm, but Afutu lunged forward, grabbing Noya's legs so she crashed to her knees in front of Dashona. Shocked, holding her injured arm, Dashona stumbled backward.

"Stupid woman!" Noya cried. "You know nothing! Only the deadliest survive! *And I am!* All the rest are stupid."

The four of them stared at her.

"Oh, sorry," she mocked. "Guess I should have better manners. But you know what? I don't!"

"How did the argument start?" Aminata pushed, "the argument between your two leaders."

"Isn't it strange that the men are always chosen as leaders?" she said, turning to Aminata. "For instance, why is he chief, and not you? See, that's how it's done, right there."

"So you started it."

"No, they did." She purred at Afutu, arching her back as she leaned into him, her hand on his leg. "If I was your lover, you'd forget you had a bad leg. You'd forget everything. We'd make love like two eagles, soaring into the black sky, tearing at each other."

"So you seduced one of the leaders."

Turning back toward Aminata, the woman laughed. "No, I seduced both of them. They were brothers, and there's no feud like a family feud. Of course, they needed proof, but that's easy to supply."

"How old was your son?" Dashona interrupted.

"My what?"

"Nothing."

"You should treat that cut. The poison is slow but effective."

Dashona pressed her hand over the cut. "There aren't any others, are there?" It was hard to tell how much the woman said was true, but they were better off having her talk. They might learn something useful, and it kept her occupied.

"There are now!" the woman said, spinning around. "And it makes things much more interesting. I love a challenge. So when did you four arrive?"

"Our boat was damaged," Sohko said. "We need to repair it."

"That's why you're up on this ledge? You thought there were boats up here?" Turning to Afutu once again, she smiled. "You'll tell me the truth, won't you? These others, they don't like me much. But you're different: you're special. I knew it as soon as I saw you. You're a champion. We were made for each other, you and I, the best with the best. It's too bad they don't appreciate you the way I do." She moved into him, pressing herself against him, trailing her fingers down the middle of his chest.

Taking her by the shoulders, he moved her away but held on to her. Throwing back her head, she screamed. "Yes! I knew it; I knew it when I saw you." Leaning toward Dashona, she laughed, a strange sound, like a parrot imitating a person laughing. Then she turned back to Afutu, but this time he pushed her away completely. "It doesn't matter, lover," she crooned, "I know what you like."

The air was heavy with raw discontent when Dashona got up and walked past Noya.

"Where are you going?" Noya called after her, but Dashona didn't stop or respond. Instead, she knelt down at the edge of the rock ledge, searching the forest below. There was no sign of the man's body, or even a mark in the trees where he fallen. His face, she couldn't forget his face in that last moment, as he turned to look at them. It couldn't be coincidence. She looked back at the woman who was now watching her very carefully. Even with the different hair and the wild face paint, it was obvious: the same chin, the same eyes, the same fullness in the upper lip, the way they had both turned their heads, with the same jerky movement, at the same instant.

"He was your brother."

The woman whirled on Dashona once again, running at her, one hand reaching for Dashona's hair while the other slipped her knife out of her sash, but this time Sohko was there to grab one hand and Afutu to grab the other. Noya wrenched herself free momentarily, but they grabbed her again, tying her hands behind her back while she screamed, thrashing wildly.

"He wasn't even armed," Dashona remarked.

"Oh, he was armed. He had everything. That was his weapon. *Why can't you be more like your brother? He's so talented. Why can't you be nice like your brother? He has so many friends, and you don't have any.* He had more than his share of everything, but, in the end, it wasn't enough, was it? He tried to talk to me. *Oh, let me, the great one, tell you how you should be, because you have so many problems, and I don't have any.* That's what he said. *You need to change,* he said, just like that, as if someone gave him permission to tell me how to be. Well, no one tells me how to be. I was his opposite, you know. He liked to settle arguments; I liked to start them. We balanced each other, you know. But then, he tried to change me, but changing me would mean changing him, and he hadn't thought about that." With a hard laugh, she looked off into the distance beyond the ledge, addressing him. "You knew it at the end. It wouldn't work anymore. It would kill you being half of one thing and half of another, no better than any other fool on this earth." She looked back at Dashona. "I knew all that when he came to talk to me, to make me change. So I did him a favor. He died still all one piece. There are very few who can claim that." Her eyes blazed, even as she struggled.

Dashona nodded. Oddly, she did understand. It was what she had noticed in the murdered man: his peace. He would live on, a spirit on the ledge, looking after the people who arrived, troubled, on the beach below. His sister, however, was something else entirely. How did one dispose of discontent? It was well-fed and growing among the group on the ledge. Her arms pinned behind her where Sohko had tied them, Noya had gone from screaming fury to complete silence, but she wasn't conquered. She was waiting.

Aminata came over and sat down next to Dashona. "We should get something on that cut," she said, a little awkwardly.

"It's all right. If it was poisoned, it would have been at work on me by now. She's the poison, but I have no idea how to cure it."

"I have an idea," Aminata said, "but it's very vague. We have to do something, to fight this somehow."

"I don't know what to do."

"You're going to have to pull yourself together. We can't fight a war against a witch if you're already defeated."

"What do I have to fight with? I can't do what she does."

Aminata exhaled sharply as she stood up. "Oh well, then, I guess you'll have to drown in your tears while Sohko and I try to do something."

"No." Dashona took Aminata's arm. "Don't leave. I want to fight, but I'm not a very good warrior. I tell stories."

"Then I guess you'll need to tell a story," Aminata said. "There are many ways to fight."

They were still spread out along the ledge, later, unable to decide what to do with the woman, or with themselves, so they sat and stared out to the sea, which had looked so beautiful to them earlier in the day. Now, everything seemed confused and darkened. Even Sohko had abandoned any thought of living on this land permanently. If by some chance they made it out of all this alive, they'd head as far away as possible, as fast as possible.

When Aminata waved her over, Dashona joined them, without looking at anyone.

"Tell us a story," Aminata said, quietly.

"Oh good," Noya called, from her place against the rock wall. "I was hoping you'd tell us a story. Make sure it's a good one, uplifting, with a clear moral at the end. I always like those." She snorted, laughing.

"Quiet," Afutu called. There was something different in his voice as he spoke, not just a response to an annoying remark, but a quiet, very clear command.

"I lov -" she started, but changed her mind.

"In the beginning," Dashona said, "before there were any villages or even rivers or mountains, before there were fish or birds or the great beasts, there was stillness. It was grey stillness, like a cloud that never moves, and it sat over the earth. There was no difference between the grey of the water and the grey of the land and the grey of the sky. It was all an unmoving sameness. And it was absolutely silent. It hung like fog over the sea, never moving.

"The creators, First Mother and First Father, moved out of their cave and onto the land, but there was no life there. There was nothing. 'We need to make the forest,' the First Father said, so he took the grey fog and pressed it into sticks and planted them in the ground. But nothing grew. They were only grey sticks in a grey fog. 'We need animals to fill the forest,' First Mother said, so she formed birds and insects and monkeys, but they only sat there, unmoving. First Father made great fish, and a huge serpent to rule the ocean, but they too were still. The water never moved. First Mother-Father stood side by side and looked at their creation, and a strange feeling welled up inside them: *they were discontent.*

"It was the first emotion, and the one that gave birth to all others. They were hungry for something that wasn't, and that hunger pulled something into motion. It was a need, a vacuum that drew energy to itself, but of itself, it was still nothing. Discontent alone could not create.

"First Father broke off one of the branches of the trees, but it was filled with grey air, not life. He picked one of the great fish out of the sea, but it too was only grey fog, and it evaporated in his hands. 'How I long for these things to be more than they are,' he said, and in that moment, a new emotion was born, the most important emotion of all, the driving force of the universe: *longing*, the awareness of something more than what is and the cry of the spirit to have it. It's the power that propels every choice and drives every creation.

"'We need to call it out,' the First Mother cried, 'call it out!' and she started singing the first song, a song without any words, a song to awaken the forest, the sea, the sky. She sang, and one by one the insects sang also, then the birds, then the whales in the deep sea, then the great beasts in the forests. But it wasn't enough. So she sang her own desire, her own longing, her joy and her sadness, and she sent the song out over the sea so that the clouds formed into separate pieces. Moved by her song, First Father joined his song to

415

hers, and their harmony soared out into the grey space and ignited the universe and started the great wheel in motion. He took her as his mate, and they gave birth to the sun and the moon.

"The force that fed creation was the pairing of opposites. There can be no light without dark, no noise without silence, no thump of the heart without the pause that follows it, no stars without darkness for them to play on. The song that awakened life contained both joy and pain, for one cannot know one without being acquainted with the other. And so we are today, the children of those who sang to awaken the forest and the sea, but our inheritance is what they bequeathed to us: a mixture, an interplay, sometimes a battle, of opposites.

"The truth is, we will never be free of you," she said, looking at Noya, "or the discontent and misery you spread before you. But your energy, which used to be so focused, is now confused. You could only be an undiluted entity while your brother was alive because he was your opposite. But even darkness cannot exist without light by which to recognize it. He changed you by his death. Perhaps he gave you this as his final gift. Or perhaps you changed yourself by his murder. In either case, without him, you must now be both: what you were and what he was. With your brother's death, you must carry his light, his love, his kindness. And when you do, you will learn to suffer the crushing burden of the many lives you've destroyed. You will never be able to leave them behind, or forget them. Your brother won't let you.

"What happened here has touched us all, awakened feelings that were already there but slumbering, or purposely kept in shadow, but you changed that. You introduced us to discontent, each in our own way. It's a primitive emotion, but it forms the base on which others are built. For me, it's a push away from what I knew, and it made me see things differently. It's clearer to me now that we, all of us, have a mixed heritage. On a sunny day, it's easy to forget the storm, but it's just as real. You've lived the storm, but that's not the whole truth. Your weapon is darkness, but you're afraid of the light. First Mother and First Father gave us a birth-right of discontent and longing, driving the twin powers: to create and to destroy. It's a complicated way to be, but it's how we are. But even when we're lost in the dark, with all its terror, its despair, its seductive lies, it can never claim us completely, for it's not all we are.

"I'm only a storyteller," she said, looking straight at Noya, "but I'm good at it. If you've killed me with the cut of your knife, I'll die tonight more peaceful than I've been in a very long time." With that, Dashona bowed her head, marking the end of her story. It wasn't the traditional end of a story, but then it wasn't a tradi-tional story. For once, she didn't worry whether people liked it or not. It was her story, and she'd told it as she'd wanted.

Noya sank back against the rock, saying nothing.

Aminata nodded.

"Well told," Afutu said, but she didn't reply.

While Dashona was telling her tale, Noya worked the rope that bound her hands back and forth against the stone ledge until it broke. Once she was free, she waited, not moving or speaking, until the others were busy making their plans to return, with her, to the beach. They were talking about some baskets they'd left far-ther down the trail and which way they'd need to go to find them. At the moment they were standing up, stretching from their long stay on the ledge, gathering their things, she stood up too. But she wasn't stiff and sore; she was free. Hands above her head, in a cel-ebration of freedom from their restraints, she ran across the ledge. Dashona was stretching the kinks out of her back, her hand pressed against the rock wall, when Noya ran straight into her, throwing her down flat onto the rock ledge. From there, she skirted the oth-ers, evaded Sohko as he tried to grab her, and ran right off the edge of the rock ledge, throwing her arms straight out as she launched herself into the air, like a bird sailing into the wind.

Paralyzed by shock, Aminata stared at the figure flying off the ledge. Sohko ran to the edge and sank to one knee, hands on the edge of the rock ledge, trying to see where she'd gone.

"I can't see her anywhere," he called back.

Pulling herself up, Dashona joined the search, scanning the area below the ledge. It reminded her of how she'd searched for some sign of the unfortunate man whose throat Noya had slit so purposely right in front of them. Spread out far below the group on the ledge, the broad sea ruled the horizon, in various shades of blue, so light it was almost white at the shore and deep blue-green farther out. Above it, the sky repeated the pattern, going from the palest blue at the edges to the deepest at the top, as if sea and sky formed two halves of a giant circle. At the edge of the sky, where blue faded into white, two black hawks were circling, riding the air currents with their broad wings outstretched, their wing tips just touching sometimes, before they soared away, circling the sky in opposite directions.

"I don't think we'll see either of them again, not as people, anyway," Dashona said.

Sohko had followed her gaze. "They're shape-shifters?"

"That's absurd," Aminata said. "People don't change into birds." When no one responded, she went on, "Besides, what were they doing up here, waiting for us?"

"Maybe," Dashona offered.

"Why?"

"I don't know," Dashona said, "but these islands are full of spirits. They have their own reasons for what they do."

"Then I'm ready to leave this land to them," Aminata said. "I like land to be land, and people to be people, and birds to be birds. Switching back and forth is...confusing."

Sohko came up next to her. "Let's go find the others and fix the boat."

"They showed us - things," Afutu remarked. They were the first words he'd said in so long that Aminata had forgotten he was there. "If everything has a reason, then so did they, and if they chose to show us something, we need to think about it."

Dashona, in a moment of restraint, said nothing in reply, nor did Aminata or Sohko, so the remark, and all it entailed, went without further discussion.

On the way down the mountain, they searched for any sign of either one of the twins, but there was none. "It doesn't mean they're not here, somewhere," Aminata insisted. "The dense growth could easily hide them, or we could just miss them behind some rock or big tree or thick bushes. There could be ten people lined up behind that huge tree but we couldn't see them, right?"

Dashona nodded but didn't reply. She'd thought perhaps Afutu would say something to her on the trip down the mountain, but he walked way up ahead, with Sohko.

* * *

"I need your advice, friend. I need to know what to do. Everything's different."

"If you'd give me any idea what you're talking about, it'd help."

"I was injured, you know, in the game."

"Yes, the day everything fell apart on the beach."

Afutu hesitated, glanced at Sohko, then looked off at tree boa curled around a thick branch. "Right. Nothing worked right after that."

"Not just your leg."

"Right."

"But today, you learned something."

"Right."

"So, this is good. Mostly."

"The 'mostly' is the problem. What do I do?"

"Tell her you love her, skip the rest, and hope for the best."

"You think so?"

"Keep it simple. Less room for trouble."

* * *

By the time they got back to the camp on the beach, the sun was dying in the sea, but there was a fire waiting for them, and a fine dinner, and good friends who were worried about them. Deka and Sule ran up to Sohko and Aminata, taking their hands, drawing them along the beach toward the fire, chattering on about a river inside a cave of flashing lights, and paintings on the walls and skulls with rows of dots painted on them. Aminata held them both very close as they all sat around the fire.

Oddly, the adults didn't talk very much about the strange experiences they'd had while they were apart. Aminata ground up papaya seeds and made a paste to put on Dashona's arm. The cuts were real, though Noya had apparently lied about the knife being poisoned. Something had really happened on the ledge, but they didn't understand it, so they didn't try to explain it to the others.

CHAPTER 28
CROSS-CURRENTS

Sohko and Aminata had agreed to go back with the children to see the amazing cave, but days went by in other ways: working on the boat, gathering food, medicines, and supplies, weaving new baskets, repairing mats and tools. Then a thunderstorm went through, stopping all projects until it passed. But the children were adamant: Sohko and Aminata had to see the cave.

When they finally agreed to the trip, Asha recommended that everyone go together. "It's not getting there or finding it that concerns me. The cave is – powerful. It's hard to explain."

"Then we'll all go," Sohko agreed.

It wasn't difficult for Naaba and Abran to navigate through the rock opening, through the pool of trailing flowers, and into the cave. The others were speechless as the boat moved through the half-obscured slit and into the huge cave beyond.

"Light the torches," Naaba called, as soon as they'd entered the cave.

"It's all glistening, shining," Aminata sighed. "It's wondrous."

Farther up, Naaba handed the pole to Abran and jumped into the river to tie up the boat. One by one, the passengers slipped off the boat and swam to the channel edge, then wandered about, touching the damp, gleaming formations that dripped from the ceiling and rose from the floor, the fine webbing that joined them, the flashing mounds of crystals. The large crystals, especially, fascinated Sohko, with their angles so exact and regular they seemed to have been made by a master carver. Each facet caught the light and played with it, sending it down the length of the cut side, back at the viewer, and deep inside the crystal, all at once.

He ran his hand along the side of the crystal tower. "A thing of perfect light. Spirit light."

Deka grabbed his hand, pulling him along. "You need to see this, down here."

But she couldn't find the spot she was looking for. Nor could her brother.

"Asha," Sule called, looking for help, "where's the ledge?"

Both Asha and Naaba were already down the side passage where the painted panels had been. Holding the torch close to the rock face, Naaba could make out faint traces of color: yellow, white, black, red, but they were blurred, only streaks going from the top to the bottom. They looked very much like the other color-streaked rock faces near the front of the cave.

Abran came back around the corner with the other torch. "The ceiling collapsed in the side passage. It's just a jumble of rock pieces."

Running his fingers down the rock panel, Naaba thought he could feel the figures that had been there: the procession, the boat in the serpent's mouth, but when he looked, they were gone.

"What is it?" Aminata asked as she came up to join them.

"I'm not sure," Naaba said, feeling his own memory fading. Perhaps he hadn't seen anything there. Moving to the second panel, the one that had been covered with layers of images of warfare, he thought he might see something, but it was the same, streaked from top to bottom with colors.

"It's like a painting," Dashona said.

"No!" Deka yelled. "It *was* a painting! The whole rock was covered with pictures: people in a boat, and a sea serpent, and a procession on the land. Then that one was all people fighting, and rows of dots all around the figures, from one to the other, and across some to others, so everybody was connected to everybody else, and there was blood everywhere. And the dots were just like the dots around the skulls on the ledge: rows of red and yellow and black dots that went around the eyes and nose, and down the chin. And the three big stars at the top, remember? They were all here! Right here!"

"It was complete destruction," Abran agreed. "They, whoever they were, split into two groups and killed each other. I saw the bodies laid out in a side passage."

Even the children stared at that news.

"It's gone now. The ceiling collapsed, filling the passage."

"So," Sohko started, "you don't know exactly what you saw."

"Oh, we know what we saw," Abran corrected, "but it's not here anymore."

"Then perhaps it never was," Aminata suggested. "The colors on the rock can look like pictures, just like the formations in the stone passage look like giant heads. I'm just saying, it could have been something that looked a little like something else. In the torchlight, flickering shadows, especially with these amazing formations -"

"No!" Deka repeated, louder this time. "It wasn't shadows. It was real. And there were three skulls, and a footprint. Don't you believe me?"

Afutu spoke up for the first time on the trip. "We've been visiting a land of spirits, and they've shown us things we need to remember, not deny. They were meant for us. We were so afraid to sound ridiculous that we didn't share the visions we were given, even with our friends. It's time we talked about these things."

"But," Asha said, "these were images of rivals, battle, death, a people divided so badly they killed each other, right down to the last two, the artist and his murderer. "It was all destruction. What does it mean? Why was it shown to us?"

Dashona told them about the two people on the ledge: the light and the dark, the murder, the flight, and the two hawks. "It seemed like destruction, well, murder actually, since the man wasn't armed, but it was more than that. In the end, neither one was dead because light and dark can't be killed. You were given a different combination: a place of absolute wonder and beauty, and a story of destruction and despair."

"But the things we saw were real," Deka repeated. "We didn't make them up."

Dashona nodded. "They were real in that you really saw them, but the spirits do what they wish, and their reality isn't the same as ours. If it was important to them that you see these things, then you saw them. When it is no longer important, you may not be able to see them. Perhaps only an echo remains. And your memory, of course. In the meantime, those who sent you these things have remade this cave into a place of wonder, a fitting home."

That wasn't entirely satisfactory to Deka. "Why give a gift and then take it away?"

"It's not gone. It lives inside you, and you need to remember it, so its wisdom can guide you."

"How can it guide me? I don't know what it means."

"It's not a simple gift, like a toy. You may not understand it until later on, but it's a gift nonetheless. Sometimes, being unsettled is the first step to new understanding."

Her brother was less willing to believe Dashona's answer. "Maybe Aminata's right. It was just something we saw, something that looked like paintings in the torchlight."

Naaba looked at the boy and shook his head, understanding exactly what Sule was going through. They'd all seen the camp, the brushes and paints set out, the firepit, the carefully drawn figures on two different slabs, but not everyone wants a gift from the spirits, or is comfortable with having his reality changed by them.

"Dashona's right," Afutu said, into the silence. "We, all of us, were given something: a vision full of contradictions, like a dream that's so strong it stays all day long."

"We should leave gifts," Asha broke into the discussion, "before we go." With that, she ended one debate and started another, about what they could give. In the end, they made their choices and dropped their gifts carefully into the river, the source of life coming from within the mountain: fine shells, a carved stone figure, an arrowhead, a blue parrot feather, a carved bone hair ornament, a string of decorated marula nuts. These weren't people with many treasures, but they each gave something they valued.

* * *

When they returned to their camp, they worked with new intensity and a single goal: to be back at sea once again. Aminata was too generous to keep an argument going, but she hadn't changed her mind: the string of islands had been full of strange occurrences, not spirits. She agreed, however, that it was time to leave them behind and find the place that would be their new home. It was time to think about where this baby would be born.

* * *

Several times, Afutu tried to speak to Dashona; each time, she said she was busy. But he hadn't become a champion by giving up easily. When he found her repairing torn mats by the shore, she was alone, but she wasn't in a terribly good mood. It was difficult work for her; twice, she'd stuck her own finger with a bone needle as she pushed it through the mat. The third time it happened, she jumped up and threw the mat to the ground in frustration.

"I hate this!" she yelled, kicking at the mat.

"Dashona," Afutu said, behind her.

With a leap, she turned around, startled and flushed. "I don't know what you want with me," she snapped. "Go away. As you can see, I'm busy. It's too late. Too much. It's all too much, everything."

He waited for her to say what she needed to say.

But she was full of mixed emotions: anger, frustration, desire, all crossing over each other, like eddies in tidal pools. "Why now? Don't you see it's too late? It's too raw; it hurts too much. It eats me up inside. I'm done with it. Do you understand?"

He didn't reply. Instead, he put his hand on her arm, leaving it there.

"You don't understand," she started, but she found it hard to remember what it was that he didn't understand; all she felt was the weight of his hand on her arm, with the strength of an ancient tree locked into the earth. "It's just, it's been, and you never said anything, and that woman, and all this time, and so many days and nights and storms," she faltered, trying to find the right words, but they all flew out of her head like bats at dusk.

"I've loved you since we told stories on the beach in our village," Afutu said, slowly, carefully. "But things got in the way, and you're right, it's been difficult, for both of us. I can't undo that. But it's the past, and I've spent too long thinking about the past. Emai tried to tell me, but I didn't understand what he meant. It's only the present that we can change, moment by moment. No matter what we've gone through in the past, this moment, right now, is our chance to recreate our lives. So I'm asking you, at this moment, to be my wife because that's the way it should be, the way it was always meant to be."

She drew in her breath to answer, but something seemed to have affected all the words she used to have, for she couldn't call them out when she needed them, even though she tried. "Of course, see, but it's – you -" The words stuck in her mouth, all tangled up, refusing to come out, but after a while, she realized she didn't need them after all, and she nodded.

* * *

"Well, it's about time," Abran commented to Sohko when he heard the news. "Everyone in the world knew they were right for each other except those two."

The fine feast Aminata organized, and the songs that Naaba, Asha, Abran, and the children sang while Sohko played the hollow sticks celebrated the long vows, and everyone's simple gifts and good wishes were abundant, but there was a sense of hurry behind the festivities. Afutu and Dashona felt it too, perhaps even more than the others. Their future was waiting for them elsewhere, and they were anxious to begin it. It was Asha who reminded everyone that the whole journey, but especially their stay on these islands, had transformed them all, and they couldn't leave without recognizing, and celebrating, that fact. So when they danced, circling around the fire, jabbing their pointed sticks into the blaze and then swinging them over their heads, they celebrated not only a marriage, but also the spirits that dwelled in the islands.

The following day, at Asha's request, Naaba went up to the rock face below the cliff, and carefully pecked out a circle of eleven dots, one for each person in the group that had started off from Chahuk's island. In the center of the circle, he put another dot, the hub. Then he started marking connections between the people, all running through the hub. When he was finished, it reminded him of Komo's circles of stones, all standing there, waiting for the connections to be made between them, so they could move the wheel of life. For Naro and Ayo, he broke the lines linking them to the hub and drew a circle around their dots, with two lines pointing away from the circle. They were an unfinished part of the picture. Around the dots for Asha and Aminata, he drew circles. Under the whole thing, he drew a bar and four dots, just as Naro had shown him, then added wavy lines and two boats.

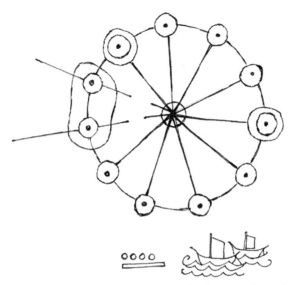

At the end of it all, he set his tools down and put his head against the rock, his hands under the diagram.

"Thank you for inviting us," he said, finally.

Halfway back down the hill, he found Asha waiting for him. "I thought you might like some company on the way back."

"That," he said, wrapping his arm around her, "would be very fine. It's strange; I thought I couldn't wait to leave, but it seems very sad, now, to say goodbye."

* * *

Four days later, they pushed the newly repaired boat into the water, declared it water-tight, and packed it up, splitting the supplies between the two boats. To start, Naaba, Asha, Afutu, and Dashona were in the yellow boat; Sohko, Aminata, Abran, and the children in the dark red one. They headed north and west along the long land, but when they tried to turn west, out toward the open sea, the current kept them locked in the grip of the land. No matter how they manipulated the mats, they were pulled right back to the land they were trying to leave.

"There's something wrong," Naaba called over to Sohko when the two boats were quite close together. "We can't get away."

"I know," Sohko called back. "Even with the paddles, I can make any headway. It's going to take us right back to the shore."

Sule sat with his arms crossed across his chest and his chin stuck out. "Is there something you want to talk about?" Aminata asked him. "Is something wrong?"

"No!" he said, turning away from her. "It's not fair," he added, though he wasn't sure she was still listening.

She was. Hands on her hips, she waited.

"Fine," he said, handing her a pure white crystal as long as his hand. "I took it, even though Asha said not to. It was nice. Why can't I have something nice? What's wrong with that?"

She watched the sunbeams play along its surfaces. "It's very beautiful, you're right. It's a treasure. So what's the problem?"

"I pretended to drop it in the river, in the cave when we were leaving gifts."

"Oh. Well, that's a lie, and a lie has to be fixed." Handing the crystal back to him, she added, firmly, "You have to fix it."

With that look, there was no room for argument, so he reached over the side of the boat and dropped the crystal into the sea. As soon as it left his fingers, he felt lighter, clearer, though without her, he wouldn't have been able to part with it. "Do I have to tell everyone?"

"No, I don't think so; the problem's been fixed."

When the current let them go, they set the mats to catch the wind. They were heading west, back out to sea, looking for a land they'd never seen but they knew was waiting for them, somewhere, not so far away.

CHAPTER 29
SIGHTS FROM THE CAMP ON THE HILL

In southern Mexico between the areas now known as
Coatzacoalcos and San Martin Pajapan, on the Gulf of Mexico

On the flat area on the hill, the boy was building a long curving line of sticks, a pretend river on which he set various rocks and
pieces of wood, as boats and crocodiles. He was arranging for a crocodile to come up and attack one of the boats when he heard a long
moan behind him. With a sigh, he turned around to see what was
going on, but it was only his mother, again. It's all she did, as far as
he could tell, just stare out at the sea. Every once in a while, she'd
moan or cry out, but mostly she sat on a flat rock and stared. He'd
have to bring her in out of the rain when a storm came through, and
get her to eat something, but she never thanked him. She never
even recognized him. So it was easier to make a world where the
enemies were clear, and the battle was straightforward, like the warriors in the boat, about to kill the mighty crocodile.

She hadn't always been like this. He could remember when
she sang beautifully, all the traditional songs that his people loved.
His father was a great hunter, a man who was so skilled at reading the signs of the game that other hunters followed him, because
they were sure they'd find the game and find their way home again.
But the Chief was jealous of this following. There were arguments.
Things had happened. Dead animal feet and hair were left in their
food baskets. Their hut was destroyed while they were at a celebration in the village center. Masked men hid in the shadows, watch-

ing them, following them. So they'd left one night. Two days later, they'd run into another group fleeing the village. At first, it was all right. They all helped each other out. His father knew all the trails, and they looked at him as the leader. But then, they'd seen the spectacular shooting star one night, streaking through the night sky with its long, fiery tail bright against the darkness, and the others thought it was a bad omen. Maybe it was. The boy shut down the memory and went back to his river and the warriors fighting the crocodile.

His mother cried out, louder this time, and pointed out to the sea. Irritated at another interruption, the boy looked out where she was pointing, and he gasped. Jumping up, his river battle forgotten, he ran down the hill toward the river.

"Ayo! Naro!" he yelled, as he ran down the boulder-strewn hillside.

Neither one heard him. Naro was walking next to the river, stopping sometimes to cross over to the other side, trying to find a good spot for a system of ropes and clay-lined baskets that would allow them to haul water up to the site more efficiently. They'd had a camp farther down the hill, close to one of the main tributaries of the giant river, but it flooded during a rainstorm. On their way to higher ground, they'd found the boy and his mother. Since she was completely panicked by the swampy conditions, they'd moved up the hill, where the tall trees grew, with their bright green bark and huge branches with orchids growing in the notches. From their camp on the hill, the view all the way down to the sea was very fine, but other parts of life, like hauling water and getting around, were very difficult.

"Ayo! Naro!" the boy called again. "Where are you?"

Far below them, Ayo was collecting certain kinds of bark, grasses and reeds that she wanted, tying them in bundles that she carried on her head. The berries and root pieces for dyestuffs she tucked into leaf envelopes that she folded into her sash. She'd gathered as much as she could carry and started back up the hill when she thought she heard a voice, but the area was full of birds singing, and the river talking, so she wasn't sure. But the second time she heard it, there was no doubt. Setting aside her bundles, she pulled out the signal conch, blowing a long note, then two short ones.

Even with the sound of the river, Naro heard the signal. Setting his measuring rope down, he climbed the bank on the far side, where he could get a clear view. At that moment, the boy saw him.

"Naro!" he yelled, breathless, across the river. "Look! Down there!"

"Easy, Chel. Catch your breath. I heard Ayo -" With a sharp intake of breath, he stared at the shore where the boy was pointing. There were two boats there, very close to the mouth of the great river. They had masts, and mats on them. "Where's my signal conch?" he yelled, rummaging through his bag. Finding it at the bottom, he drew it out and blew a series of long and short notes, a pause, two more long notes, then three short blasts.

Ayo blew an acknowledgement. Since she was the closest, she'd have the first look at the visitors. It would be easy to see without being seen, especially if these people were unfamiliar with the area. The closest place with cover was a hillock that overlooked the wide span of dark beach. The grasses there were tall enough to hide her as she knelt back on her heels, watching. As the boats came closer, she shook her head. Those boats - there couldn't be other boats that looked like those. Those boats, that looked so small against the huge sea, those boats – she knew those boats, and the people who should be in them. But how could it be that the people she most wanted to see were right there, not far from shore? Perhaps it wasn't so strange, after all. Hadn't she and Naro looked at this place and seen an echo of their homeland, where the mighty river flowed into the sea? Hadn't it called out to them as the place they'd been searching for, for so long?

Watching the boats come closer, she moved out of the grasses and onto the shore. There, she blew three long blasts on the conch, then paused and gave a broad wave. A flurry of activity broke out in the boats, with people lining up along one side, leaning out with their hands shading their eyes, craning to get a clear view. A shout of recognition. A returning call: three long blasts. Then two calls, one from each boat, in slightly different pitches, with the same three long blasts. Then, from high on the hill came Naro's call as well, and Ayo blew hers again, so that they all overlapped, the long notes of the four signal shells calling out to each other over and over again.

Ayo directed them to a lagoon, where the water was calm and the boats would be protected from the rough winds and waves. When they threw the anchor stones down and jumped into the water, they looked at their friends, the fine green land, the cloud-ringed mountain rising in the distance, and shouted with joy. After a very long time, they'd come home to a place they'd never been to but knew as soon as they saw it, as if the river and the sea from their old home had been transported here, and had waited for them. But it was different, too, because they were different, and the place had to be not just what they had known before but what they had become since.

"Does someone have to stay with the boats?" Naaba asked, reluctantly.

"No," Sohko clapped him on the shoulder. "Nobody's going to be left behind this time."

AFTERWORD

The camp became a village, their village. Shortly after they'd settled in, Aminata had her baby; later, Asha had hers. There were other joys too, and some tragedies, just as there are in every village, but mostly the days were good for the group of friends who had come so far together.

Sohko was a fine chief, just as everyone had expected, but Naaba remained the explorer, just as Emai had predicted. When he'd get restless from too much time in the same place, he'd head up the great river to see what lay around the next bend, or up into the mountain highlands. Sometimes he'd take Chel, Deka, and Sule with him. One day, though, he went alone, up into the mountains where the ancient forests called to him. It was hard to explain what he was looking for; it didn't have a name. So he wandered, sleeping in the trees, feeling the forest breathe, taking in its smells. Giant mahogany, oak, conifer, and fig trees crossed the space between the earth and the sky, decorated by snakes and vines and purple magnolia flowers and parrots.

As he followed the river, he came across several small waterfalls, where the river spilled out easily across the rocks in white plumes, but when he heard the thundering roar of the water up ahead of him, he knew he was coming to something very different. By the time he reached the edge of the falls, the sound was deafening. The water swirled momentarily at the top, as if uncertain about the plunge ahead of it, then divided into separate streams as it moved around sharp rocks at the top. Some parts seemed to hover as they fell, dropping in waves, forming a misty halo around the torrent. Then the streams rejoined and the whole broad sheet of water crashed into the pool below, sending spray flying back up and falling back down again in waves.

Carefully, Naaba found his way down the wet rocks on the side of the falls, searching for the place he knew would be there, the secret place behind the wild curtain of water. Stepping from stone to stone, he slid behind the falling water. Over the ages, the water had hollowed out a space behind the falls, and he was able to walk along its far stretches without getting soaked by the spray.

He ran his fingers over the stone, looking for the right spot. When he found it, he took out a measuring string and a charred stick. On the wall, he marked the center spot, then ran the string around in a circle, marking spots along the way. Like the last one he made, this diagram was a circle, with smaller circles along the circumference, but this time, he didn't put all the connecting lines through the center. He put them between the people, because they were all connected directly to each other. It was a wheel of a completely different kind, held together by a web of complicated ties. The three who had gone back he put on one side, and the babies on the other, including the one who had left them already.

It was only one moment in the turning of the wheel. There would be others.

"Thank you," he said, with his head bowed against the stone.

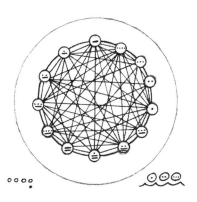

9413908R0025

Made in the USA
Charleston, SC
11 September 2011